D1052716

The Abyssinian

The Abyssinian

Jean-Christophe Rufin

Translated by Willard Wood

W · W · Norton & Company

New York London

Originally published in French as *L'Abyssin*

Printed in the United States of America

The text of this book is composed in Centaur MT with the display set in Ondine
Desktop composition by Thomas O. Ernst
Manufacturing by the Haddon Craftsmen, Inc.

Library of Congress Cataloging-in-Publication Data
Rufin, Jean-Christophe, 1952–
[Abyssin. English]
The Abyssinian / by Jean-Christophe Rufin : translation by Willard Wood.
p. cm.
ISBN 0-393-04716-4
I. Wood, Willard. II. Title.
PQ2678.U357A62913 1999
843'.914—dc21 99-25126
CIP

W. W. Norton & Company, Inc., 500 Fifth Avenue, New York, N.Y. 10110
www.wwnorton.com

W. W. Norton & Company Ltd., 10 Coptic Street, London WC1A 1PU

1 2 3 4 5 6 7 8 9 0

I

The Castaway's Order

I

The Sun King was disfigured. A slow leprosy that in the Orient commonly corrupts oils had introduced itself under the varnish, where it was spreading day by day. On Louis XIV's left cheek, the one extended in majesty toward the viewer, sat a large blackish stain, a hideous star projecting its rusty brown filaments out to the king's ear. A closer inspection revealed dark haloes on the body as well, but, except for those spotting his hose, these were less unsettling.

The painting had been hanging for three years in the French consulate in Cairo. It had been executed under the master's personal supervision in the Paris workshop of Hyacinthe Rigaud, the author of the original portrait, and been sent on by sea. By great misfortune, neither Cairo nor any of the stations in the Levant within striking distance could currently boast a master painter, and thus the consul, Monsieur de Maillet, was on the horns of a cruel dilemma. Either a portrait that did grave injury to the king was to be allowed to remain on public display in the reception hall of the consular building, or the painting would have to be confided to inexpert hands, with a good chance of being ruined entirely. The diplomat turned the matter over in his mind for a period of three months before deciding on the bolder course. He would attempt the repair.

To perform the operation, Monsieur de Maillet chose a druggist then living in Cairo's Frankish colony who was said to be skilled at restoring canvases damaged by the climate. He was a tall fellow, somewhat stooped, his face swallowed almost to the eyes by a dense black-and-gray beard, his hair a mass of tightly coiled astrakhan curls, who moved his massive bulk with brutal energy while flapping his long limbs. Yet when he turned to his work, his gestures became extremely precise. He was known as Maître Juremi, and his one flaw was to be a Protestant. The consul disliked the notion of entrusting the king's image to a fanatic, capable at any moment of some desperate attempt. But the man had the reputation of being an honest subject, in itself rare among Cairo's turbulent foreign community. And besides, Monsieur de Maillet had no choice.

On seeing the painting, Maître Juremi declared that the work would take ten days. By the following morning he was perched on a seven-foot scaffold with a young Nubian slave from the consulate at his side, stirring great stoneware pots that reeked of turpentine and poppyseed oil. The consul had insisted on being present anytime the painting itself was touched. Therefore, every morning toward eleven o'clock, once the mixtures had been prepared (for only the freshest of materials could be used), the servants called the consul, and Maître Juremi would then embark on the work of restoration under the diplomat's supervision. He attacked the stains on the drapery of the purple tunic first, where they were least noticeable. The immediate results were highly encouraging, as the varnish lost none of its gloss, the colors reemerged unaltered, and the blots vanished almost entirely. Monsieur de Maillet had every reason to be optimistic. Yet each time that Maître Juremi brought one of his small calf's-bristle brushes toward the surface of the royal painting, the consul emitted a succession of open-mouthed moans and whimpers such as a patient in the dentist's chair might give at the approach of the tongs. On several occasions the sessions had to be brought to a halt, having proved too painful.

The day finally came when the cancer that had eaten away at the king's cheek had itself to be addressed. Monsieur de Maillet, wigless, in a light calico dressing gown, agonized on a small bench he had had placed in front of the painting. His wife held his hand, pressing it to her bosom. The pair looked upward with imploring eyes, for all the world like a family group watching the crucifixion of a loved one from the foot of the cross. It was midafternoon in the month of May, and for three days a hot wind from the Nubian desert had flooded the city with dry heat. Maître Juremi, a gray skullcap on his head, seized a fine brush that the young slave held out to him and lifted it toward the august countenance of the king. Monsieur de Maillet rose from his bench.

"Wait!"

The druggist stopped in mid-gesture.

"Are you absolutely certain that . . . ?"

"Yes, Your Excellency."

In his emotions Maître Juremi displayed the same surprising contrasts as in his gestures. He was strongly tempted to give vent to his temper but managed, at the cost of intense concentration, to rein himself in. The effort was visible on his face. At the same time he grumbled under his breath, snorted, whistled like an overfired oven, yet at no point exploded, even expressing himself with a gentleness surprising in a man who was so clearly overwrought.

"I am simply priming the surface," explained the druggist. "Observe, Excellency, that my brush barely touches the canvas."

Had the decision been left to him, Maître Juremi would have dabbled the fourteenth Louis's nose with scarlet paint and scrawled dog's ears on his periwig. As a Protestant, both he and his entire family had suffered calamity at the hands of this king. That he treated him with the deference he did already surpassed all understanding. Not for the first time, Maître Juremi had sworn to himself that if the day's session was called off with nothing accomplished, he would send the whole business to the devil.

The consul, perhaps glimpsing what tremendous storms roiled behind the restorer's bright glance, fell back on his bench, saying, "Go ahead then. If you must."

Clamping the fingers of both hands between his teeth, he shut his eyes tightly.

At that moment, two hard knocks sounded at the door. The painter stepped back, the Sudanese slave rolled his large eyes toward heaven, and Monsieur de Maillet reopened his, which were pink with emotion. A fraught silence settled over the room, as though the great king himself, annoyed at the indignity about to be visited on him, had hurled two terrible thunderbolts from the heavens.

Three more knocks fell on the door, more heavily this time. There was no doubt about it. Despite the consul's explicit and repeated instructions that he not be disturbed during these sessions, someone had taken the liberty of knocking at the great oak double door leading to the hall and offices. The diplomat, checking to see that his dressing gown was properly closed, walked briskly to the door and jerked it open. In the doorway stood Monsieur Macé. Under his superior's wrathful glance, he seemed to snap at the waist, making an extreme, almost a foolhardy, obeisance, for from the perspective of geometry and logic he should have fallen face-first to the floor. He saved himself, however, righting his body with great promptness, and spoke in the modest yet firm tone that had earned him his chief's favor.

"The aga of the janissaries sends Your Excellency a message. He has expressly noted that it concerns a matter of unusual urgency. The Turks have a special word for things that may not be put off. I can only think to translate it by the imperious obligation in which I find myself to disregard your clearly stated instructions on being disturbed.

Monsieur Macé was known as a "language child," that is, a graduate of the School of Oriental Languages in Paris. On receiving a diploma, the scholars were sent, as Monsieur Macé had been, to join an embassy, prior to becoming diplomats or dragomans. The consul regarded this young man with particular favor, finding to his satisfaction that he knew his place. Not being of gentle birth, Monsieur Macé approached all questions with reserve, at once displaying his limitations and a judicious awareness of them.

"Was there any letter?"

"No, Excellency. The aga's messenger, who was unwilling even to dismount, informs us that his master is waiting for you now, at his palace."

"So the dogs now summon me, do they?" said Monsieur de Maillet under his breath. "With good reason, I hope, or the pasha himself will hear of it."

Monsieur Macé approached the consul, then pivoted on his heels so as to stand shoulder to shoulder with him, both men presenting their backs to the others in the room. The young man then spoke, using the whisper one uses to disclose a state secret in a public setting. Maître Juremi shrugged at this breach of conduct, performed as though it were the height of good manners, a trick that, among career diplomats, soon becomes second nature.

"The aga is holding at Your Excellency's disposal a French prisoner arrested yesterday in Cairo," whispered Monsieur Macé.

"And is that any reason to interrupt us? Every week they capture one of the pitiful wretches who come here to try their luck. What concern is it of mine if . . . ?"

"Only," murmured Monsieur de Macé even more softly than before, so that the consul had practically to read his secretary's lips, "he is no ordinary prisoner. It is the man we have been waiting for, the king's messenger."

Monsieur de Maillet gave a startled exclamation.

"In that case," he said loudly, "we must waste no time. Sirs," he went on, addressing chiefly Maître Juremi, "our session must come to an end."

The consul left the room with a mixed expression of dignity and displeasure on his face, though inwardly certain that anything was better than the torture he had been about to undergo.

Maître Juremi, alone with the young slave, swore savagely and tossed his paintbrush back into the pot. Several droplets of the precious pink unguent destined for the royal cheek splashed onto the boy's black forehead.

A good walker could in those days make the tour of Cairo in three hours. It was still a small city, one that travelers universally found ugly, worn, and charmless. From afar, the fretwork of its slender minarets and tall, tufted palms lent it a certain character. But as one entered its narrow streets, the view was blocked by ranks of two-story houses, undecorated except for the *mashrabiyya,* or cedar lattices, jutting dangerously above the passerby. The city's salient structures—the palace of the beys, the Citadel (where the pasha lived, and one side of which opened onto Rumayla Square), the many mosques—all disappeared in the confusion of the whole. Devoid of open spaces or general views, deprived of air and light, the city seemed to push all beauty, all passion, all happiness behind blank walls and dark gates. Few people were to be seen on the public ways, except in the neighborhood of the bazaars or those of the city gates through which the merchants came from the surrounding countryside. Black forms, draped in veils, slipped rapidly past, before restoring the streets to the possession of their resident beggars and scabby dogs.

Rarely did a stranger venture into the old parts of Cairo. Although Europeans had been granted protection by the Ottoman sultan ever since the treaties of capitulation in the sixteenth century, signed with France by Khair ad-Din Barbarossa, and were therefore free to trade and enjoy certain rights, Christians nonetheless felt threatened. The Egyptians were constantly quarreling among themselves: the pasha was pitted against his militia, the janissaries against the beys, the beys against the imams, the imams against the pasha—unless the alignment were entirely the reverse. If the Muslim factions reached a truce and pretended for a moment to be reconciled, it was always by making common cause against the Christians. The matter was never allowed to go very far, and a thrashing or two would restore order—or at least the usual state of discord. But this sufficed to make the Franks, as they were then called, consider it prudent to leave their assigned quarter as seldom as possible.

The ease with which the young man walked on that afternoon through the narrow streets of old Cairo was therefore all the more surprising. He had stepped onto the street a few moments earlier from a perfectly ordinary Arab house, closing a simple plank door behind him, and navigated through the maze of streets with the unhurried familiarity of a native. Yet he was clearly a Frank and took no pains to hide it. All morning the *khamsin* had blown its sandy breath up from the desert, and the air was stifling and dry even in the perpetual gloom of the narrow streets. The young man, wearing a simple cambric shirt with an open collar, cotton knee breeches and supple boots, walked bareheaded and carried his navy-blue wool doublet over his arm. Two old Arabs, crossing him in front of the Mosque of Hasan, greeted him amiably, to which he responded with a single word, spoken in their language, as he continued on his way. Although he was not by any means an official, since he was not Turkish, everyone in the city knew that the young man was called Jean-Baptiste Poncet, and that he held a high position in the citadel with the pasha.

Solidly built, vigorous, with wide shoulders and a powerful neck, he had often asked himself why fate had not picked him for a conscript oarsman in the Sun King's galleys. His head, unexpectedly on so solid a frame, was long and fine-featured. His face was smooth and youthful, framed by dark hair and lit by a green gaze. There was a noticeable lack of symmetry in his features, one cheekbone set slightly higher than the other and his eyes curiously placed, giving his glance a startling force. These irregularities added a note of mystery and power to his simple appearance.

Jean-Baptiste Poncet had become, in the three years he had lived in Cairo, that city's most renowned doctor. It was May in the year 1699, and he had just turned twenty-eight.

As he walked along, he swung a small case at his side, which contained a number of medications he had concocted himself, with his partner's help. The vials, knocking against each other, gave off a muffled clink behind the leather. To the crystalline tinkling that accompanied his steps, Jean-Baptiste took pleasure in imparting a merry rhythm. He looked in front of him, smiling peacefully, untroubled by the knowledge that he was being watched from behind many of the blinds and wooden lattices. Most of the houses were ones in which he was received, either to exercise his art or, quite often, as a simple guest, to take tea or dinner with his hosts. Knowing a large portion of the city's small secrets—and a small portion of its large ones—he was used to being a favorite object of the general curiosity, particularly among women, in the darkened seraglios where desire and intrigue were fomented. He accepted this state of affairs without excitement either to his vanity or to his passion and continued to play, though perhaps with a lessening sense of enjoyment, the exotic role of the free-roving animal, on whom the eyes of a thousand hunters are trained, tracking its every movement.

Pursuing his course, he passed near the perfume bazaar and finally reached the banks of the Khalij, or Cairo Canal. He walked upstream for a short time along the rivulet, which was dry at this season but which a storm could bring to a boiling frenzy at others, then started across the bridge spanning it. The spot was always filled with people, in part because of the shops and houses lining the bridge itself, in part because it provided the only path between old Cairo and the Arab quarters. On that day, however, the crowd was particularly dense, and Jean-Baptiste made his way through with difficulty. Reaching the middle of the bridge, he realized that something unusual was going on: clouds of thick smoke were billowing from one of the houses. It had started at a cloth merchant's, he was told, where an earthenware stove had spilled and scattered its coals. A horde of Egyptians were loudly throwing water onto the fire, drawing buckets from a nearby well and carrying them on the run to the smoldering house. The situation was under control and no catastrophe was expected. But in a town where little ever happened, people had flocked from all sides to watch, and getting across the bridge was virtually impossible. Jean-Baptiste elbowed his way forward. At the entrance to the bridge, on the far side from where he had arrived, a two-horse carriage was stopped in the middle of the crowd. Drawing up to it, Jean-Baptiste saw that it bore the arms of the French consul, to which he reacted by shouldering the gawkers aside all the more roughly, unwilling to linger.

While officially registered as an apothecary, Poncet held no diploma of any sort, and his practice of medicine was strictly illegal. The Turks raised no objections, but his compatriots tended to hold him liable, particularly when there was a licensed doctor among them—luckily, there was none in Cairo at the moment. Constantly under the threat of being denounced, he had already been obliged to leave two cities for this reason. It was therefore only prudent to stay away from the representative of the law, which in everything concerning the Franks meant the consul.

Just as he was passing the carriage, his head tucked into his shoulders and his face slightly averted, he heard an imperious voice calling him: "Monsieur, if you please! Monsieur! Could you spare us a moment?"

The person Jean-Baptiste feared was the consul. The voice, fortunately, belonged to a woman. He approached the carriage, and a lady leaned her head out the window. She was perspiring profusely from the close heat, and her rouge had run, leaving the lead white that coated her face exposed and cracking. Intended to fend off the ravages of time, her artifices had precipitated them instead. Rid of her dripping facepaint, she might have presented the smiling, straightforward face of a fifty-year-old woman, in whose blue-eyed glance there remained traces of beauty, and an air of soft and timid kindness.

"Can you tell us what has slowed our carriage so? Are we in any danger?"

Jean-Baptiste recognized the consul's wife, having seen her once or twice in the gardens of the French legation.

"A small fire was kindled in one of the houses, Madame, and has drawn a crowd of onlookers, but all should return to order shortly."

Expressing her relief, the lady thanked Jean-Baptiste and withdrew her head into the carriage, where she settled herself back into the cushions and resumed beating her fan. It was then Jean-Baptiste noticed she was not alone. Across from her, lit by the sun slanting through the gap made by the Khalij, sat a young girl.

It would be no exaggeration to say that the flaws of the one set off the virtues of the other: they were exact opposites. The cosmetic layers that caked the face of the elder woman contrasted with the pure complexion of the younger, and the lady's fidgeting anxiety stood in opposition to the calm and serious immobility of the girl. Had Jean-Baptiste been asked to describe her he would not have known how to begin. Of all that his first exposure to beauty had revealed to him, he was conscious only of a general impression. A single detail stood out, both absurd and adorable: she had tied her ringlets with blue silk ribbons. Jean-Baptiste looked at the young woman with astonishment, and though he was generally easy in his manner, he failed, in his surprise, to compose his face. The carriage lurched forward as the coachman lashed his whip, and the silent conversation of their eyes was interrupted, leaving Jean-Baptiste standing alone on the bridge speechless, troubled, and elated.

"Confound it!" he said to himself. "I have never seen her like in Cairo before."

And he continued his walk, at a somewhat slower pace, toward his house in the Frankish quarter.

2

The consul, Monsieur de Maillet, was born into the minor nobility of eastern France, where his family continued to put forth a few sparse shoots. It would be inaccurate to say that his family had slid into ruin, because they had never had much to start with. Hedged in on the one side by an enterprising bourgeois class and on the other by wealthy peasants, these gentry preened themselves on neither doing nor owning anything. What kept them from making painful comparisons was that they belonged, if only at a mediocre level, to the nobility, a fact that transfigured all other aspects of their mediocrity. Their salvation, as they never doubted, would come from above. When some member of their lineage, no matter how distantly related, rose in rank (it was bound to happen someday), then they would all rise. The miracle did not produce itself immediately, but when Louis Pontchartrain, who was a first cousin to Monsieur de Maillet's mother, became the Sun King's minister and then his chancellor, it was clear that the long-awaited event had occurred. No man reaches such heights unaided—even if he has earned his place solely on merit. He must have many men about him, men he has placed and maintained, and may on a particular day call into action. Their devotion is all the greater for their having been nothing beforehand. Pontchartrain knew this and did not forget to use his family.

Monsieur de Maillet emerged from his pious and idle youth having learned little from books and less from life itself. His powerful uncle saved him from nothingness by obtaining the consulship in Cairo for him.

While grateful to his uncle, Monsieur de Maillet also had strong feelings of apprehension. He knew he could not repay the debt solely by his own efforts. Someday this man of enormous power would ask him for a great favor, a favor that he might not be able to perform without putting himself in danger. And Monsieur de Maillet did not like danger.

The Cairo consulship was one of the most enviable posts in the Levant.

The French embassy to which Monsieur de Maillet reported was in Constantinople, at a considerable remove. And the fact that Cairo never received delegations passing on to other, more distant, parts greatly simplified his duties. The task consisted simply in legislating over the few dozen troublesome merchants and adventurers in Cairo's foreign colony. These men, stranded there after what was generally an extraordinary sequence of events, had the audacity to consider courage a virtue, money a source of power, and the duration of their exile grounds for glory. It was Monsieur de Maillet's task to remind them that the only power was the law, which did not look favorably on them, and the only virtue nobility, which they would never possess. But the essential thing, as Pontchartrain reiterated tirelessly, was always to get along well with the Turkish powers-that-be. This coincided with France's overall diplomacy, which was to support (albeit surreptitiously) the Ottoman alliance against the Holy Roman Empire. It also helped maintain civil order, as nothing so held the Frankish community in line as to know that the Turks might, at a nod from the consul, sweep in and expel a foreign troublemaker.

It should also be added that the consul paid no rent, received an annual income of four thousand livres, with a further six thousand five hundred livres for the expenses of his table and domestic servants, and the right to import one hundred barrels of wine a year at two and a half piasters duty per barrel, offering the chance for a considerable profit. These benefits, which made Monsieur de Maillet rich, provoked an extreme gratitude in him. He renewed his protestations of service on a monthly basis, in letters that traveled to his protector via the French East India Company ships laying over in the port of Alexandria. The main ingredient in these missives was certainly praise; but fearing that a diet of honeyed words would in the long run cloy and perhaps even disgust, the consul diluted his encomiums with various subjects borrowed from the local situation. The digressions could sometimes reach the proportions of modest memoranda, such as the one (of which he was inordinately proud, though he never learned his minister's reaction to it) in which he examined the possibility of digging a canal to join the Mediterranean and Red Seas.

Monsieur de Pontchartrain always answered these letters, making comments and sometimes adding a few notes on the political situation. In his last dispatch, already more than a month old, the minister had for the first time expressed what seemed a direct order. The consul was to expect a visit from a Jesuit priest, who was arriving from the court at Versailles by way of Rome. The minister asked Monsieur de Maillet to kindly comply with any orders the ecclesiastic might bring with him. He was to consider them as representing the wishes of the council and King Louis XIV himself.

Monsieur de Maillet fretted about this business. If a messenger had to bring the orders himself to avoid the risk of writing them down, their degree of secrecy must be extreme. Yet as time passed and still the Jesuit did not appear, Monsieur de Maillet recovered his peace of mind. The policies of kings were a mysterious matter and might constantly change course. Other developments had undoubtedly occurred to draw the Jesuit more urgently in another direction. Or he could simply have gotten lost en route.

Now, however, it seemed that this unlikely traveler had reappeared, half naked and a prisoner, in the hands of the aga of the janissaries. The aga had no hesitation in releasing his captive to the consul, who vouched for him personally. But the affair had already stirred considerable curiosity. The pasha and all the foreign powers in the city would not let the matter rest until they had explained the mystery of this envoy, who had arrived from the Sun King covered in mud and had the temerity to announce to one and all that he was the bearer of a political message.

Monsieur de Maillet revolved these thoughts in his mind as he paced the reception hall of the consulate. He had ordered a place set for his guest at table, and the two of them would shortly dine there in private. The consul's wife and daughter would pay their respects to the clergyman briefly before retiring to let the two men talk. Hurried steps could be heard on the staircase as the Nubian valets ferried bucketsful of cold water upstairs for the traveler's bath. From all appearances, the former captive was taking his ease. Impatient, Monsieur de Maillet began to feel a slight irritation toward his guest. He stopped his pacing and sat down on the bench opposite the painting he was having restored. What he saw stunned him. The king's face was unblemished. The stain was gone and the king's complexion had returned to its initial purity. On examining it closely and with great attention, the consul could make out a slightly redder area where the blotch had been. On a child's face, it might have been taken for the evidence of a recent slap. On the august countenance of the king, this shadow could only be a slight excess of rouge, applied to indicate that the sovereign was in good health and that his people had every cause for optimism.

For the space of a moment, Monsieur de Maillet thought he had witnessed a miracle. For the Jesuit to materialize and the stain to disappear seemed to indicate that a divine providence was taking an active hand in the affairs of the house. Then he realized the truth and rushed over to yank on the bellpull.

"Tell Maître Juremi to appear here first thing tomorrow morning!" he yelled at the porter.

That insolent heretic had dared to restore the painting while he was away! The results were successful. Thank heavens! But what calamity had been narrowly averted! The work merited payment—the fee had already been agreed on—but the man's disobedience would have to be punished. With scoundrels of this sort, there was no other way to maintain authority. The consul would offer the apothecary a choice between a week's imprisonment and a fine, to be deducted from his fee. The consul had not the slightest doubt that the man would choose the fine. The restoration had been successfully accomplished, a triumph sweetened by the expectation of paying less than full price for it. By the time Father Versau came down for dinner, the consul was able to receive him in exceedingly good temper.

"My friend," said the Jesuit, clasping both the consul's hands in his, "I'm undone by your welcome. It is as though I were returning to life. The bath, the clean clothes, the orderly house—if you could only know how I have dreamed of these things."

Tears of gratitude filled his eyes. And if what Machiavelli has said is true and we love others for the good we have done them, the consul's lively sympathy for this man—on whom he had just lavished so many kind attentions—can cause no surprise.

"I paid my respects to Madame de Maillet in the hallway," said Father Versau, "and I learned that she was not joining us for dinner. I would on no account trouble the arrangements of your house."

"Not at all, not at all. We have things to discuss in private. Let us take the opportunity to conduct business during dinner."

"Certainly. I also encountered your daughter, Mademoiselle de Maillet, for whose grace and discretion you deserve to be complimented. How did you manage to educate her so well in a foreign land, where I would imagine that tutors are rare and schools even more so?

"She remained in France until the age of fourteen. We brought her out to join us only in the last few years."

The two men barely knew each other, yet their conversation was already proceeding along lines of established familiarity. The priest admired the king's portrait and "its excellent state of preservation in this humid climate." He went on to ask the consul a few concerned questions about his health and the responsibilities of his post. At last they sat down at table and the conversation turned to serious matters.

"Father, I am most eager to know the details of your journey. Did you not mention that you lost everything in a shipwreck?"

"A terrible shipwreck. I would be dead at this very moment, but for the extreme bounty of Providence."

He then entered into a long account of his leaving Rome. Not wanting to reach the Levant on an Italian boat, he had taken passage on a Greek galley, and it was only once on board that he discovered the thorough incompetence of both captain and crew. The ship had gone aground within sight of Cyprus. The Jesuit, seeing that disaster was imminent, had ordered one of the ship's boats lowered and boarded it with a few others. The currents drove them against a rocky, wave-battered coast, and their skiff was splintered on the shoals. Father Versau felt a pang of regret at being consigned to a watery tomb, thereby reducing, as everyone knows, his chance of being resurrected from the dead on Judgment Day. He placed the problem in God's hands, however, along with his life and the fate of his order, and died. His last memory was of his death in the cold, dark, turbulent water. Next he knew, he was waking up on the sands of a small creek, his arms wrapped around a beam that had been spat up from the sea along with himself. He was as solitary, naked, terrified, and cold as Adam on the day of his creation. But God had not abandoned him. There were fishermen living along the shore. They rescued him, clothed him to the extent they were able, and brought him two days later to the coast of Egypt, where they habitually went to set their nets. At his request they dropped him off on the beach near Alexandria. Finding himself on Ottoman territory without a safe-conduct, Father Versau chose to avoid the city. He made a detour through the desert around Alexandria and reached the Nile somewhat farther south, where he boldly negotiated his passage to Cairo with a crew of boatmen, knowing that he had not a penny to pay them.

"The rest is already familiar to you," he said modestly.

During the telling of the priest's story, Monsieur de Maillet had uttered a thousand exclamations of surprise and dismay. Now, looking at this frail stick of a man, he wondered how he had possibly survived so many hardships.

"My adventures," said the Jesuit in a graver tone, "are relevant only insofar as they explain my arrival here and the condition in which you first found me. The crux of the matter lies elsewhere."

"Ah! Of course," said Monsieur de Maillet. "The king's message!"

Father Versau straightened in his chair, blinked once or twice slowly, and resumed the conversation with a touch of solemnity. Monsieur de Maillet glanced at the portrait, which suddenly seemed to herald the presence of the king himself above them.

"Strictly speaking," said the Jesuit, "I carry no message."

"But you said . . ."

The black-clad man held up his hand for silence. This would take time.

"No message in the sense of a written letter. Nothing in fact that the king ever wrote down or expressed directly. This precaution was fortunate in every respect, as you can appreciate. Given the adventures that befell me, it would have been highly imprudent to carry anything of the sort."

"I quite agree," said Monsieur de Maillet.

"But if there is no message, there does exist on the king's part a clear purpose, revealed to his spiritual director, to whom he has opened his conscience."

"His confessor, Father de la Chaise?"

The Jesuit crinkled his eyelids. Monsieur de Maillet looked at him agog, like a child who has discovered a chest full of treasure.

"This venerable man, who belongs as you know to the Jesuit order, has divulged the king's purposes only to a close and confidential group of persons: Madame de Maintenon, who zealously defends the cause of religion at the court of Versailles; Monsieur de Pontchartrain, our minister; Father Fleuriau, the director within the Society of Jesus of all that pertains to the Levant; and myself, his assistant and representative. And now you."

Monsieur de Maillet bowed his head in sign of his submission to the wishes of this powerful company, and also to hide the tears of gratitude welling up in his eyes.

"The affair can be summed up in a few words. You know that Christianity is now at war with its enemies. The Ottoman expansion has at present been contained. The next step is reconquest, and it is only a matter of time. But the gravest danger has arisen among those who claim to live in Christ. The Reformation, that hideous canker, has threatened to corrupt the work of God from within. The king of France has opposed it wherever it has reared its head: in his own country by revoking the concessions made to Protestantism by the Edict of Nantes, and in Europe by confronting—at peril to his own crown—the Protestant princes under the leadership of the traitor William of Orange. But the struggle is no longer confined to the Mediterranean and the countries bordering it. Now the whole universe has entered the battle. Christ's message must be carried to all known lands, and these must be reclaimed from the infidel. It has also to be carried to those still largely unknown lands that have emerged in the last two centuries as new battlegrounds for Christianity: the Americas, the Indies, China, and the Far East. Each time we encounter the same challenges. First it is the peoples themselves who resist us—living as they do outside the true faith, they cannot conceive the mortal danger threatening to swallow them for all eternity. But in the second place, we face the rivalry of this so-called Reformation, which is nothing more than a diabolical attempt to prevent God's true word from reaching those who most need it."

From time to time, Monsieur de Maillet nodded in assent to show that he was following the argument. In truth, the eloquence of this little man fascinated him, not least because it had appeared so suddenly when the discussion turned to issues of politics and religion.

"The king of France has learned a great deal in the course of his long reign," continued the man of the cloth. "He is able to see beyond the historically contingent. He clearly recognizes, to the wonder of his confessor, the deep import of the struggle he is embarked on and the reasons for his great temporal power. This universal contest between the forces of the True Faith and those of men still steeped in darkness is one that occupies him body and soul. He is determined to continue it until his last breath. And while there are many battles to be fought, some are more urgent than others. The Turks, as I have said, will be dealt with in time. We are on hand, we help a few Christians here to keep the flame alive. When the great edifice of Ottoman power starts to crack, we will penetrate through every breach in its defenses. But the hour is not at hand. Nearby, however, is a country that calls to us, a large country that has remained separate thanks to the vagaries of history and its startlingly mountainous terrain—a country that is still in darkness, but I am tempted to say only marginally so, a country that asks nothing better than to join our ranks. The country is a Christian one, but its faith, improperly nourished, has grown awry—"

"Abyssinia!" said Monsieur de Maillet, as though hypnotized.

"Abyssinia, yes, a land that is practically unknown and practically converted, a land that has until now swallowed up all who have penetrated it, yet which still calls us."

The Jesuit leaned forward, reaching over the table to seize Monsieur de Maillet's hand over the pewter plates bearing the remains of their meal: "The king of France wants to add to his glory by bringing this land back to the Church. His Majesty charges you to conduct an embassy there."

3

Jean-Baptiste Poncet and Maître Juremi, partners in the apothecary trade, shared a house that also served them as an atelier. It was at the far end of the Frankish colony in a small, quiet street, where they found the privacy they needed for their work.

"Halloo!" cried Jean-Baptiste pushing the door open and penetrating into the extreme disorder of their bachelors' quarters. "Are you in, you old sorcerer?"

He heard a groan from upstairs. Tossing the doublet he still carried over the back of a chair, he went up to join his friend.

On the upper floor, a large terrace looked out over an inner courtyard. The other windows all had their blinds drawn, and many were bricked shut. Poncet found his friend leaning over the balustrade, a blank look in his eyes and holding a sword.

"What are you doing here all alone with that instrument in your hand?"

"I have just killed the consul," said Maître Juremi.

"Really?"

Jean-Baptiste knew his friend better than to be perturbed.

"Really. I killed him twelve times. Would you like to see? Watch." So saying, the giant drove at the air in front of him as though clashing swords with an adversary who was backpedaling frantically. When he reached the wall, he lunged, grunting as though with the effort of driving his sword into a body. The tip of the foil pierced the plaster, chipping off a small flake and baring the red entrails of two bricks.

"Bravo!" said Jean-Baptiste applauding. "He certainly deserved that. Do you feel any better?"

"Considerably."

"Then now that you are calmer, perhaps you can explain the situation to me."

Jean-Baptiste grabbed a chair and sat down. His friend remained standing, pacing back and forth and swatting at his leg with his foil.

"I am at the end of my tether with that consul. Just the sight of him provokes me to murder."

"That is nothing new," said Jean-Baptiste smiling. "And it seems to me that I advised you from the start not to accept the work."

"Not accept it! But he summoned me."

"If he summoned me," said Jean-Baptiste, "I wouldn't go."

"Is that so? May I remind you that you are not a Protestant and therefore may live here in considerably more safety than I do? In addition, the pasha consults you and honors you as his personal physician, whereas I am nothing more than a humble preparer of plants. But that's not the question. Maillet summoned me, I went, I did the work, and now it is all over."

Maître Juremi told his friend how he had taken advantage of the consul's departure to ignore his instructions and finish the restoration of the painting.

"And was it a success?" asked Jean-Baptiste.

"I think so."

"Then everything is fine."

"Ah, but you don't know the consul. I am expecting his guards to arrive here at any moment to take me into custody. He has probably been too busy to notice as yet."

"But what can he do? It isn't a crime to perform the work you've been assigned."

"No, but His Excellency likes to be obeyed. He will insist that I am at fault, and since he is both prosecutor and judge, there is no disputing him. That old miser will sentence me to a fine and dock it from my wages."

"Pay it! At least that'll be the end of the story."

"Never! I would rather kill him and flee to another country."

On the subject of money, Maître Juremi had an entirely Protestant sense of justice. He would never take even a sequin he had not earned fairly, but he would never accept being paid a sou less than his full fee.

"Calm down, Juremi. He doesn't have the right to hold you liable to a fine. According to our statutes, he is obliged to offer you a choice between a financial sanction and a prison term. Hit him in the pocketbook instead of the chest—it will hurt him just as much. Choose the prison stint, spend two days locked up in his jail, then never have anything to do with him again."

Maître Juremi had wallowed in the sweet prospect of annihilating the consul long enough to have achieved complete satisfaction. And he recognized the wisdom and shrewdness of his friend's advice.

For a moment, they stood in silence. The hot wind had died down toward midafternoon. The fine dust stirred up by it was settling in a powdery layer, whitening the wrought-iron railing and dulling the leaves of the potted orange trees. Jean-Baptiste went inside to fetch a jar of water and two pewter goblets. They drank.

"There was a small fire, just a while ago, on the bridge over the Khalij. It made quite a commotion. The consul's wife even found her carriage blocked by the crowd."

"Ah," said Maître Juremi without great interest.

"By the way," said Jean-Baptiste, pouring himself another glass of water, "as you spend so much time at the consulate . . ."

His friend shrugged.

"Do you know the young girl who was with Madame de Maillet?"

"What did she look like?"

Jean-Baptiste could not bring himself to say that he had noticed only the ribbons in her hair.

"I couldn't see her very well."

"Was she blond, with big blue eyes, somewhat sad?"

"I think so," said the young man quickly. "Yes, that sounds about right."

"That would be the daughter of our rotten consul."

"Nature is quick to forgive," said Jean-Baptiste pensively.

"It's odd you should have seen her. Normally the young lady never goes out. In the two years she has been here, no one—or practically no one—has ever seen her. I only caught a glimpse of her turning a corner in the hallway. But come to think of it, today is the Feast of Pentecost and the two women were planning to attend mass at the convent of the Visitandine nuns. That's what it is. Except on big occasions, her father keeps her hidden at home like a treasure."

"He's right," said Jean-Baptiste. "She is one."

"The consul is a monster," was all that Maître Juremi replied.

From the lugubrious tone of his voice, it appeared that he was again ruminating his grudge.

Jean-Baptiste crossed his legs on the parapet and stretched in his chair. High over the rooftops, the square of sky above the terrace was turning violet, while the setting sun colored the long tendrils of cloud pink.

This brief, dazzling encounter with a young girl above his station brought back thoughts of Venice, Parma, and Lisbon. But in those cities, anything was possible. . . .

Jean-Baptiste had grasped early on the advantages of a roving life. Being outside the caste hierarchy of a particular locale, the traveler is allowed the dignity of a free man and the chance of speaking on an equal footing to all.

Whatever his origins, a wanderer may, if he is clever, become a prince's friend or a princess's lover. At least he can envision the possibility. Poncet, who lacked neither cleverness nor imagination, had often proved this true in the cities where he had lived.

But as soon as he resumed his place within his country's order, as here within the Frankish colony in Cairo, he was nothing more—whatever pains he took to hide his ancestry—than the son of a servant girl and an unknown man. Differences in social station became once more a formidable obstacle, robbing him even of the pleasure, before such an apparition as he had seen today, of dreaming that happiness could be his. Since his arrival in Egypt, Poncet had had few encounters of this kind, but he had no cause to regret their rarity, as they plunged him into desperate unhappiness.

"Aren't you starting to grow bored with this city?" asked Jean-Baptiste.

"Hah! I would happily trade it in for another," said Maître Juremi, whose thoughts had taken a similar trend. "But where would we go?"

In every station in the Levant, as they both knew, they would confront the same discontent—not because the environment was too alien but because the representatives of their own nation had too pervasive and stolid a presence. The best would have been to return to Europe, but without a license they could not practice their trade without constant exposure to persecution.

"We should strike out for the New World," said Jean-Baptiste.

This seemed an excellent idea. In order to discuss it at more leisure, they set off cheerfully through the winding streets to the old section of Cairo and had dinner in an Arab tavern where the spring lamb was beyond compare.

~

The Jesuit priest asked for leave to retire and went to his room to rest. Monsieur de Maillet remained alone, his elbows on the table, giddy. He had stopped hearing the clergyman's explanations after his mention of an embassy. The shock had been unexpected, and the consul had managed to hide its full impact only by dint of a violent effort. Now that he was alone, he relaxed his guard and issued a stifled sob. A footman appeared and helped him onto a large bergère, where he collapsed.

The diplomat's wife and daughter were just then returning from their pilgrimage to the Visitandine nuns. Seeing the unhappy consul, they rushed to his side.

Madame de Maillet rarely left the house. In one of its rooms, set aside entirely for her use, she had set up an oratory in one corner, her tapestry and sewing in the others, and she addressed herself to each in turn. She devoted a veritable cult to her husband, which further contributed to her pessimism. The poor woman transmogrified the ordinary problems of consular life into horrific dangers, encouraged by Monsieur de Maillet, who exaggerated his encounters with the world in such a way as to terrify her. That all this would eventually lay him low was something she had expected for some time, without ever stopping to think what she would do when it happened. Now she went around in circles moaning. Her daughter, showing more presence of mind, applied her slender fingers to loosening the lace jabot constricting her father's neck.

Monsieur Macé glided into their midst. On seeing the consul's state, he suggested calling a doctor. The two ladies approved immediately.

"Yes, but who?" asked Mademoiselle de Maillet timidly.

"Plaquet?" suggested Monsieur Macé in a low voice.

The consul sat bolt upright: "Not him!" Seconds later he was once more established on the couch, claiming to feel perfectly recovered.

Such was the almost miraculous power of the man's name alone. Dr. Plaquet was an elderly ship's surgeon who had been stranded in Cairo after falling in love with an actress and following her there. The lady died, but the surgeon stayed on. Since the departure four years previously of the last real doctor Cairo had known, Plaquet had been the only licensed practitioner available to the Frankish community. Unfortunately his notions of medicine were so antiquated, his knowledge so uneven, and his methods so brutal that no one cared to consult him. Since any indisposition carried the threat of a visit from Dr. Plaquet, the French colony had for some time refrained from illness, just as a person can refrain from breathing and not suffocate immediately. As time went on, however, the merchants and ordinary people began more and more to apply to other healers: to charlatans, both Jews and Turks, and to druggists, the most famous being Jean-Baptiste Poncet. The consul, however, had expressly forbidden consulting these irregulars in medical matters. He therefore owed it to himself to set an example, hoping that in the few years he had still to spend in Cairo he might never need to resort to them. If the situation proved serious enough, he could always arrange to have himself examined in Constantinople.

As to bringing in Plaquet, never!

Everyone breathed a sigh of relief at the consul's providential recovery, and the room's atmosphere relaxed. Madame de Maillet called for coffee.

All four were soon seated in a circle, coffee cups in hand.

"It was nothing of consequence," the consul explained. "Our luncheon was . . . a bit heavy. The wine . . . to say nothing of the weather."

What more could he say? It was impossible to speak openly to these chattering women about the great secret he had just been told. Macé, perhaps? Yes, Macé would have to be let in on it. All this would entail a great deal of activity in the days to come, and he would need the assistance of someone. The Jesuit would understand: Macé was entirely trustworthy, a man who served unconditionally. The consul did take exception to the airs Macé put on when talking to his daughter. Right now, for instance, the two were turned toward each other, clutching their coffee cups. She would see nothing wrong in it, poor child. But you would swear that Macé was looking at her with more insistence than he should. Whatever is going on here, thought Monsieur de Maillet, I intend to stop it immediately.

Monsieur Macé was the only young man allowed, if not into the intimacy of Mademoiselle de Maillet, at least into her neighborhood. Although she found him terribly ugly and he left a malodorous trail in his wake, the young girl enjoyed talking to him. He was different and listened to her with great attention, and this was enough in her present state of isolation to make conversation a pleasure. As for Monsieur Macé, he had chosen his career for good and all, and would hardly compromise his chances of advancement by dallying with a young lady whose father held his fate in his hands. Yet on the rare occasions when Mademoiselle de Maillet came within his ambit, he found himself helplessly drawn to her, on account of her extraordinary beauty, grace, and youth. It was despite himself that he looked deeply at her, and despite herself that she responded with delight. This did not, in the eyes of her father, make the situation any less criminal.

"Might I have a moment in private with Monsieur Macé?" asked the consul in a severe voice.

The two ladies withdrew. Once the two men were alone, the consul began to pace back and forth, while Monsieur Macé waited quietly in the chair where he had been ordered to sit.

"There are many things I might say about your behavior, Macé," the consul started ill-temperedly, "but this is not the time. As a question of necessity—please note that I am driven by necessity and not by any consideration of your merits—as a question of necessity, Macé, I am going to entrust you with a most solemn political secret. You will show yourself worthy of it, or there is not a spot on earth where you will be safe from the wrath of the man you have betrayed."

So saying, the consul raised his index toward the portrait of Louis XIV. The young man bowed in sign of obedience, and, as he was seated this time, his nose practically touched his knees.

4

"The king," began Monsieur de Maillet gravely, "has decided, for reasons I am not at liberty to disclose, to send an embassy to Ethiopia."

"Your Excellency wrote a dispatch to that effect last year," said Monsieur Macé.

"Precisely. The minister had asked me to discuss the various ways of entering the country. The issue was already being considered at court, of course. Do you remember the conclusions I reached?"

"Two routes: the first by sea, past Jidda along the coast, and the second by land, through the Muslim kingdom of Sennar and the mountains."

"Your memory is retentive, Macé. Do you also remember my further observations on these two routes? By sea, the entrance to the country is controlled by a Muslim potentate in alliance with the Turks. The sole function of this barbarian is to prevent any white Christian from penetrating into his territory, Catholics in particular. No man has overcome this obstacle in the past fifty years. The last priests to attempt it had their throats slit and their tonsures sent, so I have heard, in a package to the emperor of Ethiopia, who had ordered their deaths."

Monsieur Macé made a grimace of disgust and fished a lace handkerchief from his pocket, which he briefly pressed to his nose.

"The land route has proved just as deplorable. The rare European travelers who have managed to penetrate the country and meet the emperor face to face—negus, they call him—have been held prisoner at his court for the remainder of their lives. More commonly, they have been stoned to death by the mob as soon as they were discovered to be Catholics."

"None of this," said Monsieur Macé sadly, "would have happened without the Jesuits."

"Hush!" said the consul, turning pale.

He walked quietly to the door and opened it to see that no one was listening in the hall.

"You know perfectly well that our visitor is one of them. What is more, he is closely allied to the king's confessor."

"But all the same," protested Monsieur Macé in a low voice, "they must know what happened there."

"It was fifty years ago."

"But what an odd mixture of adroitness and bumbling it was," the secretary continued in a whisper. "They converted the negus and practically subjugated the entire country, only to be chased out of it and banished forever. The upshot has been that no Catholic is allowed into Abyssinia on any pretext. Your Excellency does not mean to tell me that the priest now visiting this house is foolish enough to propose returning there."

"No, Macé. He is not planning to go there himself. His plan is more astounding than you are capable of imagining."

The consul's lower lip began to tremble ever so slightly. Afraid of a renewal of his earlier indisposition, he placed his hand on the oak table.

"This time they intend to send me."

"You, Excellency!" cried Monsieur Macé leaping to his feet. "But that is quite impossible!"

The two stood staring at each other for a time, pale and motionless. Slowly, a feeling of unease settled over them. It was utterly impossible, that much was certain. But why, exactly? The real reason—and the only reason—could not be voiced. One doesn't go announcing that one is afraid. How then was the consul to justify his refusal of the assignment? Monsieur Macé grasped that he had been presented a sensitive mission, his first. Here, unexpectedly, was a chance to return to the consul's good graces after his incautious conduct with Mademoiselle de Maillet over coffee.

"Your state of health . . ." said the secretary, his hand clutching at the air as though trying to catch a butterfly.

"Yes, yes," the consul picked up quickly. "My health would never withstand the journey. The climate, for one thing. And there are whole deserts to cross."

His face suddenly darkened.

"But they would never believe me. From the vantage point of Versailles, there is virtually no difference between Cairo and the sands of the Sudan."

"All the same . . ." said Monsieur Macé, his mind still racing.

"The Turks!" exclaimed the consul. "The Ottoman authorities would never authorize such a mission. Proselytizing on behalf of Christianity is forbidden here, and the Ottoman policy is for Abyssinia to remain surrounded by Muslim neighbors. Nothing frightens the Turks more than the idea of a Catholic alliance building at their rear."

"Yes," said Monsieur Macé. "If there is to be an embassy, it must be a secret one, led by an unknown."

"Moreover," said Monsieur de Maillet, not considering that he might be contradicting himself, "that will make it much less expensive. With the Ottomans, anything can be arranged for a price. But the pasha would charge a fortune to allow a consul, who has the rank of a bey, to travel on an embassy."

"At every turn the presents would have to be more extravagant."

The two men had reached a state of feverish excitement. Monsieur de Maillet dragged his assistant to a rolltop desk in a corner of the room. The heat had expanded its slats to the point where the desktop stayed stubbornly half open. Taking up pen and paper, Monsieur Macé wrote, under the consul's dictation, a short memorandum setting out in an orderly array the arguments that militated against the diplomat's traveling to Abyssinia himself. They read it over excitedly. Monsieur de Maillet poured two small glasses of sherry (the name they gave wine in that house when it turned a musty brown), and they drank a toast.

"All the same," said the consul, setting down his glass with a somber expression, as though the wine had filled him with bitterness. "To disobey the king!"

"Your Excellency is not disobeying him! The king wants an embassy. You are simply showing him why you cannot lead one."

"Then we must find someone else."

Monsieur Macé trembled at the thought that the consul might choose him. He felt no inclination to go to his death when a placid and brilliant career awaited him.

"The person we want," he hurriedly observed, "must have a good chance of success. The king does not simply want his embassy to set out, I would think. He also wants it to return. A diplomat would draw too much attention and never make it past the Egyptian border."

"Correct!" confirmed the consul. "And that is exactly what we wrote in our initial dispatch to the minister."

The two men thought in silence. The bells of the chapel rang two o'clock. The heat over the city had penetrated the curtain of greenery around the house. Sweat had turned Monsieur Macé's cotton jacket dark under the arm holes. For a moment, the consul was filled with disgust. Really, he thought, he might change his clothes from time to time!

He returned to his earlier train of thought, but the distraction perhaps influenced the direction of his mind, for he suddenly exclaimed: "What we actually need is a practical man!"

Surprised by his own idea, he stopped in his tracks. Monsieur Macé appeared equally startled by the obvious truth of this.

"Yes," said the secretary. "How right Your Excellency is. A man who would bring the negus what he wants."

"A merchant!"

Monsieur Macé's face suddenly lit up. "Sir, we received information last month, as you are no doubt aware, that a caravan from Ethiopia would be arriving in Cairo. Yet there has been no trace of it. The caravan must have disbanded somewhere south of the city. Its leader was a Muslim trader who has traveled back and forth to Abyssinia several times."

"Do you know him?"

"He was pointed out to me once in Cairo. He is perfectly modest in appearance, practically a beggar. But they say that on his last trip he brought with him five hundred thousand écus' worth of gold dust, civet musk, and ambergris, which he exchanged for goods the negus had ordered."

Monsieur de Maillet paced back and forth in a state of agitation.

"Might he still be in Cairo?"

"I wouldn't know. All in all, it is unlikely, but who is to say? He conducts his business with great secrecy. I am not even certain that he would consent to talk with us, let alone provide any information on Abyssinia."

"One thing at a time," said the consul peremptorily. "Find him. We will know how to make him cooperate."

The consul had made up his mind. He pushed Monsieur Macé toward the door.

"Go and look for the man immediately."

The secretary was somewhat disconcerted by the consul's sudden haste.

"Take my horse, a guard, money—whatever is necessary. If he is in the city, bring him back to me. By the way, what is his name?"

"The Arabs call him Hajji Ali."

"Well, my dear friend, good luck in finding Hajji Ali."

Proud of being addressed in this way but despairing of his mission, Monsieur Macé rushed into the courtyard of the consulate. Ten minutes later he was in the city.

Freshly rested, the Jesuit listened composedly while Monsieur de Maillet set out for him, in what was intended as an extemporaneous disquisition, the contents of the memorandum he had written with Monsieur Macé.

Father Versau took the consul's side after a brief discussion and agreed—much to the latter's relief—that Monsieur de Maillet should not lead the embassy to Abyssinia himself.

"In truth," the priest concluded, "no one thought that you would really go."

The consul was nettled by this remark. Did they suspect him of cowardice? He was about to protest when it occurred to him that real courage sometimes takes the form of swallowing insults without flinching. Valiantly, he kept his mouth shut.

"What alternative can you suggest to us?" asked the Jesuit calmly.

"It appears to me," began Monsieur de Maillet, "that given the disparity in power between our most holy king and the Ethiopian ruler—who, for all his crown, is only a native—there should be no appearance of a petition on the part of His Majesty Louis XIV. One never knows what to expect with people of this kind. Consider the affront to His Majesty if his embassy were to be made captives, as happened in the last century to the Portuguese embassy. Pedro de Covilham, its leader, was retained there for more than forty years and in fact died in Abyssinia. Therefore, while the rank of the envoy sent us in return is of the highest importance, the rank of our own messenger is much less so."

"Your reasoning is sound," said the Jesuit. "Our thought was that sending a genuine embassy would be the most likely way to provoke the Abyssinian sovereign to respond in kind, as we should like. But if you can suggest other ways of reaching the same end . . ."

The conversation took place on the little balcony outside the large second-floor room assigned to Father Versau. From this promontory, the two men surveyed the main street around which the Frankish colony was clustered. Every person who passed the consulate, seeing Monsieur de Maillet on the balcony, respectfully tipped his hat to him.

"It appears to me," said Monsieur de Maillet boldly, "that the best way would be to take advantage of the regular relations Ethiopia maintains with Egypt."

"And what relations might those be?"

"They are of two kinds. From time to time, the emperor sends a messenger to the Coptic patriarch of Alexandria to ask him to choose a new abun. In a tradition that goes back many centuries, the head of the Ethiopian Church, known as the abun, is an Egyptian Copt who is sent to Abyssinia for that purpose. However, the opportunity is too rare and unforeseen to be relied on."

"And the other opportunity?"

"The merchants. In some years, a caravan comes down from Abyssinia to exchange goods both in Cairo and along the route."

"I thought the negus was at war with the Muslims."

"We too, Father, are at war with the Turks, yet we stand peaceably on this balcony in conversation. States show a prudence that individuals should more often emulate. Certain ties never break."

Monsieur de Maillet spoke these last sentences with a grimace of courtesy that betrayed the enormous satisfaction he sometimes felt at being himself.

"Excellency," said the Jesuit, whose subtle smile registered his entire trust in the diplomat, "I leave it in your hands to propose a solution that will advance the king's plan."

The consul bowed his head. Inside, he was bursting with proud humility.

Monsieur Macé returned toward five o'clock. Perspiring profusely, his hair plastered to his head, the powder clotting on his cheeks, he burst into the consul's office with barely an apology.

"I have him," he blurted out excitedly.

"Our merchant?"

"Yes, Hajji Ali himself."

He got his breath back slowly, one hand pressed to his heart.

"I searched the entire city. Everyone said he was gone. By sheer luck, one of my informants had seen him yesterday."

"Where is he?" asked the consul sternly.

"On the landing. He is waiting. Let me explain something to you first . . ." Macé corrected himself: ". . . Excellency." As he regained his breath, he also recovered his sense of propriety, and it was just as well. Monsieur de Maillet did not approve of his subordinates taking liberties, whatever the circumstances.

"He is a rogue," continued Monsieur Macé, "and a sly fox. He would not let me speak a word about Abyssinia. I had to promise him . . ."

"Well?"

"One hundred écus."

The consul gave a start. "Oh, really?"

"For that price, he will talk."

"And what could he tell us that would be worth one hundred écus?"

"Excellency, I beg you to honor my bargain or I am a dead man."

"Fine, I'll pay. But what has he said?"

"Nothing yet."

"You are mocking me!" said Monsieur de Maillet, pretending to leave the room.

"Excellency, please. He will talk. He will tell us what the negus needs."

Monsieur de Maillet hesitated a moment.

"Well," he said irritatedly, "what are you waiting for? Show him in!"

Hajji Ali was one of those men whose ethnic origin is impossible to determine. Extraordinarily thin, at least to judge from his bony hands and hollow cheeks, he had delicate features, a hooked nose, heavy-lidded eyes, and a coppery complexion that would have made him seem a Yemeni in Yemen, an Arab in Egypt, an Abyssinian in Ethiopia, and even an Indian in India. He could even have passed for a European tanned brown by the tropic sun. He was clad in the blue tunic worn by Arabs and shod in green babouches. His right ear was pierced with a golden ring. Taking the consul's hand, he held it flat between both of his, made a sort of triple obeisance first, then placed his right hand on his heart, and ended by kissing his own fingers.

Monsieur de Maillet was in the habit of allowing the varied but, as it seemed to him, always tiresome forms of greeting to unfold without resistance on his part. He indicated a bench, and his guest sat down on it cross-legged.

The conversation started slowly, with Monsieur Macé interpreting for both of them. Hajji Ali praised the decoration of the consulate, the handsome appearance of the king, to judge from his portrait, and the refreshing quality of the hibiscus flower syrup he was served. He ended his remarks by observing in a melancholy tone that a sedentary man, no matter how great his wealth, must forfeit the company of the stars overhead while he slept. Monsieur de Maillet agreed politely. They were getting nowhere.

At a sign from Monsieur Macé, the consul extracted a leather purse from the rolltop desk in the corner. It contained the promised sum. Monsieur de Maillet gave it to the camel driver, who promptly caused it to disappear. Hajji Ali then began to talk about the negus. The present emperor was named Iyasu, the first of that name. He was about forty years of age. He was a great warrior, although his kingdom was currently at peace. He had fought many great battles.

"There is nothing that the Ethiopians need," said Hajji Ali, in answer to a question Monsieur Macé must have asked him earlier. "Their country supplies them with every necessity."

"Yet I understand," said the consul knowingly, "that the emperor has commissioned you to bring back certain things from Egypt."

Hajji Ali's answer was short.

"He says," Monsieur Macé translated, "'Not things.'"

"What does he mean, 'Not things'? What is it then?"

"I cannot say, Excellency. Animals, perhaps?"

"Ask him."

Monsieur Macé translated the question, and the merchant threw his head back and laughed. During this prolonged and noisy bout of hilarity, the two men observed the blackened stumps of gold-capped teeth at the back of the caravaneer's mouth. Finally the consul grew impatient. Hajji Ali slowly recovered his self-possession and wiped his eyes.

"May we know the reason for such gaiety?"

"Your question is apparently the source of it," said Monsieur Macé.

"I tell you he does not want things and you say, 'Animals?' It is very funny!" hiccuped Hajji Ali, still laughing.

"Sir," said Monsieur de Maillet angrily, "I fully share your sense of amusement. But what I would learn, since you have contracted to tell us, is what you intend to take back to Ethiopia if it is not things or animals."

Hajji Ali once again looked serious. "I am looking for a man."

Monsieur de Maillet exchanged a quick glance with Monsieur Macé. "Well, a man! And what man might that be?"

"That is a state secret. I may not tell a soul," said the merchant, in a tone that brooked no argument.

There was a long silence, during which Monsieur Macé signaled to the consul to go back to the desk for another purse. Monsieur de Maillet silently and angrily refused. Hajji Ali, his eyes half closed, pretended to see nothing. Finally, tiring of the contest and judging that his goal was not far, the consul gave in. He produced a second purse, which disappeared under the merchant's tunic.

"Last year," said Hajji Ali, as surely prompted to action by the purse as a mechanical toy by its key, "I was sick."

The consul despaired of this beginning. "Get to the facts."

Monsieur Macé judged it wiser not to translate these exclamations and to let the camel driver work up to his subject at his own pace.

"I was sick and I came to Cairo for treatment. The Arab doctors were unable to find a cure for me. I don't trust them anyway. It has always seemed to me that the Frankish doctors are more skillful. I made inquiries in your colony, and someone gave me the name of a friar. I went to see him. He was dressed as my people are, but his robe was brown with a rope around the waist."

"A Capuchin," interposed Monsieur de Maillet impatiently.

"Very likely. There are many of them here. This one was an old man who was nearly blind. I asked if he could heal those who believe in Muhammad and was told yes. In point of fact, he cured me."

"I am glad to know all this," the consul told his interpreter. "The man should understand, however, that his precious state of health engages little of our concern. Ask him what it has to do with our business."

"I returned to Abyssinia by the September caravan," continued the merchant. "No sooner had I arrived than the emperor summoned me. He made the unusual request of seeing me alone. During our interview, he informed me that he himself was ill, and his illness was identical to the one I had been cured of by this Frankish friar."

"And you have returned to Cairo for a doctor!" said Monsieur de Maillet, his face purple with emotion.

Hajji Ali assented with a respectful bow.

"May we know . . . whether you have found him?" asked the consul.

"Unfortunately," said Hajji Ali with an air of exaggerated sadness, "the old Frank who cured me last year died during the dry season. He was extremely old, and his heart . . ."

"What will you do now?" asked the consul.

"I will wait. Allah provides, if one has faith."

"Your piety is commendable," said Monsieur de Maillet somewhat impatiently. "But how does the business now stand . . . in worldly terms?"

"Other Frankish friars—of the same sort as the doctor who cured me—have promised me another doctor soon. They are waiting for one of their order to arrive from Jerusalem, a man with a great reputation for healing. Even now he must be nearing Alexandria. He should be here within ten days at most."

"How fortunate!" said Monsieur de Maillet.

"I too am glad this man is coming," the merchant continued, "because the remedies the earlier doctor gave me have run out and I need a new supply."

"Would it be possible to know the sickness in question?" the consul cautiously asked Monsieur Macé. The question was translated at length to the merchant, no doubt with many circumlocutions.

"My illness is not a secret. But as you know that the negus also suffers from it, I may not reveal its nature without betraying him. You should be aware that it is not a fatal illness, but that it causes great discomfort and tends to sour one's disposition, which is unfortunate in a sovereign."

The conversation continued along polite and insignificant lines for some time. Monsieur Macé brought the merchant back to his lodgings toward six o'clock, after they agreed to meet again the next day.

Monsieur de Maillet was pleased beyond all expectation. He showered congratulations on his secretary, which Macé received with bended back. In one day they had managed to revise the plan for an embassy without traducing it, yet in such a way as to spare Monsieur de Maillet's life. They had discovered the negus's weakness, along with a way to get a messenger into his presence. Moreover, the messenger was to be a Catholic friar, which could only rejoice Louis XIV. Both men gave themselves extremely high marks for diplomatic skill. The only thing needed to cap their victory was to bring the good news to the Jesuit.

"By the way," said Monsieur de Maillet, "what do you imagine the illness is?"

"In my opinion, Hajji Ali has a skin condition. You undoubtedly noticed that he was constantly scratching himself on his right side. When he reached out his arm for the cup of tea, I thought I noticed a sort of rash along his elbow, looking something like the lichens we see on the barks of trees in our forests."

"Well," said the consul, "it does not make much difference whether it is his skin or some other part of his body."

Thereupon, they went upstairs to speak to Father Versau. The Jesuit listened to their account politely, his hands folded over his stomach. But when Monsieur de Maillet reached the part about the Frankish doctor, the small black-robed man flew into a terrifying fit of rage. What amazed them in the first place was that so frail a body could unleash such a storm of violence. Later they tried to figure out what horrible mistake they had made to provoke such an explosive response. It was then that Monsieur de Maillet remembered that it had all started the moment he said the word "Capuchin."

5

The Capuchins, whose habits are recognizable for their cowl, or *cappuccio* in Italian, are reformed friars of the Franciscan order. Having run afoul of the curia in the Holy Land, which held jurisdiction over them, the Capuchins in Egypt had declined precipitately in number and seen their political power drastically reduced within the space of ten years. This was well known to Monsieur de Maillet. He also knew that to avoid being eliminated from the country entirely, the Capuchins had resorted to a devious stratagem. They had gone to Rome to ask the pope to intercede personally. They convinced him that thousands of Abyssinian Catholics, the converts made by the Jesuits fifty years earlier, had been driven out of the country by the negus's persecution after he expulsed the Society of Jesus. These victims of the Jesuits' zeal and the Ethiopian heretics' cruelty were barely managing to survive, according to the Capuchins. They were dispersed across the inhospitable south of Egypt between the land of Sennar and the Abyssinian border. The Capuchins claimed to protect these lost Catholics, whose existence the friars strongly confirmed, though no one else had ever seen them, and petitioned the pope to grant them official title to the mission. Innocent XII looked favorably on this order of simple, poorly educated friars, not unmindful that many were Italian, and granted their petition. With the pope's support, the Capuchins had returned to Egypt two years earlier. They migrated southward and opened a hospice in Upper Egypt. From having been practically absent from the country, they were now back in greater force than ever before.

Monsieur de Maillet also knew, though without giving it much importance, that the Capuchins' plans did not stop there. Their real goal was not simply to succor the Abyssinian Catholics in exile but to convert Abyssinia itself. The pope had encouraged their plans and created a fund to supply the needs of Capuchin missionaries to Abyssinia in perpetuity. This put them in direct competition with the Jesuits, who had never accepted their defeat in Ethiopia and believed that they would one day be returning there.

There were so few Jesuits in Egypt, and they lived so peaceably and with such apparent goodwill toward those around them, that the consul had misjudged how serious was their rivalry with other orders—at least among the upper echelons. Father Versau's wrath at the mention of the word "Capuchin" brought Monsieur de Maillet's error vividly to his notice.

"It is out of the question," the Jesuit explained vehemently, "for a message from the king of France to be transmitted by Italians. Moreover, the mission is the responsibility of our order and ours alone. The king's instructions on this point are unmistakable. And though my natural modesty has so far kept me from disclosing it, I may tell you that as I was passing through Rome to come here, I met with His Holiness the pope in person."

This fact raised the Jesuit's prestige even further in the eyes of Monsieur de Maillet, though it would hardly have seemed possible at first blush. The man presently seated across from him, not content with receiving his orders from the lips of the king's confessor, had betaken himself to the Supreme Pontiff and, separated by no greater distance than separated the two of them now, conversed with him. Admiration filled the consul, and with it a painful sense of shame at his gaucherie. He was prepared to hear the Jesuit's words in a spirit of total submission.

"The pope, to whom I represented the king of France's design, declared himself entirely in accord with it. Furthermore, he gave his blessing to any actions the Society of Jesus might undertake to rescue Abyssinia from the heresy into which it has unfortunately sunk."

Night falls quickly in the tropics. The blue twilight that now filled the room gave the cleric's words added solemnity.

"The truth of it is," he went on piously, "that for the spiritual reconquest of a vast people to proceed as an act of true faith, it must be performed by a universal and uncontested power standing far above earthly ambitions. Only the king of France, the greatest Catholic monarch of the age, possesses such power and can accomplish such a project with lofty disinterest. All the rest devolves from this one great conception: the pope recognizes it as sacred, and our order will execute it in all humbleness."

The priest paused for a moment and went on with a note of testiness in his voice, "Whereas an enterprise set in motion from below, led by generally ignorant priests, citizens of a weak nation, cannot help but be influenced by all-too-human motives."

The priest punctuated his last sentence with a sigh. Monsieur de Maillet, utterly devastated, held his breath.

"Your business has begun promisingly," the Jesuit resumed in a loud voice, his tone once again friendly. "To place our embassy in the hands of a physician, who would travel in company with this merchant, is an excellent idea. But the doctor must be French, and a priest of our order must accompany him."

Their talk was interrupted at this moment by servants carrying in torches. The spell was broken and the subject dropped.

Dinner was attended by general high spirits. The Jesuit told a thousand stories of his travels. The ladies questioned him about Versailles and Rome. He shone brilliantly, directing his attention most particularly toward Mademoiselle de Maillet. The girl's father was touched to recognize the native propensity in priests of this illustrious order for guiding the souls of the young.

Father Versau expressed a wish to see the two Jesuits he knew to be in Cairo at that moment. Might he meet with them on the following day? Monsieur Macé promised to convey the priest's message to them. The party broke up early and the consul was left alone in his study. He reflected at length on the terrifying fact—one he had at first refused to believe—that the Jesuits were not only foolhardy enough to send an embassy to Abyssinia, but wanted to go there themselves, when the entire country held them in hatred. But the worst for Monsieur de Maillet was that he now had to find a Frankish doctor in the colony, and there were none.

~

At seven in the morning, the cool of the night was peeling away in strips, as the city filled with warm light. The large trees of the Frankish quarter resonated with birds, busily singing in the last remnants of shade. The dust still stuck to the ground but once stirred up by footsteps remained suspended in the air.

Maître Juremi walked on the sandy edge of the road, passing from the shade of the plane trees into the bleached patches of sunlight and back. He was as happy as a dolphin skipping between the cool ocean and the warm air. Whistling tunelessly, he carried a small cloth bundle. The consul's flunkies had shown up the night before, as predicted, to deliver a summons for him to appear at the consulate.

In the end, Maître Juremi had accepted the wise counsel of Jean-Baptiste. He had packed a small sack with toilet articles, a clean shirt, and a pocket Bible, and was setting off for jail as gaily as a man on his way to an afternoon of fishing.

At the entrance to the consulate, a servant came and politely took him into custody. He led him to the second floor; then, passing through a low, hidden door in the upper hall, they entered a small room. It was wonderfully cool, its windows opening onto the leafy structure of a vast mulberry tree. In the center of the room, and occupying most of its space, was a table laid out for a meal. Light caromed off a white tablecloth embroidered with the Maillet crest, glinted among crystal glasses, and lit up a carafe of fruit juice, two porcelain cups, and a loaf of fresh bread. The lackey pulled out a chair for Maître Juremi and invited him to sit down. The druggist refused. Some misunderstanding was at work here and it was bound to be discovered soon. Maître Juremi started to tell the lackey that it was a mistake, that he just wanted to go to jail, but the servant disappeared, leaving him standing in the middle of the room with his bundle, trying to calculate all the ways this misunderstanding was going to cost him, as it was bound to do shortly.

The consul arrived before long, looking unwell. His eyes were red, and he had applied a great deal more makeup and powder to his face than he should have. It was therefore particularly surprising to discover that his mood was affable.

"Maître Juremi! How delighted I am to see you! Now why were you not offered a seat? Please, do sit down!"

Startled, and without relinquishing his distrust entirely, the druggist folded his long body onto a dainty chair. The consul ordered mint tea and lavished small attentions on his guest, offering him milk, sugar, a stirring spoon, etc. He poured the fruit juice into their two glasses with his own hands. Maître Juremi started to regret that he had not stayed with his rapier—one solid stroke would have put an end to the entire comedy.

"The work you performed was excellent," said Monsieur de Maillet, raising his eyebrows and adding in spite of himself, "though it was done in my absence."

Maître Juremi could think of no response. To give himself composure, he stuffed an entire pastry into his mouth and waited, muzzled, for what was to follow.

As he was not an articulate man even under normal circumstances, it could hardly be expected that words would suddenly spring to his lips now.

"Your business takes considerable talent," the consul went on, "combining herbs, making them into different pastes, coatings, and varnishes, no?"

Maître Juremi tipped his head to one side, then the other, shrugged his shoulders, and continued to chew.

The consul had something on his mind, but what could it be? The diplomat drained a large cup of coffee in a single draft, and the druggist judged that the issue would soon be on the table.

"These mixtures can be put to many uses, no? Have I not overheard that you even make . . . remedies?"

Now we are getting down to it, thought Maître Juremi.

He started to breathe more heavily, like an antelope suddenly sensing that the bushes behind it are stirring.

"Don't be afraid," said the consul, fishing out a small handkerchief yellowed from frequent washing and wiping his mouth. "My predecessors often acted strictly toward certain of your colleagues who practiced as apothecaries or physicians without the requisite licenses. I myself may have been cautious, but it is perfectly understandable in the circumstances—there are so many charlatans in these parts. What do you think?"

Maître Juremi hiked up his eyebrows twice, which Monsieur de Maillet took as a sign of assent.

"But my mind is henceforth made up," he continued. "I have seen you at work—on a painting, it is true, but nonetheless. And the information that I have received about you is uniformly excellent. If you tell me that you make herbal remedies, believe me, you will have my full support. I am a man of my word, did you know that?"

"Yes, Excellency," said Maître Juremi with some difficulty.

"Then speak to me frankly. Are you familiar, as is widely claimed, with the herbalist's pharmacopoeia?"

"I believe so," said the druggist.

"He believes so! What modesty! I have heard it said that you do more than appears, that people from all parts of the colony visit you, that even the pasha consults you."

Maître Juremi looked down at the floor.

"Do not regret it!" insisted Monsieur de Maillet. "It is well. Excellent. I never suspected such talents in you, Maître Juremi. Your modesty is too complete. Madame de Maillet had to inform me, as I suffered last night from a slight indisposition, that she herself, my own wife, and without my knowledge, had called upon you six months ago, and that you had cured her."

Seeing the terrified expression on his guest's face, the consul spoke in even gentler tones.

"Do not be afraid, truly. I am at a loss as to how to convince you. I offer you my sincere congratulations. And what is more, my encouragement."

Monsieur de Maillet rose, walked toward the window, then turned and looked at the druggist. "Would you be capable, for instance, of curing skin diseases, one of those leprous conditions that often afflicts black men here?"

"How can I put it, Excellency," Maître Juremi finally mumbled. "There are two of us."

"What do you mean?"

"I have a partner."

"Fine. I am well aware of it. Kindly answer my question all the same."

"The point, Excellency, is that medicine is more his domain. He prescribes a remedy, which I then prepare. In the case of Madame de Maillet, for instance, I described your wife's condition to him, and he told me what she would need. I prepared the unguent and brought it to her. That was the extent of my involvement."

The consul walked back to the table and resumed his seat.

"I see," he said. "Then I should really be talking to your partner."

"That is what I have been trying to say to Your Excellency."

The warmth that Monsieur de Maillet had invested in the conversation sank by several degrees.

"What was his name again?"

"Poncet, Excellency. Jean-Baptiste Poncet."

"And where can I find him?"

"We share a house. He lives on the upper floor, while I live on the ground floor."

"And your laboratory?"

"Ah! Your Excellency would be hard pressed to distinguish between what serves us in our lives and in our work. I can hardly describe to you . . ."

The consul remained thoughtful for a long moment.

"Do you think," he finally said, "that your friend would be willing to undertake a lengthy voyage?"

"You would have to ask him, Excellency. He is . . . an unusual young man. If I were not his partner, I would even say that he . . . has a certain genius."

"Genius! You don't say!"

These adventurers have no qualms about anything, Monsieur de Maillet thought to himself.

"Could you bring him to me?"

"Certainly, if you request it. We are subjects of the king, and you are his appointed representative."

Even from a man of no consequence, Monsieur de Maillet could never hear such professions of faith without a gladdening of his heart, and he could never remain ungrateful to a person who offered his loyalty so sincerely. Here, he thought, is the very harmony that binds a monarchy together: a welcome authority over grateful subjects.

Maître Juremi smiled within himself. He had often noticed that he knew no middle ground between impulsive rebellion and utter obsequiousness. It was the mask he wore as a Protestant. Monsieur de Maillet would have been highly surprised to learn that the man before him was one of the fierce emigrants William of Orange had used to break through the Stuarts' defenses on the coast of Ireland. Yet the wound he bore on his stomach was a remnant of that engagement, and Maître Juremi felt a great inclination to draw up his shirt and expose his saber cuts to the consul.

"In that case," said Monsieur de Maillet, "tell your partner that I expect him here at eleven o'clock."

"As Your Excellency wishes. And yet . . ."

Maître Juremi hesitated. The consul did not seem ill-intentioned, and there was little risk in having confided Jean-Baptiste's true profession to him. It was his friend's character that was more likely to provoke difficulties. Had Jean-Baptiste not said just the night before, "If he were to summon me, I wouldn't go"?

"And yet?" said Monsieur de Maillet impatiently.

"And yet as I know my friend Poncet well, I might suggest another course."

"Which is?"

"I believe that if Your Excellency were to call on him at home, or rather at the home that the two of us share, my partner would be infinitely grateful to you and could refuse you nothing."

"I call on him! The fellow grants audiences then?"

Maître Juremi judged it prudent to say nothing.

It was strange, absurd, even revolting, thought the consul. But as this was an emergency and the man did have the upper hand—in his own way and for a brief instant—one might as well swallow one's contempt.

"Will he be there in an hour?" asked Monsieur de Maillet, his fists tightening.

6

The carriage, drawn up on the wooden cobbles of the courtyard, stood waiting. It was a splendid vehicle, built in Montereau and brought over from France in two separate ships, the wheels in one, the coach and shaft in the other. The consul used it for his official visits to town, finding that it gave him added authority among the Turks. After deliberating for the entire hour he had allotted himself, Monsieur de Maillet finally resolved to take his carriage to the doctor's. The man lived only a few dozen yards away, and it would have been easy, in fact perfectly natural, to go there on foot. It might even have kept the visit more discreet, but it would also have made it more suspicious if anyone noticed. No, the best way to avoid drawing too much attention to the whole business was for the consul to set out in his carriage, to stop in front of the town house of an important merchant he sometimes visited, and to make a detour across the street to where the apothecaries lived, pretending to have no other motive than curiosity. The consul asked Monsieur Macé for his opinion, found his own judgment confirmed, and the two men set off around ten o'clock in the morning.

In order for his outing to seem all the more normal, the consul ordered his coachman to proceed outside the colony, take a turn around town, and return and stop "in front of the town house of Monsieur B."

"So, Macé," said the consul, slightly nettled, "what have you discovered in our files about the great personage we are about to visit?"

"Very little, Excellency. The man lives quietly. We do not even know if Poncet is his real name. He arrived here three years ago. We know that he first lived for six months in Alexandria, having fled Venice. He has boasted several times that he practiced medicine in Marseilles, in Beaucaire, and in Italy beforehand. We have good reason to suspect that his papers are false. His birth certificate comes from Grenoble, where that defrocked monk who practiced forgery with such unusual talent was apprehended last year. Your

Excellency, having been alerted to these facts at the time, graciously agreed to extend his protection over Monsieur Poncet, notwithstanding our ignorance of the place, date, and circumstances of his birth."

"What does his birth matter!" hissed Monsieur de Maillet between his teeth.

As far as the consul was concerned, only a nobleman had a birthplace, on land where he owned both men and soil, and which bore his name. The rest were born wherever they could manage, and the only interest the matter held was anecdotal.

"Have we any clear idea why the man should be wandering from place to place?" he asked. "Perhaps this Poncet is as much a Protestant as his partner."

"I believe his displacements have been provoked by denunciations. He practices medicine and pharmacology without a license of any kind. As to his religion, we are quite certain that he is a baptized Roman Catholic."

"Yet I have never seen him at chapel."

This was a reference to the small church attached to the consulate, where the colony gathered every Sunday.

"Well, but at least a quarter of our community are no more observant than he."

"I know, and one day we will have to find a remedy."

"The priest says the man used to go there from time to time outside of services when he first arrived in the colony. Apparently, he even brought flowers to the church once."

"Has he ever taken confession?"

"Never."

The consul shrugged and looked out his window impatiently.

Monsieur Macé shuffled through the yellowing papers on his lap. The open windows brought the warm air of the Arab city washing through the carriage with its smells of coffee and dried spices. The crowds in the narrow streets practically jostled the carriage at times. Children yelled out jibes and took off running. Women, always gathered in groups, cast inquisitive glances into the carriage from behind the close protection of their cotton veils.

"Not many citations," the secretary continued. "Disturbing the peace: he and his partner got to drinking one night to celebrate something or other. There was a complaint for dueling, but it turned out they were just clashing swords for the fun of it. Poncet goes about a great deal among the Turks, attends to the pasha, a number of beys, the chief qadi of Cairo, numerous merchants . . ."

That was precisely what made the affair delicate for the consul. The favor in which the apothecary stood with the Turkish authorities gave him considerable independence. The consul knew from experience that it was dangerous to provoke men who could arouse the ill will of the natives over a trifling incident and create a diplomatic brouhaha. Poncet was undoubtedly aware of this. And the man might authorize himself on that account to lace his behavior toward the consul with considerable insolence.

"Your file is exceedingly thin, for which you can hardly be congratulated," said the consul haughtily, though he did not in ordinary times attach much importance to gathering information about the members of the foreign community.

The carriage had stopped, its circuit accomplished, before a private house. Its rich proprietor bustled out with exclamations of surprise and pleasure. The diplomat was disagreeably forced to express his equal joy at seeing the thickheaded trader, but to regret that a small matter, one that merely piqued his curiosity, claimed him across the way. So saying, he took Monsieur Macé's arm and crossed the street with determined dignity.

The house shared by Poncet and Maître Juremi was of far lesser consequence than the one it faced. It consisted of no more than a collection of two-story structures attached one to another. The facade onto the street would have formed an uninflected wall had not an entire wooden apparatus been appended to it, a scaffolding forming a sort of arched gallery at street level through which one could walk in the shade; above was a balcony acting as a visor against the sun to keep the rooms behind it cool. The residence of the two druggists was not otherwise set off from the houses on either side except as a section of the entire block, identical on the outside to those around it. This little neighborhood housed the least prosperous elements of the colony in close and unsanitary proximity: new arrivals, bankrupts, widows, and mixed-race children of unofficial status, whom the consul sometimes had the kindness to tolerate within his community.

The door to the druggists' house stood open. To avoid standing in the street suspiciously, the diplomats entered without waiting for an invitation. Maître Juremi hurried up to them and ushered them past the narrow entrance hall into a vast, dark room that occupied the entire ground floor of the house. The scene was one of indescribable disorder, far too heterogeneous to be made sense of visually. On first sight, one noticed mostly the bronze mortars, gleaming with yellowish reflections. Clay retorts set on glowing coals spewed columns of smoke into the air, but the smoke, weighted by mysterious and heavy substances, sank back in horizontal layers and crept around the walls. In one corner a worn sheet was stretched over the surface of a straw mattress. The ceiling was low, blackened by soot, and from it hung a hundred or perhaps two hundred wicker baskets stuffed with dried plants, withered fruits, and crusts of bread half-gnawed by rats.

"I take great honor, Your Excellency, in welcoming you to our laboratory," said Maître Juremi, who, with his tall, broad frame, almost brushed the ceiling beams.

"Your partner is in?"

"Upstairs."

Through the gloom, a shaft of light drifted down from above, and a plank staircase led up through the opening. The consul, with Monsieur Macé in tow, ascended the stairs.

The room above turned out to be as bright as the room below was dark. It was lit by four large windows, opening onto the balcony on the street side and a terrace on the other. The ceiling had been removed—or else had never existed—providing an unobstructed view of the rafters and the grayish underside of the roof tiles.

The space was entirely filled with leaves. Full-sized trees, rooted in large wooden tubs, towered upward into the light and moist heat. A giant euphorbia reached practically to the rooftree, while a lustrous ficus, various trees with hairy trunks, and others covered with sharp spines commingled their branches. In the gaps left open by these large specimens appeared a multitude of smaller plants. The floor was almost completely covered with pots except for a few narrow paths, one leading to the French windows onto the terrace, another to the windows onto the balcony and the street. There was also a table piled high with books, and a small wardrobe in the one dark corner. At an intermediate height, either hung from the wall in copper and tin planters or suspended with lengths of cord from the joists, were dozens of other plants of all kinds—succulents, umbellifers, lichens, and orchids, all thriving peacefully.

The consul and his secretary were momentarily struck speechless. In the extraordinary jumble of this veritable greenhouse, one could hear the fluttering and chittering of small birds. Maître Juremi had stayed below. Aside from their two selves, the visitors could make out no other human form in this earthly paradise.

"Come in, come in, dear sirs," a voice invited them from somewhere high in the room.

The two diplomats took a few steps forward, as the floorboards moist from frequent waterings, squeaked under their feet. Toward the back of the room, at head height, hung an empty hammock.

"I will just finish this delicate graft and join you directly," said the voice. "Do take a seat in the meantime—there are two stools near the table."

Monsieur Macé, whose eyesight was good, motioned the consul to observe where a ladder was set against the top of the highest tree. On the last rung stood two legs in supple leather boots.

"Well, well," said the consul in a loud voice, betraying little irritation, "take all the time you need!"

He motioned to Monsieur Macé, and the two made their way across the floor, stepping over pots, catching their stockings on unnoticed thorns, toward the table, where they sat down as the voice had ordered them to.

"There is only the shortest season for these cuttings," the voice went on from the top of the ladder. "And in our trade, everything depends upon hybrids. The plant in its wild state is only our raw material. Ah! Ah! Ah! This little wire has gone and broken again. Please excuse me."

"We understand," said Monsieur Macé, beginning to fear that the consul would be unable to hide his anger much longer.

"Yes, it is only the raw material, as I was saying. We need to cross species, make one serve as a support for another. To us, Nature is only a starting point. We have the ingredients. What we need now is to explore the world of combinations."

On the table were piled a disparate set of works, which the consul leafed through nervously: a treatise on botany, the odes of Horace, and several quarto volumes in Arabic.

From a stout tree branch hung two fencing foils, while on the floor below them lay gloves, chest protectors, and face masks: all the equipment necessary for fencing.

"You are welcome to start the discussion of our business. I am Jean-Baptiste Poncet. Apparently you have something to tell me."

"Sir," said the consul, rising to his feet, "the matter I have to discuss is of the utmost urgency or you can be certain that I would not have come to visit you. My wish, in all honesty, was to see you. However, as long we are able to hear and understand one another, it may do just as well."

"Truly," said Jean-Baptiste in a warm and sincere voice, "I am grateful to you for letting me complete this task. Otherwise, all the work I have done would come to nothing."

"Monsieur Poncet," said the consul abruptly, still standing with his head raised toward the roof, "is it true that you practice medicine?"

"Ah! Your Excellency, I have always known that this moment would come. We will hide the truth from you no longer. It has been a source of chagrin to me that we have not been able to speak of this earlier. There was no pleasure in having to hide in order to practice an art which, after all, is for the common good. Yet I knew that you were hostile. As you are here, I will in a moment show you specimens—"

"Listen, Poncet! My question is simple and straightforward. I have no intention of imposing a sanction on you—to the contrary! I will ask you again, and I expect you to answer me simply: do you practice medicine?"

"Yes."

"Could you treat, for example, those skin diseases that the natives have, those leprosies and funguses?"

"Nothing could be simpler. That is not to say that there exist any miracle cures. Each case requires individual treatment."

"Enough on that score," said the consul, cutting him off. "Let us move on to another question. I have come with the solemn proposal that you undertake a diplomatic mission of great importance."

"This wire, this wire. Juremi!" the man cried out from the top of his ladder.

"Did you hear me?" asked the consul.

"Yes, yes. Go on."

"Would you agree to carry a message for the king of France?"

"What is it?" asked Maître Juremi in a loud voice, his head appearing from the depths below.

"It is this copper wire. Could you bring me a new spool of it, like a good fellow. The one I have keeps breaking."

"Monsieur Poncet," said the consul, maintaining a tenuous hold on his composure, "I am speaking to you on matters of the highest importance. Can you not spare me two minutes and climb down from that tree?"

"I have almost finished. There are only two or three knots left, but if I stop now the whole thing will be ruined. But you needn't worry. I have heard everything you said. A diplomatic mission for the king . . ."

"A mission that would make you one of the most glorious instruments of Christianity, of the pope himself."

"I have already told you," said Poncet in a voice devoid of the slightest trace of enthusiasm, "I will do anything it may please you to request, Consul. But I have little stomach for official matters."

"Let us look at the business in different terms. It is a question of giving medical treatment to a sovereign."

"Louis XIV?"

"Not exactly." The consul sniggered, impatient at such naïveté. "A sovereign to whom the king of France would send you. Do you understand? There is glory in treating the body of a great king, is there not?"

"You know, when we doctors look at a body, there are no kings."

Monsieur Macé glanced at the consul and saw the same tide of discouragement rising in him as he felt in himself, a feeling that might at any moment burst into a flood of invective or tears.

"Now, Consul, I am moved that you have come all the way here. Whether or not a king is involved, if you ask me to treat someone, I will do it for you. I only hope it is not too far away. I have a great deal of work on hand and it would hardly be possible for me to leave for any length of time."

"In that case," exclaimed the consul, falling back into his chair, "I am afraid all this is useless."

"Go on all the same."

"What I propose," said the consul in ironic tones, "is more than a brief house visit. I estimate that it will take you more than six months to reach your patient's bedside."

"Six months! What can you possibly be talking about?"

"To treat the negus of Abyssinia in his own home," said the consul.

There was a long silence in the branches of the tree, then the visitors saw the ladder shake and a set of feet start down the rungs.

Jean-Baptiste soon reached the ground. He brushed away the little leaves that clung to his shirt and hair and walked slowly toward the diplomats.

He looked much younger than Monsieur de Maillet had imagined, probably because of the strong hold on the public mind of a doctor as a wise old man.

Beyond this, the consul took little note of the physical aspect of the man now facing him. What he noticed was his manner, and it displeased him. There was no constrained mimicry as though sketching the first motions of a ritual politeness, and no sign of respect, let alone subservience. There was nothing studied about his expression, which was open and natural. The two visitors, powdered, sweating, and bewigged, took pains to give themselves a posture of authority. Their interlocutor gave them (as he did to all creatures) a look that was strong, curious, frank, and sympathetic, which seemed to them the height of insolence. Confronted with so singular a character, Monsieur de Maillet maintained himself more than usually on his guard. Monsieur Macé felt himself immediately invaded by a lively hatred.

The consul and his secretary both detested freedom—the one piqued because it could not be brought into submission, the other regretful at never having embraced it—and they both recognized it now in front of them. Jean-Baptiste, after a moment's silence, advanced a last step toward them and said with a smile:

"The negus of Abyssinia! Now that, sirs, is something we should talk about."

7

Madame de Maillet stood at the front steps waiting for her husband. In the breathless heat, she nervously agitated a large paper fan decorated with Chinese roses. The carriage returned at eleven. The consul stepped out with his assistant. Madame de Maillet ran up to her husband.

"Dearest, I beg you to take some rest. You never stop. The climate is dangerous. Your heart . . ."

"Have no fear for me," said the consul, "but rather for the affairs of state, which are in grave difficulty. And tell me where I may find Father Versau at this time."

"He has been closeted in his rooms for more than an hour with the two Jesuit priests who came to visit him this morning."

The consul made his way toward the second floor, motioning Monsieur Macé to follow.

The vast room assigned to the Jesuit opened at the back onto a small paneled study with low ceilings. Here the ecclesiastic spent the better part of his day. Monsieur de Maillet knocked and was admitted, with Monsieur Macé at his heels. They joined a table at which three black-robed clergymen were already seated.

"Allow me to introduce you to Father Gaboriau, whom you know, and Father de Brèvedent, whom you have not yet set eyes on, I believe," said Father Versau.

The diplomats greeted the two clerics. Father Gaboriau had lived in the colony for fifteen years at least. He was a portly man, with square, reddish hands and a face to match. He taught class to the children of the Frankish community. Several generations of children, riveted by the chaotic lineup of his upper teeth, which sprouted in all directions, had tried hard to understand how they could close on an equally obstreperous set of lower teeth. Yet each time the good father stopped talking, the miracle recurred and the saurian maw closed placidly. The only consequence of this mandibular deformity was that the father, irreproachable in all other respects, showed a marked preference for liquids. The consul, whose virtual monopoly on the wine trade we have already noted, was largehearted enough to supply spirits to the clerical orders at cost. The profits he thereby forwent remained relatively trivial as long as the men of the cloth kept their consumption within reasonable bounds. Father Gaboriau was the only one to abuse the system. While Monsieur de Maillet's piety forbade him to believe the priest a drunkard, there was nothing to keep him from considering him the near equivalent of a thief.

The other Jesuit was the opposite in every way. He was tall and frail of limb, without being thin, and his complexion was waxy. He wore small copper-rimmed glasses perched on a minuscule nose. The attenuated central portion of his face only emphasized the forehead that bulged below the line of his close-cropped hair and the prominent mouth and chin. These protrusions seemed to consist more of flesh than of bone: his great lips hardly closed and his neck skin was already starting to hang down at the chin. This stooped man with his forehead and spectacles, with his bony hands accustomed to turning yellowed pages, was instantly recognizable as a scholar.

"You are quite right," said the consul, bowing. "I have not met Father de Brèvedent."

"He arrived only two months ago, and the Turks, as you know, have made great difficulties for us. Officially, we may have only one of our number here in permanent residence. The rest must be simple visitors. As far as the authorities are concerned, Father de Brèvedent is therefore only an ordinary visitor."

Brèvedent smiled timidly and watched the consul out of the corner of his eye without turning his head.

"Now then," said Father Versau, "have you discovered a likely envoy?"

"Yes, Father," said the consul, "I have found one, though it was far from easy. He is a Frenchman, a Catholic, a doctor, possessed of a strong constitution and an innate sense of adventure."

"Clearly the answer to our prayers," said the Jesuit, looking around the table for approval. "Has he accepted definitely?"

"How shall I say. . . . He will be here following luncheon. His decision is not yet final. I thought it best not to press him. You will have the opportunity to communicate the details of the mission to him directly. And we shall all be present at his induction, should you approve of him, which can only strengthen his commitment."

Monsieur de Maillet thereupon gave a detailed description of the man in question. He walked a careful line, skillfully as he fancied, between praising the individual's virtues and exposing his bizarreness. He judged it prudent to forewarn Father Versau of their candidate's apparent age.

"He looks youthful, but our police reports tell us that he is older than he appears on first sight."

With a laugh, the consul added, "It must be the effect of a cordial he makes from plants and administers to himself by way of experiment."

"A youth potion?" asked Father Gaboriau, who had been dosing himself with vegetable juices all his life with little success.

"I suppose. It is otherwise difficult to explain his extraordinary state of preservation. . . ."

They continued to discuss elixirs for some time, until a footman sent by Madame announced that lunch was served, and they all went downstairs.

Mademoiselle de Maillet joined them at table. Spurred on to shine in conversation, Father Versau depicted in almost every detail the mission to Ethiopia ordained by the king of France. The consul felt the disclosure vain and possibly harmful. He promised himself to speak to his daughter that very night about the strict discretion to be maintained on this subject. The meal, in the meantime, was a very lively one. Father Versau told all that was known about the Abyssinian emperors, one of whom had been converted by the Jesuits at the beginning of the century. They had left accounts of their stay in Ethiopia, as well as of their subsequent expulsion and the great persecution of Catholics that followed. The ladies voiced their indignation at this. He then described all the dangers that the mission would face, and the terrible cruelty of the climate and the peoples on its path. Lunch ended in a sort of voluptuous stupor. The consul had to admit that the house had rarely known such animation or, despite the seriousness of the subject, such gaiety. The two visiting Jesuits only came off the worse by contrast: one of them, Brèvedent, never gave up his air of contriteness, while the other, turning redder than ever, had nodded off after the third glass of wine.

Just as the group were rising from table, the steward came in to announce Monsieur Poncet. The ladies withdrew, and it was decided to receive him in the audience hall, under the portrait of the king, while taking coffee.

Poncet entered. He had not bothered to change his clothes but had simply slipped on his dark blue doublet over his shirt, leaving it unbuttoned. No hat, no lace cuffs, no cane. His black hair hung free, his curls swaying when he turned his head. His slender hands, the tips of his fingers tinged green, began to walk through the air the moment his conversation took an animated turn. He saluted the consul and the three priests, looking them each in the eye. The consul performed the introductions. Father Versau, seated in a large armchair almost directly under the king's portrait, spoke majestically.

"Monsieur Jean-Baptiste Poncet," he started solemnly, "can you state for us officially whether you will agree to journey to the king of Abyssinia and deliver him a message from the king of France?"

Poncet's face brightened into a broad smile.

"Sirs, I find you in something of a hurry," he said, laughing. "Consider that I am still standing, that I have worked all morning, that I have come here on foot, the only person in the streets, or practically so, at a time when the heat deters others from stirring. Moreover, I see here coffee and biscuits . . ."

"You are right," said the consul, whom a sense of urgency had distracted from his duties. "Please take a chair. What may we offer you? Macé, if you would be so kind, a cup of sweetened coffee for Monsieur Poncet."

The young man soon had everything he required. He drank his coffee slowly, turned the conversation to the portrait of the king and the way it was restored, and spoke of the trees he had seen in the consulate garden on the way in. When the conversation was flowing, the others contributing to it easily, he returned abruptly to the business at hand.

"So, gentlemen, you wish to send me off to treat the King of Kings? The idea is a good one, I swear to you. Excellent, even. The more I think of it, the more clearly I see that only a doctor could enter that country without being put to death immediately. But what makes you think that the present emperor needs my services?"

"We have it from the most reliable source," said the consul. "The negus himself has sent for a medical practitioner. A messenger is in Cairo at this very moment who has been charged with bringing him a doctor, and you are to travel with him."

"Let us hope the king does not die before I reach him! Well, it cannot be helped."

"The attempt must be made in any case," the consul added.

"The medical question is one aspect of the business," interpolated Father Versau, speaking now in more familiar tones, "but there is also the message we would like you to bring."

"And what exactly might that be?" asked Jean-Baptiste.

"Very well," said Father Versau, pleased that the conversation was finally coming to essentials. "You will first win the emperor of Abyssinia's confidence by treating his complaint. You will then solemnly announce that you are also—and above all—the envoy of His Royal Highness King Louis

XIV. You will explain to him that the king of France takes a great interest in the Christian kingdom of Abyssinia. We expect you to convey in every detail the unequaled greatness, surpassing power, and saintliness of the French monarch. The negus must quite simply be made to understand that the princes of the Western world have, almost to the last one, consented to pay homage to the king of France. Furthermore, it is in the interest of the king of Ethiopia to bask in this great light himself and turn toward it."

"Handsomely put," said Poncet, "and I hope I manage to convey the message, but what practical consequence do you foresee from all this?"

"What we would like," said Father Versau, "is for the negus to send an embassy to Versailles in return. The embassy should be a brilliant one, led by a man who has the emperor's entire trust, and augmented by the representatives of several noble families in his entourage. Finally, and this is of crucial importance, it must include several young Abyssinian boys who would study at the Louis-le-Grand preparatory school in Paris. They can then attest to the great glory achieved the world over by our language, our culture, and our sciences."

"Will you give me a letter to this effect?" asked Poncet.

"An official letter," the consul interposed, "affixed with all the requisite seals and ribbons."

"But," Father Versau continued, "you must hide it jealously. The message is to be delivered only to the negus himself."

"I believe I understand," said Jean-Baptiste. "Now, if you will take the trouble to consider matters from my point of view, I think we can say that the diplomatic mission is additional."

"Additional?" queried the consul, startled.

"Yes, additional. You will all agree that I am not primarily a diplomat by trade. If I go there it is to cure the emperor of his disease. That is what we must discuss."

"And what is to discuss?" asked the consul. "You simply tell us yes or no, and there is an end of it."

"Your pardon, Excellency," said Jean-Baptiste, "but there appear many details still to consider. The first is to know what I will receive by way of fee."

"Fee!" exclaimed Father Versau. "You are being asked to carry out the king's will. The honor—"

"Every man wants what he has least of," Poncet cut him off with a slight cough. "And what I lack is money."

The consul looked at Father Versau with a horrified expression.

"How am I to treat the poor for free," Jean-Baptiste continued, seemingly untroubled by the loud silence around him, "if the rich won't pay?"

"Sir," said Father Versau finally, "the emperor wants a doctor: he will therefore pay you himself. Our only contribution can be toward the cost of your voyage."

"I accept your reasoning," said Poncet, biting down on a cinnamon biscuit. "I will apply to the emperor for the fee. But let us examine the costs."

There then followed an involved discussion during which the doctor extracted from the consul a promise—it would be put in writing—to bear the cost of all the accouterments of travel, and to reimburse him for the work missed and clients lost in consequence of his long absence. The value of the medical instruments he brought would be paid to him beforehand on the likelihood that they would all be destroyed or damaged en route, and he insisted on a provision of warm clothing and weapons. Additionally, there was the cost of providing mounts for the expedition, and of paying the ransom that each kinglet would exact for crossing his lands.

The consul agreed to all the items, while horrified at the expense. He resolved to write that very day to his relative Monsieur de Pontchartrain to have the expenditure endorsed.

"Well then, I accept," said Jean-Baptiste finally. "I will go to Abyssinia whenever you like."

There was visible relief around the room.

"I would just like to add one detail," said Father Versau, determined that the agreement should overlook nothing.

He motioned to his colleague with his hand, saying, "Here is Father de Brèvedent, who will accompany you."

"A Jesuit in Abyssinia!" said Poncet. "But their emperors have been denouncing you as enemies for fifty years. Father, this is a risk that I would not ask anyone to take."

"You are not asking him to take it," said Father Versau firmly. "Our orders are from the king. And as you have pertinently pointed out, the affair happened fifty years ago. Things may very well have changed. You can be sure in any case that there is no question of taking Father de Brèvedent with you in the guise of a Jesuit. No one here knows him. He is simply a traveler. There he will be, let us say, your servant."

Poncet exchanged a brief glance with Father de Brèvedent, who looked as pleased as if he had just received a bastinado.

"A servant it is, then, as long as he agrees," said Poncet.

He then turned toward the Jesuit. "We shall call you . . . Joseph? How does that suit you, Father?"

Brèvedent lowered his eyes to the floor.

"As long as we are choosing the expedition," said Jean-Baptiste, "I have a partner that I am hard pressed to do without. Now if it were at all possible for him to accompany us . . ."

"A Huguenot!" the consul exclaimed sharply.

At this, Father Versau rose to his feet.

"Sir, I believe we have acceded to your every request. Do not presume any farther. It would be unthinkable to include a political emigrant in a matter that so closely concerns the king and our church. This is easy enough to understand. Let us talk of it no more."

Poncet, who had not even consulted Maître Juremi, decided the battle was not worth pursuing. He let matters rest there.

Both sides solemnly renewed their agreement. The consul accompanied Poncet to the front hall. When he returned, a visible satisfaction had come over the men in the room. The consul joined in the chorus of thankful exclamations. Macé, in his usual style, shot the dove on the wing:

"Now," he said darkly, "we have only to persuade Hajji Ali to break his agreement with the Capuchins."

Standing on the steps of the consulate, Jean-Baptiste took a deep breath. The scent of pine, volatilized in the hot air, carried to him from the Azbakiyya gardens nearby. But beyond the smell of the oasis, beyond the smell of the desert, coming to him from where the winds had their source, and borne down from the highlands along the course of the great river, he seemed to detect the aromatic gums and spices of the land of Punt, the fragrant country he was being sent to explore. Abyssinia . . . he had dreamed of this land. In Venice, his friend Barbarigo had told him of the adventures of João Bermundez, the companion of Cristovão da Gama, Vasco's son, who had sped to the aid of the Ethiopians a century ago when a Muslim invasion threatened. Traveling there himself had remained a dream, and Jean-Baptiste would never have dared to implement it. But now his good luck, which he firmly believed in, was offering him the means to go there. He had been longing for a new world, and what world could be newer than this legendary and inaccessible land? Rather than empty and unknown, it was rich and coveted, freighted with gold and history.

Born at a time of misery, in the France of the insurrectionary Fronde, and having neither wealth nor station, Jean-Baptiste had been offered every opportunity for sadness and despair, yet he had decided long ago that he would never succumb to such feelings. And it would be difficult to imagine a merrier existence than he led, or one less bound to routine or subject to outside constraints. The very moment he started to feel bored with this city, knowing it too well, his fate intervened, as in an Arabian tale, and transported him to the country of his dreams.

Marveling at this turn of events, Jean-Baptiste walked slowly down the steps of the consulate. He had often passed in front of the consulate's small garden but had never had a pretext to go inside. He stopped to look at it now. To the right of the short gravel alley was a bowling green, in the center of which burbled a small stone fountain. He walked toward it. Behind the fountain, he noticed a small tree he had never seen before. Even distracted by his reverie, Jean-Baptiste looked at the world with a botanist's eye. He knelt by the bush and examined its leaves. Then, partly to look up its name later in his books and partly to have a souvenir of this day, he took a wood-handled budding knife from his pocket, intending to cut off a small branch. First casting a glance around him to make sure that no one was watching, his startled eyes locked with those of Mademoiselle de Maillet, standing at a window on the second floor, her elbows resting on the sill. She had so little expected him to raise his eyes that she felt as entirely surprised as he.

In his present good spirits, Jean-Baptiste interpreted this second meeting in as many days as a happy sign. He smiled. She was still wearing her blue ribbons. Having espied this familiar landmark, Jean-Baptiste felt free to look more deliberately at the young girl's delicate features: her small, straight nose, and her pale, limpid eyes from which all gravity disappeared when she answered his smile. But no sooner had the young girl revealed her rows of white teeth to him, inflaming his sight, than she withdrew. Jean-Baptiste stayed momentarily with his knee on the lawn, then stood up, waiting for her to reappear. The window remained empty. He slowly walked back to the alley, then out onto the street, and from there home, taking his time.

The extraordinary voyage that had just been proposed to him once more filled his imagination. Mademoiselle de Maillet's sudden appearance, which yesterday had plunged him into melancholy, today added to his joy. Everything was possible again. He felt himself once more a free and unfettered traveler, as he had in Venice, in Parma, and in Lisbon. Just thinking this made him imagine pleasure. It was all he asked for.

8

Alix de Maillet had been an ugly child until the age of fourteen. Raised in a convent near Chinon after her parents went to live abroad, she was subject to cruel nicknames all through childhood because of her tubby form and red cheeks: "Poppy-cheeks" and "Turnip-face" were two she remembered. But the corollary to being thought unsightly was that others looked on her with a certain indulgence. No one was afraid or jealous of her, and, at the cost of repelling others by her appearance, she was rewarded by their affection. The early years of her adolescence only confirmed this state of affairs. Her body promised to undergo its transformation without any improvement to her proportions. She had entered convent school ugly at the age of six and would leave it ugly at the age of fourteen, to rejoin her parents in Egypt.

It was then, inexplicably, that beauty came over her, the way a rash spreads over a person's face at the onset of fever. She grew long and slender. All her stores of unattractive fat melted into sap and made her shoot upward. Her red cheeks turned paler, and so much white was blended with their pink that her complexion became one of extraordinary freshness, and satiny to the touch. She loosed her thick blond hair, which, having been tied in a chignon or braids since childhood, had acquired the dark tones of oak. By misfortune, her beauty had settled on her at a time when she was alone, and there was nothing to signal it back to her from the outside world. The way her parents looked at her was nothing to judge by, she had no girlfriend to reflect her image, and the mirror alone told her nothing. She felt a transformation in progress and even thought she saw her premonition confirmed when she looked at herself. But she also wondered whether the awful solitude she lived in might not be misleading her. In her family's fine house in Cairo, she saw no one and, more important, no one saw her.

At first she had maintained a girlish correspondence with a few old school friends. But when no answering letters arrived or they came only after a long delay, she stopped expecting them and soon no longer wrote any herself. She took a few piano lessons, but her ancient instructress collapsed in the street one day on the way to the consulate and died after lying unconscious for ten days. Father Gaboriau tried to teach the young lady Latin, a language she understood better than he, having been a good student at the nuns' school, and mathematics, which did not interest her. She begged her father to let her stop these lessons. The one thing she had left was reading. The library at the consulate was fairly well stocked. She enjoyed the natural sciences and classical tragedies. She was strongly encouraged to read edifying texts, among them the fables of La Fontaine and Fénelon's *Télémaque.* And she discovered novels all on her own, a genre her father condemned although he had not read any and did not hide them. *La Princesse de Clèves,* with its heroine oppressed in love, opened a new world for her, one she never again relinquished. One doesn't have to be beautiful in order to dream, as she had proved all through her childhood. Her body had for a time preoccupied her, seeming to offer the chance to find happiness in this life, but in the end it had only led her to uncertainty and self-doubt. And so she reentered the world of her imagination with voluptuous pleasure. There, at least, she was the fairest of them all, and received praise on all sides.

After lunching with the Jesuits, the young girl sat down at her bedroom window and looked out at the foliage of the lindens in the consulate garden. She thought of Abyssinia, which she had just heard described, and of the worlds around her, so close yet inaccessible, where other young girls were probably dreaming, and which she might easily have been born into. She fantasized that her skin was black. Looking at the gold bracelet against her milk-white wrist, she wondered how that same yellow radiance would look against a dark ground. Flitting from one thought to another, she slipped away from the objects around her and, leaning her elbows at the window, entered the deep reverie that was now her natural state, in which hour after hour slipped away unnoticed.

Suddenly she heard a noise on the front steps, directly below her. It was her father seeing someone to the door. She watched the man go down the stairs. From behind she could see that he was slender, hatless, his head surrounded by curly hair, and his feet shod in soft leather boots. He stopped on his way down the alley. She continued to watch him. At that moment he stepped aside from his path, walked across the grass, and knelt by the strange little tree she had already noticed herself, thinking that it looked like none of their common plants.

She could now make out the visitor's profile. It was the young man she had seen the day before on the bridge over the Khalij, the one who had looked at her so strangely. His gestures, which were resolutely simple, had a striking elegance. She noted the ease with which he knelt down, how he pulled a knife from his pocket, grasped a branch. At the consulate, the rare people she encountered belonged to one of two apparently incompatible worlds. There were the men of circumstance—educated, polite, full of their own importance, stiff, precious, and incapable of a natural gesture, especially a practical one. Then there were the men of the people, those who did everything but counted for nothing. Whether cooks, coachmen, or guards, they were as coarse as they were skillful, to the point where one preferred them to stay quiet and in the shadows. The young man before her seemed to blend elements of both castes: he had the figure of a master, and the ease of a footman.

At no time as she watched him did she feel any apprehension about being seen. Alix believed herself to be in the world of dreams still, where the sleeper is never unmasked by her own invention. Yet this young man turned his eyes toward her. How long had it been since she had felt the sensation, so natural to those who live in society, of being examined by an unknown person? Possibly she had not even felt it once since leaving childhood, or perhaps only with the old priests her father sometimes invited to dinner. But this bold incursion, by a man who yielded gracefully to inspection himself, who maintained his natural stance and his expression of open astonishment, this she had never experienced. In her confusion, she offered a smile in answer to his own. Terrified, she then took three steps back from the window, regretting it immediately. Her hands clasped behind her back, feeling the wooden door of her bedroom, she stood still for a long moment, breathing hard, her feelings in an uproar. She already missed the warmth of that gaze. Hers had been the reaction of a child who runs away at the thought of danger, just at the point of enjoying a delightful experience.

Why did I step back? she asked herself. That young man does not scare me. I'm not afraid, I'm not. Besides, he looks extremely honest and polite, or my father would never have invited him here. How could I be doing anything wrong by looking out the window? And what shame could there be in watching a visitor leave the consulate?

Thus she reasoned with herself for a long moment. When the struggle at last concluded and one of the scales had tipped the balance in its favor, she rushed back to the window. The stranger had disappeared.

She waited, saw that he did not return, and faced back into her room. Heat battened on the house. Outside, the trees swaying in the tepid wind brought some relief, but inside there was none. She looked at the bed with its green moiré spread, the pillow embroidered with her initials, the little table covered in green baize, the cabriole chair, the books, the few porcelain dolls. These familiar objects, which had soothed her on so many days, were essentially the jailers of her solitude. The man's look had unmasked them. Unwilling to draw any consolation from them, she stood and sobbed, her face in her hands.

"Green!" said the consul categorically. "You heard me correctly. And after two days of horrible pain, he fell to the ground, like rotten fruit."

"Give me a moment to translate, Your Excellency," said Monsieur Macé, waving his hands.

Hajji Ali leaned back, a horrible expression on his face.

"He wants to know if the patient died," the secretary translated.

"No," replied Monsieur de Maillet learnedly. "Or at least not right away. He suffered for a very long time first. He begged to be killed for mercy's sake. However, we Christians are not allowed to sever the body from the soul."

"I would have done it," cried out Hajji Ali, brandishing a small dagger that appeared suddenly from under his capacious tunic.

"Tell him to stay calm," said the consul, backing away, "and to put down that object."

Hajji Ali mopped his forehead with his sleeve and turned to the diplomat more evenly, looking him in the eyes.

"Are you certain that you are telling me what truly happened?" he asked.

"Am I certain? I only have it from my honorable colleague in Jerusalem, who wrote it in his own hand to Monsieur de Ferriol, our ambassador in Constantinople, who has sent me word of it just now by express messenger. He arrived this morning, and you will find his horse still in a lather in my stables."

Macé translated.

"A Capuchin friar," said Monsieur de Maillet slowly and distinctly, as though he were driving home a difficult lesson, "who has been passing himself off as a doctor, recently left Jerusalem. He boarded a boat for Alexandria and Cairo. It must be the very same one, no?"

"It must be," said Hajji Ali.

"Three patients that he claimed to have treated for leprosy were brought into the consulate after his departure. My colleague saw one of them alive, but the other two were dead. The limbs of two had turned green, and one had lost his altogether."

"Enough," bellowed Hajji Ali, burying his mouth in his elbow, convulsed by retching. "Don't tell me the whole thing again."

"I only repeat it because you refuse to listen. And you continue to doubt the story."

"It is just that there are other Capuchins, and it may have been they . . ."

"Let us drop the subject," said Monsieur de Maillet, rising to his feet. "I warned you. If you want to take the chance of bringing a charlatan to the negus's bedside, let it be on your head. After all, it won't be mine that rolls."

"But what choice do I have, if I don't take this Capuchin?"

The consul resumed his seat. This was taking longer than he had expected.

"There is a Frankish doctor in the colony who is a perfectly capable man."

"Really?" said Hajji Ali, his features lighting up with excitement. "Who is it?"

"An apothecary. He treats the pasha himself."

"Oh, yes! I have heard of him," said the trader. "But all the same, for a Frank to get his references from the Turks, don't you think it a little strange?"

"What do you mean, his references from the Turks! And what about my reference? No, no, I formally recommend this man to you. He has doctored my own wife."

Hajji Ali looked doubtful still.

"The Capuchins warned me against him," he said finally.

"And on what grounds, if you please, do they spread calumnies?"

"He is not pious."

"He is not pious!" exclaimed Monsieur de Maillet, rolling his eyes with impatience. "In the first place, it is false: he goes to church. In the second place, what does piety have to do with the question? If he is a good doctor, what does anything else matter?"

"Nothing happens in this domain without the help of God," said the camel driver, shaking his head.

"What can you be thinking of? You are a Mahometan, the doctor is a Catholic, and the negus is a heretic. What sort of God is ever going to make sense of that?"

"God is God," said Hajji Ali, bringing his fingers to his lips and looking into the air.

"Then take the Coptic patriarch of Alexandria with you and ask him to perform a miracle," shouted the consul.

The man, as Monsieur de Maillet could now sense, was drawing him into territory where he would soon be defending the most repugnant atheism just to make a case for his candidate. He held silent, and the merchant remained for a long time absorbed in his thoughts.

Hajji Ali had no idea whether to believe the story about the courier from Jerusalem. In his world, which was the world of the desert, things were not less true for seeming incredible, and he took care not to provoke what might be supernatural powers.

What he knew for certain was that the consul had a strong and unaccountable wish to see him break with the Capuchin friars and take this Frankish doctor instead. He made a quick calculation of his own interest and saw that it did not lie with the ecclesiastics. For one thing, they promised him nothing and even acted as though doing him a favor. Moreover, they endangered his caravan. Not only the Turks but every native power along the way would likely be alarmed by the friars. The Frankish doctor would be a lesser target for suspicion . . . and if his government was so eager for him to go, then perhaps they could agree on a price.

Hajji Ali started to wail and bemoan his sorry plight.

"Kindly ask him why he is moaning," said the consul angrily to Monsieur Macé.

"He says he is thinking about the great cost to him of changing his plans and bringing a different doctor."

Glory be, the consul breathed to himself, we are finally there.

The discussion continued for another half hour. Monsieur de Maillet was obliged to return three separate times to the drawer of the little rolltop desk. There were the camels to be changed, the messengers to be sent, and the prayers to be offered up. But at the end of the day, the matter had been settled honestly between them, and everyone left satisfied.

When Father Versau learned of the happy outcome of the negotiations, he announced that he would leave the following day. His route lay toward Damascus, where he had other business awaiting him. Dinner was eaten quickly and in silence. Father de Brèvedent came back after nightfall to receive his superior's final instructions. The two priests held their conference on the second floor.

Monsieur de Maillet retired early, overcome with fatigue.

Not far away, in one of the last small streets of the colony, Jean-Baptiste and Maître Juremi had supped with great gaiety and drained a bottle of their best wine. At ten o'clock they went out onto the terrace. The sand-laden wind drew a veil over the stars and trapped the day's heat in the air around them. From every part of the Arab city came the sound of tambourines and ululating voices, the season of weddings being still in its final days. Dogs howled back and forth.

"No, no," said Maître Juremi, continuing their discussion, "there is no question of my taking part in this business."

"But the consul would never need to know. I won't say a word. My manservant and I leave town, and we meet you a little farther down the road."

Juremi, holding his pewter goblet in one hand, raised the other in a gesture of authority.

"It's useless! The answer is no."

"Then we are going our separate ways?"

They had first met in Venice five years earlier. Jean-Baptiste was looking for a fencing master. He had happened on this great hunkering French émigré, black-haired and fractious, living under an assumed name. His students knew him as Maître Juremi.

"So it appears," said the Protestant glumly.

He turned away. Though an emotional man, he disliked showing any sign of his feelings.

Before setting himself up as a master-at-arms, Juremi had worked at every trade under the sun and remembered with particular fondness a period he had spent making preparations for an apothecary. Jean-Baptiste had put the alembic and assay scale back in his hands, and Juremi had given up trading in sword cuts. The two had entered into partnership and fled together to the Levant.

"This world!" burst out Maître Juremi all of a sudden, pushing back from the balustrade. "It looks as though it is all my fault."

He took two angry steps along the terrace, then turned back toward his partner.

"We are separating not because I refuse to leave here," he said, "but because you accepted an engagement unilaterally and, I think, a little hastily."

"Weren't you saying only yesterday," said Jean-Baptiste in self-defense, "that you wanted to leave Cairo and set out for the New World?"

"The New World! And not on orders from that consul, either. If I ever travel to untouched lands, believe me, I won't be going with Jesuits in tow."

"Oh, the Jesuits," said Jean-Baptiste, "they are nothing but a means. Do you think I have any use for this mission? I don't give a fig for their embassy and the king's service. But if they are asinine enough to outfit me with horses, arms, and equipment, do I have to be even more asinine and refuse the offer?"

"It makes no difference. You are bound to it now."

"Bound? You are joking. Nothing says I have to do what they expect of me. If a place strikes my fancy, I'll stop there, and if a road draws me on, I'll follow it. Their embassy can go hang itself. I am curious to see Abyssinia, and that's the only reason I am going. Besides, if I find the country suits me, I might very well stay there."

They were silent for a long moment. Maître Juremi, still not saying a word, went back into the house, where a candle was burning. He took down two swords and grabbed up the leather chest protectors. Since turning to pharmacology, fencing had become simply a pastime to while away the summer nights with. They stood en garde.

"Come on," said Jean-Baptiste before they crossed swords. "I know you well enough—you'll go."

"No, sir, you will not make me change my mind," said Maître Juremi, "but I wish you a safe journey."

As soon as their two swords clashed, the gloom that had seemed ready to pounce on them was dispelled.

9

Preparations still had to be made for the caravan to Abyssinia, which would be led by Hajji Ali and include Poncet and his manservant Joseph. Everything was to seem as natural as possible so as not to awaken the suspicion of the Turks. The consulate, therefore, could take no part in it, nor could Jean-Baptiste show too active an interest. It was Hajji Ali who bought the camels and the mules, and their saddles, bridles, and pack harnesses. The arrangement was that Monsieur de Maillet would pay the outfitting costs, at whatever price the trader quoted. This gave Hajji Ali the opportunity for added profit, and with it he bought as much merchandise as he could safely load onto the animals. Once in Abyssinia, where the goods could be exchanged for gold and civet musk, the trader could increase his investment tenfold.

The consul drew up an official letter for the negus. He had it translated into Arabic by Monsieur Macé. As a further precaution, he had Macé check the translation with a learned Syrian monk, Brother Francis, who lived in the Arabic quarter. When it was done, the French seal was affixed to it and it was handed over to Poncet. There were still presents to be gathered for the rulers whose land the caravan would cross. The tariffs were set according to a strict schedule, which had been in place since time immemorial.

For his part, Jean-Baptiste busied himself collecting a medical arsenal to deal with every imaginable contingency. Monsieur de Maillet had given him a new and spacious flask case in which to stow his medicines securely. Jean-Baptiste also chose the expedition's weapons. A large musket was installed on Joseph's saddle, while the powder and caps were left in Poncet's keeping. Other than a pair of swords, Jean-Baptiste had two pistols bought for him, which he packed in his saddlebags.

As the preparations went on, the consulate developed into the operation's headquarters. The members of the caravan met there discreetly each night before dinner to discuss the day's progress. The so-called manservant Joseph had stopped wearing his Jesuit habit so as not to draw attention to himself. He had not yet assumed his valet's disguise, since the consulate's own servants, some of whom might be spies, would be quick to suspect him. Hajji Ali, Poncet, and even Maître Juremi (who was not taking part in the journey but was helping with the preparations all the same) came and went at the consulate without being announced. Monsieur de Maillet allowed these liberties because he knew they would soon end.

The bustle was tiring to Madame de Maillet, but delighted her daughter, Alix, who for once had the pleasure of seeing a few visitors around the house. Most of all it gave her the opportunity to catch sight of the young man she had surprised in the garden, several times and at close range, and to learn his identity. Jean-Baptiste was always extremely circumspect toward her, and took care not to cause her any embarrassment by addressing her directly. Yet Alix soon had the startling and delicious impression that they were communicating as surely as if they were talking face to face.

The first time she had this sensation was the day the men held a lengthy debate on whether mules or camels could carry the larger load. Jean-Baptiste maintained that, conventional wisdom to the contrary, camels carried less cargo than the humble mule. He and Hajji Ali argued the question, while the consul, Monsieur Macé, and Father de Brèvedent all voiced their opinions. In keeping with the new tenor of the consulate, in which all doors were now open, Alix entered the room where the conversation was in progress. She stayed off to one side, seated on a stool with her embroidery, observing the visitors. She felt immediately that the young man was speaking to no one but herself. The impression was strange. Jean-Baptiste's words seemed to ricochet off the solid mass of the men facing him, whom she saw backlit and from behind. The words reached her as smooth and as rounded as pebbles in a riverbed, their syllables indistinct, their original meaning erased. All that was left was their music, which was addressed to her for no other purpose than to delight her—a task in which it succeeded wonderfully. Had the two been holding an actual conversation, she would have had to attend to the meaning of his words, whereas this silent interchange was made up of pure emotion.

From time to time the young man glanced in her direction. His eyes seemed to look far in the distance, to a point well beyond the window. The others probably saw it as nothing more than a mannerism of the kind a speaker uses to collect his thoughts. But she felt with absolute certainty that his gaze was resting on her. And she knew that the light, reflecting off her face and long blond hair, carried her image, her whole self, into the dark chamber of his eye and on into the man's secret heart. But the play of looks and glances, if it inflames the imagination, does not appease the passions it arouses. Far from assuaging Alix's desire to approach the young man, these troubling signals only increased it. He for his part did nothing to bridge the distance separating them, while she was prevented from doing so by both her station and her sex.

One afternoon, though, using her mother as a shield against moral blame, Alix managed virtually to address the young man as he entered the consulate. The two ladies were strolling in the small garden. As Jean-Baptiste reached the alley at their height, Alix spoke up loudly enough for him to hear, pointing at the shrub next to which she had seen him kneeling.

"Mother, why do you not ask this man, who knows so much about plants, the name of this bush, which we noticed yesterday and which is unfamiliar to us?"

Jean-Baptiste stopped, bowed to them easily, and offered his reply in an untroubled voice.

"I, too, have noticed it. Curiously, it belongs to a species that is unknown in Europe and that even John Ray fails to include in his herbal. The only mention of it I have found is in an old Egyptian text. The species is apparently common farther south. The plant never grows any taller than this one, and blooms only once in its life, with bright red flowers that last only a few moments. Some point to it as an explanation for the Bible passage about the burning bush."

He spoke these last words looking straight into the young girl's eyes. It was she, all of a sudden, whose cheeks took flame. He bowed immediately and left.

Madame de Maillet, who had not noticed her daughter's confusion, came back repeatedly to this explanation of the Bible, which delighted her. It was only the following week when she told the story to her confessor that she discovered such symbolic and scientific explanations of the scriptures were the work of cabalists and philosophers, who were equally irreligious.

On the eve of the caravan's departure, Alix realized suddenly that these days of happy disorder were coming to an end, that she had never spoken to the young man directly, and that he might die in the course of his perilous journey. Was there anything she might do? As usual when on the point of passing through the door that would take her out of the realm of dreams, Alix hesitated. She felt how little talent she had for real life, and told herself that all the feelings, all the looks, and all the thoughts she had imagined as belonging to the young man probably had come from herself. Besides, had he ever made an attempt to speak to her or send her a letter? At her first overture, he would surely inform her of her error. What do you want, Turnip-face? Who does this Poppy-cheeks take herself for? As long as she sought no confirmation, she would suffer no rebuff. Alix could then preserve intact the whole store of phantoms and sweet dreams she had collected over the past happy days. What more could she hope for?

Jean-Baptiste, for his part, was beset by perplexity. He was about to embark on a journey that he looked forward to passionately. It suited his taste for adventure and exploration. He was engaged in enthusiastic preparations for it. Yet now, having met this young woman, he felt qualms, and a shadow had fallen over what should have been his unalloyed happiness.

After the melancholy of their first encounter on the bridge over the Khalij, and the cocky daydream of the second at the window of the consulate, there had come a succession of visits and daily encounters. Jean-Baptiste had had time to contemplate at leisure what at first he had glimpsed only fleetingly and to observe this young girl closely. He now even knew her first name. Far from dissipating the grace and mystery of his first impression, their proximity over the last days had only confirmed his initial sense, nourishing it and making it so vivid that her image filled even his dreams. It had reached the point where he started to miss Alix when he didn't see her.

The disparity in their social stations, which had struck him so forcibly at first, and subsequently had seemed possible to ignore, had reasserted itself. An unbearable wall had risen between them, though their glances constantly wandered across it. Jean-Baptiste was in despair.

This period of preparations and daily meetings lasted only a short week. Dominated as it was by the excitement of the caravan's departure, it had offered Jean-Baptiste little time to analyze his feelings. Besides, in whom could he confide? Maître Juremi shied away from such subjects and knew no middle ground between hushed Protestant gravity and barracks-room coarseness. Aside from Juremi, Jean-Baptiste knew no one in Cairo who could play the role of sympathetic listener, though he himself received all the town's confidences. He suddenly saw himself as the most solitary and unhappy of men, a new sensation for him, overtaking him just as he was embarking on a heady journey. For the first time he felt the paradoxical sweetness that results from extending compassion toward oneself. On the eve of his departure, in the late afternoon, he set out for the Arab city, crossing two wedding processions at al-Azhar Mosque, and entered the Roda gardens.

With its ancient potbellied sago palms, its great mango trees with twisted trunks, and its rough, austere acacias, it was the spot in Cairo that best approximated the Mount of Olives, where a man who was shortly to take leave of everyone he knew might go and meditate. Yet Jean-Baptiste had hardly arrived in this solitary place before he felt how little talent he had for despair. The lush plants of the garden exhaled their oily perfumes into the air rising off the sun-heated ground. Old, barefooted gardeners pensively watered the beds of young plants, and the water flowing over the dry ground made a soft and delicious sound. The days were still long. At that hour the sun was gone, but the purple-shadowed light would last far into the evening. Jean-Baptiste sat down on a bench, laughed at the stupidity of having forfeited a whole hour of his life to melancholy, and swore he would never do it again.

He then tried to look at the situation as dispassionately as possible. First, he had to admit his lack of experience. Although he had long been enjoying women's favors effortlessly, he had never known love except as he awoke it in others. From these one-sided passions he had learned little, except how to escape the inconvenience of a violently jealous husband. One outraged spouse had even forced him to leave Venice in disastrous circumstances. Since arriving in Cairo, he had behaved cautiously and managed to extricate himself unscathed from the intrigues that lovely and desirous Ottoman ladies had tried to draw him into. One bey had even befriended him and offered him his eldest daughter in marriage. There was a condition attached to it, of course: Jean-Baptiste had to convert to the Muslim faith. The young man used his religious objections as a pretext to end the affair, which, on his side at least, involved no deep feelings.

Fortunately, he was lucid enough not to take these frolics and diversions for love, a feeling he readily admitted to never having known. This caused him neither sorrow nor regret, it was a simple fact. No woman had ever made him feel the lasting sense of unrest, the capture of the whole mind, the subjugation of the heart and senses that must indicate love. Accustomed to seeing only the bright side of what happened to him, he had been mostly pleased that no passion had ever come to place limits on his freedom. His first reaction at being hounded, at the very moment he was embarking on an adventure, by the tender and troubling image of Mademoiselle de Maillet had therefore been one of displeasure.

An old man, slouched on his donkey's back, was slowly coming up the road. Across the still, quiet evening came the old man's clucking encouragements and, in answering rhythm, the muffled sound of the donkey's hoofs. The panniers hanging at the donkey's sides were filled with prickly pears. As the man neared, Jean-Baptiste signaled to him, handed him a piaster, and received four of the fruit in return. He began peeling one with his budding knife, still sitting pensively on his bench.

Now he no longer regretted being in the grip of love, for it was clearly love this time. But what could he do? The only solutions that came to mind were futile. If he stayed on in Cairo, the consul would be furious. The man would persecute him and most likely force him into exile again. It was absurd in that case even to think of the consul's daughter. The child had responded to him as she did because she lived in isolation, but she was nonetheless a young lady of privilege. A man such as himself could never entertain any thoughts toward her, especially if he abandoned the diplomatic mission that had briefly given him standing in her world. If he left, on the other hand, he would probably never see her again. This was most likely the best solution. Everything passes, and travel helps bury memories, the bad with the good, by flinging handfuls of new impressions on them.

Something told him, however, that he could bridge the two courses that seemed irreconcilable, that he need renounce neither his desire to see Abyssinia and distinguish himself there nor his impulse to win the unreachable Alix de Maillet, whom he believed in every fiber of his being to have been created only to meet him and make him happy.

The prickly pear was sweet and juicy. He liked the contrast between the small hard seeds and the soft flesh. He picked up another. It still had its spines, and pricked him. It is because it pricks that it is so sweet, he thought.

It was one of those meaningless sentences that sometimes find their way into a train of thought. What he must have meant was that the spines of the cactus protect its fruits from the animals that covet their sweet flesh. But his mind, made clumsy by the problem that obsessed it, seized on this paradox and transposed it to his situation. He was dazzled by it, as though he had experienced a revelation. That's exactly it, he thought, dropping the pears. There are extraordinary obstacles between myself and her, and only extraordinary circumstances can surmount them. If I were staying on in Cairo, I would never have seen her, never have approached her, and nothing would have been possible between us. But the mission entrusted to me, by putting me in the way of great dangers, can also provide me with a great triumph. I go to Abyssinia, I cure the negus, I return with the embassy as requested, and I accompany it all the way to Versailles. Louis XIV knights me and the consul can no longer refuse me his daughter. There. Today prickers and tomorrow, thanks to them, sweetness.

The young man stood up and, mumbling to himself, strode quickly toward the garden's gate. With the broad outline now in mind, the rest should come to him without much effort. He developed a plan of action easily, judged it to be excellent, and swore that he would hold to it.

Everything now appeared to him in a new light, especially the diplomatic mission he was charged with. At first he had thought it served only the interests of the king of France and the pope, but he now realized it could also bring about his own happiness. The business was becoming altogether more serious.

10

On questioning the boatmen in Bulak, Cairo's port on the Nile, Monsieur Macé learned that two Capuchin friars were making their way upriver from the delta on a rotten felucca. They were still three days away from the city. The news of their impending arrival spurred preparations on. The caravan was set to depart in two days, on a Monday. The day before, Father de Brèvedent asked the consul if he might conduct the weekly mass at the consulate himself. The consul agreed, privately reflecting that it was growing more difficult all the time to imagine this cleric as a workingman. As it would have been impolitic to use the main chapel, which anyone in the colony could attend, the mass for the travelers was celebrated in the reception room, under the king's portrait. Other than the members of the de Maillet family, those present were Father Gaboriau, Monsieur Macé, the dragoman, a Monsieur Frisetti, and Jean-Baptiste. As usual, Jean-Baptiste made no sign to Alix, but he exchanged a last, long look with her, in which she read—to her astonishment—much joy.

The consul was oblivious to the young doctor's behavior except to note that he lacked any knowledge of even the most basic liturgy. This detail confirmed his already strong belief in the man's scandalous impiety.

The ceremony performed, a light meal was served in the drawing room next door. Congratulations were exchanged. It was at this point that Jean-Baptiste asked the consul for a last, private audience.

"Now then," said the consul testily when they were alone, "what is it?"

"I am obliged to inform you, Excellency," Poncet began, "that my partner is unable to remain in Cairo after my departure. The remedies he prepares are always made according to my instructions. Alone he can do nothing. He is therefore returning to Alexandria, where an apothecary has been asking him for some time to join his workshop."

"Fine," said Monsieur de Maillet. "And how, if I may ask, does this concern me?"

"I am coming to it. My partner's removal to Alexandria is only temporary. When I return from Abyssinia . . ."

The consul lowered his eyes.

". . . yes," continued Jean-Baptiste in a determined voice, "when I return from Abyssinia, Maître Juremi will return to Cairo and we will resume our business."

"An excellent plan."

"In consequence . . ."

"In consequence?"

"We are leaving our house just as it is."

"I see no difficulty there. Do not concern yourself for the rent," said the consul resignedly, believing he now knew where Poncet was headed.

"The matter lies elsewhere. I have already counted a year's rent in the expenses I submitted."

"Then everything is in order!"

"No," said Poncet. He paced twice around the small room, then bore down on the consul and stood over him, taller by a head. "The house is nothing, but its contents are infinitely precious. All our equipment is there, which is again not much. But we have grown a great number of plants that are of incalculable value, plants we have painstakingly hybridized over the past years. They must not disappear."

"It seems to me that I could instruct my servants to water them . . ."

"Water them! Your servants! How little you know about these things, sir!" said Poncet, rolling his eyes skyward. "Do you truly believe that it just takes a few drops of water, sprinkled at any odd time by any odd person, to keep such a treasure alive?"

"Yes, I suppose," stammered the consul, "that is what I believed."

"Well, it is not so!" Poncet thundered. "That is why we are paid as we are: because of all we must know about this strange botanical world, next to which human intrigues are of laughable simplicity. You can hardly conceive the depths of patience, intuition, and memory required to make these plants grow in reasonable concord, when they are by nature furiously hostile to one another."

As always when caught up in a subject, Jean-Baptiste emphasized his words by waving his arms energetically.

"One species, for example, may die if the temperature rises by a few degrees. You know this, and you believe you are solving the problem by opening a window. Catastrophe! The plant is caught in a draft and you come back the next day to find it dead."

His tone allowed the full, tragic weight of this event to be felt, and Monsieur de Maillet's eyes opened wide with horror.

"And another," Jean-Baptiste went on, making the consul start, "absorbs all the water that you give it. It gorges on liquid, its leaves are swollen, plump, turgescent. It looks like a goatskin filled to the brim, and every day you toss a bucket of water at it. Then before you know it, the plant has entered its dry phase. There is no outward indication of this except a few, virtually imperceptible signs, which botanists have worked more than a century to discover. From one day to the next, a single glass of water poured at its foot can make the whole plant rot. There are also incompatible plants that must be kept apart or they will devour and strangle each other, fight one another to the death with all the might of their branches. One thinks—"

"I believe I understand," the consul interrupted, anxious to rejoin the others. "Who would you like to take care of your charges?"

"I need someone who is educated and can read well, because we have written everything down. We have notebooks in which every species is described, along with its situation, its origin, its illnesses, its hunger, its thirst, and its respiration. But that is not all. There are learned men who cannot touch a plant without making it die. Although for us it takes tremendous effort to know plants, they know us instinctively at first glance. If you were to put Macé in charge of our house, for instance, it would be a tomb within a week."

"Then who?" asked the consul, crestfallen to see the candidate he was going to propose rejected.

"I have already said that plants recognize some humans as favorable by the signals they give off. Eventually we botanists learn to recognize these persons as well. I see only one person here whom Nature has so marked."

"Well, at least there is one," said the consul, who was impatient to settle the matter. "His name, pray, that I may inform him of his new duties immediately?"

"Mademoiselle de Maillet, your daughter."

Having delivered this bomb, Poncet stepped back two paces and waited. The consul was speechless.

"My daughter," he said finally in a tone of offended dignity, "is placed entirely above such work by her station."

"Yet Nature has granted her the capacity for it."

"What Nature allows is of little consequence, if society forbids it. Abandon this idea immediately, I pray you, and find another candidate."

"There are no others."

"Then your plants will die, and we will reimburse you their value."

"It is not a question of money," said Jean-Baptiste seriously.

He approached the consul and spoke placidly to him:

"Consider that you are being asked for nothing very serious. My partner and I will be gone by tomorrow. The house will remain empty. Your daughter will find a large shelf on which are two thick notebooks, where everything has been written out in Latin. The rest will take care of itself: she has the grace that plants look for and will instinctively discover what they need."

"I see that you continue to insist when the question is closed. My daughter will not go."

"In that case," Jean-Baptiste exploded, "I will not go either. You can find someone else to sniff at the negus's scabs."

"Have some respect, sir! You are speaking of a king."

"Yes, of a king and his scabs. I entrust them to your good care."

Jean-Baptiste made a bow and opened the door.

"Poncet!" said the consul. "That is quite enough! Your unending blackmail has gone too far as it is. Listen to me and close that door."

The doctor did not move from the doorway.

"For a week now you have been making us jump to your every whim, but there are limits. I tell you in all earnestness: you may make whatever arrangements you like for your house except what you have just proposed to me, which is unthinkable. Then make your departure for Abyssinia, otherwise . . ."

"Otherwise . . ."

"Otherwise I will have you arrested immediately. My authority over the members of our nation in this city is absolute. I will show you no pity in my use of it."

"Then have me arrested immediately."

"Don't try me!" barked the consul.

Poncet was already extending his hands for the shackles.

"What are you waiting for?"

The noise of their argument had attracted Monsieur Macé and Father de Brèvedent, who now intervened and calmed the two men down. Poncet went home a short while later. Before leaving, he told the consul that his proposal would stand, and that the diplomat had the whole night to think about it.

Monsieur de Maillet was undone by this latest incident. He refused to unburden himself either to his secretary or to the Jesuit and went up to his quarters immediately to rest. His wife soon joined him, worried at seeing him so upset. She found him stretched out on his bed, his head propped up on two pillows. With a feeling of relief, he confided to her the indecent proposal the young man had made.

That Madame de Maillet was a person of honor was beyond doubt. She regarded her high birth with the same proud awe as her husband did his. But women are often better able than men to distinguish what is essential from what is merely accessory. Gently, and with a great deal of tact, she suggested to her husband that his interests would be injured less by agreeing to Poncet's latest request than by opposing it. If the apothecary did not leave, he would continue to seek out the consul at home, and the ensuing complications might test the consul's health sorely. While if Monsieur de Maillet accepted, the inconvenience would be minor, practically nonexistent.

"The house will be empty. It is common knowledge that it is full of plants and scientific books. We will send Alix there with Father Gaboriau on the pretext that she is botanizing, and no one will think anything of it. As to our daughter, a little outing would do her good, and some physical activity as well."

"But how the devil did he manage to observe her in the first place?" said the consul, sitting bolt upright. "Is it possible that they have conducted a secret relation in this house?"

"Don't fret, *mon ami.* Our daughter has a strong natural sense of modesty, as I can vouch. He has spoken to her only once, and I was there."

Briefly, she recounted the little scene in the garden.

"And that," went on Madame de Maillet, "is where he discovered her propensity for horticulture. I can assure you he is right. When one of my little potted plants suffers from the heat or dryness, I always give it to Alix. She takes it into her room and gives it back to me a few days later green and healthy again."

Madame de Maillet argued so ably that her husband conceded. He thought to himself that Poncet had no chance of returning from his journey. Even if the man's proposal harbored some disreputable plan, he would never have the opportunity to execute it. Relieved at overcoming this final obstacle, though it was in part of his own making, the consul sent his young Nubian servant to Jean-Baptiste's house with a simple note: "My daughter will botanize at your house every morning with Father Gaboriau. Now, leave."

2

The Journey to Abyssinia

I

The Sun King's mission to Abyssinia left Monday morning at eleven o'clock. Hajji Ali led off on a camel, his head wrapped in a new muslin headcloth. Following him came Jean-Baptiste, mounted on a spirited horse and wearing a wide felt hat with a white plume. And finally there was Joseph, so-called, the false manservant and true Jesuit, hidden under the shadow of a straw hat, whom they found waiting for them at the city gate, sitting his mule crossways. Five pack animals brought up the rear, a mix of camels and mules, loaded with the baggage, led by a handful of Nubian slaves.

For the sake of discretion, there were no farewells at the consulate beyond those that had taken place the night before. Jean-Baptiste passed under the windows of the legation shortly before nine o'clock on his way to join the others. Monsieur de Maillet and his wife signaled to him from the balcony. They were deeply moved at the sight of this poor boy, fated in all likelihood never to return, saluting them almost tenderly, with grateful tears in his eyes. The truth of it was that Jean-Baptiste cared nothing for the two old crabs but hoped that, from behind one of the windows on the second floor, Alix was watching him.

Next came their farewells to the Turks, which were long and fulsome. The pasha, who had provided the caravan with all the necessary safe-conducts, cried over the departure of his doctor. But he was used to obeying him in everything and feeling the better for it, and he assented once again to do his bidding, even if the course prescribed was a bitter one. The pasha, Husayn by name, was a man of some fifty years of age, worn out by a life made up in equal parts of great hardships and excessive pleasures. Egypt seemed to him the least pleasant country and the most difficult to govern. The unending imbroglios between the military factions and the beys made him weary. He alternated between an attitude of indifference—during which time the level of unrest would rise—and cruelty, when he would suddenly tire of his adversaries' maneuverings and decide to behead a few dozen of them. Thanks to Poncet's good offices, the oscillation between these two poles had been damped somewhat: there had recently been fewer riots and fewer death sentences. Now that Poncet was leaving, there would again be a few more. But all of this was fated to occur, and the pasha felt no call to alter destiny.

Other wealthy personages, both Turks and Arabs from among Jean-Baptiste's clients, held out purses full of piasters to him, praying for his speedy return. But common people in Cairo were no less distraught by the physician's departure, as he never refused his help to the poor. A small crowd of cripples, beggars, and humble folk had gathered at the news of his departure and now accompanied him through the narrow streets, making the scabby dogs asleep in the shade run in terror before them and the women leaning at their blinds raise their veils abruptly. Jean-Baptiste promised them he would return, finally having to make a show of anger to persuade the crowd to let go of his legs so that he could advance.

Slowed by these emotional scenes, the travelers crossed the city, making numerous detours. Maître Juremi, who followed on horseback as far as the ramparts, bade the caravan a solemn farewell. According to the precepts of his austere God, there was no call to succumb to emotion. Every day during the preparations, Jean-Baptiste asked his friend if he had changed his mind about coming, and every day Juremi told him not to think about him anymore. After all, they were just two adventurers that life had thrown together for a time to work their skulduggeries in concert and now they would go their separate ways. Jean-Baptiste was too intent on accomplishing his goal at this stage to deviate from his course, and his companion had his own reasons for following a separate path. They would simply have to resign themselves to it. When Maître Juremi clasped Jean-Baptiste's hand in his own hamlike fists a final time, it was with little show of emotion. He shook it perhaps a bit longer than usual and left without a word.

The little troop left the city by the Carpetmakers' Gate and found Joseph lurking under an arch of the Aqueduct of the Pharaohs. It was nearly three o'clock in the afternoon. The sun was already casting a yellow light on the stones. Little by little as they walked westward, their shadows stretched out behind them on the ground. They crossed the Nile on two large ferries rowed by oarsmen who were stripped to the waist. The camels, terrified, tugged at their hemp halters. They were still in the middle of the river when the light began to fail and the water turned the color of ink. They could see the gray mass of Cairo spiked with Ottoman minarets growing more distant on one bank, while on the other, behind a curtain of dark green palms, they saw the monstrous mass of the pyramids. At nightfall they reached the village of Giza and entered its narrow labyrinth of clay houses, where oil lamps burned with a yellow glow.

A cousin of Hajji Ali welcomed them into his courtyard, which was paved and shaded by a mimosa tree. He invited them to sleep on the roof terrace of his house. Cairo was already far away, and the night was dark, cool, and moonless. They slept well.

They left the next morning early. An immense, silky plain extended along the river, looking like a green cloth patched here and there with black squares. Thousands of peasants, alone or in small, bright groups, toiled on these newly plowed fields. Others drove oxen ahead of them along the roads and carried their wooden plows on their shoulders. The little caravan cut across this fertile strip and came out into the desert at the level of the pyramids. They plodded slowly past the pyramids' base, enjoying the warmth and silence of the morning. Jean-Baptiste had often come here to daydream during the years he lived in Cairo. Twice he had climbed the pyramid of Cheops before dawn in order to watch the sunrise from the summit. As they neared the Sphinx, Jean-Baptiste quietly rode off from the caravan and made a circuit around the sandstone colossus. When he reached its head, he stood facing it, remembering that the Arabs called it Abu al-Hul, the father of terror, and were in mortal fear of it. He looked into its shadowy eyes and said:

"We will meet again, I swear."

Then he rode on at a gallop to rejoin the caravan.

The second night they slept under the stars, rolled up in their sleeping skins at the edge of the sands, where the desert meets the cultivated plain. And over the next two weeks, as they made their way slowly up the Nile Valley toward Manfalut, they settled into the regular travel rhythm of a caravan. They rose with the sun, drank very sweet tea brewed over a fire of twigs, packed the loads onto their animals, walked in silence in a state of near-hypnosis, looked for a campsite, unloaded, ate dinner, and slept.

Manfalut, where they arrived after a fourteen-day walk, was a large town that seemed hardly to rise aboveground, its low houses of cut stone seeming almost a part of the desert floor. Once inside Manfalut, however, they discovered every convenience they could hope for. They took up lodgings with a Jewish trader who rented out the top of his house to travelers.

It was here that they would meet the large caravan with which they would join up for the journey into Nubia. Hajji Ali knew that it was expected "soon," but as time is counted in the desert, "soon" might mean in only slightly less than an eternity. Days passed, and their wait dragged on in the torpid village, crushed under the heat.

More than the dangers that lay ahead, Jean-Baptiste was concerned with the company he would find in the course of this long trip. Hajji Ali had about as much conversation as his camels. He spent hours poking at his black teeth with a small pointed stick, and whenever he managed to excavate even the smallest shard of food, he made a horrible sucking noise and thanked the Prophet. To every question of Poncet's, the caravaneer replied that it would be revealed in time, God willing. He refused to give any information about the journey, Abyssinia, or the emperor. Jean-Baptiste quickly became convinced that the trader did not trust him as a doctor. The man had agreed to take Poncet because the consul pressured him to do so and made it worth his while, but he seemed to be waiting for some opportunity to put the young man to the test.

With Father de Brèvedent, Jean-Baptiste found his exchanges slightly more interesting. He could address only brief orders to his supposed servant in front of Hajji Ali, and could never bring himself to do so without lowering his eyes. But during their enforced idleness at Manfalut, he made a point of bringing the priest with him into the countryside to look for plants. They would venture out sometimes toward the Nile and the silty lowland, where they discovered new species of reeds and freshwater algae in the canals, and sometimes toward the desert, where they collected succulents and watched scorpions fight. It was soon apparent that Father de Brèvedent had a solid grounding in the sciences. Jean-Baptiste had stowed in his pack a small bronze sextant given to him by one of his Turkish patients. The Jesuit taught him how to use it and, almost apologetically, topped off his practical demonstration with a learned discussion of astronomy. When they had gotten to know each other somewhat, Brèvedent made an admission in the same terms of extreme modesty that he always used:

"I even invented—but when I was young, a very long time ago—a machine, now don't laugh, a perpetual motion machine. It was nothing much, but apparently it amused natural philosophers considerably. I even built a model of it out of wood and metal."

Jean-Baptiste made enthusiastic sounds and pressed him for details.

"I don't remember very well," answered the priest. "It seems so long ago."

Then, blushing, he added:

"The journal of the Academy of Sciences was kind enough to honor me with the publication of my plans."

It was possible to imagine a better traveling companion than this melancholy Jesuit who considered astronomy almost a frivolous occupation. But one has to make do, and Jean-Baptiste, who could not live without friendship, readily extended his own to Father de Brèvedent. At dusk they could be seen returning side by side, boon companions, their shirts wet with sweat, carrying baskets full of plants and animals they had found. Over one of their shoulders hung an empty goatskin from which they had both drunk during the day. When they arrived back within sight of the town gates, they reassumed the roles of master and servant.

Now that he knew the quality of Father de Brèvedent's mind, Jean-Baptiste grew more mortified every day to see this delicate, cultured man, whose health was frail, trotting back and forth to the well, panting under the weight of the water buckets, and bowing low to Hajji Ali, who treated him like a worm. How can he accept such humiliation, Jean-Baptiste wondered. It must be all the more galling to a man who has long been accustomed to using his mind freely.

Yet Poncet never lost sight of the purpose of their trip, and grew increasingly concerned as the large caravan failed to show up. This could have the gravest consequences.

~

Alix de Maillet was at first highly surprised by the mission so unexpectedly thrust upon her. Her father explained the entire business. For several moments, she felt unable to understand it, then was flooded with joy. She spent the morning in her room humming and turning the crank of her hand organ. A mission! It was the first time anyone in the world had given her a responsibility to carry out on her own. All her prayers had been answered. She would finally be able to leave this house, of which she had gone over every inch like a prisoner in a cell. Additionally, she would have the run of the place where she was going, since it was unoccupied. Her father's description of it as a maze of plants and objects aroused her lively curiosity. Along with excitement she felt a certain fear. Would she carry out her mission successfully? Would she not find herself confronted with objects and living things—albeit plants—that were hostile, incomprehensible, and ready to let themselves die? The risk seemed considerable enough to make her anxious, but in the end she felt confident. Besides, the place would not be totally foreign to her. The house belonged to Jean-Baptiste Poncet. She was going to enter the precincts where he lived, and despite her disappointment over his departure and silence, she expected to relive the same emotions in the house that she had felt in the presence of its owner.

Father Gaboriau, joylessly enrolled in the business, came to fetch Alix the day after the caravan's departure—the plants could not be left uncared for any longer than that. The consul granted them the use of his cabriolet, and the two set out at eight o'clock for a two-minute journey. That very morning, Monsieur de Maillet began to let all his visitors know that his daughter would henceforth be botanizing with Father Gaboriau in the apothecaries' old house. He wanted the matter to be public, and therefore to appear all the more natural. The Jesuit had the carriage stop at the entrance to Poncet's house, and he made no secret of the fact that he now had the key to it. They opened the door to the first room, Maître Juremi's lair. The Protestant had neatened it to some extent before leaving, which is to say that he had removed the bedclothes and put away the dishes scattered everywhere. On the table in the middle of the room they found a letter addressed to Father Gaboriau. The priest asked the girl to read it to him, as the light was too dim for his weak eyes. It proposed that as the Jesuit was no longer as young as he had once been, he was not to trouble himself with climbing the stairs to the second floor. A chaise longue had been prepared for him in that very room, which the two now saw in a corner. As a delicate touch, the apothecaries had also left in the corner a large demijohn with a spigot at its base, filled with a stimulating medicine they had specially concocted to cure the priest of the full panoply of his ailments. Upstairs, Mademoiselle would find two large registers containing all the instructions pertinent to caring for the plants.

The priest tasted the medicine and grimaced with pleasure.

"Is it bitter?" asked Alix.

"My child, it is a medicament, and one must accept it as it is."

If the drink had not been recommended by physicians, Father Gaboriau would have sworn that it was alcohol. When he had taken his full glass, he lay down on the chaise longue and instructed his pupil to set to work promptly upstairs.

She climbed the steps and discovered, as her father had done a few days previously, the dense profusion of plant life occupying this unexpected greenhouse. The plants had exhaled their humid breath during the night. The air in the room was warm and moist and smelled of decaying wood and forest flowers. The small birds perched near the rooftree were chirruping.

The young girl walked slowly down the narrow path between the pots of plants, running her fingers lightly over the branches. Coming to the table, she sat down at one of the stools. The place was truly extraordinary and entirely in keeping with the young man who had created it—whose presence she seemed to feel all around her. She drifted off into a sweet daydream, from which she emerged on seeing the two thick registers on the table, which reminded her of her duties. She opened the first volume. It was an austere treatise on horticulture printed in Holland some twenty years before. Her heart sank at its thickness. By the time she had read and translated the whole thing, the plants would be long dead. But as she looked through the first pages, she came across a small piece of paper sticking slightly beyond the edge like a bookmark. On it was written: "Give the big ones a bucket of water a day, the little ones a glass, and the succulents half a glass a week. Open the windows during the day and close them when you leave. As for the rest, do what seems best. And above all, talk to the plants as you would talk to me. . . . Jean-Baptiste."

Alix burst into laughter, then clapped her hand over her mouth, afraid that she might attract the priest's attention. From below came only the sound of regular breathing: Father Gaboriau was asleep. She folded the slip of paper, hid it between two books on a shelf, and set happily to work carrying out the simple and agreeable task before her.

2

Two days after the mission's departure, Monsieur de Maillet received a visit at the consulate from an unusual-looking man who introduced himself as Brother Pasquale.

On seeing him enter his study, the consul shuddered. He was clearly a Capuchin friar, wearing the unmistakable habit of his order with the knotted cord at his waist and the large hood hanging down his back. In his ample robes it was hard to make out his figure clearly, but his broad shoulders, great height, and calloused hands gave him the appearance of a woodcutter who had taken up orders. His terrifying appearance was completed by a large, square head, framed with a curly black beard and set with small, glittering eyes. He spoke in a strong Italian accent, rolling his r's and carving out his words with all the brutality of a butcher hacking the fat off a side of beef.

"I am superior of our community," he announced, bowing to the consul.

If this boor is the superior, thought Monsieur de Maillet with disgust, what do the rest look like?

The monk explained that he wished to meet the man Monsieur de Maillet had named to lead an embassy to the negus of Ethiopia.

The consul pretended surprise, disclaiming any knowledge of the matter. But the Capuchin reached under his robes and pulled out a paper from which he read the first paragraph of the secret letter given by the consul to Poncet and stamped with the seals of the kingdom of France. Monsieur Macé, who was present at the interview, saw Monsieur de Maillet's face turn deathly pale and thought his chief was going to faint. But the consul mastered himself and found the strength to ask the friar where he had obtained the document.

"But it was you, Consul, you yourself who sent it to us," said the Capuchin, his smile revealing a depleted set of teeth.

"I never sent you anything of the kind!"

"Your secretary, I see him here, I think. To make certain of his translation he bring it to one of our brothers, no? Brother Francis, maybe you know him?"

The consul turned to Macé and skewered him with his glance. If he could have struck him down, he would have done so without hesitation. The man's error was so gross, so unpardonable, that he doubted whether a punishment could be found that would expiate his guilt completely. The consul had ordered Macé to have the translation of his letter verified by an old Maronite monk named Brother Francis, who lived in town behind the slaughterhouses, and who was known as an authority on languages. But this incompetent, this oaf, had gone to the wrong monk and shown the letter not to the harmless Syrian friar, but to a Capuchin.

For his part, Monsieur Macé finally held, though most unhappily, the key to what he had considered all along a diplomatic enigma. That the consul should disclose his official letter to the negus to the same Capuchins he had excluded from the expedition at great pains had seemed to this language child, who was in truth only a tyro, the very sort of subtle ruse that gave these Oriental chancelleries their Machiavellian reputation. Now he had discovered the atrocious truth.

Monsieur de Maillet had in the meantime recovered his wits. There would be time afterward for settling accounts. What mattered at the moment was to find out what this boorish friar wanted, given that he held so strong a card. Sorting through his recollection, the consul noted with some satisfaction that the king's letter to the negus made no mention of the Jesuits.

"This embassy, it is a very good idea," continued Brother Pasquale. "I come with a proposal to help you. We have brothers of our order in High Egypt and in Nubia also. We can help you very much."

The friar then entered into an explanation of why his order had a direct concern in all that related to Ethiopia. The pope himself had charged the Capuchins with the holy mission of converting Abyssinia. In fact, the Holy Father, not two weeks before, had officially named the superior of the Franciscan order as the pontifical legate *a latere* to Abyssinia. In this, the consul recognized Innocent XII's proverbial duplicity. While giving his blessing to the Jesuit mission, which was supported by the king of France, this conniving pope had simultaneously appointed as his legate to Ethiopia the superior of an order he knew to be directly in competition with the Jesuits. In other words, he was sending in the same direction two ecclesiastical camps between whom there was precious little love. And may the best man win!

But this was no time for deliberation. The consul sensed the danger and reacted with extraordinary promptness. In moments like this, he had to admire himself. Ah, if only Pontchartrain could see him this very instant, his face once more composed, feigning surprise and disappointment!

"Great God above! Brother Pasquale, how terribly unfortunate! I did indeed have you informed of our plan through my secretary. But as Brother Francis offered no response, we took it as a simple acknowledgment of our embassy. Nothing suggested that you might care to participate in it. They have now been gone three days and we have no way of catching up to them."

"Unfortunate, yes," said Brother Pasquale, shaking his head. "In a few days only, two occasions have disappeared. We have two brothers who are ready to go with an Arab merchant. He comes here to bring a doctor for the negus. Now he has vanished."

"Can it be possible?" exclaimed Monsieur de Maillet, perspiring through every pore. "I can well understand your displeasure."

He continued to make consoling sounds, but the Capuchin, who was not one to speak when he had nothing to say, bowed abruptly and walked out. He had understood that there was nothing else to be learned for the moment.

That life was full of coincidences was a fact Brother Pasquale was ready to admit, and besides, he knew the Orient well enough not to pry into every last circumstance. But the mission did seem to have left in a terrible hurry, and the consul had been too perturbed for a man acting in good faith. The Capuchin headed toward the Arab quarter to continue his investigation.

Inside the consulate, Monsieur de Maillet tore off his peruke as soon as the cleric was gone, his head awash in perspiration, and turned on Monsieur Macé. Before he could give vent to his high dudgeon, the secretary fell to his knees on the parquet floor with the sound of a nut cracking. No one ever implored the consul for his pardon in vain: Monsieur de Maillet decided that he would simply withhold his secretary's pay for two months.

~

The big caravan finally arrived in Manfalut. It made its entrance in the small hours of the morning while the town was still asleep. The previous night, the great market square had been nothing but a deserted stretch of gray sand with a few skeletal dogs prowling over it. In the morning it was covered from end to end with couched camels, bundles tied with rope, and lengths of cloth stretched between wooden stakes for shelter. A crowd of men in blue tunics, wearing turbans or headcloths draped loosely over their shoulders like scarves, moved from place to place shouting. Tin teapots were set to boil on wood fires. A heavy smoke, blue with grease, hung at head level, rising from braziers where sheep carcasses were roasting.

Hajji Ali knew the caravan leader well, a certain Hasan al-Bilbessi, and he was able on the strength of his connection to conclude some business immediately. He exchanged his five mules for two camels, on the pretext that they were less expensive than in Cairo and a better choice for the deserts they would soon be crossing. Unfortunately, the two new animals could barely carry the loads of the mules they were replacing. The upshot, as Hajji Ali informed them with an ugly smile, was that Joseph would no longer have an animal to ride and would have to walk on foot in the sand beside the pack animals—just like the Nubians, only they were used to it.

Father de Brèvedent accepted the news of this further humiliation without demur. He even persuaded his companion to raise no protest, arguing that it was better not to awaken any suspicions. Jean-Baptiste began to notice that the Jesuit took an inordinate pleasure in being submissive, and the somewhat dutiful sympathy he had felt for the man at first had now largely evaporated. It was clear that the cleric shared his enthusiasms only superficially and from politeness. Brèvedent always maintained a cautious reserve. Despite the pleasure he claimed to derive from his walks with Jean-Baptiste, it was soon apparent that he in fact preferred to avoid them. What he truly wanted to do was hide behind a stand of prickly pear and perform the spiritual exercises that strengthened his faith.

The extent of the two men's dissimilarity was driven home one day in a brief conversation. Jean-Baptiste had questioned the supposed Joseph about his call to the priesthood. The cleric answered with naive self-assurance.

"It is all very simple. I was born into a wealthy and privileged family. Everything was easy for me. I only had to learn what I was taught. The plan of creation was laid out for me effortlessly through the language called science. God showered His Providence on me. He gave me everything, and I simply wanted to give it all back to Him."

"And I," said Jean-Baptiste, "am in the opposite position. I was born with no family and very poor. At the age of six I was sent to work for an apothecary. His daughter taught me the alphabet the way you might teach a dog to roll over. That is all the education I received. The rest I learned myself, in any way I was able. So, to follow your formulation: God gave me nothing and I am quits."

The Jesuit looked at him with an expression of terror, as a student might look at another student who has just committed an infraction, afraid of being made to share his punishment. Clearly he considered Poncet, if not the devil incarnate, at least one of his minions. This had been his prejudice from the start, implanted by Father Versau and the consul, who had poured endless pious warnings into his ear. That day for the first time, Jean-

Baptiste realized he was alone. He keenly missed Maître Juremi: his friendship, his passion for truth that sent all hypocrisy flying, his generosity, and his rare and precious humor.

The caravan left Manfalut two days later. It counted some one hundred and fifty animals, extending in a long, slow procession with Hajji Ali, Poncet, and Joseph walking somewhere near its middle. They marched two leagues east and stopped at the village of al-Kantara. They next crossed a stone bridge over a narrow watercourse they took to be a branch of the Nile and camped the following evening in the desert near some gigantic ruins representing the legs and feet of a seated pharaoh whose head and torso had been worn away by erosion.

Thanks to the favor they enjoyed with the caravan leader, Hajji Ali and Poncet were able to claim two of the best spots, between the colossus's toes. The indentation in the enormous blocks of stone formed a kind of cave to protect them from the night chill.

Joseph prepared dinner for his masters. Poncet came to keep him company by the fire while he was stirring the soup. He found the Jesuit looking even more worried than usual.

"I joined the camel drivers earlier," said the priest, "and I overheard some of their conversation."

"Well, what were they saying?"

"That there is another Frank in the caravan."

"It's perfectly normal," said Poncet, unruffled. "European traders travel to Upper Egypt often, and even to Nubia."

The Jesuit's comportment was starting to irritate him: his hangdog expression, his constant worrying, and his humorlessness. With little prompting, Jean-Baptiste too would start booting him in the backside.

"Imagine that you were alone in the middle of a large caravan like this," whimpered Father de Brèvedent, "and that you knew—because it is common knowledge—that there were two other Christians in it. Would you not seek them out immediately?"

"There are many adventurers traveling in the Orient who would rather pass unnoticed by their countrymen," said Jean-Baptiste impatiently.

"Then let us go looking for this man ourselves. That way we will know whether he is avoiding us or hiding anything."

In the end, Jean-Baptiste gave in. He was tired of arguing, and this damned priest's anxiety was catching. He agreed to take a look around camp. Joseph turned over his stirring spoon to a Nubian, warning him not to let the soup burn. As there was little time before nightfall and the caravan was large, they split the task between them. The Jesuit went to one side of the stone colossus and Poncet to the other. Darkness was quickly coming on. The sun, almost at the horizon, had turned into a red ball, flattening itself against the already black disk of the desert. The raking light, diffracted by the dust of camp, surrounded the bustling figures in a hazy nimbus. The two men each inspected as many groups as they could before dark but found no one who looked like a Frank. The Jesuit was still far from reassured. He had been warned by Father Versau to expect some plot on the part of the Capuchins and saw their shadow behind this business of the mysterious traveler.

The following days were hard. They crossed a rocky desert without coming to any watering holes. Joseph's condition was painful to see. Staggering under the heat, he came at every stop to plaster his parched lips to the goatskin hanging from Poncet's saddle. On the second day, his buckle shoes fell apart and he was forced to walk barefoot on the burning ground. The soles of his feet turned into a mass of bloody blisters in one day. Poncet unpacked the leather trunk in which he kept his medicines and coated the poor man's feet with an unguent to dry his sores and relieve the pain. But when he rose to his feet the following day, the Jesuit turned pale and almost fainted. Jean-Baptiste offered to let him ride his camel, but Joseph would hear none of it and walked tight-lipped the entire way.

That man, thought Jean-Baptiste, truly has a passion for obedience. There must be nothing he fears so much as freedom.

Luckily the sky clouded over somewhat during the next few hours. The heat was less intense, and the ground in that part of the desert was coated with fine dust, which was easier on bare feet. That night in camp, Hajji Ali came to tell them that they were only a day's march from a large oasis where they planned to spend several days. He then joined the leader of the caravan for dinner: Hasan al-Bilbessi had slaughtered an injured camel, and its stringy meat was cooking over a large fire.

The next day was again extremely hot, and Joseph once more suffered prodigiously. That night at last they reached the large palm grove the Ancients called the Parva Oasis and the Arabs al-Wah. This was the farthest point on their route still under Egyptian control. A small archipelago of palm groves linked to one another by narrow bands of vegetation lay scattered over an arid sea of rocks. The whole might have covered the area of a large town. Many springs filtering through the dark earth nourished a bright crop of tall, dense grass. A number of plots, surrounded by low walls of flat stone, were farmed for senna and colocynth. Through the palm grove, groups of dark-skinned children passed along the path, laughing and carrying large, misshapen gourds on their heads, which made them look like hunchbacks. Hajji Ali stayed according to his custom in another palm grove where he was known to an obliging native woman as a regular customer. For Poncet he had found a hut of woven palm leaves that even had a bed. They watered the camels at a small pool, afterward hobbling them and leaving them to graze. Jean-Baptiste ceded the bed to Joseph and slung his hammock between two palm trees.

3

When they had been in the oasis for two days, Hajji Ali came to sit beside Jean-Baptiste and amiably offered to prepare tea for him. They chatted idly for a good hour before the trader asked the Frenchman to come into the straw hut for a moment.

"Take a look," said Hajji Ali when they were inside.

He slipped one arm out of his loose tunic and pulled the garment back to reveal that his arm, shoulder, and the upper part of his back were eaten away by a scabby ulceration of the skin.

"How long have you had this ailment?" asked Poncet.

"About three years. The condition comes and goes."

"Do you scratch it?"

"Constantly, day and night. Only the Prophet can keep me from it. But as soon as his eyes are turned elsewhere, I claw at it until it bleeds."

Poncet told him to put his clothes back on. They emerged from the hut, and Hajji Ali resumed his seat by the teapot. The doctor went over to his baggage, stacked near the hut's door, and brought back a vial sealed with a cork stopper.

"Paint your sores with this every morning and evening. We'll talk again in three days."

Hajji Ali kissed his hands, carefully took the vial, and, thinking to join duty and pleasure, went off to have his alma coat him with medicine.

Brèvedent, who had witnessed the scene from a distance, came to sit next to Jean-Baptiste. The priest had apparently recovered from his afflictions of a few days earlier, but his attitude was still suspicious and fearful.

"Why did he wait so long? He could have shown us his condition before we left," grumbled Brèvedent, looking after the cameleer distrustfully.

"Of course not. Think what would have happened if my medication had proved ineffective before we left Cairo. The whole journey would simply have been canceled, on the presumption that I could not cure the negus either. Whereas at this stage, we have already paid Hajji Ali, and we have put ourselves in his hands. If he has to leave us behind, it will be much more to his advantage now."

The two were silent, and Jean-Baptiste guessed that the Jesuit's mind was more than ever beset by dark thoughts.

In point of fact, Father de Brèvedent had little confidence in Jean-Baptiste's medical ability. Their botanical excursions had allowed him to see how thin was the apothecary's knowledge. Several times, Brèvedent had even proved better informed than he. Jean-Baptiste was not in any way disconcerted: "Botany is not the same thing as medicine. What counts there is a sort of enthusiasm, an intuitive sense of the affinities between living things, the ability to discover the vital and necessary correspondence between an ailing man and the plant that will restore him."

This gibberish, as far as Brèvedent was concerned, was in the same category as magic. He had grave doubts about the effect that these imaginings would have on Hajji Ali today and on the negus tomorrow. But it was too late to go back, and the Jesuit had linked his fate for good or ill with this strange herb doctor.

To change the subject and lighten the atmosphere, Jean-Baptiste directed the conversation toward the name of the oasis, al-Wah.

"I think it comes from *al-haweh,* the air. The name would derive from the coolness of the air here and the breeze that constantly makes the palm leaves rustle."

Brèvedent, on the other hand, leaned more toward *halawa,* sweetness. They decided to have their philological differences arbitered by a native. The first one they met was an old man driving a pair of donkeys. Their panniers were full of dates, and he walked behind his animals prodding them with a stick.

The Arabs love their language, and a good quarrel about words is always welcome. The old man listened to the two travelers, his wrinkled mummy's face cracking into a broad smile. After each of the Franks had briefly expounded his theory, the old man poked Brèvedent in the chest with his stick, as though it were a fencing foil, and said:

"No!"

Then he did the same to Poncet.

"Al-Wah," he said, pronouncing the word in its native form, and he beckoned them to follow.

Walking in the lead, with Jean-Baptiste and Brèvedent behind him and the two donkeys pulling up the rear, he led them across a clearing, past a small field of colocynth, and into a grove where the understory consisted of a dense growth of leafy, dark green bushes. Pointing at the small trees with his cane, the old man said three times:

"Al-Wah!"

It was a kind of holly, though its glossy leaves had few prickles.

"Moses' rod," said the old man. "Al-Wah!"

And he pointed at the bush.

"Khalid ibn al-Walid's stick, al-Wah!"

"Who is Khalid ibn al-Walid?" asked Father de Brèvedent humbly.

The old man frowned, as though the question were proof of great and distasteful ignorance.

"Great general," he said. "Exterminator of Christians!"

"Really?" asked the Jesuit, embarrassed.

"Before, the water here was bitter. Khalid ibn al-Walid struck the springs with his staff. The water became pure. Al-Wah!"

They thanked the old man and returned to the hut in silence.

"So now," said Father de Brèvedent, seeing his companion lost in thought, "what supernatural correspondences does this plant suggest to you?"

Jean-Baptiste made a vague gesture. When they reached camp, he continued on alone through the oasis.

He had recognized the bush as the one that grew, lost and alone, in the garden of the consulate. It was the one he had been about to take a branch from when he looked up to discover Alix. At the memory, he drifted off into a sweet daydream.

For two weeks, Alix had been coming every day, and things had settled into a pleasant routine. Father Gaboriau fell asleep in the chaise longue after taking his cordial. Alix went upstairs to talk to the birds and plants. As Jean-Baptiste had predicted, she sensed instinctively what each plant needed, encouraging the smaller ones and lopping back the conquering ardor of the larger ones with a few strokes of the pruning shears. She had also found the time to leaf through the books and to grasp hesitantly by their pommels the swords still hanging from a branch. She had even dared to stretch out in the hammock. The whole setting spoke of absence. Sometimes, according to her mood, Alix felt Jean-Baptiste's presence everywhere there was a trace of him. At other times he was horribly missing, like the head torn from a now-lifeless body.

It was only after two weeks that, having become familiar with the house, she ventured onto the terrace above the inner courtyard. Though all the blinds were closed, someone could be watching from behind a window, and she was afraid that gossip of some kind might reach her father's ears.

At first, she spent only a few minutes on the terrace. Nothing seemed to move behind the facing windows. Growing bolder, she eventually brought out a chair and spent a good half of her mornings outdoors.

She was there, on the fifteenth day after the caravan's departure, when she heard a small noise behind one of the shutters. She started, then froze. Best not to seem afraid or run away as though doing anything reprehensible. The scratching resumed. It came from the window closest to the terrace, less than three feet above her head. All of a sudden, the shutters drew back and a woman appeared in the opening. With a finger to her lips, she cautioned Alix to make no sound, as the startled young girl was clearly on the point of screaming for help. Alix steadied herself, and the two women looked at each other in silence. The person in the window was of mature years—she seemed to Alix to have alighted on those distant shores of life that, at her young age, one swears never to reach. That is to say, she was a woman of over forty. She had the thick, handsome features of a peasant, set in a full face. Her eyes, smiling and empathetic, gazed forthrightly at her friends in solidarity with them and shone toward all others with the proud courage of the poor. She wore a servant's simple dress of dark brown cloth, from which her rounded arms, strong shoulders, and firm bosom overflowed as from a basket too full of fruit.

"A friend! a friend!" she whispered, gesturing with one hand, while the other stayed at her lips.

When she saw that Alix had regained her calm, she continued in a low voice, "Go see if the priest is asleep."

The young girl did as she was told.

How does she know about the priest? she wondered, as she cautiously made her way downstairs.

Father Gaboriau was snoring happily. She went back out to the terrace and nodded yes.

"I am going to come down," the woman announced.

The young girl did not dare argue the point. She watched while this sturdy woman climbed lithely out of the window and jumped onto the terrace with the quiet grace of a cat. She was taller than Alix, though she wore flat-heeled sandals. She smoothed the creases from her dress with two swift passes of her palm, then approached the young girl. Grabbing Alix's two wrists with friendly authority and holding them out slightly from her body, the woman examined the girl with wonder.

"Then it's true that you are beautiful!" she said.

Alix blushed deeply. Fat red poppy, she thought.

"More beautiful than he said," the woman added.

There was something tender and consoling in her face. Perhaps it lay in the fact that the woman's joyful smile so closely coexisted with the wrinkles at her eyes and mouth, which spoke of tears and hardship. To her simple gaiety these added the gravity that comes of deep attachments.

"Who?" asked Alix.

"Juremi, of course," said the woman, laughing.

Mademoiselle de Maillet could not keep her face from briefly registering her disappointment.

"Since he is the one who talked to me about it," she added enigmatically.

She took Alix's hand, led her to the chair, and made her sit down. She herself perched against the balustrade.

"I have been watching you for two weeks. I know everything about you, your name, who you are in love with. That's unfair. I should tell you something about myself. My name is Françoise, and I live in this house. When the two gentlemen were living here, I came every day to prepare their meals. Is this reassuring to you?"

"Yes . . . no . . . I don't know," said Alix, confused.

"Of course, it was a bit cruel," said Françoise. "I could have spoken to you long ago. Do you think I enjoyed seeing you moon around not ten feet away from me?"

A heavy strand of hair dropped from Françoise's black chignon to her temple, and she tucked it into place again. Alix saw that her hands were red from hard work, her nails close-cut and broken, yet they were a woman's hands, the skin evenly covering the network of veins, making them smooth and graceful.

"But you have to understand," said Françoise. "I had my orders. Well . . . you can always disobey orders. But I had given my promise."

"Promise? What did you promise, and to whom?" asked Alix.

"To Juremi. He made me swear that I would wait until you were settled in here, and that I would make sure that the priest was fast asleep every day. By the way, is there still plenty of that drink they set out for him?"

"About half a demijohn, I'd say."

"Remind me to fill it up again when the time comes."

"Have you more of it?" asked Alix, whom the prospect of running out of the cordial had been tormenting for several days.

"As much as you could ever want. It's the same rotgut the consul your father sells us at twenty piasters!"

Françoise laughed quietly, her head thrown back. Her teeth were perfect, the enamel white as pearl, and all of them in place. Then she grew serious again.

"I promised all this to Juremi. Only then was I to give you the letter."

"Letter!" burst out Alix.

She no longer understood. Juremi, a letter? She was starting to grow apprehensive.

Françoise hushed her and listened for any sounds from the sleeping man below. Hearing nothing and seeing that the girl was on tenterhooks, she reached into her dress and pulled out an envelope.

"How curious you are! Here you have waited patiently for two weeks, and now a few extra moments seem too long! Take it."

Alix snatched the letter and read the envelope: "For Mademoiselle de Maillet." It was in the same hand as the note she had been reading over and over since the first day, Jean-Baptiste's.

4

The long caravan formed up again slowly after three days. As the countries ahead, lying ever farther to the south, were subject to intense heat, and as the moon now rose over the desert in the evening, the decision was made to travel at night. The caravan would get under way in the afternoon as the sun was sinking. Wells would also be growing scarcer, and provisions even more so. They would take food for eight days. At the last moment Joseph was given a sack to carry on his back, the camels being loaded to the utmost limit.

Hajji Ali maintained an inscrutable expression. He came and went, overseeing the loading of the caravan, shouting orders, lashing out with his whip. Several times he passed directly in front of Poncet but gave no indication of whether the treatment for his sores was working. The Frenchman refrained from making the slightest inquiry before the three days had elapsed.

The caravan creaked into motion, and they walked along slowly in the gentle night air. The moon seemed to shed a dusting of light that molded to the surface of objects and pricked shadows into relief. The swaying camels, the men walking in rapt silence, the hundreds of muffled footsteps on the sand lulled the senses almost irresistibly. It took an effort not to fall asleep.

At dawn, when the sky on their left started to streak with violet light, they reached their first water hole and made camp. It was no oasis, just a few trees and a well that was heavily tainted with alum. The water had a foul cast and tasted horrible. The men cooled their heads and faces in it. But one would have to harbor a strong desire to die of something other than thirst to drink it.

The third full day of Hajji Ali's treatment had come and gone. Once camp was pitched, the camel driver came toward Poncet with a grave expression, passed in front of him, and joined a group of men a few yards away who had gathered around the well to perform their ablutions before morning prayer. They had bared their chests and their heads. Hajji Ali now slowly did the same. He kept on his baggy trousers but took off his shoes. He splashed himself with water, rubbed himself down, spat, and, picking up his tunic and headcloth in one hand and his boots in the other, he approached Poncet. The doctor saw that the entire treated surface was clear, though still slightly raised, an effect that would disappear within a few days. The disease was gone. Hajji Ali gave Jean-Baptiste a respectful bow, pulled on his tunic, and went on his way toward a quiet spot where he set out his prayer rug.

Joseph, who had witnessed the whole incident, secretly made the sign of the cross.

"Great God! A miracle!"

The remark irritated Jean-Baptiste, as it seemed to belittle his skill.

"Do you know what the cabalists say?" he asked. "He who believes in miracles is a fool."

Father de Brèvedent looked at the ground. "And he who does not is an atheist. You can meditate on that tonight when we take the road again."

The following days and nights passed in the same way. The desert ship slowly gathered speed for its crossing of the high solitary wastes. Several times they slept in the middle of the vast open landscape, with no other shade than the stretched skin of their tents. The heat under the tent cloth was like an oven. In contrast to the early days of the journey, the hours of rest were now more painful than the hours of walking, when they at least enjoyed the cool of night. They reached another well, whose water was fresh and good, and they were able to fill their water skins.

Since testing Jean-Baptiste's skill at medicine himself, Hajji Ali had become more respectful toward him. He was still not a talkative companion, but he answered the Frenchman's questions willingly enough and sometimes even volunteered information he thought might prove useful. One day Hajji Ali came up to Poncet just before the daily march.

"Up to al-Wah, there was another Frank in the caravan. Did you know that?"

"We heard about it, but we never saw him. Who was it?"

"I don't know. He is ahead of us now by two days' journey."

"Who is he traveling with?"

"He rides a camel, and another man follows with the packload. But the man is alone."

As soon as the camel driver had gone, Joseph came up to ask for the news. Jean-Baptiste, partly from pity and partly to avoid any further displays of the Jesuit's despair, told him that everything was fine.

There followed more days of enervating rest and more nights of plodding under the blinding light of the full moon. They finally climbed onto a desert plateau and, after making their way across it for an entire stage, discovered the wide valley of the Nile below them at sunrise, gauzy with the mists that had risen off the fields during the night. At a bend in the river lay a large city. The low mass of its mud-brick houses was offset by the green squares of its gardens and the heavy towers of its minarets, very different in kind from the slender Ottoman arrows of Lower Egypt. They had reached Dongola, the first city in the kingdom of Sennar. The caravan stopped at its outer walls. Hajji Ali and Poncet entered the city at noon, the doctor's manservant following at three paces. They brought their letters of recommendation and their gifts to the prince who ruled the city in the name of the king of Sennar.

He was a small, frail man, almost lost from view on a throne covered in brightly colored fabrics. He welcomed his visitors effusively and asked Poncet if he would kindly treat his youngest daughter, a child of eleven, who was going blind. The young princess was called in and arrived on the arm of a servant girl, who now had to accompany her everywhere. The child's eyes were gummed shut by a yellowish humor. The governor explained that it was sometimes necessary to tie her hands behind her back at night because if she even touched her eyelids, the catarrh worsened. Jean-Baptiste ordered Joseph to fetch his medicine trunk. He took a red powder from it and prescribed that it be dissolved in a quantity of very pure water and that the girl's eyes be washed with the solution three times a day, and a wad of cotton imbibed with it attached to her eyes at night.

The next morning the girl's eyes were dry. Three days later she was able to open her eyes normally and her sight was returning. The governor, deliriously happy, told Poncet that there was nothing he would not grant him. The doctor answered that he wanted only the governor's protection. During the week they stayed in Dongola, they were treated with magnificence and lodged in the palace. They were served the haunch of an antelope and the breast of an anteater. They were spared hippopotamus cheek, to the governor's regret, as it was out of season. Poncet was obliged to treat a quantity of other patients from among the great lords and their families. The governor put a horse at his disposal and a donkey at his servant's. The two Franks were thus able to see the city and admire the extraordinary fertility of this part of the valley. The bank of the river was two or three yards higher than the water's surface at this point, and the land was not flooded annually as in Egypt. If the crops were irrigated, it was thanks to the great and incessant industry of men, and the cunning design of their water wheels, their hollow trunks, and their weirs. On his return to the palace, Poncet complimented the governor on his agricultural projects and expressed his admiration for the rigorous administration of the district. The little man responded enthusiastically.

"The city is yours if you care for it. Stay here as my doctor and tomorrow I will give you twenty acres in the valley and thirty families to work it. You will have a house in town, and a stable filled with camels and Arab horses. You will be happy, believe me."

Hajji Ali for once proved useful. He reminded the governor politely that the Frankish traveler was on his way to visit the negus of Abyssinia, and that for all the generosity of his offer it could only be put into effect on their return. The peoples of the Nile considered the Abyssinians as water-masters, since they controlled the source of the river and could deviate it or make it run dry at will. To provoke the "the Father of Waters" was unthinkable. The governor bowed.

Meanwhile, the news from Poncet's patients was excellent. Every day brought a new account of some spectacular recovery. Father de Brèvedent grudgingly recognized that whatever its source, the young man had a genuine healing power. He was attuned to the suffering of others and skilled at relieving it, but his rapport extended even to their most innocent moments. He needed only to look at a child to provoke a smile. Even animals seemed to find his presence calming. The fearful, mangy dogs in the street, who normally steered clear of people, followed him instinctively through the town, though he never fed them. His rapport with all God's creatures had more in common with the inanities of Saint Francis and his followers than the austere severity of Saint Ignatius of Loyola. The Jesuit could not possibly admire such childish foolishness. On the other hand, Poncet's gifts could—like the local languages and beliefs, and like everything else that served no purpose—be surreptitiously used to advance the cause of the true faith. Poncet certainly provided an excellent passport to Abyssinia, and Brèvedent had only to make the best of it.

Finally, everything was ready for their departure. They had been invited to the palace for a last evening of festivities. The caravan would not roll out until the next morning: because of the dangers they would face in the adjoining regions, they had decided to travel during the day.

Poncet was just taking a rest in his room when he heard a scratching at the door. Probably a messenger come to beg him to attend a sick person in town. When he went to see he discovered a little black boy with a shaven head, runny nose, and frail, half-naked body, who held out a note to him. Poncet opened it. It was written in French:

"Come meet me. The child will show you the way."

The words were written in capital letters as though to disguise the handwriting, and the message was unsigned.

Poncet decided to wake up Father de Brèvedent, who slept in a room on the ground floor, and ask him to come along. Then he went to his trunk, already packed and ready to go. From it he pulled a sword, which he strapped to his side, and a long dagger, which he gave to the terrified Jesuit. The child led them through the streets as the shadows deepened in the gathering twilight. The inner recesses of the town teemed with people. The heat dropped at about the same time the bats started to circle through the dusk, and it was then that the townspeople emerged from their windowless houses, which stayed cool as cellars all through the day, and talked back and forth from one doorway to the next.

Jean-Baptiste tried to keep a mental map of their path through the streets but soon had to give it up. They finally arrived at a narrow square where three small alleys came together. At one corner was a teahouse of the kind found throughout the Middle East, its two square windows covered with a wrought-iron grill. They entered to find the room practically empty, its floor and the earthen benches around the walls covered with threadbare red-and-blue rugs. Small oil lamps, placed on chased copper platters, diffused a warm glow. A man sitting in the shadows at the back of the room rose at their entrance, and Poncet put his hand on the hilt of his sword.

"Friend," said the man.

Poncet froze. He looked at the tall figure looming in the darkness.

"I recognize that voice. . . ."

The stranger approached, uncovered his head, and stood revealed in the light from the tables.

"Maître Juremi!" said the Jesuit.

Jean-Baptiste, who had recognized his friend at the first sound of his voice, sprang toward him and wrapped him in his arms. There were shouts of joy. Not only was Poncet delighted to be reunited with his old companion, but it meant that he was no longer alone—Joseph having proved a negligible companion. Maître Juremi ordered coffee all around, emptied the cups out the window, and poured each of them a dram of white liquid from a small flask he took from his pocket. They toasted their reunion.

"So the Frankish rider was you all along," said Jean-Baptiste.

"I couldn't make myself known as long as we were still in Egypt. It wasn't that I didn't want to, believe me."

Now that their eyes had grown acclimated to the feeble light of the lamp, Poncet could see the change in his friend's appearance. His face was much thinner, his eyes deeply recessed.

"And once I arrived here, I preferred to let you go about your business with the governor and only show myself just before your departure. What do you think? Will it be difficult for me to join the caravan?"

"I'll see to it," said Poncet. "Now that we are back together, let's not be separated again."

They went on with their happy outpourings. Maître Juremi refilled their glasses. They drank them down in one gulp and went on laughing and joking.

"You have to tell me all about your journey," said Jean-Baptiste. "When did you decide to come along? And how did you manage to stay hidden in Manfalut?"

Maître Juremi, taking a long pull at his drink, waved a hand to indicate that he would soon answer. But the Jesuit, who had kept quiet all along, suddenly intervened in a high-pitched voice.

"You will excuse me," he said, "but I believe this man's presence would not be in conformity with our agreement."

His natural tone of command had somehow returned. He was no longer the obedient manservant he had been playing at. Maître Juremi only then seemed to take note of his presence.

"What does the old crow want with us?" he said, looking at Father de Brèvedent with open hostility.

"We are here," the priest continued, "by order of the king and on instructions from His Most Holy Eminence the pope. The mission is our responsibility and ours alone. The consul said as much before our departure: there is no question of our embassy being joined by a . . . someone who . . ."

Maître Juremi's face had assumed such a terrifying expression that the Jesuit lost the will to finish his sentence.

"Tell him to shut his mouth or I'll brain him!" thundered Maître Juremi, pounding on the copper table. The sound, like a crash of cymbals, brought the owner of the teahouse running.

The Jesuit turned his assault on Jean-Baptiste, who appeared calmer, and with whom the decision would rest in any case.

"Monsieur Poncet, you have made a commitment you are bound to honor. However far we travel, we will eventually return, or so I trust, and we will have to justify our actions. If we take this man in our caravan, who will ever believe he joined us here without your consent? They will say that you planned it all along."

Maître Juremi let out a roar and drew his sword.

"I'll split the rat in two!" he bellowed, as he rushed toward the Jesuit.

Poncet slipped between them. The shouting continued. Bystanders were now crowding to the windows to see the extraordinary sight: a quarrel between two Franks. Jean-Baptiste managed to disarm his friend. He pushed him back toward the rear of the room and turned toward Father de Brèvedent.

"I never made a commitment," he said, "to abandon a friend in distress when deserts lay on all sides. Be advised that while I had nothing to do with his coming here, I take every responsibility for seeing that he remains with us."

Tugging Maître Juremi by the sleeve and pushing Joseph ahead of him, Jean-Baptiste started toward the door.

"Let us go to the governor's immediately to arrange the necessary papers," he said.

They parted the crowd at the teahouse door and made their way back through the now-dark streets, guided by the same little messenger who had led them before.

The governor owed Poncet a debt for the recovery of his daughter and could not refuse the Frenchman a favor. He wrote a letter recommending Maître Juremi to the king of Sennar and the negus of Ethiopia. Hajji Ali, who watched unhappily as the two Franks were reinforced by a third, understood that opposition would be futile. As for Father de Brèvedent, he became Joseph once more and offered them no further counsel. His lower lip fell and his jaw sagged again, giving him his usual look of despondency. He became even more taciturn than before, and Jean-Baptiste wondered whether, despite the little sympathy the Jesuit had ever shown him, he was not simply jealous to see the two friends reunited.

At any rate, the manservant Joseph benefited from the Protestant's joining the caravan. What with the two additional camels Juremi brought and the presents they left behind with the governor, the servant no longer had to travel on foot.

The priest continued to believe that Maître Juremi's arrival had been staged for his benefit by Poncet and his friend. In fact, nothing could have been farther from the truth. While the caravan plodded along, the two went over every facet of their recent activities. Maître Juremi had felt remorse at allowing his friend to face so many difficulties alone and had decided to accompany the journey early on. But to avoid complicating matters with the consul, and also to keep Jean-Baptiste from having to tell lies—a practice Maître Juremi held in strong aversion—he preferred to say nothing and join the expedition once it had left Egypt.

Jean-Baptiste, for his part, had had an inkling from the first about this mysterious Frank who stayed hidden so close to them, but he had not known for certain until the very last.

They also spoke of Cairo, where Maître Juremi had stayed on one more night after his friend's departure. He had left the house just as the carriage bringing Alix and Father Gaboriau had turned into the street.

"Are you sure," asked Jean-Baptiste testily, "that she received my letter?"

5

Now that she knew the kind of drink he had been prescribed, Alix was quick to urge Father Gaboriau to increase the dosage. On this day they had no sooner arrived at the apothecaries' house than she made him swallow a large glassful in one draft. The priest was asleep in less than five minutes. At the first snore, Alix jumped out onto the terrace and called up to the shuttered window:

"Françoise! You can come!"

The blinds opened immediately, and Françoise climbed down to the young girl on the terrace. They set up two chairs in one corner and sat down side by side.

"So," asked Françoise, "has the letter I gave you yesterday made you happy?"

Alix blushed. Though she hardly knew the woman who was now looking at her with such kindness, she trusted her instinctively. The hours of the early morning had seemed endless, and Alix had been burning with impatience for the moment when she could confide everything to Françoise, who she felt understood her.

"Here," she said, handing the letter to her friend. "Read it yourself."

Françoise took the two sheets covered with Jean-Baptiste's close script and read the following:

Dear Alix,

I write you in great haste, sitting on a trunk, my belongings in disorder around me and my mind burdened with the thousand small cares of packing for the journey—hardly the best conditions for expressing one's feelings. Yet mine are so clear to me at this time, and the plans I have made because of them so definite, that I do not expect to be at a loss in formulating them. My one fear is that I will present them too abruptly and at a time when you are not ready to hear them. For this reason I have taken the precaution of having this letter reach you after some delay—forgive me, please. You are reading these lines: that means that you have come to my house and feel at home there, that my beloved plants are all around you, and that you have met Françoise, who has won your confidence as she deserves to. All of this, Alix, makes it easier to talk to you. We are sharing the same space, even if we are not there together. We have friends who can help us meet. Never have we been closer to one another now that distance has freed us from all that kept us apart when we were near each other.

Protected by being at a great remove, I have less trouble telling you quite simply how I feel. I have not dared to do so in these last days, and the circumstances were all against it. Yet I have seen no one but you and spoken to no one but you, even when I seemed to be addressing others, and you were in all my thoughts.

Our knowledge of each other is too recent for us not to remember all its stages. From the first moment I saw you on the bridge over the Khalij, I was overcome by your beauty and the grace of your whole being. Since I have approached you and watched you, ever since we exchanged glances, this first emotion has only grown stronger. And as I am not used to having such strong feelings, I was at first worried, even irritated, before happily giving in to them. I wish I had enough time to describe all the charms I find you to have, yet this sheaf of paper could not hold them all. Since I do not have the leisure to describe every one of your qualities, I prefer to say nothing that might lead you to think that I have neglected some of them. Dear Alix, I adore everything I have seen of you, and I can also say that I love just as passionately the strength that you are still concealing but will soon show.

Why tell you all this when I am going away? If my feelings are so strong, shouldn't they offer me good reason not to leave? And if I go all the same, what is the good of expressing them? These are the questions that have been on my mind these last days, irritating me all the more because I refuse to concede the slightest place in my life to melancholy. After turning the thing over in my mind unendingly, I have finally come to see it under a different light, so that my departure now seems a happy event. Yes, Alix, you have read me correctly, and I want to convince you of it: this journey is our great chance. If I had stayed in Cairo nothing could have happened between us. But there is nothing I may not hope for if I succeed at the challenge set before me. The victory would lift me toward you, and, if you are willing, make us equal and therefore free. Since I made my vow to fulfill this mission for you and you alone, I feel the strength to overcome every obstacle that could possibly come between me and my purpose. Every step that takes me farther from you brings me closer. I have no doubt as to the outcome of my undertaking: I will return. My only hope is that you will have enough patience to wait for me. In the countries through which I am traveling even as you read this letter, Alix, you should know that if you cannot join me, you also cannot abandon me. I take constant pleasure in the feeling that you accompany me. And there, on the desert roads, bound by no law, I find the hardihood to kiss you.

"Well," said Françoise, finishing the letter, "what a lot of rigmarole just to say that he loves you."

"But," said the young girl, disturbed, "he has hardly met me. We haven't spoken . . ."

"And how do people fall in love, according to you? By spending lots of time every day with someone they don't like?"

"No, of course, but how can you know . . . that he is being sincere?"

Alix was making a visible effort to utter the thoughts she had confronted the night before.

"A man who leaves on a journey like this has little reason to lie," said Françoise.

"He might have written the letter as a sort of challenge, or from nostalgia, or even boastfulness. After all, it costs him little to ask me to wait."

"Do you believe that for a moment?" asked Françoise.

The young girl lowered her eyes and seemed to reflect. A tear rolled down her cheek.

"Of course not," she said. "I am only trying to convince myself of the contrary because every part of me tells me that he loves me . . . as I love him."

"Would it be so bad simply to accept that?"

"If it is the case," said the young girl, pursuing her thought, "I will be wretched no matter what happens."

"And why should that be?" said Françoise.

"Think of it," said Alix sharply, turning her tear-filled eyes on her friend. "If he does not return from this voyage, I will be heartbroken forever. And if he returns . . ."

"Anything will be possible—he has said so."

"You don't know my father!"

What a child! thought Françoise, moved. "You are looking too far ahead," she said gently. "Wait only until he returns. And trust him for the rest. All the same, a man who has forced the gates of unknown kingdoms, won the confidence of native princes, and advanced the aims of the king of France and the pope might just be able to bring around even the stubbornest father."

Alix looked at her with the mix of tenderness and defiance we reserve for those who tell us faithfully what we want to hear.

"Come here each morning. We'll talk. The time will pass more quickly," said Françoise.

She then took the young girl in her arms, stroked her hair, and let her cry a bit more.

~

All went well until they reached Sennar. The caravan arrived in the city after traveling for ten days through the Desert of Bayuda. As they progressed southward, the vegetation gradually reappeared. They had entered a region the Arabs called Rahmat Allah, "God's Mercy." The mercy lay in there being no need, as in Dongola, to irrigate the soil. Here it was done by the tropical rains. Everywhere were green pastures and fair-sized trees, and in places even the beginnings of forests. Thanks to the bounty of the heavens, the farmers enjoyed a degree of leisure and walked beside their donkeys singing.

Sennar, the capital, was on the banks of the Blue Nile, which flows down from the mountains of Abyssinia, its waters heavy with powdered schists. It was a large mercantile and agricultural city with richly provisioned bazaars, handsome mosques, and a palace that served as the permanent residence for the king and his court. All of it was built of stone and covered in red clay.

The journey through the last section of desert passed without incident. After the initial joy at their reunion, Maître Juremi had settled back into his usual sourness and taciturnity. The Jesuit and he maintained an armed truce. They avoided each other and addressed themselves only to Poncet, who thus found himself in the disagreeable position of having to mediate between the two men. Joseph's situation was admittedly the most unpleasant of all. While his enemy disported himself as a master, he was forced to play the humble role of servant, loading and unloading the animals, preparing food at every stop, and filling the goatskins at the wells. Furthermore, Hajji Ali was now giving him orders. Poncet had asked him not to, but now that they were in foreign lands, the camel driver had lost all fear of the Franks. Despite the man's apparent respect for Jean-Baptiste, he still tried to extort small payments from him at every opportunity, amounting in the end to considerable sums. During a halt in the middle of the Bayuda Desert, Hajji Ali decided to try a new form of blackmail. He arrived at the Franks' tents with Hasan al-Bilbessi, whose face was veiled impenetrably by his headcloth to reveal only his sand-reddened eyes.

"In two days," said Hajji Ali, "we will arrive at Guerry. It is an inspection station for smallpox."

He explained that the king of Sennar, who greatly feared disease, had established quarantine posts on his borders to keep out possibly infected travelers.

"Hasan says he knows the commander of the border post well," Hajji Ali went on. "He will let the Arabs pass, but he'll be afraid of you. We will have to leave you there and go on alone. Unless . . ."

"Unless what?"

"Unless you give us something to change this functionary's mind."

Hajji Ali named an exorbitant sum. This was followed by a song and dance in which the camel driver relayed their counterproposals in dialect to Hasan al-Bilbessi, who would shake his head in stubborn refusal like a peasant. The price finally came down, but they were obliged to pay it. Two days later they arrived at the border post to find the buildings deserted. The fear of epidemic had apparently evaporated and the quarantine had been lifted. But neither Hajji Ali nor Hasan would restore the money, having very likely divided it between themselves already.

At Sennar, things started off well. They went straight to the palace to give the king their letters and presents. As at Dongola, the king no sooner learned that Jean-Baptiste was a doctor than he asked him to treat a relative of his. Then things started to go wrong.

The king called Poncet and Maître Juremi, whose letter of recommendation identified him as an apothecary also, into a small chamber behind the throne room. The monarch was whippet-thin, his skin the matte black of charcoal. His small eyes had the restless cruelty of a man who, having ordered many horrible acts, expects an even more atrocious retribution to be visited on him at any moment. Hajji Ali was not asked to join them for the consultation. The king would explain the situation to them in Arabic, a language that both Poncet and Maître Juremi understood well. A guard led in an adolescent boy who, though probably no older than fourteen, was already taller than the two Frenchmen. On the king's order, the young patient took off his gold-embroidered black tunic, revealing an extraordinarily thin body. Every muscle could be seen under the smooth layer of his skin, like a machine where all the gears are visible. His stomach was distended and the navel extruded like a chicken neck. The most remarkable aspect was that the boy seemed to be in good health, except for his excessive thinness.

"This is the son of my third wife," said the king. "We don't know what he has. Everything passes right through him. If he eats millet, out comes millet. If he eats sorghum, out comes sorghum. If he eats meat, out comes meat."

He looked expectantly at the doctors to hear their opinion.

"What do you think?" Poncet asked his friend.

Maître Juremi, who had argued with Joseph that morning, was in an irascible mood.

"Simple," he said. "Let him eat shit."

Jean-Baptiste was so unprepared for this answer that he burst out laughing. He checked himself almost immediately, but the damage was done. The king thought they were making fun of the boy or, more seriously, of himself. He asked Poncet to translate what the apothecary had said. Jean-Baptiste said there was no need to, then invented something, but the monarch remained dissatisfied.

Poncet gave the king's son every attention. The drugs he administered allowed the boy to retain more of what he ate even by the next day. But the king's trust in them, like a dish that has cracked but is not yet broken, had been damaged so fundamentally that there was no hope of restoring it.

Then something happened that would hardly have mattered in ordinary times but, acting on the still-invisible crack, managed to widen it to the point where a break occurred. Father de Brèvedent precipitated the calamity.

Ever since the Frank shadowing them had been identified, the Jesuit had felt some relief. He was still dismayed to be traveling with a Protestant, but at least it had not turned out to be a Capuchin. He managed to convince himself that the danger from the rival order was past and that they had shaken off the Capuchins thanks to their hasty departure from Cairo.

Brèvedent was so confident of this that he formed the idea of visiting the house built by the Capuchins in Sennar for their small community of monks. If Poncet would join him they could go as master and servant. The two might then gather news about the area and even learn what schemes the monks were hatching with regard to Abyssinia. Poncet agreed. Maître Juremi stayed at the house in town that Hajji Ali had rented for them while the other two set off on foot to the monastery.

It may seem strange that the king of a Muslim state should allow a Catholic hospice in his capital, but the explanation is simple. In getting his permission, the Capuchins had used exactly the opposite arguments they had used with the pope. In Rome, they had described their mission as the rescue of the Catholics who had been hounded from Abyssinia after the Jesuits' expulsion and who had taken refuge in Sennar. But in Sennar it was well known to all, and to the king in particular, that no such Catholic refugees existed. The Jesuits had succeeded in converting no one in Abyssinia other than the negus, and even he only for a short time. They left as they had arrived, entirely alone. The workings of power are such that had there been any Catholics in Sennar, the king would never have allowed Romish priests to minister to them, for fear of an uprising. But since there were none, and since the priests vowed, on pain of excruciating torture, not to try to convert any Muslims, there was no harm in admitting this handful of peaceful foreigners. They ran a school for children, cared for the sick, and, having the pope's ear, gave the king of Sennar a link to Europe.

Poncet, with Joseph at his heels, crossed the wooden threshold of the monastery and entered a vast courtyard. Pruned orange trees, planted in large round tubs, had been set out across the powdery red ground. The Capuchin who welcomed them showed not the least surprise at their visit. He ushered them into a windowless room that, like all the others, gave onto the courtyard. He invited them to sit on low stools with seats made from woven leather strips. Four other friars joined them. Their habits, similar to the one worn by Saint Francis, took on an Arab aspect in this setting. With their deeply tanned faces, their black beards, and their stocky frames of peasants from the Abruzzi, they could easily have been taken—had it not been for the small cross they wore around their necks—for natives of this Nubian kingdom.

One of the friars introduced himself as the superior. His name was Raimondo. He introduced his companions, all wearing the same severe expression as himself. He then pointed to two other monks, who held back slightly and eyed Poncet with suspicion.

"These two brothers are visitors. They arrived yesterday morning from Cairo."

"Yesterday morning!" said Poncet. "Which way did you come? We should have seen you in Dongola."

"More than one caravan travels to this city," said Brother Raimondo. "They came down the Valley of the Nile as far as the second cataract, then crossed the sand desert to the north of us."

"That is a much longer way," said Poncet.

"It all depends on the season. When the Nile is not in flood, a rider can gallop through the valley and travel quite fast."

Jean-Baptiste asked when they had left Cairo. He calculated that their departure had followed his own by ten days.

6

Returning from the monastery through the shadowy streets of Sennar, the so-called Joseph worked himself to a high pitch of terror. Father Versau's direst warnings in the days before the expedition's departure, with their repeated evocations of the Capuchins' guile and devious machinations, were now coming true in the most unexpected way. The warm night seemed to teem with unexpressed menace. The Jesuit thought of the days and days of travel that had brought them to this country: they weighed on him like so many slabs of granite between himself and the light. The Franks could cry out, or die, and no one would come to their rescue. As these sinister thoughts revolved in his head, the Jesuit released loud exhalations like a whale. Irritated, Jean-Baptiste hastened his pace to be out of earshot. The young man was unfairly heaping on Brèvedent, who had only led them into the lion's den, all the anger he felt at the Capuchins' blackmail. It was in this state, one of them fulminating and the other in despair, that they walked back into the house where Maître Juremi was waiting for them.

He was sitting peacefully in the courtyard on a stack of wicker hampers reading a book in the light of a small reflecting lamp. Poncet and Joseph each sat down on one of the trunks facing him.

"The Capuchins know everything," said Jean-Baptiste.

Father de Brèvedent kept his eyes gloomily on the floor.

"You mean . . ."

Maître Juremi indicated the Jesuit with his chin, his eyes never turning away from Jean-Baptiste.

"No. Luckily, that's one thing they don't seem to know about."

"Then what?"

"The main thing: that we are traveling on an embassy for France."

"We'll have to ask them to keep it quiet," said Maître Juremi, rising stiffly from his improvised seat.

The mud walls enclosing the courtyard reached only to head level. Beyond this frail barrier they could hear the sounds of evening: distant conversations and children's shrieks, nearby murmuring, dogs barking, the sound of hoofs. The night was moonless. Above, in the deep sky, star-spangled and oppressive, a high wind was blowing.

"What exactly do they want?" asked Maître Juremi, standing motionless.

"They want two of their friars to accompany us. They visited the consul in Cairo shortly after our departure and still hope to profit from Hajji Ali's mission."

"And if we refuse?"

"They'll tell the king of Sennar everything. Think what it means. The king is Muslim. He'll allow a doctor for the negus to pass through his country, but never an embassy from a Christian king."

"And?"

"And we would probably be imprisoned, first of all. But the Capuchins have hinted that it wouldn't end there. The common people here trust them, especially if it should ever come to spreading bad reports about other foreigners. They'll say that we are sorcerers, and my box of vials will support that. The mob will clamor for our heads and the king will accommodate them."

"What did you tell them?" asked Maître Juremi.

"That we had to arrange things with Hajji Ali, that we would do our best. I said we needed two days."

"Bravo," said Maître Juremi. "So what can we do in those two days?"

Poncet raised his eyebrows to indicate that he had no idea. They pondered the possibilities in silence. Jean-Baptiste felt no real anxiety, although the situation was critical. At this moment, when their mission seemed utterly compromised, he was annoyed at the setback to their plans but remained certain that their journey would eventually succeed. At the heart of his confidence may have been the thought of Alix.

"Let's bring a Capuchin with us," said Maître Juremi in all seriousness, "and let's chop him to bits as soon as we get far enough away from here."

Father de Brèvedent started. As usual, rather than address the Protestant directly, he spoke to Poncet.

"Any inclusion of the reformed Franciscans in our enterprise would run directly counter to the terms of our mission. As to killing priests, such a thought can only be the product of a deeply irreligious mind."

"Well, let him suggest a different solution," said Maître Juremi.

Poncet stood up, walked a few steps into the small courtyard to the edge of the light, then came back to his companions. Planting himself in front of them, he said:

"We must leave tonight."

"Leave!" said the other two, for once in accord.

"Yes, leave. That gives us two days and two nights. We must find a way to fool the Capuchins' spies into thinking that we are still in town. In the meantime, we'll get as much of a head start as we can."

"We have no knowledge of the region," said Father de Brèvedent.

"The caravan doesn't leave for a week," added Maître Juremi.

"We won't wait for the caravan. Hajji Ali will be our guide."

The answers were coming to Poncet even as he spoke them, as to a candidate at an oral review who is too nervous to think but still hears himself give the correct response.

"Stay here," he said. "Pack your personal belongings—the bare minimum. I am going to get Hajji Ali."

Before they could say a word, he was gone. In the pitch dark, Jean-Baptiste bumped into shadows and tripped over the paving stones of the little street. Fortunately, the large sandy esplanade where the caravans stayed on their way through town was straight ahead. He picked his way through the cluster of tents toward Hasan al-Bilbessi's. There, as he had expected, he found Hajji Ali in palaver with the leader of the caravan and several other traders, all sitting on rugs laid directly on the ground. After a round of greetings, and after sipping down a glass of very hot tea as slowly as his impatience allowed, Poncet asked if he might have Hajji Ali's company for an important matter. The camel driver took his time before finally allowing himself to be pried away from his friends, and Poncet led him back to the house.

"What is bothering you all of a sudden?" asked Hajji Ali ill-humoredly.

"We have to set out tonight," said Poncet.

Hajji Ali bared the stumps of his teeth in what might have been an ironic smile.

"Tonight?" he said.

"I am not joking."

"That's unfortunate," said Hajji Ali mockingly. "And will you be traveling alone?"

"No. With you."

"Wonderful! Truly we must thank the Prophet for his prohibition on fermented drink, as it puts the strangest ideas in a person's head."

"I have taken no fermented drink," said Jean-Baptiste, "and I advise you to listen carefully to my words or tomorrow you will be whipped and thrown into prison."

"Whipped! And by whom?"

"By the king."

Hajji Ali looked grave.

"Now, you remember that the French consul in Cairo did not want you to travel to Abyssinia with the Capuchins."

"I remember it well."

"He was right, and what he said about them was true. But they are tenacious. They sent two of their number in pursuit of you to get revenge, and now they have found you."

"Here?"

"Yes, here. Those priests have a house in this city. The king looks favorably on them and gives them his protection."

Hajji Ali felt the beginnings of fear. It could be seen in his slumping body, and in the way his features gradually assumed a pitiful expression, as though he were about to beg for mercy.

"But what can they possibly hold against me?" he asked.

"They hold something against us all, and they want to stop us. Tomorrow they will tell the king that we are not doctors at all but charlatans, and the king will believe them. And they will tell him that we are envoys of King Louis XIV of France and we will be thrown into prison."

"Ah! Ah!" groaned Hajji Ali, as he made a quick calculation of his share in the general misfortune.

"And you, who have lied to the king and presented us as Frankish doctors, you will be thrown into prison and whipped."

"But," said the camel driver, "I'll say I didn't know."

"The Capuchins have talked with the consul in Cairo. They know that you know."

He looked hard at Hajji Ali.

"And if they say nothing, we'll be the ones to mention it."

Although he made the statement with as merciless a countenance as he could muster, Jean-Baptiste was not especially convincing. Hajji Ali was adept at reading men's characters, and he instinctively knew that Poncet would never do such a thing, even to his worst enemy. The result, oddly enough, was for the threat to achieve its aim by a circuitous route. All the camel driver's mistrust was drawn to it, while an aura of truth was cast over the rest of what Jean-Baptiste had said. Hajji Ali believed that the three Franks were in real danger and assessed where his own interest lay. It took him little time to realize that he would draw no benefit from their disappearance. Of course, if it happened in the middle of the desert, he could at least take their belongings. But the king of Sennar's first act on imprisoning the Franks would be to clap hands on their goods.

No, rightly considered, Hajji Ali's best interest lay in bringing them to the negus. The emperor of Abyssinia was bound to be pleased with Poncet and would reward Hajji Ali with a handsome emolument. At the same time, the trader would earn the gratitude of the Franks in Cairo. Clearly his interest lay in saving the travelers. Additionally, if the Franks were forced to flee Sennar, they would necessarily leave behind part of their baggage, and Hajji Ali might have the usufruct of it. His decision was therefore made. He still had to paint it as a terrible sacrifice, though, so that Poncet would compensate him for it as liberally as possible.

Hajji Ali began to moan. He mopped his face of the sweat that had appeared on it at the talk of whips and prison. He mentioned money. Fifteen minutes later, a bargain was solemnly struck. The four of them would set out together—the three Franks and Hajji Ali—taking five camels and as few trunks as possible. Each traveler would carry his personal effects on his own camel, along with his weapons. The baggage camel would carry mainly the presents for the negus and the medicine trunk. Everything else (including their many scientific instruments, the presents for local potentates, and all their spare clothing) would be brought that very night to the house of a widow whom the camel driver knew and habitually sought consolation from on his passage through Sennar. She would hide their excess belongings and keep them safe against his return. Finally, Hajji Ali insisted that the camels become his property from that day on. The Franks would make him restitution for their use by the payment of a large lump sum.

In return, Hajji Ali consented to be rescued from his current difficulties. He would even have Hasan al-Bilbessi cover for their flight. If anyone asked the caravan leader about the Franks, he would say that they had gone botanizing along the river, and that Hajji Ali was suffering from migraine and had shut himself up in the hammam. Afterward, they would see.

The four then lay down to rest, though none was able to sleep. Hajji Ali, who had gone off to speak with Hasan al-Bilbessi, returned at two o'clock with a camel, and they lashed the two trunks to its saddle. Then, carrying their personal gear and saddlery, the three Franks slipped into the street behind the camel driver. They harnessed their camels, which were tied up at some distance from the caravan, and set off down the road into the inky blackness of the night. Luckily, Hajji Ali knew the way well. There being nothing so reassuring as flight, they no longer felt any fear, and they proceeded for several hours at a cautious walk. Now the city was far behind them and the sound of the dogs had grown quiet. A breath of moist air came up from the left, where the river must be: they guessed that they were traveling up the course of the Blue Nile. At the first light of dawn, they saw mud huts springing up from a bed of reeds ahead of them, and startled cattle snorted by the river's edge, as if to put the last remnants of the cold night to flight. Here a log bridge spanned the Nile. They made for it and, once safely across, spurred their mounts to a gallop toward the purple light of the east.

~

The routine adopted by Alix and Françoise of meeting secretly each morning on the terrace of the druggists' house was threatened from the very quarter they least expected. Father Gaboriau, that peaceful man who had proved so amenable to his treatment and had offered them so little trouble, suffered a stroke. Alix came down one day at the usual time to find him half out of his chaise longue, one of his hands hanging down, one of his eyes too wide open, his mouth askew.

The poor man survived, though he remained unable to move or speak. His loss almost put an end to the women's budding friendship. The consul took it as a pretext to call an end to the botanical outings, which he had authorized only under the most odious constraint. His daughter delicately pointed out that they had made a commitment toward "that laboratory's owners." Her father shrugged. These were nice terms for a pair of thieves. The matter almost came to an argument, as Alix resisted his wishes with unexpected force. She finally persuaded him to let her continue her duties there, henceforth accompanied by Madame de Maillet, her mother. Françoise stayed hidden. On the first visit, Alix made her mother listen to detailed botanical explanations—of her own invention, naturally, having no others—in which she managed to incorporate a number of Latin terms made up for the occasion. She stood for an endless time over each humble succulent, suddenly metamorphosed into a unique specimen. The poor woman found herself prodigiously bored, and returned home with a headache and aching feet. She summoned the energy to accompany her daughter to the druggists' house a second time, but it was to be her last. The air of the greenhouse, she declared, was bad for her health. However, she recognized that it provided the greatest benefit to her daughter.

Madame de Maillet persuaded her husband that Alix's passion for plants was harmless and that there was more to fear from opposing the sentiment than from gratifying it. The consul allowed himself to be convinced. Not a whisper of disparagement had reached him from the colony at large concerning these visits, and he had even been complimented by a certain merchant whose son had started keeping an herbarium of his own. Alix was afraid of having to stop her visits altogether or of being chaperoned much more closely. Instead her father simply gave her permission to go alone, and she was able to meet Françoise without supervision.

It was a period of great happiness. The young girl felt a complete transformation in herself. The first sign of it had been her firmness and resolution toward her father in the management of this affair.

In the beginning, they were absorbed mainly with the superficial. Alix had been deprived of friendship just at the age when it is most necessary. She needed to take stock of her own beauty and of her new body, which she still looked at uneasily, as though she were harnessed to a high-spirited team whose strength frightened her.

It was a time for trying new hairstyles, which they undid hastily at noon before Alix went home. Often, Alix brought clothes she had smuggled from the consulate in a sack, outfits of her mother's for dress-up. In the shade of the orange trees she would parade along the shady terrace past her friend, laughing. Françoise taught the young girl not only general notions of beauty, but how to value each detail at its worth and give it its full due. Alix was blossoming.

Looking back on this time later, she was extremely grateful to Françoise for having shown such patience and gaiety during the long period when she was so naively absorbed in discovering herself.

Imperceptibly, they moved on to other things. Alix was aware of her assets, had stopped doubting them, and knew their limits. From that time onward she developed a new ease, a deep confidence, which she had the cleverness to mask by preserving the modesty of her speech and behavior. Her mother, in her customary way, noticed nothing. Though Alix had often regretted not being closer to her mother, she now realized how little the poor woman had to teach her. What a difference with Françoise, whose life might have been written into a novel!

She had been born near Grenoble, and her father was a prosperous grain merchant. Her parents took little notice of her, and Françoise retaliated by running off with a man thirty years her elder. He had not settled into a trade, although he had worked at them all. He spent a great deal of money despite not being rich, the very opposite of Françoise's father. Her lover was well-spoken, and he knew the Orient and Italy. He took her with him, and it was the start of endless adventures, which she narrated in small pieces, like tales from *The Thousand and One Nights*. First came flight, fortune, travel, and poverty. The two were in love. Then followed exile, lies, gambling, and more poverty. By the time they arrived in Cairo they no longer saw eye to eye. The next chapter went from bad to worse and ended with the man's death, alone, in a squalid corner of the Arab quarter. From this picaresque existence, Françoise drew portraits, stories, and a few rules of conduct. She uttered her precepts as though she herself had no further use for them, her fires having gone out from age and indifference. But Alix noticed that when Françoise spoke of her employment with the apothecaries, she never mentioned Maître Juremi without emotion.

"Do you love him?" the young girl finally asked her.

"I have asked you for frankness and owe it to you in return," Françoise answered. "He is a good, courageous man, and, yes, I believe I love him."

"Have you told him?"

"Oh, you obviously don't know him! He is sullen and irascible. I have thought twenty times of talking to him. I would stay awake all night and think what to say. Then I would arrive, he would look at me with his dark eyes, and my courage would ebb away. You see: I pretend to be a woman of the world, but I am not even as far along as you. . . ."

This simple admission only increased the value of everything else Françoise had told her. She had made a clean breast of her bold escapades as well as her moments of weakness, and of the passion she had followed to its conclusion as well as the one she had not yet dared reveal.

Alix admired her. Such a feeling toward a servant would have scandalized her father, but Alix saw the matter differently. Françoise was a free woman, one who had bought her freedom at a high price and regretted nothing.

Until this moment, Alix had thought a woman's only choice was to submit, but Françoise's life provided an alternative. Under the older woman's influence, Alix's dreams began to grow more adventurous and more chaotic. Whenever Alix fantasized her own freedom, she saw herself riding horseback beside Jean-Baptiste. At first she thought it was only because there was no one else in her circle to compare him to. But Françoise convinced her differently.

"When a man has taken such a firm a hold of your dreams, he is not to be dislodged that easily," she said, shaking her head.

7

They walked for twenty-one days. In the early stages, they were sure they were being pursued by the king of Sennar and his troops. They expected to see signs of his might everywhere, in their fearfulness assigning him much greater power than he had. It took a week to convince themselves that they were not being followed—much less preceded—by the king's formidable agents, to whom they practically attributed wings. The truth was that they were simply lost somewhere in the enormous kingdom of the desert. Their real enemy was neither the invisible ruler nor the devious Capuchins but the country through which they were passing, where they found no water, food, or rest.

The land was flat. Vast expanses of arid country dotted with sunbaked rocks alternated with valleys along rivers of sand. Water ran there only once a year, great torrents of it, which the soil absorbed before it could join other watercourses. The vegetation in these strange valleys was dense, composed of bamboos and reeds, prickly pears (then in bloom), aloes, and acacias. A thick carpet of *kantuffa*, a dense, thistly bush, made stopping there unpleasant and even blocked their passage at times.

Having reduced their baggage to a bare minimum, the fugitives had no protection, neither a tent, nor a hammock, nor a blanket. They slept on the ground. In the desert, they had to be careful of spiders, scorpions, and poisonous snakes. In the denser vegetation of the valleys, when they could force their way through, they found large constrictors. They were also attacked by mosquitoes and every other species of insect devised by the Creator to chase man out of the wilderness and send him back to his own kind, however much he might fear them. One of the first days after they fled Sennar, Father de Brèvedent was bitten on the ankle by a giant spider. Poncet gave him medicine to relieve the pain, but the swelling spread to his whole leg, and he developed a fever. Traveling became extremely painful for him. But the sickness abated and the priest recovered, though very slowly, and he was noticeably weaker afterward.

During all the time they thought they were being pursued, they avoided the villages, which were in any case no more than small clusters of herders' huts. The travelers visited the wells to fill their goatskins only at night. When they finished the sack of dried beans they had brought from Sennar, they caught a calf that had strayed from its pasture. Hajji Ali put it to death according to ritual procedure, then ordered Joseph to dress it. Killed by a Muslim, butchered by a Catholic, and devoured by a Protestant, a more ecumenical calf could hardly be imagined, unless a rabbi had been invited to gnaw on its bones. They loaded the uneaten sides onto their saddles. Unfortunately, a young shepherd had seen them and given the alarm. A swarm of black men armed with assegais and short bronze swords descended on them. Poncet considered it best to flee, given the number of their assailants, but Maître Juremi leaped to his sword and cried:

"To me, sirs!"

Jean-Baptiste grabbed a weapon as well and went to his friend's defense. They attacked the first two natives who approached them. Surprised at the swiftness and near-invisibility of the rapiers, the two assailants allowed themselves to be pierced through, their eyes wide with astonishment. Two others replaced them. They were visibly amused by these incomprehensible and practically immaterial encounters. The clash of the swords excited them. The other natives drew up in a large circle to watch these single combats as though attending a celebration. The two strangers exerted themselves behind their long steel rods, which fluttered through the air like dragonflies' wings. Their opponents parried the blows with heavy spears, and some carried small leather shields. When a touch was scored, they were replaced by two more challengers. The outcome was no longer in any doubt, as the black men in the circle now numbered more than two hundred. They stamped on the ground with their bare feet and made the heavy bracelets around their ankles jingle. The circle around Poncet and his partner was practically closed. When weariness overcame them, their attackers could simply collar them, disarmed and out of breath. Looking away from his duel by chance, Poncet suddenly saw Joseph. The crowd had not surrounded him. He was standing beside the camels, his arms dangling at his sides, unable to decide what to do.

"The pistols!" Poncet shouted at him.

The Jesuit still seemed staggered.

"In my saddlebags! Get the loaded pistols and fire them!"

The circle slowly closed. Poncet could soon see nothing but the dust rising from the ground under the rhythmic trampling of innumerable thin, naked legs.

Suddenly, two gunshots rang out. The natives stopped in their tracks. For thirty seconds all was silence, then they took to their heels, leaving their wounded and a number of their weapons behind.

Father de Brèvedent was still holding the pistols, looking with horror at the smoke drifting from the muzzles.

"Well," said Maître Juremi, walking up to the false Joseph, "that's what you might call a triumph. With two pistols you could carve yourself a kingdom out here."

He smiled at the Jesuit.

"And with only the slightest persuasion, I'm sure they could all be turned into Catholics."

The Jesuit shrugged his shoulders.

They found Hajji Ali, who had decided to watch the encounter from a distance, in the middle of a thorn bush. He begged Poncet to treat his many and deep scratches, and endured the swabbing like a martyr. Of the four voyagers, he was the only one to emerge wounded from this brief and victorious campaign.

Jean-Baptiste now estimated that they had traveled beyond the reach of the king's vengeance and that it was better to travel openly, for by prowling on the outskirts of villages they raised the natives' suspicions more than if they simply acted as normal travelers. Their lives immediately became easier. The tribesmen, they discovered, entertained a harmless curiosity toward them, and people came from far and wide to see their white skins. Some, after fearful deliberations, even touched them. Always, the natives showed warm hospitality toward them. The ones who attacked them had simply been angered at having their property taken on the sly. When asked in a friendly way, they were inclined to give anything they had. They offered the travelers huts to sleep in, millet cakes, and large bowls of milk mixed with fresh cow's blood, a dish the Africans considered the height of refinement. As a simple gesture of goodwill, they even offered them the loveliest young girls from among their kin. Poncet and Maître Juremi, after their long hours in the saddle, had no other thought when they climbed into bed than to fall sound asleep. They would invite the proffered courtesans to lie down beside them, but soon were snoring in earnest. Before drifting off, they always took care to show their bedmates their full anatomy. It was explained to them that one of the main duties of these young women was to report the next day to the community at large on the color of the travelers' most private parts. The natives seemed to have trouble conceiving, in the absence of firsthand testimony, that the same strange white color should extend even to the farthest reaches of the foreigners' bodies.

Father de Brèvedent, who had been advised by his companions to follow their lead and not on any account refuse the honor shown him, would spend the night reciting the acts of contrition, afraid he might at any moment fall prey to the Beast. Only partially recovered from the swelling on his leg, and weakened by the hardships he had endured, the Jesuit ruined what was left of his health by these feverish vigils. Maître Juremi observed sarcastically that there was no need, to preserve one's chastity, to take Saint Ignatius's injunction *perinde ac cadaver*—like a cadaver—literally. It was no use.

Hajji Ali would never have troubled his head with such scruples, but for the moment he was still scarred by the thorn pricks and yelled in pain at the slightest touch. All he could do was make belittling comments about the savages' customs and hypocritically regret that Islam had not yet enlightened them.

They walked in this way from village to village for five days until they reached the large town of Grefim, which lay wrapped in the shade of palm trees and adorned with flowers and fruits: guavas, pomegranates, avocados, and oranges. Parrots and other brightly colored birds perched in the trees, providing an agreeable change from the vultures that had been the travelers' only companions in the sky for days on end.

They still had two short days' journey through the desert before they reached the long fertile valley of Simyen, which took them to Serke. Surrounded by white hills planted to cotton, the city was a great seat of commerce. In the center of town was a busy market, overflowing with produce from the surrounding area and brightly festooned with the cotton cloth woven in the town and dyed with raw pigments: carmine, indigo, and saffron. An odor of spices floated over the market, and a great variety of aromatic goods from Ethiopia was displayed in the stalls. The city was situated along a narrow stream with a bridge across it. On the far side lay Abyssinia. The outline of its high mountainous region could be seen disappearing into the dusty haze.

They crossed the bridge at six in the evening. Though nothing around them had changed, their spirits lifted when they set foot on the far shore and they shouted with joy. Poncet opened the medicine trunk and produced a special vial he had set aside for the occasion. They sat down under a kapok tree whose giant roots formed triangular buttresses in the shape of shark fins that made perfect arm and back rests. Jean-Baptiste uncorked the vial and toasted their arrival in Abyssinia. He took a large swallow from the bottle and passed it on to Maître Juremi, who followed suit. It was the same medicine that had brought such voluptuous pleasure to Father Gaboriau in his chaise longue. Hajji Ali, a less observant Muslim since arriving in the Christian lands of the patriarchate, drank a double dose. Joseph refused to drink. They encouraged him to. Ten minutes later he vomited his first blood. Extremely worried for the priest, Poncet asked the camel driver how far it was to the next town on the Abyssinian side where they could safely stop to look after the sick man in the shade of a flame tree, or even in a house if they could find one.

Hajji Ali told them there were no villages nearby. The best plan was to follow the road, as they were not very far from the capital. The merchant clearly wanted to reach the city as quickly as possible and considered a servant's life too inconsequential to delay their journey.

The Jesuit agreed fully, making light of his indisposition.

"We are about to climb toward the highlands," he said. "The cool air up there will do me more good than staying down here in the sweltering desert."

An hour later they had reached the foothills and started up a wide valley with a lush growth of bamboo and ebony trees. As they climbed the narrow path, the vegetation grew thicker and thicker. They stopped at dusk in a clearing by the trail. A terrifying roar awakened them in the middle of the night, followed by high-pitched screams. As the moon had set and the night was dark, they decided that the safest course was to stay together and wait for morning to investigate. At dawn they discovered two of their camels missing. There was an enormous puddle of blood where one of the animals had been attacked and eaten by a lion. The other camel turned up several hundred yards below them, where it had fled in terror at the lion's attack, after breaking its head rope.

With another of their camels gone, one of the company would have to walk. The Jesuit volunteered. He was thin and feverish, and his legs were starting to swell. Poncet curtly refused.

"Please, let me," said Father de Brèvedent. "Don't show me any favor. Remember that I am only a servant. If you treat me indulgently you will arouse suspicions."

This time they did not listen to him. Maître Juremi shoved the priest roughly toward his own saddle and started to walk alongside the caravan.

They walked in the valley for several more days. Its vegetation grew more and more luxuriant, and they sometimes came across sycamores ten feet in diameter. At night, they took turns standing watch, pistol in hand, sitting by the fire only a few feet from where the camels were tethered. Then, at the very head of the valley, they emerged into another, larger valley that seemed to contain and extend the first. The altitude made the air agreeably cool in the morning, while the nights were cold and humid. Breasting the short rise dividing one valley from the other, they looked back to discover a sumptuous panorama behind them: the flocked green surface of the mountain was incised with a long, winding scar, retracing the path they had just followed. The entire mass of rocks and trees, like a wave crashing against a sandy shore, rolled, heaved, and cascaded down to the gray expanse of desert, which they could now see from their great height. Scattered palms in the distance and the white patch of a few cultivated fields seemed like spray hurled by the wave of vegetation and drifting in its backwash.

Along the sides of the new valley grew mainly juniper and wild olive. They heard a lark sing and saw a number of jays and woodpeckers in the trees. The path climbed in a series of steep switchbacks, and they could sometimes see it loop twice or three times above them. They had still not passed a single dwelling since arriving in Abyssinia, nor had they met anyone except a few poor creatures, hairy and half naked, who scurried along the trail carrying huge burlap bags full of charcoal.

At night they continued to mount guard, although the wildlife seemed less threatening as they went on. During the day the only animals they saw were troupes of large black monkeys with thin bodies and arms as long as their legs—in fact the monkeys seemed as dexterous with either limb. Finally, they left the forest and entered an open prairie where the ground was carpeted with yellow flowers. A few trees still grew here and there, an odd mixture of conifers and dwarf baobabs. Higher up, above a sizable escarpment, a vertical wall led to the ridgeline. This was the edge of the high plateau. As they drew closer, they could see this blackish palisade rising above them, running along the crest like a rampart. At its base were large blocks of basalt that had split off and rolled to a stop down the slope. Clear, cool springs welled up through the brown rock immediately underlying the lush grass. In this green amphitheater, dominated by the ring of basalt that fringed the high plateau, they sank into a blissful enjoyment of their setting. Lying on the soft grass, drinking the clear water, warmed by the sun and cooled by the gentle breeze, they spent almost a whole day in silence, half asleep, looking off into the distance. Until then, survival had been their only thought, and their eyes had been fixed on the ground ahead. Now they found themselves absorbed in admiring the sky.

Jean-Baptiste felt that each of them was praying. This was plainly the case with Hajji Ali, who knelt facing Mecca. Father de Brèvedent kept his eyes half closed as though listening to the song of sacred trumpets echoing the power and glory of the Almighty from the depths. Deprived of the church and its ritual pomp, he was the one who had the most difficulty of all of them in adapting to the solitary wastes.

Maître Juremi, sitting off to one side on a large boulder, was shaking his head, moving his lips, and looking at the sky from time to time with a severe expression. Poncet knew his friend well enough to recognize that this was his way of praying, for Juremi believed that he was constantly in God's sight. Prayer was simply the moment when he and God had something specific to talk about. And the Protestant never minced his words: he thought the Creator had as many responsibilities toward his creation as the other way around, and maybe more, since, as he put it, "He started it, after all." Whenever he believed an injustice had been committed, Maître Juremi upbraided God directly, argued his opinions, and even gave the Deity summary orders.

Jean-Baptiste for his part gave thanks to the invisible powers of the sky and earth, confessing once and for all that he knew neither their names nor their faces. For a long moment, he thought about Alix with the delicious feeling that his road had already brought him closer to her.

8

Before tackling the last rock outcrop between themselves and the high plateau, the three Franks took off their European clothes—their torn and stained trousers, and their shirts immersed a hundred times in wells, puddles, and mountain streams, and stiff from deeply ingrained dirt. All three then put on Arab clothes, consisting of a long blue tunic and a headcloth. Hajji Ali counted on presenting them at first as simple camel drivers. The Abyssinians, who were used to such caravans, would leave them in peace.

Two hours later, they were at the foot of the wall of columnar basalt. They walked along it until they found a break in the rank of organ pipes, aligned like the stakes of a palisade. At the end of a steep path snaking through the basalt blocks they found a village perched on the extreme edge of the high plateau.

The first thing they saw above the thickets was an octagonal church, its pointed roof surmounted by a cross. A service was in progress inside as they passed. Through the still, clear air came the echo of treble voices raised in psalm.

The town was no more than a large market center inhabited by slaves and herdsmen. The locals walked bareheaded, a length of goatskin draped over their shoulders and a white cotton cloth wrapped around their waist. The complexion of these men was lighter than that of any black men they had seen until then.

In the distant days when Sennar was still Christian, this village had served as a customs post for the active trade between the two countries. This explained the wall they had passed on their way into the town. Hajji Ali brought them quietly to the house of a trader he knew, who greeted them with a conspirator's whisper. In the twilight, dressed as they were in their Arab shirts, no one had looked at them twice. Hajji Ali, who was known in the town, had been careful to uncover his face so that he would be recognized.

The following day, their host arranged to buy their camels and give them mules in return, since they would be crossing no more deserts. The exchange was sealed with only a little extra coin on their side. Father de Brèvedent, whether from the excellent night he had spent under the stars in the trader's courtyard on a bed of woven sisal or from the comfort of seeing the cross on top of the church, appeared to feel much better in the morning. Hajji Ali went off to pay the *awid,* a toll collected on behalf of the emperor by two of the town's functionaries, and they once more took up their route in the early afternoon.

At first they traveled over a gently rolling moor covered with flowering heather, wild oat, and reeds. They then found themselves in an airy cedar forest, like a cathedral nave framed by the regular pilasters of the tree trunks and roofed by the high vault of their branches. The mules traveled at a slow trot without urging, making a pleasant change from the woozy swaying of the camels. The air was hot under the direct sun, but so pure after the dusty warmth of the desert that it seemed brisk and lively. When they entered even a small shadow, whether from a tree or a passing cloud, an unexpected freshness pounced on them, reminding them surprisingly of Europe. The effect on the travelers of this change in the elements was not particularly favorable. Their bodies had taken considerable abuse from the tropical dryness and miasmas, and now, in a period of relative calm, all the damage done to their health was coming to the surface. On the first night they stopped to rest in a tiny hamlet of a few huts. Maître Juremi called Poncet over and bared his leg for him. Above the ankle, in a crater of reddened flesh, stuck out the head of a guinea worm, like the tip of a slender white cord. Jean-Baptiste sent for a feather, around which he gently rolled the first segment of the parasite, then wedged the whole thing in place with a bandage.

Jean-Baptiste himself was in poor shape. He was shivering, and his joints and back ached. He lay down that night with his teeth chattering. In the morning they saw that the Jesuit's condition had worsened. His lips were dry, he was racked by fits of coughing, and his forehead was beaded with icy sweat. And even Hajji Ali, used as he was to these journeys, asked Poncet to give him medicine for a stomach pain.

They had no time to dawdle in the hamlets. Their safety lay in the capital, Gondar, which was now only five days' journey away. Only half conscious, their senses impaired by fever, they covered the last portion of their journey in a state of numbness that only increased the fantastical character of the country. The lapses in their memory, combined with their blurred perceptions and the long emotional reverberations from the illness in their bodies, left them with a powerful but chaotic impression of the landscape.

The high, rolling plateau over which they traveled seemed to be the natural base of the earth, like an ordinary chalk amphitheater by the sea coast. And when the path they were following led them to the extreme edge of the plateau, the valley they looked down on, from which a haze of dust and water vapor drifted upward, did not so much speak of their own considerable altitude as it seemed to reveal on the contrary a monstrous abyss opening onto the smoking entrails of the earth. The next moment, if the path veered slightly away from the lip of the precipice, they might see a craggy mountain rising from the surface of the plateau, its lower slopes covered with vegetation, its summit bare, cold, and lifeless. In some places, the peaks looked like gigantic monuments of gray stone, from which blocks were coming loose.

At times, the two effects happened together. One side of the path would drop away into a deep abyss, while the other rose toward the solitary heights of a porphyry mountain.

Other than in the peasant hamlets where they stopped at night, they saw no one on the roads between. A pair of eagles soared above them all one day. And they saw elephant droppings, although they never saw the animals themselves. One day they encountered a herd of *agazar*, a wild goat considered a great delicacy by the Abyssinians. Hajji Ali urged Poncet to kill one with his pistols, but the Frenchman felt too nauseous to try.

Finally, they arrived in the town of Bartcha, a half day's journey from Gondar. There Hajji Ali learned that the emperor was not in the capital at the moment, having gone off to quell a rebellion in one of the provinces.

"There is no point in arriving too early in Gondar," said Hajji Ali. "Better that you should wait here for the king to return. A friend of mine will hide you in his house. I will go on to the city and come back for you when the time is ripe."

Poncet had little faith in the camel driver's words. He could not forgive him for having stolen everything they had. Other than the presents they had brought for the King of Kings, their property had all fallen into the trader's hands. He even had the gall to remind them that the Arab shirts they wore belonged to him, and that he expected them back as soon as the emperor had paid them their first gold. Regretfully, Jean-Baptiste watched Hajji Ali go, afraid he might abandon them altogether.

Luckily, their health improved. Maître Juremi had his guinea worm rolled up slightly more each day. He would soon recover. Only the Jesuit's condition truly worried them. The house Hajji Ali had found for them was made of wooden poles daubed with a mixture of mud, straw, and cow dung. The floor was of packed dirt. All in all, it was hardly the best place to tend a sick man. Lying on his pallet, poor Joseph seemed to sink a bit more into the earth each day. The man had overestimated his own strength. His extreme devotion to his mission had made him believe that he, a scholar used to the comforts of a quiet library, could endure the hardships of the road like a convict on a chain gang. But his growing weakness had prepared his body for disease the way drought readies a stand of pine trees for fire. The Jesuit truly was in a pitiful state. His tall, gaunt body was twisted like a vine. He breathed through his open mouth, his lips scorched by the heat and his own feverish breath. Jean-Baptiste and Maître Juremi took turns sitting at his bedside. Yet for all the Protestant's kindness to him during this period, the Jesuit continued to express his holy revulsion at the heretic's presence whenever he was conscious. And for as long as he still believed he would recover his health, Brèvedent clung to the idea of accomplishing his mission. For hours on end, in dreary tones at times seeming to arise from the depths of his delirium, he would describe his great plan of converting Abyssinia.

"What we need first," he said, "is to understand the Abyssinians' mores, customs, behavior, and language. Yes, the language. First. As soon as we arrive there, I'll study the language. I learned the rudiments of it in France. But no one speaks it really. Language is the only avenue of persuasion. Then, their beliefs . . . must know them perfectly . . . that is the great secret. In Europe, church ceremonies have replaced pagan rites . . . but keeping the same dates, the same places, the same images."

Sometimes he would clutch whoever was at his bedside, in the end even speaking to Maître Juremi, whom he mistook for Poncet.

"We won't repeat the errors made by our predecessors, will we? The king must not be converted before we have made a start on the people and the clergy. . . ."

Opening up his soul in his death agony, the Jesuit showed how much his modesty and willingness to accept humiliation were the obverse of his great pride. He behaved in strict obedience to his order and renounced all personal desires, but he did so in the service of a vast historical design and a collective ambition to wield power. He had agreed to fetch water the better to rule over a king and his empire. Despite the encouragement and skillful attention of Jean-Baptiste, the Jesuit's illness gained ground, and the priest soon knew that he was dying. Once he had accepted the idea, his passion for obedience took a new turn. He had submitted totally to the demands of his holy mission, but now he espoused those of Providence instead: he abandoned himself to the illness that a divine fate had sent him. Further treatment was useless. He died two days later, as docile to the call of death as when Hajji Ali had barked orders at him.

Poncet and Maître Juremi wanted to bury the priest in the courtyard, under the acacia tree that shaded it. Their host refused, saying that the ancestor who had built the house was buried there, after having died a violent death. To profane his tomb by putting this bad companion in it for all eternity was out of the question.

That night, therefore, they slipped out through the narrow streets to a bean field and dug a deep trench on the edge of the moor where they buried the Jesuit. He was laid to rest in his Arab shirt—Hajji Ali could always whistle for it. Referring to his Bible, Maître Juremi intoned a brief service, while Poncet, the only Catholic present, being unfamiliar with the ceremony and not knowing what to do with his hands, threw dirt onto the body without waiting for the end of the psalm. The man had shared his life for many long weeks, and he was moved to see him disappearing into a hole. Jean-Baptiste had given him his friendship and could not be sure it had been entirely rejected.

"No one ever ran farther to escape from freedom," said Maître Juremi, after he had closed his Bible.

This was to be the poor priest's epitaph.

Walking back toward the house, the two friends traveled in thought to the mysterious continent of lost childhood, of dead hopes, and of the vanished past. When they spoke again it was to agree that the Jesuit's life had been even sadder than his death and that, although they had mourned him sincerely, they did not miss him.

By the next day, the pall had dissipated. A new tone of gaiety had even sprung up between them, which they resolved not to abandon. Hajji Ali returned after being gone for three days. Dressed in the Abyssinian style in a white tunic embroidered with a band of bright color, perfumed, his hair drawn back, he was unrecognizable. He reacted to the news of Joseph's death as though they had reported the loss of a mule. He made no comment and went directly to the matter at hand:

"The King of Kings returns to Gondar today," he began. "We may now solicit an audience."

"At what time?" asked Poncet, glad at the prospect of leaving the house.

"It is not a question of hours but of days."

"Of days! Is the king not anxious to be treated?"

"Certainly. But before he reveals to the court that he has called for Frankish doctors, he must prepare their minds for it. He must make clear that those who have pretended to treat him up till now have failed."

"I would think that they had had all the time in the world while we were traveling here either to kill or to cure him," said Jean-Baptiste.

"Perhaps," answered Hajji Ali, his equanimity in keeping with his new appearance. "Yet they have observed my return and suspect the mission I was on. The queen's entourage are hostile to the Franks and have decided to make one final attempt. You should know that the priests and soothsayers who make up this party want revenge for a humiliation they received from the king. At the time he was setting out on his last military campaign, a comet of unusual brightness and with a particularly long tail was seen in the sky. The soothsayers prophesied that the king would lose the battle and never return. But he won and he is back. They are looking for a way to recover his favor."

"And what means do they plan to use this time?"

"They arranged last week for a great saint to travel in procession from Lalibela. He is a monk who has not eaten or drunk for twenty years."

"Twenty years!" said Jean-Baptiste and Maître Juremi, in tones of mock reverence.

"It is nothing to joke at. This is entirely genuine. The saint can be seen by all. He lies under a canopy. Four monks carry his litter. Before him goes the patriarch, surrounded by a dozen monks singing and holding up a tall golden cross. Behind him walk thirty young warriors with bare feet."

"And a dozen mules carrying barrels of mead?" said Maître Juremi, snickering.

"The monk has been in prayer since his arrival," Hajji Ali went on, sidestepping the controversy. "This morning he saw the negus, and raised a great icon of the Virgin over him. Tomorrow he will return to give him the word of God to drink."

"To drink! But in what form?" asked Jean-Baptiste very seriously.

"The matter is shrouded in secrecy. He says many words no one can catch—this must be the heart of the secret, because his actions are simple and well-known. Two officers responsible for overseeing all that the king ingests have watched the procedure and described it to me. The saint writes a word, whose nature remains a mystery, onto a pewter amulet. He then dips the metal into a bowl of holy water where the ink from the word is dissolved. The water is then drunk by the king."

"How many times is the operation repeated?" asked Jean-Baptiste, somewhat subdued.

"Only twice."

"And how many days are they giving themselves before effect is supposed to show?"

"The king has let me know that if he is no better in a week, he will call on you to treat him."

"What if, by some fluke, he is cured?"

"By some fluke!" said Maître Juremi. "But in fact there is nothing more likely. If the treatment doesn't work at once, they need only increase the dose by soaking an entire Bible in a pint of *eau de vie*."

"If he is cured," said Hajji Ali, "we will leave."

"Without seeing him?"

"You have to understand that the king takes a great risk by seeing you, even though people know that it was he who sent for you. Since the Jesuits tried to convert the country during the reign of his grandfather, the negus is no longer entirely free. The clerics and all the others who oppose Catholicism watch him carefully. At the slightest misstep, they will resume their intrigues to free themselves from his iron grip. Everyone knows that the Frankish priests still hope to enter the country by fair means or foul, and they are wary. Without the excuse of receiving medical attention, the king would rather send you away to preserve peace at home."

Having imparted this disturbing news, Hajji Ali left them to return to the palace. They remained alone. Their confidence had not been shaken, but they were unhappy at having to remain cooped up behind the walls of their courtyard.

One of their host's sons went to the market and brought back a sample of every plant that was being sold there. The two set about identifying and preserving them with great interest, as there was no country on earth with more aromatic species, odorous resins, dyes, and spices. Using his mortar, his filters, and an improvised retort, Maître Juremi followed Poncet's directions to pound, distill, and make tinctures and emulsions. They partially restocked the medicine chest, which their journey had seriously depleted. If they had to return now without seeing the king, at least they would bring back these botanical discoveries.

Three days after Hajji Ali's visit, the trader they were staying with came to tell them that they would have to move to a new house that evening. When night fell, they walked the last distance separating them from the capital, disguised in their long Arab shirts. The mules with their meager baggage following behind. In Gondar, they were taken in by another Muslim, whose house was in the Arab quarter, and they were shown into two modestly furnished rooms with grilled windows opening onto a narrow street. The man carried in meals to them himself, counseling them to be patient.

It was from this austere retreat that Hajji Ali retrieved them a week later. He had arranged for Abyssinian clothes to be sent to them the day before: short tunics of white linen, and light cotton cloaks to drape over their shoulders. The next morning, Hajji Ali appeared on a small bay horse, its harness elaborately decorated with pompoms and plumes. Slaves followed behind him, leading two more horses by the halter. Poncet and Maître Juremi, now dressed in Abyssinian costume according to Hajji Ali's instructions, mounted in turn, and the small procession set off at a light trot and dancing obliquely toward Koscam Palace.

9

"Go on!" said Monsieur de Maillet impatiently. "Don't forget that the letter must be finished today if it is to reach Alexandria by the next mail. Where were we?"

Monsieur Macé sat at the rolltop desk, pen in hand. His eyes were still cloudy from the bad night he had spent, and the weeping humors they exuded were apparently quite appetizing to the mosquitoes that invaded the town at the start of the dry season. Men and women were driven away from him and insects attracted. Unfortunately, he failed to make the obvious deduction and revise his personal hygiene.

"Let's see, let's see," he said, looking for where he had left off reading. "Here we are: '. . . and this same Capuchin father who previously asked to send monks of his order with our embassy obtained an audience with me yesterday. I may confess to Your Excellency . . .'"

"No! That is not diplomatic language. A consul does not confess himself to a minister."

"We might put: 'Your Excellency should be aware . . .'"

"A slight improvement. Go on."

"Your Excellency should be aware that there was nothing courteous about our interview. I prevailed on myself to hear him out, although Father Pasquale, who was clearly beside himself, crossed the line of polite and respectful discourse on a number of occasions."

"Not bad at all," said Monsieur de Maillet, standing with one leg outstretched, pleased with the sound of the letter and at the same time admiring his apple-green silk stocking, freshly arrived on the galley from France.

"Following our last interview, he sent men in pursuit of our envoys' caravan. The Capuchins caught up with our mission in Sennar, where they reiterated their demand. Our envoys, taking advantage of a moonless night, appear to have fled and, despite all efforts at finding them, disappeared leaving no track."

"Are you using the singular?"

"I beg your pardon, Excellency?"

"With the word 'track.'"

"Yes, I believe so, Excellency."

"Make it plural. I have trouble conceiving that they would hop along on one foot in single file to leave just one track."

"'. . . despite all efforts at finding them, disappeared leaving no tracks.' With an *s*."

"Excellent."

"'The Capuchins, alerted by the sudden flight of the French mission, pursued their investigations and succeeded in uncovering the identity of the supposed servant Joseph. The matter will be brought to the attention of the pope himself, or so I am assured by Father Pasquale.'"

"Let us not mention that oaf's name so often. Say simply: '. . . or so I am assured by the Capuchins.'"

Monsieur Macé made a note of the amendment.

"'If I could suggest two conclusions that Your Excellency might draw at the present time from this unfortunate affair, they would be the following: first, that our envoys were still alive and in good health a month ago in Sennar, which is about where we anticipated they would be at that date.'"

Monsieur de Maillet wandered to the window and looked out into the garden.

"'And secondly, though this is admittedly more tenuous, that these questions of religion have introduced a complicating element into our diplomatic mission. The rivalry between the two religious orders and the frank hostility of the Abyssinians toward the Catholic clergy have jeopardized a mission which, in and of itself, raised few difficulties. In other words, as I might put it almost too bluntly, the Jesuits, who at first benefited this plan by their efforts, are now compromising it. I fully believe that in ordering this mission His Majesty wished to act in the interests of Christianity as a whole.'"

It was the fourth time since the previous evening that they had reread this letter. The consul never tired of hearing the political portion of it, which seemed to him so bold and clairvoyant. At that moment, his daughter appeared briefly on the steps of the consulate, distracting the consul's attention somewhat. How he would have loved to share these diplomatic jewels with her, so that she might preserve in her mind a clear image of her father's genius against the day when Time's implacable wheel carried him off.

"'It is therefore incumbent on us to discover,'" Monsieur Macé continued, "up to what point the interests of the king of France in this matter coincide with those of the Catholic faith. As soon as the embassy we await has returned, I will consult Your Excellency to learn how I am to proceed. Shall we continue to admix affairs of state with those of religion? Or, where diplomatic and even commercial ties hang in the balance, shall we act on His Majesty's sole behalf and in the primary interest of his kingdom?'"

"I believe it is perfect now," said Monsieur de Maillet sanctimoniously. "We will reread it one more time after you have added the corrections, and then it can be sent."

Monsieur Macé rose to his feet and returned to the stifling cubbyhole that served as his office.

The consul, holding himself slightly back from the drapery at the window, watched tenderly as his daughter left "to do her botanizing," in the household's phrase. He admired her graceful figure, her light step, her more serious and less childish air.

It is time, he thought, that I made marriage plans for her.

~

"This beast is doing its best to throw me!"

Maître Juremi used all his weight to control the little horse, which pranced under him with fear-crazed eyes. Hajji Ali motioned to a slave, who grabbed the horse's halter.

"This is no time to go sprawling," said Jean-Baptiste, who gripped his reins with both hands and managed by dint of a concerted effort to keep his horse at a walk.

They had just emerged from the Arab quarter and crossed the stream that separated it from the city proper. They were no longer veiled by their Muslim headcloths and were plainly revealed to one and all as white men. Yet the crowd that streamed through the narrow streets of the city remained impassive and showed not the slightest curiosity toward them. There were several reasons for this. In the first place, the two Franks, whose skin had been darkened by long exposure to the desert sun, had very nearly the same complexion as Abyssinian Christians. Secondly, several dozen foreigners lived in Gondar, and the inhabitants had grown accustomed to their physiognomy. Most were Greeks and Armenians, with a few southern Slavs among them, who had fled the Ottoman yoke and been granted protection by the emperor. And lastly, although the travelers would only gradually discover it, the Abyssinians dislike making a show of their emotions or revealing any part of their thoughts. At any rate, the two friends proceeded through the streets unaware of this, harboring the delightful impression of belonging to this fabled country, which they had dreamed of for so long.

Maître Juremi, whose thick, graying beard gave him the aspect of a sage, and Jean-Baptiste, looking like a young lord with his very dark and curly hair, fresh complexion, and elegant carriage, pranced side by side, anxious but filled with happiness.

As they slowly climbed toward the palace, the white figures of the crowd parted to let them pass. Men and women alike wore a simple cloak draped around their slender silhouettes. With their chiseled features, large almond-shaped eyes, and upright posture they looked for the most part haughty and aristocratic. It was easy to recognize the slaves from subjugated countries, whose features were coarser and backs more bent—either naturally or from carrying a heavy burden—and who chattered away among themselves.

The city was still full of armed soldiers, moving through the streets with their spears and leather shields, and of prisoners brought back from the recent campaign. As they passed a bare, grass-covered space, most likely a parade ground or place of assembly, Maître Juremi turned back to Jean-Baptiste.

"Here is the explanation for what we heard the day before yesterday."

A group of some twenty Shangalla warriors, whose armies the negus had recently defeated, were moaning on the square. Some were sitting on blocks of stone, while others were standing with their arms outstretched. Five or six were lying on the ground covering their heads with their hands. All of them, in the middle of their black faces, had two bloody stains in place of their eyes.

"The punishment for traitors," said Hajji Ali.

Brought back by the victorious army, the rebellious chiefs had been tried and sentenced to blinding by the high court. The punishment had been carried out two days before, and the prisoners' shrieks as their eyes were put out were heard throughout the town, and even in the house where the two travelers were waiting.

They continued on toward the palace. Jean-Baptiste, who twisted in his saddle several times to take in the horrible sight, noticed that the crowd pretended to pay no attention to the victims. If a prisoner, in the darkness he moved through, happened to grope his way toward an Abyssinian or place himself in his path, the passerby would simply step aside to avoid him with no more concern than if he had had to jump over a puddle or make way for a stray animal.

The palace was nearly invisible, surrounded as it was by tents and temporary structures against its walls. It was a massive building of cut stone, flanked by square towers with cupolas. With Hajji Ali to lead them, they were allowed to enter the great vaulted gateway without exchanging a word with the sentries. They dismounted, giving their horses to a guard, and walked down a dark corridor. After waiting briefly in a frigid antechamber, which smelled of dank stone, they were ushered into an audience hall whose two tall windows opened onto the courtyard below. A dozen personages were lined up along the walls waiting for them. Hajji Ali made a deep bow, which his companions imitated in all respects.

One of the figures broke away from the group. He stood slightly ahead of the others, wearing a black cloak embroidered with gold thread and a necklace of the same metal. His face was round, his hair close-cropped and curly, his beard short. Not as tall as Maître Juremi, he must have been about the same age. He spoke to them in a loud voice.

"He asks," said Hajji Ali, "if you are Franks."

"Who is he?" whispered Jean-Baptiste before offering his answer.

"He is Ras Yohannes, intendant general of the kingdom, the most powerful man after the emperor."

"If by 'Franks' you mean Catholics, the answer is that we are not, Excellency. We are subjects of the great King Louis XIV, but not of the great priest of the Church of Rome."

During the long days of waiting, Jean-Baptiste and Maître Juremi had discussed at length their answers to the questions that were most likely to be put to them. As Father de Brèvedent was no longer there to take offense at it, they had decided to take a high hand toward Catholicism and even make themselves out to have some enmity toward it, the better to distance themselves from the Jesuits. This was a somewhat risky game, though no more than any other.

"Where is the country from which you come?" asked the ras, or lord, after a period of reflection. The strangers' first answer, as translated by Hajji Ali, seemed to disconcert him somewhat.

"Beyond Sennar and Egypt, Excellency, on the other side of the great sea."

Jean-Baptiste knew that the Abyssinians' knowledge of geography was limited to these two countries. They were aware of the existence of other peoples, and had heard tell of the Portuguese and the Italians, but they had no concept of where their countries lay.

"Are there lands in these regions that are not under the rule of the man who calls himself the Chief of the Christians?"

Jean-Baptiste recognized the propaganda spread fifty years before by the Jesuits in an attempt to establish the pope's great power in the West.

"Your Excellency surely knows that there are fortunately many. The pope claims to govern men's souls. He does not govern their countries. Kings, ours among them, extend their protection to many kinds of subjects within their borders, even those who, like ourselves, do not recognize the authority of the pope."

Whether because of the torture victims they had so recently seen or for some other reason entirely, Maître Juremi, aware of the extreme danger of the conversation, had a constant and overwhelming urge to rub his eyes.

"Then you do not believe in Christ?" another asked suddenly. The question had come from a tall old man coiffed in a red toque, who stood to the left of Ras Yohannes.

"We believe in him, and we worship his teaching," said Jean-Baptiste. "But we do so in our own way, which is not the pope's. In consequence, our beliefs are condemned as severely by the pope as your own."

A ripple passed through the ranks of the assembly. Maintaining the majesty of their bearing, the dignitaries looked around at one another. In places there was whispering.

"Are you priests?" asked the same old man.

"Not at all."

"Yet we hear that you claim to effect cures."

"We claim only to serve our fellow man by putting the properties of the plants and animals placed on earth by God at the time of the creation to the best use possible."

"Then do you believe that it is possible to cure without prayer?"

"Prayer is a call for miracles, and we perform none."

"Do you not believe in miracles?"

Jean-Baptiste was tempted to give the same answer he had given earlier to the Jesuit but thought the better of it.

"We believe in the miracles reported in the Bible and performed by the Son of God. We do not know of any others."

"Yet great saints have also accomplished miracles," said Ras Yohannes.

"Perhaps this points to a limitation in our faith," said Jean-Baptiste. "We hold firmly to all that Christ said and to all that is written in the four Gospels. But we do not likewise agree to the accuracy of all that mere mortals have said. We do not believe, for instance, that a saint once converted the devil himself, nor that an ill and hungry monk could by means of prayer cause roasted quail to rain down on his plate."

These two examples had been given to Jean-Baptiste by Father de Brèvedent, who had heard them from the lips of Jesuits expelled from Abyssinia. These stories of a saint who triumphed over Lucifer and of a monk who produced quail were apparently points of controversy within the Coptic clergy itself. This time, there was a perceptible commotion in the assembled ranks. It seemed that Jean-Baptiste had touched on a sharp and deep disagreement between those present. Ras Yohannes ordered silence in the room. The men grew quiet. Then a little man stepped forward from the group of dignitaries. He was dressed in the saffron robe of a monk. His bulging eyes must have had very weak sight, and he seemed to look around as though in a fog.

"How many natures does Christ have?" he asked in a shrill voice.

This was the central question, the one over which the Jesuits had long battled, the point that had caused the Ethiopian Orthodox Church and the Church of Rome to split and go their separate ways twelve centuries earlier, a theological matter of virtually unravelable complexity. Strangely, the two travelers had made no provision for this question in all their preparations for the interview, as though it had been too obvious, or too indelicate, as though no one would have dared to raised so bold an issue. Maître Juremi looked at Jean-Baptiste and saw an expression of deep surprise on his face.

10

"How many natures does Christ have?" the monk asked a second time.

A heavy silence settled over the room and all eyes turned toward Jean-Baptiste, who said nothing. Then suddenly, as though struck by an inspiration, he straightened.

"How many natures does Christ have? But that is a question, sire, that I should ask of you!"

He allowed Hajji Ali time to translate his words, then went on.

"Each of us must speak only of what falls within his area of knowledge. For my part, I am a doctor, and my friend is an expert at preparing medications. The only other thing we know is the handling of those steel rods that, at home, we carry at our sides. Ask us what you will, sire, concerning plants or weapons, and we will do our best to answer you. But the question you have asked us surely concerns another such theologian as yourself. We are prepared to be instructed in this matter."

Jean-Baptiste ended his answer with a dignified bow. Dressed in his white cloak, with one hand on his heart, he looked at the ras and the assembled company with a disarming candor.

Inside, he was in agony, as though he had just traveled a narrow path along a ridge with sheer drop-offs on either side. His heart was pounding, and a cold sweat ran down his back. But he forced himself to show nothing of this.

There followed a long silence. The only sound was the chorus of complaints that rose from the courtyard, in which the voices of men and women mixed.

"Prepare to see the King of Kings," said Ras Yohannes finally in solemn tones. "As you claim to have the skill to cure him, and as His Majesty has kindly agreed to submit to your prescriptions, you will be admitted to his presence. I must inform you, however, that our emperor does not enter directly into relations with anyone, still less with foreigners. You may not touch or approach him, but only see him and hear the man through whose mouth he speaks."

"But that makes it impossible," said Jean-Baptiste. "How do you expect . . ."

The ras raised his hand to silence him.

"Those are the conditions. Do you or do you not have the power to heal?"

Jean-Baptiste was in despair at the terms imposed on him, less because they affected treating the king, whose ailment Hajji Ali had more or less described to him, than because they would affect his diplomatic embassy. How was he to convey a message to the negus?

The ras would brook no contradiction, so much was clear, and Poncet accepted the terms as laid out. The dignitaries filed from the room, and the three travelers were left to wait for their audience.

"You never mentioned these details," said Jean-Baptiste sharply to Hajji Ali. "We will be unable to speak to the king?"

"In public he must remain inaccessible," said the camel driver. "That is the law. He is not even allowed to touch the ground. When he mounts the throne, he is carried on the back of a mule and touches his foot to the ground only when he reaches the rug on which the throne is set. As the mule also climbs onto the carpet, she often deposits dung right in the middle of the Persian motifs. It makes no difference—everyone is used to it. In fact, you are lucky. Things have changed considerably. In the old days, you never saw the sovereign at all. This one's grandfather appeared publicly only two or three times a year. Otherwise, he kept to himself behind an arras."

"Why does the negus not talk?"

"That is the way it is. The king has an official to take the place of each of his organs. There is the king's eye, who reports back to him on all that he sees at court, and the king's ear, who listens on his behalf. There is the chief of his right hand and the chief of his left, who govern his armies. And you will hear the *serach massery*, the man who repeats his words aloud."

"Does he at least make his children himself?" grumbled Maître Juremi.

"Be serious—we haven't much time," said Poncet. "What happened to the saint who hasn't eaten in fifty years? Are we in competition with him or has he been sent packing?"

"Twenty years," said Hajji Ali punctiliously. "He has not eaten in twenty years. Ah, the Prophet, now, would never countenance such levity. . . ."

He kissed his fingertips and raised his eyes skyward.

"The emperor," he went on, "no longer confides his trust in the holy man."

"Are you certain?" asked Maître Juremi. "We don't want to take the bread from his table."

Poncet shot him an angry glance.

"I apologize," said Juremi. "The long wait has made me nervous."

"Save your gibes for when they put our eyes out," said Jean-Baptiste brusquely. He himself was hardly calmer than his friend.

At that moment, two guards came to lead them away. The three followed them through a succession of small dark rooms, all cold and empty. After a short wait in the last of them, they entered the audience hall. It was a vast room whose triple-vaulted ceiling rested on five thick, round columns arranged in a quincunx in the center and on the sides. The majority of courtiers were all the way in the back, standing. In the rows progressively closer to the king, there were more and more people sitting down: the reason for this was that they were out of the negus's line of sight, and custom required that all those whom the king could see must remain standing, even if the audience went on for hours.

The monarch was seated at one end, in a kind of alcove, on a throne that was itself set on a carpet. The mule, apparently, had deposited the monarch there cleanly this time. The king was separated from the first row of courtiers by a space of several yards. The foreigners were led to the front in silence. It was at this point that they heard the roar of lions rising from the courtyard—these were the captive lions for which the King of Kings was famous. And from the other side they heard the same plaintive chorus they had heard earlier during their interview with Ras Yohannes.

As they had agreed beforehand, Poncet and his colleague imitated Hajji Ali in his every gesture. When they arrived in front of the king, the camel driver kneeled, then, with his arms before him, sank down onto his stomach until he was stretched out at full length on the stone floor. The other two followed suit. Maître Juremi unfortunately knelt too far forward, so that his outstretched hands touched the royal carpet. Two officials roughly drew him back. The three remained prostrate until the "King's Mouth" informed them that the sovereign granted them his authority to appear standing before him. They were then able to observe him.

Iyasu, King of Kings of Abyssinia, appeared to them from the height of his gilded wood throne tapestried with Indian cloths. They could see clearly neither his body, which was wrapped in a large scarlet coat, nor his face. His long hair, bound by a muslin headdress knotted at the nape of his neck, fell down along either cheek. All that could be seen was his thin nose and his large, shiny, staring eyes. His mouth was hidden in the folds of a yellow silk scarf, loosely rolled around his neck.

When he spoke, the sound of his voice was barely audible, until it was taken up by the official charged with the loud and clear expression of the royal will. Jean-Baptiste noticed that during the audience Hajji Ali stopped translating. An Abyssinian dragoman standing to the right of the King's Mouth was responsible for putting all official pronouncements in Arabic. The audience was extremely brief. The negus confirmed his desire to seek counsel from the foreigners for his bodily complaint, about which no details were given. Poncet conveyed to the "Right Hand" of the king a written message he carried from the pasha of Egypt. The King of Kings responded that he was pleased to enjoy continued good relations with that governor, both on account of the trade between the two countries and the authorization Egypt gave the patriarch of Alexandria to send the abun, or metropolitan, on which the Church of Abyssinia depended.

The pasha's letter, which was read by the dragoman, was short but full of praise. In it, Poncet's skill as a doctor was specifically noted. Poncet then vouched for Maître Juremi, who was not mentioned by the pasha. The Protestant placed the presents they had brought for the king in the hands of another official. As private individuals, the apothecaries were not expected to make magnificent gifts. On the advice of Hajji Ali, they had chosen a box containing a set of straight razors with ivory-inlaid handles, and a Gobelins tapestry measuring approximately three feet by five and depicting a stag hunt. The presents disappeared instantly behind the alcove.

The negus, without offering any thanks, dismissed them. He said that he would expect their prescription on the following day. Ras Yohannes, who had taken a station near the throne, added in menacing tones that the medicine would be tested first on three slaves, then on two officials, and only then given to the negus himself. If there was a mishap during any stage of this process, the consequences to the two foreigners would be severe. Finally, he informed them that they were free to move about the city and the country. They might speak to anyone they chose, but if they uttered a single word resembling an attempt to proselytize the Catholic faith, they would be dealt swift and appropriate punishment.

The visitors prostrated themselves a second time and left the audience hall shaking as badly as if they had been tortured.

They were returning to the house of Hajji Ali's Muslim friend when a messenger, on foot and simply dressed, ran up to them to say that the two foreigners were to pack their trunks, load them onto their horses, and follow him. Packing was the work of a few moments, since Hajji Ali had robbed them of everything. They threw their few remaining items into a sack: their ragged European clothing, their books (which the Arab was unable to read), their medicine chest, and of course their beloved swords, which were swaddled in cloth. The messenger led them to a stone house adjoining the outer wall of the palace, on the side opposite the one they had entered earlier. It appeared to have been built as a guardhouse. The entrance was through a narrow hallway that led to a flight of steps. They climbed the stairs after the messenger, who opened a heavy door by struggling with an enormous lock. He showed them into a room of modest size. Light entered through a large window oriented toward the morning sun. There were two beds strung with braided leather, two stools carved from wooden blocks, a table, and a shard of glass by way of a mirror.

The question on Poncet's mind and on his friend's was to know what would happen to the enormous key. Would it be given to them, in which case they would feel at home here? Or would it be given to someone else, which would mean that they were prisoners? The messenger left it in the door. As he did not speak Arabic himself, they learned nothing more from him.

When the friends were alone, they fell back on their beds and lay there for a long time in silence.

"Do you feel at all like Jonah," said Maître Juremi finally, "deep in the belly of the whale with hardly any chance of getting out alive?"

"One thing at a time," said Jean-Baptiste, stretching. "We have crossed some hurdles already—let us look to the next ones. Tonight we will prepare a salve for the king, since Hajji Ali assures us that the negus has the same ailment as himself. Afterward, we'll see."

So saying, Jean-Baptiste fell asleep, and Maître Juremi gladly copied his example.

They were awakened by a faint tapping on the door. The glare outside had lessened and a bluish shadow seeped in from the street. It was already late in the afternoon. The young man who entered their room was about twenty years old, short, and very thin. His face was scarred by smallpox, and the disease had thickened his skin. His features were coarse, his nose in particular, which was short but round like a ball. At the same time, his dark eyes brimmed with intelligence and humor, a smile played on his lips, and his gestures were graceful. With these traits, along with his dark and wavy hair, he might have been taken for Jean-Baptiste's unlucky brother.

"My name is Demetrius," he said in Arabic.

It was clear that he spoke Arabic as a foreigner. He told them that he also spoke Greek, his native tongue, but they were unfamiliar with it, and Italian, which the Frenchmen had both learned in Venice. It was in this language that the conversation continued.

Demetrius introduced himself as a personal servant of the emperor's. Hajji Ali was very busy and could no longer attend them continually, whereas Demetrius could accompany them as often as they wanted. From anyone else, they would have understood this to mean that he was their new jailer, but the young man was so cheerful and so pleasant that they accepted his statement at its face value, and even with a certain pleasure.

"Would you like to visit the city? I can take you out to dine, or we can have your meal brought here."

It was still early and they had seen almost nothing of the capital, so they agreed to follow their guide into town.

They went on foot, and as all three wore the same cotton clothes, the two Frenchmen had the joyous illusion of no longer being strangers but of moving freely among a people like themselves. Demetrius, smiling as ever, inadvertently corrected their perception.

"As long as I am with you, you have nothing to fear," he said. "The priests won't dare to kill you."

At these words, the two foreigners began to look at each passerby with suspicion. The Abyssinians seemed uniformly indifferent to them. They neither turned their eyes away as they passed nor stared at them. One would have sworn they failed to notice them at all.

From time to time, the little streets they followed opened out onto a major thoroughfare. Down one of these came a long procession, and they stopped to let it pass. The cortège was led by priests in scarlet cloaks wearing tall, gold-embroidered hats. They carried heavy staffs mounted with incised, openwork crosses, in which the cross pattern was repeated infinitely and woven into figures that themselves joined to form crosses. It was as though the metal had crystallized like frost around the elemental form. Behind the priests came warriors carrying spears and black shields, with cutlasses at their belts. Some wore narrow bands of scarlet cloth knotted around their forearms. Demetrius explained that this was a badge of honor, and that each ribbon stood for an enemy killed. In the midst of the stern, silent soldiers arrived what was presumably the procession's centerpiece. It was a long pike to which a wooden crosspiece had been fixed, and it was carried by a strong Abyssinian, taller than any of the others by a full head. On this rack hung a sort of jacket, made of dark and silky cloth. It had two sleeves and its tails fluttered behind it in two tattered strips. It looked like the stained and threadbare formal clothes that a beggar might wear. From this strange relic a pink liquid dripped.

"Oh, I imagine you are going to be indignant," said Demetrius, looking at them with concern.

"It looks . . ." said Maître Juremi, his eyes opening wide with horror, ". . . like a hide."

"To appreciate the laws of this country, there are nuances you must grasp," said Demetrius. "Different kinds of punishment exist. The one you see here is rare, fortunately, because the crime it punishes is rare. Traitors belonging to the enemy are condemned to have their eyes put out."

"We have seen that."

"Yes. And it is only when they are friends, men of our own camp, members of our own family, as it were, that the punishment is to be skinned alive."

At this, Jean-Baptiste and his friend looked again at the vile hide floating in the wind and turned away nauseated. Bringing up the rear of the procession was a group of smiling women and children, who clapped their hands in silence.

The three men resumed walking. Demetrius could feel that the two foreigners were deeply affected by what they had seen.

"Don't be upset," he said. "You have arrived just at the end of a victorious military campaign. The prisoners are being punished, the traitors unmasked, and bravery rewarded. But life is not always so lively."

"We are pleased to hear it," said Maître Juremi. "So when the time comes for our skins to be paraded through the streets, we can take consolation in the knowledge that we will be providing the public a rare entertainment."

"Your skins will never be paraded through the streets!" said Demetrius, bursting into laughter. "That is totally impossible."

"And what if our medicine is ineffective?" asked Poncet.

"Nothing of the kind will happen to you. You are guests of the emperor."

"Weren't the Jesuits also guests of the emperor?" said Maître Juremi.

"Oh, but just a moment," said Demetrius, holding up his finger. "The Jesuits were not skinned alive, so far as I know. The law was applied to them strictly."

"Which is to say?"

"Which is to say that they were stoned to death. You will see when we go back down two piles of stone in the middle of a square. The last Jesuits executed are still buried there. No one is allowed to touch the piles."

"So we run the risk of being lapidated," said Poncet, who was beginning to enjoy his conversation with this earnest and forthright boy.

"Come, come, you don't run any risk at all," said Demetrius, taking each of them by the arm and making them walk beside him. "The emperor protects you, and I am his servant. Let's move on to a new subject. You'll see that this country offers many other pleasures."

11

They ate dinner in an enormous room set slightly below street level. After entering through a low door they were greeted by a middle-aged woman, tall and wearing a long white cotton dress embroidered with a multicolored cross. She had the grave beauty they had come to recognize as one of the common traits of this imperial race. She showed them to a narrow alcove separated from the rest of the room by muslin curtains. Dim shapes could be seen moving behind these veils. It was the custom in Abyssinia never to eat in public, for fear that a stranger's look might introduce evil spirits into their bodies through the food. During meals, therefore, the inn was transformed into a series of adjoining cotton-walled cells where small groups of diners gathered, screened from the eyes of outsiders. Once the meal was over, the veils were pulled aside and the whole room came into view, with the various groups sitting on stools or carpets around colored wicker tables. The travelers dined on a flat cake a cubit in diameter. It was made of teff, a cereal grown in the Abyssinian uplands and allowed to ferment until it was tangy. The whole was then covered with a quantity of heavily spiced sauces. Drink was served to them in round, long-necked pots. It was a smooth liquor of honey and water that seemed harmless but befuddled their minds in an agreeable way. As the veils were removed and the other diners gradually appeared, Poncet and his friend marveled at the regular and beautiful features of the men and women around them. Naturally enough, as they examined the other diners with interest, their looks clearly indicated their partiality for the women.

"Be careful," said Demetrius. "The customs here are extremely simple. These people do not recognize adultery as a sin, but the one thing they hold to unreservedly is their dignity. Always treat women with haughty respect, even to the point of a slight disdain. Avoid looking at them. This will not keep them from noticing you. No one looks at you, yet everyone sees you. The thing to remember if you don't want to make my task impossible is this: that a stranger's glance, in this country, is of the greatest danger. The moment you find yourself alone with any of these women, even if she is married or a princess of the blood, you may have your heart's desire. But beforehand, don't look at her."

The impression made on the two travelers by the skinned human hide was still so strong that they immediately stopped looking around them. With exaggerated show, they bent all their attention on Demetrius.

The young man spoke Italian fluently. He explained to them that he was almost the only person in Gondar to speak it, and that he had learned it from his mother, who was Greek but whose mother had been Sicilian. Like other families of merchants, his had come to Abyssinia by way of the Red Sea and remained there more or less by force of circumstance. His mother had had five children, two of them fathered by an Abyssinian. Demetrius was one of the mixed-blood children.

"For a long time I was the most beautiful child in all the city," he said, looking at them from his deeply scar-pocked face. "Then there was the epidemic. Many died. My life was saved, and that's all that matters to me. After my parents died, the king took me into his service, and he has shown me great kindness ever since. Did you know," he went on, an expression of naive awe stealing over his face, "that he is an extraordinarily humane king?"

"I believe," said Jean-Baptiste, "that we have had some very convincing demonstrations of that trait."

"What?" said the young man. "You are still thinking of those earlier incidents. That's not right. A monarch shouldn't be judged on the basis of such details. Iyasu, as I can attest, is a good king, perhaps the best Ethiopia has produced in a very long time. Would you like an example of it? There is an ancient custom here that when a negus ascends to the throne, all his siblings—or at least the ones who might have a claim to power—are imprisoned on top of a mountain. You have seen the inaccessible hummocks that rise from the plateau? There they remain jailed their whole lives. If they escape, they are mutilated, because it is written that only a person who is whole may rule. Well, when Iyasu was declared emperor, his first act was to form a procession to go to the foot of Amba Washine, where the princes were imprisoned. He ordered them released and awaited their arrival. You cannot imagine what they looked like! The collection of men that came down off the mountain was pitiful in the extreme. There were old men in rags, covered with lice, as thin as Job—these were princes of the blood from the third generation before Iyasu. There were also children, one with his ear cut off because he had so melted the heart of a slave that she had hidden him under her cloak to help him escape. Truly these men are to be pitied, since they were not traitors or miscreants, only princes. The custom was unjust, of course, but it was also dangerous, something Iyasu understood perfectly well. The more valiant of the captives had nothing in their hearts but hatred for the king and wanted to topple him by any means. If an enemy force had ever managed to capture the prison, it would have found any number of legitimate heirs to the throne there, each bent on getting his revenge. This has happened in the past. Well, Iyasu freed all the prisoners without a moment's hesitation. He ordered them to be given clothes and food. For two whole days, there was nothing but tears of joy and gratitude."

The mead had loosened the speaker's tongue and disposed his hearers to listen to him peaceably. Comfortably seated on thick carpets, lulled by the sound of a *krar* played by an old man, the two Frenchmen listened to Demetrius, enjoying his lively talent for mimicry.

"Didn't these princes dry their tears of happiness before too long?" asked Poncet. "And had ambition and jealousy been uprooted from their hearts entirely?"

"In fact, they had! Our king has had no other dealings with his family since except to receive regular homage from them. There was only one cousin who mounted a rebellion."

"And he was skinned alive," said Maître Juremi.

"Then you know the story?" asked Demetrius, somewhat surprised.

"Just the ending."

The young man laughed loudly.

"There is not only the family," he went on seriously. "The balabat—our aristocrats and princes—and the governors, the tribes, in fact everyone in this large country, are always threatening the king's power. And that is without counting the Gallas. Those who give us the least trouble are our Muslim neighbors. They may isolate us from the world, but, at the moment, they are not at war with us. Our king, though, is never at rest. Such is the duty of all kings, but the present one has shown so much strength and energy that he ranks as the greatest we have had for a very long time. He has wooed the princes, placated the tribes, pushed the Gallas back, and imposed respect on the Muslims. His achievements are phenomenal."

"You'll excuse me if I am disrespectful," said Poncet, somewhat lightheaded, "but I don't see how the living statue we met earlier today can have accomplished all you say. Is he not completely under the thumb of his lieutenant general and all his priests?"

"The king?" said Demetrius. "You make me laugh! They are afraid of him. They hate him because he has taken their power away. The high clergy have never been under such firm royal control. The king takes little interest in theology, but he does want to maintain his authority, and he knows that it depends on preserving the unity of his church. He prevents schisms from developing between the clerics and the balabat. He keeps them all at his feet. And if he maintains the pose of a living statue during his audiences, it is the better to force the priests, princes, and nobles to stand before him, as you saw, until they drop from fatigue."

"Isn't there anyone in that bunch who has more influence than the rest and can convey a message to him directly?" asked Jean-Baptiste, still thinking of the diplomatic mission he held from the consul.

"Among those you have seen? No, no one. But there are other channels."

"Through you, for instance?" asked Jean-Baptiste, looking at Demetrius.

"You do me too much honor even to imagine such a thing."

They returned home through the dark streets, somewhat waveringly. Demetrius saw them as far as their door. Before going to bed, Jean-Baptiste searched through his medicine chest for the notebook in which he recorded the ingredients and proportions for his concoctions. He put a small graphite rod in one pocket and the notebook in another.

"Tomorrow I am going to start taking notes," he said, lying down fully clothed.

"What for?" said Maître Juremi, yawning wide enough to dislocate his jaw.

"In the first place because it is interesting. And then because that's how we'll find a way out of this country."

~

It was still pitch dark when Jean-Baptiste heard the key scraping in the lock. He groped for the sword he had concealed under his bed. The door opened slowly. In the opening stood a person carrying a short candle in a clay candleholder.

Jean-Baptiste waited, poised to spring. Suddenly he saw the flash of a sword blade as the massive shadow of Maître Juremi leaped soundlessly toward the door. The Protestant reached the intruder in an instant and put the tip of his rapier to the man's heart. The stranger raised his hands, lifting the candle and lighting his face. It was Demetrius.

"What do you want at this time of night?" said Maître Juremi in a loud voice.

"Shh! please!" said Demetrius, whispering. "Don't make any noise, and take your sword away."

Maître Juremi stood aside. Demetrius entered the room.

"Get dressed," said Demetrius quietly.

"We are."

"Then follow me. You have nothing to fear."

The two friends looked at each other for a moment. They put away their swords and followed the young man. He did not go out of the house but went through a door they had noticed earlier but thought must lead to an attic. Instead it opened onto a narrow hallway. They passed through two more doors and realized from the size of the stone blocks in the wall that they were inside the palace. Demetrius walked in front of them up a narrow winding staircase, its slit windows letting in a cold wind from outside. They emerged finally onto the crenellated battlements looking out over the palace ramparts. The sky was clear and cloudless. From the city came only the glow of its sentry posts and watch fires. The vault of heaven was so dense, so evenly pricked with stars, that it seemed a silky cloth shining from every point of its double weave of nothingness and stars. Since arriving in the Abyssinian highlands, the travelers had often been lulled into forgetting that they were far from home, but the sky always reminded them. Through the crenels, they could see the Southern Cross.

Demetrius led them along the full length of one facade before ducking under one of the small cupolas marking each corner of the castle. The cupola formed the roof above a small square room. It was furnished with a wooden table and four stools. On one of them sat a man. He was dressed in a simple white tunic clasped at the waist by an embroidered belt. He leaned one elbow on the table and bent toward a candlestick, but he straightened himself at their arrival. From his eyes and the shape of his nose they recognized him as the living statue, the impassive god, before whom they had prostrated themselves that very morning: it was the emperor. Poncet had a moment of hesitation. Should he stretch out at full length on the floor of this narrow room, an uncomfortable prospect? Jean-Baptiste was perfectly prepared to go through the worst contortions if it meant he would be allowed to retain his skin. But the king indicated the stools on either side of him and without the least self-consciousness readjusted one that had been perched askew over two rugs.

The two Franks made brief bows, then took their seats beside the king. Without the paraphernalia of state, the King of Kings appeared no more majestic than any of his subjects, although this was not to say little. He had the grave, noble bearing common to all Abyssinians, but the monarch added to it an air of sadness, even bitterness, which was discernible whenever his face was at rest. At the sight of the two foreigners, he produced a large smile, which was immediately replaced by his former look of melancholy. Physically, he was a small man for his race and extraordinarily thin. He looked to be about forty years old, and his carriage was slightly stooped. There was no trace in his eyes of the feverish spark that might indicate, slumbering within, a savage heart. No, this was just a tired, weakened man, one it would be easy to pity if one did not know that just the day before he had ordered the most terrible tortures.

"I am happy to see you," he said in a soft voice.

Demetrius translated his words into Italian.

"Your Majesty does us a great honor . . ." Jean-Baptiste started.

The king interrupted Demetrius's translation.

"Don't bother," he said. "There is no point. They are not here."

Poncet remained speechless.

"You answered the priests well," the king went on, his expression still indifferent.

They noticed that he constantly scratched himself on the arms and stomach.

"Yes, your words were reported to me. They were skillful. I do not believe in the miracles they speak of any more than you. They have never been known to cure a fever. All their ceremonies of divination are nothing but a masquerade. You probably know that they foretold my defeat at the time of the comet. It's always the same thing: they are eager for my downfall and they call on the stars to give themselves courage. But tell me, what is your religion, which is neither the Catholic faith nor our own?"

"It is called the Reformed Church, Your Majesty," said Poncet.

"The Jesuits never spoke of it during their time here."

"And for good reason: they are our worst enemies."

"I believe you," said the emperor.

Then, turning his tired gaze toward Maître Juremi, he added quietly:

"Yet I could have sworn that this man was one of them."

"A Jesuit!" said Poncet.

Maître Juremi turned pale.

"Yes, or a priest of some sort. That would be in keeping with their methods," said the king, once more examining Jean-Baptiste. "I know that you are a doctor. But he joined your caravan later, like a thief—or a priest."

Maître Juremi was on the point of jumping to his feet. Poncet held his arm firmly.

"Luckily," said the king, "Hajji Ali has told me the whole story. I understand that this man is your partner and that it was the Franks who refused to let him join the caravan. Don't worry. I trust you. Apparently you are skilled at medicine, and that is really all that interests me. We have little time, and I must show you my illness."

The candle flame projected their shadows onto the stone cupola. With its high, domed roof, the room seemed like a cave. But dawn was starting to break, and in the darkness above they could make out the bluish rectangle of a narrow window opening to the east.

The emperor stood up, unfastened his belt, and slipped off his tunic in a simple movement. Poncet approached and examined him in silence.

"You can touch it," said the king, observing the doctor's hesitation.

Poncet asked Maître Juremi to hold up the candle and started to probe the affected area. I am lucky to have had a look at it, he thought. This lesion has nothing to do with Hajji Ali's.

On his thorax and on the upper part of his abdomen, the king had a large, oozing plaque that was in places cracked and suppurating. The doctor looked for other areas that might be affected but found none. He turned the patient this way and that several times. For anyone observing this group from a slight distance, it would have been a surprising sight: the naked, stooped King of Kings, humbly exposing his thin frame and extensive sores for all to see, while beside him the heavy warrior's figure of Maître Juremi quietly held the lamp and Jean-Baptiste, trying to understand, touched the sick man gently, less concerned with obeying a king than fulfilling toward another the duties of brotherhood.

"Is it painful?" asked Poncet.

"Yes," said the emperor. "But the pain is nothing. The worst is the itching."

At a signal from the doctor, he put his clothes back on.

"Imagine those audiences that last several hours," the king continued. "I have one obsession: to dig my nails into my flesh. But I must not move. Those dogs know that I am ill, as someone has spoken out of turn. That is all they will know. I don't want them to see me in pain or making a gesture because my illness forces me to. My will must appear intact. Otherwise they will tear me to shreds."

They sat down again around the table.

"Have you taken any treatment?" asked Jean-Baptiste.

"I have tried a few things. Baths, and mud plasters, and a powder given to me by the old woman who was my mother's midwife—she claims some knowledge of medicine."

"And?"

"It has grown worse and worse."

"What about . . . " Poncet hesitated. ". . . the great saint who hasn't eaten in twenty years?"

"What? You didn't hear? I had him watched night and day. They found him on the day after his arrival, just a little before dawn, on all fours in the kitchens gorging himself on olives. I ordered him to go on with his digestion back at his monastery."

The four of them laughed.

"Your Majesty," said Poncet, "we will prepare a salve for your illness. Must we have it tested first by your slaves?"

"No. Give the priests any medication you like—something harmless—and send me your prescription directly through Demetrius. Be sure to tell him how I am to use it."

"You must abstain from all other treatments while taking ours."

"Have no fear."

"And we must absolutely see you in two days to judge the effect of the medication."

"These meetings are dangerous. No one must know of them. And we must not have any more than are necessary. I will try to arrange another for two days from now, but do not grow impatient. And keep this in the strictest silence."

Dawn had come. The room was filled with a blue light that made their faces look dull and gray. The emperor left them through a small door. They went out the other side, made their way back along the ramparts, and soon found themselves once again in their house.

"Do you know what his illness is?" asked Maître Juremi when Demetrius left them alone.

"I'm afraid I do, and it's very serious."

~

After the grave and joyous period of their first confidences and the period of intimacy that followed, Alix and Françoise settled into something of a routine, tending to Jean-Baptiste's monotonous plants. Their discussions began to follow predictable avenues and to reflect a growing pessimism. They could see themselves always stuck there, in a house that had at first palpably evoked the men they waited for and had gradually become the setting for a painfully protracted absence. Neither bore up well. Two or three times they quarreled over nothing, and though peace was soon reestablished it served to warn them that their meetings could not go on for long without some change. Then Alix had an idea.

"What would you say if I persuaded my mother to take you into her service?" she asked Françoise. "You could come work for us and we would see each other at the consulate. I would show increasing friendship toward you, and you would be assigned to my company. We could go for walks and even come here, but we wouldn't always be obliged to meet in this place."

Françoise applauded the idea. Now they had to find a way to persuade Madame de Maillet. The plan, even before it had borne any fruit, reintroduced a spark of animation into their lives.

Alix began by telling her mother that she had taken an interest in a stray Frenchwoman. The poor woman, who lived in a hovel near the medicinal garden, helped her tend the plants and carry water. At first, the young woman asked her mother for a few piasters with which to pay for the occasional help. Then she began to describe the poor person's misfortunes, letting drop in the course of their conversations that the woman was not of bad character but that fate had abandoned her penniless in this cruel city. Together, mother and daughter bemoaned the sorrows of this world, and Madame de Maillet blessed Providence for having preserved them from such an unhappy destiny. The two had little to talk about, and Françoise became their favorite topic of conversation. One day when Madame de Maillet asked her daughter for news of their protégée, Alix, who had decided to bring the issue to a head, said in even tones:

"Oh, her mind is quite at rest. She has come to a decision."

"What decision?"

"I forget whether I told you. A Turkish merchant, quite a rich man, has asked her to marry him. This would provide her with security. Of course, she went back and forth a long time. He is apparently quite old and ugly. But she would be his fourth wife and would therefore share with three others the inconveniences of the marriage."

"Horrors!" said Madame de Maillet. "And must she also forswear the Christian faith?"

"That is just what causes her the most hesitation. She is very religious, and having to renounce Christianity would certainly be a blow to her."

"Well," said Alix's mother. "And what did she finally decide?"

"The Turk convinced her that embracing Islam would be no great burden. You simply say that God is Allah and Muhammad is his prophet. That is all you have to do. Christ is recognized as a kind of saint, a precursor of Muhammad, and you are allowed to go on praying to him. In short, the Moor convinced the poor woman that she would lose little by converting, while ensuring that she would eat her fill every day."

"My daughter," said Madame de Maillet, her eyes wide with anxiety, "this woman will be lost. One mustn't believe a word these infidels say. They have captured the Holy City, destroyed our churches by the thousands, and put any number of Christians to death. We must prevent her from becoming a Turk at all costs. Not only would she die in this life, for those men are exceedingly crude with their wives, from what I hear, but she would be consigning herself to hell for all eternity."

The two women sought some way to avoid this terrible outcome. Finally Alix suggested that Françoise might enter into their service. Her mother considered the idea.

"Yes," she said. "I have thought of it. Since our laundress returned to France I have often asked Monsieur de Maillet to replace her. He has always answered that there was no one in the Frankish colony capable of filling the position. I think he is driven by motives of economy—when it comes to spending the nation's money, your father has always shown great moderation."

"I am afraid this is a false economy," said Alix, to whom the idea appealed. "The two Nubian slaves who have taken over the laundry have already ruined the color of several dresses, and are always burning the linens with too much washing soda."

"Not to mention the ironing, a true massacre! But your father, unfortunately, pays no attention to it. The only time I have ever heard him complain was a few months ago, when his beautiful apple-green silk stockings turned brick-red because of being put to soak with one of my capes."

"There, you see?" said Alix. "I am sure we could make him see the advantages, or rather the savings, that would come from having a true laundress. My father will say that he hasn't time to find a candidate. So much the better as we have one all picked out."

Alix argued so convincingly that her mother agreed to propose the matter to Monsieur de Maillet. Although she would likely have done nothing to save a human life, which is in God's hands, the pious woman willingly undertook to save a human soul when it seemed on the point of straying from the true path.

"How do you intend to put the matter to my father?" asked Alix.

"I know him well. It is no use hiding things with him. I'll tell him the whole truth, just as you have told it to me."

Alix managed not to smile, but when she later reported her mother's words to Françoise, the two had a good laugh.

Monsieur de Maillet allowed himself to be swayed and granted his wife the use of a laundress for a trial period of two weeks. Françoise presented herself at the consulate, was briefly introduced to the consul, a man far too preoccupied to attend to the household help, and soon won the heart of Madame de Maillet. From the first day the new laundress worked hard. Two weeks later the consul, unobservant though he was, had to admit that the house was transformed. His clothes sparkled once again. Using extracts from the plants at Poncet's house, Françoise had even managed to restore the consul's stockings to their original color. The ladies now wore white lace, rather than the yellowish stuff of before. Most important, Françoise had gently but firmly taken hold of Monsieur Macé's two suits, one after the other, which had both been filthy. The consul noticed one morning when his secretary entered the office with a sheaf of papers that something was missing. He looked around the room, unable to find anything out of the ordinary. It was only when he sighted down his nose at Monsieur Macé, who was standing directly before him, that he realized that his secretary no longer smelled. Françoise was hired.

As planned, Alix and she pursued their friendship in the consulate. The young girl went off each morning to take care of the plants. Alix went alone and spent less time with them than before. Then she would return and wander through the house. The portion occupied by Monsieur de Maillet comprised only the ceremonial wing, that is, the room where the king's portrait hung and a few adjoining offices, as well as the apartment on the second floor for visiting dignitaries, which was most often empty. Madame de Maillet for her part rarely left her room. All the rest of the house—cloakrooms, hallways, Alix's bedroom, boudoirs, kitchens, pantries, and laundry room—provided propitious places for the two friends to meet. The different settings gave renewed charm to their complicity, and the need for discretion added piquancy. With both of them on the alert, the two women found a thousand opportunities for conversation in the vast house.

12

The morning following their unexpected consultation with the emperor, Jean-Baptiste and Maître Juremi busied themselves preparing two medicines. One would go to the king and the other to the priests for their experiments.

That afternoon, Demetrius took them outside the city to a large church where a votive feast was under way that drew thousands of people every year. The sun shone brightly. Torture was the last thing on anyone's mind. Stretching as far as the eye could see, a crowd of women and children dressed in white and carrying black parasols trotted along on little donkeys. Old men walked by leaning on their tall shepherd's crooks. Many priests and monks in brightly colored cloaks passed carrying processional crosses. The highest dignitaries took shelter from the sun under large red and black parasols fringed with jingling silver bells, carried for them by young slaves. Everyone was walking toward a forest of cedar trees. The lower branches of these trees came twisting down to the ground, and children used them to swing on. The church itself could hardly be seen. Octagonal in plan, its rounded thatch roof rested on the lopped trunks of a row of large cedars planted eight feet from the walls. By adding a log floor between the trunks and the church, this natural colonnade had been turned into a circular gallery.

Demetrius took off his shoes, and the travelers did likewise. They managed to penetrate into the first enclosure of the church, where they saw icons dating from a number of different periods. Some seemed purely Byzantine in influence, but most had traces of a style that was particularly Abyssinian. The eyes seemed to have a life of their own, independent of the faces, which they governed entirely. The saints were depicted as light-skinned, a sign of holiness and a mysterious mark of the sacred similar to the use of a dead language for prayer. But the likenesses were drawn from native models, so that the stiff, hierarchical figures of Christ and the mother of Christ had the features of ordinary women and children.

Once back in the capital, Demetrius took them on a visit of the palace. He showed them the courtyard they had passed through on their way to the audience with the king. At a sign from the young man, the guards allowed them to approach the cage where the negus's four lions were sleeping. There were a male and three females, one of them very young, imprisoned behind thick iron bars. Poncet was worried for a moment that Demetrius planned to tell them some story of torture and sacrifice involving the animals. Instead he informed them that the beasts belonged to the emperor and to the emperor alone, that he fed them meat every morning, which a slave threw into their cage in his presence, and that nothing was allowed to disturb their rest. The travelers felt relieved.

Finally, during the afternoon, Demetrius brought them several flattering invitations to dine in aristocratic houses in the city. They accepted one for that very night and found that their hosts had provided everything imaginable to honor them: delicious foods, quantities of mead, and a small group of musicians and singers. Poncet, who had taken many notes that afternoon, was able to pursue his observations of local customs. He noticed that men customarily made little effort to lift food to their mouths. A female dinner partner would generally prepare a mouthful for the man beside her and, as Abyssinians used neither spoons nor forks, feed it to him with her fingers. Poncet was seated next to a large, impassive woman of ripe years, whose stout figure could be made out under the flowing shapes of her embroidered cotton dress. He watched with genuine terror as the slave girl set down the flat cake and sauces at the table and his neighbor kneaded a portion of it into a ball with her long, gold-ringed fingers. She then dipped it into the red liquids, which were virtually swimming with hot peppers, and stuffed the whole thing decisively into his, Jean-Baptiste's, mouth. Opposition was useless, despite the burning sensation he immediately felt. He accepted the second mouthful with his eyes full of tears. The same treatment was being meted out to Maître Juremi at the hands of a graceful young girl on his right. The other men appeared in no way shocked at these signs of forwardness. But they reproved Poncet and his friend in the strongest terms when either tried to stop the force-feeding on the paltry grounds that he was no longer hungry.

This ordeal continued until their torturers concluded that the two had eaten their fill—or perhaps until the moment when, on the basis of past experience, the cruel ladies judged that their charges were about to collapse. Their insides on fire, the Frenchmen were doused with floods of mead, overheating them completely. The guests then began to disperse around the house. Some went out onto the terrace to drink coffee under the moonlight. But Poncet's stern companion motioned him to follow her, while Maître Juremi went off in another direction with his own companion.

They both thought they were being led to a washroom of some sort, where they might splash water on their faces, as their eyes were still stained with tears and their lips inflamed by the strong spices. Instead, they found themselves in dark apartments hung with tapestries and strewn with cushions. Their hostesses silently undressed, then, just as they had taken over the management of the travelers' nutritional needs, so they addressed their other desires. After a brief effort at resistance, the two were convinced of the wisdom of Machiavelli's dictum: That which cannot be avoided must be actively sought. And so they took the practical view and lent their support to the undertaking. After their many long days in the desert, voluptuousness was an experience they had practically forgotten, and one they were surprised but not sorry to rediscover in this unexpected form. Somewhat later, they returned to the drawing rooms where the other guests were scattered. Demetrius offered to accompany the two Franks home. Poncet and Maître Juremi bowed to the men, who appeared delighted, though the husbands of their hostesses were in all probability among them, and again to the women, who accepted their respectful obeisance with grave dignity.

The two went to bed more perplexed than ever. Far from erasing Alix from Jean-Baptiste's mind, these carnal exercises made him miss her all the more keenly. He dreamed of her and, blending the sensations he had just experienced with his recollections of the young girl, passed a night in delicious ecstasy.

On the following day, they rose late and went to visit the spice market, where they saw displayed in bulk all the rare plants of which they had seen samples thanks to their Muslim host in Bartcha. They spoke with the merchants and even met two men from the countryside whose business it was to collect aromatic and medicinal plants in remote and often inaccessible areas. Questioning them about the uses of various grains and leaves, Poncet and Maître Juremi discovered with horror that the best-studied branch of pharmacology in this country was the field of poisons. The tendency was one they knew only too well from Europe, where the science of death philters had very early on become exact and empirical, while its poor offspring, medicine, remained an approximate, highly debatable, and, some claimed, much less useful science.

That night they went to dinner at another house. Armed with the previous day's experience, they drank little and insisted on stuffing food into their mouths themselves. Before this show of appetite, the women considered it useless to intervene, and the two were able to stop when they wanted.

After the meal, they stayed close to the slave girl who served coffee and bombarded their neighbors with questions on Abyssinian literature. What began as a ploy to shield them from further feminine advances actually introduced them to the great passion of Abyssinians for poetry, which they had not suspected.

Demetrius had considerable difficulty translating into Italian the bits of verse that were recited for them. He explained that the beauty of this poetry lay in what the Ethiopians called the contrast between wax and gold. Wax is the material of the mold into which the golden jewel is poured. The shape of the mold is ordinary and its substance base, but once it is broken the hidden treasure appears. The words of poetry appear deceptively dull at first, but by a subtle play of emphasis, their surface meaning disappears to reveal another, which is deep, brilliant, and wise. The translations never managed to capture this transmutation. But Jean-Baptiste and his friend listened to their fellow guests recite verses, first in their waxen form—and here they saw a mimicry of boredom and despondency—then, adding imperceptible variations in tone and meaning, the Abyssinians would speak the golden phrases, and their features would radiate admiration and exquisite pleasure.

Everyone left highly delighted. Jean-Baptiste and his companion congratulated themselves on the way home for having acted reasonably and preferred the pleasures of poetry to all others. This allowed them to retire early and keep their minds clear. Before going to sleep they had a final conversation on how they would act toward the emperor. Jean-Baptiste again proposed to his friend that they keep to the surface of things and discuss only the symptoms of the negus's illness. But Maître Juremi, who was driven by a keen passion for truth, suggested that his friend be more honest and allow the sovereign at least to glimpse the possibility that his illness was more serious. Wax or gold, it always came back to the same thing. They fell asleep without having decided on a course.

Toward dawn, as they had expected, Demetrius woke them up, and they went to visit the emperor again in his tower.

They found him in a state of excitement. As soon as they entered the room, Iyasu said to them with a broad smile:

"You have cured me."

Jean-Baptiste and Maître Juremi remained impassive.

"I no longer scratch myself. The shooting pains are gone. The largest scabs have fallen off and the oozing spots have started to dry up. If I could brush aside my convictions—and yours—I would say that a miracle has occurred. Look."

He started to remove his long tunic as though it were a shirt, leaving the belt knotted and drawing his arms out of the sleeves one after the other.

Poncet examined the lesion.

"It is much better," he conceded.

"You don't seem very enthusiastic," said the king. "I understand. You are cautious. You want to be sure that the response holds up. You are right, but let me tell you that even if the relief is only temporary, I am already extremely grateful to you. You have given me hours of peace after months of unbearable torture."

"Your Majesty," said Poncet, "what we see is truly encouraging. There is every reason to believe that, since your illness is responsive to this treatment, we will see further progress in upcoming days. But . . ."

Here Poncet looked toward Maître Juremi like a soldier about to embark on a painful mission.

". . . there are certain things that you should know," he continued.

"I am listening."

"The complaint from which you suffer may be alleviated. Its effects may be reduced to nothing, even for a considerable time, but it cannot be cured. The sickness will return. You will have to learn to live with it and, no doubt . . ."

He allowed a moment to pass in silence. The king looked at him steadily and without blinking. Jean-Baptiste heard himself say the end of his sentence, surprised by it himself.

". . . to die from it."

Demetrius, after he had translated these words, looked at the king for a response. It did not come immediately. The negus stood up, walked toward a corner of the room, almost disappeared into the shadows, then turned back to them.

"I don't like what you are telling me, but I like your language. It is not the speech of flatterers and charlatans. You are right to think that I am able to hear it."

He paused for a beat, eyeing the candle flame, then once more looked into Jean-Baptiste's eyes.

"How long before this illness does away with me?"

"I don't know," said Poncet.

"Not true," said the king sharply, in tones of anger and authority. "How long?"

Jean-Baptiste was flustered.

"I believe . . . I know of no instance where a person suffering from this disease has lived . . . more than two years."

The king heard his sentence pronounced in perfect stillness. He roused himself slightly, made the silence last.

"Death," he said finally, "matters little to me personally. I could die tomorrow. I am ready."

He sat down again, as though to make his words less solemn.

"But," he continued, "I have my duty. My eldest son," he continued, "is only fifteen years old. He is still weak and easily influenced. I am uneasy about the education he has received from the priests and the court during my long absences. I may quit this life only when I have safely secured the throne for him. Otherwise, three generations of kings will have worked for nothing."

He stared fixedly at the candle, as a drop of tallow ran down its side.

"Two years!" he said.

He rose and walked to a chair by the door he entered through. On it lay a white shawl, folded into a rectangle. He threw it over his shoulders and wrapped himself in it tightly.

"When my grandfather inherited the crown," he went on, "this country was in a state of complete anarchy. Our enemies had devastated it, our vassals had regained their freedom, and the priests had imposed their will on the sovereign. In the countryside, the people were dying of hunger."

He turned and walked toward them.

"There were peasants who ate their own dead."

Poncet lowered his eyes. Maître Juremi stared into the shadows.

"Such was the state of this country. Everything had still to be done. Royal authority had to be restored, our enemies driven back, the lords brought into submission, the priests held in check. Fasiladas, my ancestor, began the process gloriously, founding the city around us, Gondar. He made it a new capital, far from the corruption that had overtaken Axum, where the court had been for centuries. Then came his son, my father. He was just as upright, just as glorious, and just as determined. In succeeding him, I have had the good fortune to enjoy a long reign, restore our heritage, and bring it to fruition. I have reduced levies on the people and abolished the tolls that divided the country into isolated areas as much as brigands ever did. More than anything, I have applied the rule of law. The law is harsh, no doubt, but it is the law of our fathers, known to each of us, and before it all of us are equal."

Dawn was slowly approaching. A violet cloud bisected the window: there was night above it, and a pale liquid below.

"We accomplished all of this alone, you understand. Alone. We have long ceased expecting help from our neighbors. They are Mahometans and they hate us. But we also had to protect ourselves from those we always considered, though from a distance, to be our friends and brothers, that is, our Catholic family across the sea. When the Turks attacked this country a century ago, the reigning king thought he could call on the Portuguese for help. And they came. Cristovão da Gama, son of the great Vasco, even gave his life for us. But they saved us only to send their Jesuits to us in the aftermath. When the priests arrived, no one knew yet who they were. Our ancestors welcomed them with open arms. Were they not our brothers in Christ? When they spoke of our obeying the pope and rejoining the Catholic community, we made no objection. Think of it! We had suffered so much at being cut off from the world . . . the prospect of being reunited with it was a joyful one. We asked only that they set forth the theological arguments proving that their interpretation of the Gospels was superior to ours—surely a reasonable request. Our priests entered into the controversy with an open mind. But they brought their great erudition, and the Jesuits, who were so sure of themselves, had to confess that they did not know the answers to our questions. They returned to Rome somewhat affronted.

"The pope sent back other priests who were more learned and also more unscrupulous. We took them for our brothers, but their actions were those of enemies. Our greatest weakness at that time was the king. The poor man was easily influenced. He fell under the Jesuits' sway and made a number of terrible decisions. In the end, acting on his sole authority, he ordered the wholesale and immediate conversion of the country to Catholicism. We finally understood, although too late, that there were other evils than those from outside our borders, namely those inflicted on us by our supposed friends. I will spare you the detail, but there were numberless instances of the pernicious influence of these Frankish clerics, of their desire to subjugate our minds, impose a new faith on us, cripple us with dissension, and conquer us by perfidy. The most terrible civil wars that our country has ever known date from that period. The king's authority, which until then had survived even the worst challenges, now collapsed, and all because a monarch had pretended to embrace the faith of these strangers in a moment of weakness. The people then sought refuge among the priests, who were unable to protect them. Our enemies took advantage of the inner turmoil here. What followed was the chaos I described to you, which three generations have scarcely managed to erase."

He grew calmer and continued more softly:

"That is where things stand, and why I need time."

Day was practically upon them. The king approached Poncet and placed his hand on his shoulder. The hand was dry and light, almost weightless.

"When I see men like yourself, I think it a great shame that we must refuse everything that comes to us from the West. Before the Muslims forayed from the desert, our civilization and yours were one. Greek was spoken at the court of my ancestors. But we are still too fragile to risk opening ourselves to our supposed brothers, who persist, as we well know, in wanting to convert us. They do not understand that to do so would be to destroy us."

He drew back his hand and started to walk toward the door.

"Thanks to you," he said almost joyfully, "my life now has hope. I knew what I had still to accomplish. Now I know how much time is left me to do it."

The king left, and his visitors remained silent, almost despondent. Then Demetrius, anxious at the daylight streaming into the room, accompanied them back to their house. They asked to be left alone while they changed their clothes, agreeing to meet the young man again in two hours.

As soon as the door was closed, Maître Juremi pounced on Jean-Baptiste.

"Are you mad? Whatever possessed you? We agreed that you would dampen his optimism and prepare him to face a long illness. But why the admission? Why the prognosis?"

"I know," said Jean-Baptiste, his head sinking into his hands. "When I looked at that man . . . I couldn't bring myself to lie."

"Lying is one thing. But why tell him the whole truth?"

"There was something in him that commanded me to say it all."

"It wasn't in him, it was in you," said Maître Juremi. "To tell a king his fate! What craziness! You took yourself for a god, my friend. It's perfectly simple. It was pride and nothing else, a great swelling of pride."

"I don't think so," said Poncet in a small voice. "I think it is the opposite. When I speak to him, he is not the king. I speak to him as I would to . . . a brother."

"A brother you have just stabbed."

He had hardly finished speaking when three knocks resounded at the door. The Protestant went to open it. Two officers of the guard had come to arrest them.

13

The guards, looking fierce and speaking only their own language, led Poncet and Maître Juremi to the palace, not by the secret way the two had used at night, but making a complete circuit of the walls to enter by the ceremonial gate.

They crossed a narrow antechamber and found themselves in the reception hall where they had first faced questioning from the ras and the priests. The same dignitaries were in attendance, but arranged this time in two groups, while on the stone floor between them lay three bodies, covered by a sheet. A cleric spoke, and a dragoman stepped forward, the same who had translated their public audience with the king into Arabic.

"You gave us medications, made by your own hands," he said, "and intended for the use of the king. These slaves tasted them. All are dead."

Jean-Baptiste was greatly relieved. He had feared something far worse. The "official" medications were simply mixtures of water, flour, and beet juice coloring, which had been prepared in front of Demetrius.

"Tell these gentlemen," said Jean-Baptiste, "that our recipe is simple, and that before we sent our samples, we gave an equal portion to Lord Demetrius, of the emperor's service."

At Demetrius's name, and even before the interpreter had started translating, there was a stir in the hall. The two apothecaries understood that the young Greek was being sent for. He arrived shortly, perspiring, and carrying a small box. In it was a portion of the substance given to the priests.

The young man made a long speech, and though the Franks were unable to follow it they interpreted its spirited tone clearly enough. Suiting his actions to his words, Demetrius opened the box, scooped out a gob of the preparation, and made a great show of eating it, afterward offering it to all around him. The priests affected an air of disgust, and after a short discussion the assembly broke up. Once the room had emptied and the door shut, the sounds of a tumultuous conversation could be heard.

Demetrius explained with a smile that the incident was closed.

"I hope the king will at least condemn them to death for having poisoned these three unfortunate men," said Jean-Baptiste.

Some soldiers had entered the hall quietly and were dragging the corpses out by the heels.

"A person can be condemned only for killing a man, and slaves are not men," said Demetrius seriously.

At this, the two doctors and their guide also left the room. Since it is easy to grow accustomed to the misfortunes of others, particularly when they are ratified by an entire society, they quickly forgot the victims of this political machination and only laughed at its absurdity.

This business helped them understand how the king exercised power in the midst of so many dangers. The only men in whom he confided were those who, like Demetrius and Hajji Ali, came from a foreign country. Some had been captured and imprisoned in the course of raids or military campaigns. Just as the Turks used abducted Christian youths for their janissary corps, the negus took young Muslims who had been raised as Christians into his service and they gave him their utter devotion. They were useful in the capital and everywhere else in the country too. For confidential missions beyond its borders, he used Muslims who owed him everything, like Hajji Ali, or else Armenians and other Christians from the Levant who were subjects of the Ottoman caliph.

During their time in Gondar, Poncet and his friend learned to detect the emperor's protective shadow, which they were never without. In addition to Demetrius, there were always discreet and nearly invisible witnesses beside them in the streets where they strolled, the houses where they had dinner, and the countryside where they botanized. Taking the innocuous aspect of peasants, vagabonds, or merchants, they extended the king's might over the Franks.

The weeks they spent in the capital gave the travelers the opportunity to witness many scenes of daily life, to observe the strangeness of the local customs, and to engage in a few more voluptuous encounters—though their moderation in this department almost gave them a bad name. They also visited many churches, discovered the native painting tradition, and came to appreciate the music of the country, which had at first repelled them. They understood its beauty better when they saw it in the context of dance, for which it provided a setting and a support.

They soon learned to tell the provenance of many objects, whether of wood, of hammered copper, or of wicker. The wide diversity of their manufacture reflected the many cultures coexisting within the patchwork empire. Poncet filled an entire notebook with his scrawl, and he managed to buy another one, thanks to the resourcefulness of Demetrius, for the Abyssinians were unfamiliar with paper and wrote only on parchment.

They continued to see the king, though less often than at first so as not to arouse suspicion. They were able to chart the gradual retreat of his symptoms, if not of his illness itself. The king never questioned them again about his prognosis. On the other hand, he asked them countless questions about the customs, sciences, and politics of the Western nations.

The day finally came when Demetrius announced that the negus was setting out again on a military campaign. The king of Sennar, seizing on an insignificant border incident, had declared war on Abyssinia. The young Greek told them it was far less dangerous to follow the king than to stay behind in Gondar. The court might take advantage of its relative freedom to hatch further plots against the two foreigners, who were rumored to have wormed their way dangerously into the king's favor. Pretending to take the medicine of the Frankish doctors that the court officially passed on to him, the king let it be known that his condition had improved, and finally that he was cured. He rewarded the two foreigners with several presents of great value. They were also earning money from their other patients in town. Over time, Jean-Baptiste and his partner had been called to attend to many people from all walks of life. They had even been officially summoned to treat the queen for a complaint, which they did successfully, and the priests were thoroughly enraged.

When the question came up of whether to accompany the king on his military campaigns, Jean-Baptiste judged that the moment of truth was at hand. However interesting his stay in Abyssinia proved, he could never forget the real reason for his journey and the vow he had made himself. He had to return with an embassy.

The likelihood of this was in no way assured, for the Frenchmen now understood why the negus so distrusted the Jesuits and the Western powers. And had the emperor not said to them himself that it was still too early for his country to open its doors? This was the political barrier to the prospect of an embassy, but there was also another and more personal one. So far the Franks had reaped only the advantages of their strategy for gaining access to the emperor, but now they were starting to sense its disadvantages. Their efforts to win the king's trust and friendship had met with far more success than they had hoped for at first. The sovereign liked them. He was bound to them by ties of trust and affection, and gave incontrovertible proof of it, directly or indirectly, every day. But the game they had played was not without danger. Their friendship with the emperor might make him accede to their solicitation for an embassy; on the other hand, and this was just as likely, it might make him detain them at his side for their whole lives, as had happened to many travelers before them. Jean-Baptiste decided that he would speak to the emperor at their next interview. All day he thought of Cairo, his house, and Mademoiselle de Maillet. Fanned by his reflections, his longing to return grew so strong that he felt in himself the energy to convince even the most steadfast opponent.

The king did not always receive them in the domed room at the top of the palace walls. Often Demetrius led them out of the city to join the sovereign in his hunting tent at the edge of the forest where he pursued leopard and lion during the day.

They now spoke almost on familiar terms, though the king never lessened his distance or dignity, a mark of his natural majesty. That night he honored them with his company at dinner. The three of them—Demetrius was still bound by the rules governing subjects—dipped their hands into the same dish of sauce-covered flat cake, or *injera.* They spoke of the upcoming campaign and of the king's departure. The meal ended. A soldier brought in a ewer and a basin, and they rinsed their fingers.

"Your Majesty," Jean-Baptiste began when they were once again alone, "now that we have spoken of your departure, allow me to say something about our own."

The words were ambiguous. Yet at the glance the sovereign shot him, Poncet knew he had grasped that they were not talking of departing in the same direction.

"Your Majesty summoned us. We have done what it is in our power to do. From the first we have kept Hajji Ali abreast of our intentions. Now it is time for us to return to the country we came from."

A servant brought in coffee in small cups. The king served his guests with his own hands. He took his time, plucking two tiny leaves from the aromatic plant the Abyssinians call "Adam's Health" and dropping them into his coffee.

"How strange!" he said. "I was just going to discuss with you tonight the terms of your settling here. The rule we have abided by for many centuries is a strict one: strangers are welcome, but they must then stay in our country. You know the trouble, the tragedy even, that has ensued every time we have strayed from this principle. I intend to maintain it."

Poncet looked at his companion and read the disbelief in the Protestant's eyes as he waited for what would happen next.

"I have no intention of restraining you," went on the negus, "nor of making you live a life of seclusion, which, I well understand, you might find difficult. It is therefore my intention to offer you an official position—which I will have the court ratify—and a level of compensation in keeping with my high estimate of your worth."

"Your Majesty," said Poncet amiably but resolutely, "I am sorry. We cannot accept. We have told you since the outset that we must return to Cairo."

"It is true," said the emperor, "that you have told me this. Or rather, the pasha of Cairo wrote to that effect in his letter of commendation. Well, that counts for something. It is perhaps the only circumstance, in fact, where the principle I mentioned to you may be set aside. The pasha of Cairo is a Mahometan. As such, I consider him my enemy. But he is an enemy with whom we do business. He fears me, because of my power over the Nile. I need him, because he authorizes the new patriarch to travel here when the abun dies. It is our tradition, and it is more useful now than ever to have a monk who does not speak our language at the head of our church, someone who has never stepped outside his monastery in Egypt before coming here to stand trembling in front of me. Therefore, because of my word to the pasha of Cairo, I can allow you to leave."

"We are very grateful to Your Majesty."

"Allow me to ask you a question all the same," said the king.

Poncet bowed his head. While the sovereign had opted not to impose his will by force, it was clear that he had not yet given up trying to persuade them to stay.

"Why do you prefer to serve this infidel, this Turkish dog, who is unlikely ever to show much gratitude toward you, rather than a Christian prince who cannot refuse you any favor?"

"Your Majesty," said Poncet, "it is not for the pasha of Cairo that we are returning."

"Why then?"

The young doctor thought to himself, Now we are coming to it. He drank a mouthful of coffee and went on.

"As you know, Maître Juremi and I are partners. He follows me, but it is I, in fact, who want to go home."

"Well then," said the king, "it is to you, Jean-Baptiste, that I address the question."

"Here it is, Your Majesty," said Poncet. "I am in love with a young woman."

The king laughed. It was one of the first times that they had seen him do so. He laughed noiselessly, his head thrown back. Demetrius waited respectfully for the conversation to resume.

"Fine," said the sovereign at last. "I imagine that she will be extremely proud to take up residence at my court, covered in gold. Cairo is very hot, from all I hear, and women prefer our climate. Have your wife join you in Gondar."

"She is not my wife," said Jean-Baptiste.

"You can marry her here."

"To tell the truth, Your Majesty . . . we have not reached that stage."

The king laughed his strange laugh once more.

"What stage have you reached?"

"This young woman, Your Majesty, is of a station much higher than my own. Her father holds an important position with our government. We love each other."

Jean-Baptiste felt a twinge as he said this, as though he might be tempting fate. With the superstition of a lover, he was afraid of fate on this score as on no other.

"But I still have to convince her family, which will not be easy."

"Tell them that she will live here by a great king, and that you will be one of his high officers."

"Ah! Your Majesty, do you not know men any better? They have no imagination, and anything that is not directly before their eyes does not exist for them. I know full well that an appointment to your service has all the dignity of many posts that fill the sons of our great families with pride. But that will not be enough to convince the father of the woman I love."

He stopped for a moment while Demetrius finished translating, then went on, his head swaying from side to side like a man who is thinking aloud and duly considering each idea as it comes into his mind.

"I can see that Your Majesty is doing everything possible to help me, and I am grateful for it. In truth, there is something . . ."

"What is it? Speak."

"I don't dare speak of it because I know that my idea runs counter to your own most firmly held convictions."

"Say on. If I must refuse, at least we will neither one of us regret that there was something that we failed to try."

"Then here it is," said Jean-Baptiste finally. His words came in a rush; he spoke like a man dropping his load to the ground with a toss of his shoulder. "The father of my beloved is a diplomat. If I could rise to a similar station he would be bound to recognize me, if not as his equal, at least as someone belonging to the same world. One way this might happen is for Your Majesty to recommend to King Louis XIV of France that he name me his permanent ambassador to Abyssinia. I might then return here and still represent to the woman I love the brilliance of my position. While it would be greatly inferior, I am sure, to the position Your Majesty might offer me at his court, it would have the great advantage of being one that her father will understand."

"An embassy!" said the king.

A gust of air, passing at that moment under the skirts of the royal tent, raised a whirlwind of sand off the floor and brought the conversation to a pause.

"You know that this is not our custom," said the sovereign. "When we have something to say to our neighbors we send messengers as discreetly as possible: merchants, pilgrims, even beggars sometimes. When official representatives have been sent to us, such as those sent from Portugal in earlier times, we have bristled at their arrogance, and we have not let them leave our country to return home."

"I know," said Poncet.

The king paced around the table, passing his hand absently over the rough cloth of the tent.

"You are also aware that these priests, the ones you call Jesuits but others as well, prowl on our borders dressed as Arabs and seize on the least pretext to enter our country. When I was a child, my father sent for a doctor from Cairo as I have done you. Two monks arrived. He welcomed them in a friendly way, though with some suspicion, and asked which one was the doctor. They answered calmly that the doctor had not been able to start on the journey with them but that they had come on ahead."

"And what became of them?" asked Jean-Baptiste.

"When the people learned that Frankish clergymen had returned here, a crowd started to form. Our priests and princes put the king in quarantine for fear that he would be converted, as had happened once before to our great misfortune. Civil war threatened to break out at any moment. The king, my father, did not hesitate. He delivered the two strangers to the crowd, and they were stoned to death in front of the palace. This is just to say that an embassy may bring fanatics in its wake, men who will stop at nothing to enter this country though we do not want them here."

"Exactly!" said Jean-Baptiste, still pensive, seeming to articulate his immediate thoughts. "Name an ambassador you already know, one who shares your antipathy for the priests and gives his word never to bring them into the country. That puts the matter on a whole different footing. It seems to me, Your Majesty, that you actually have little to fear. On the contrary, to have an envoy from the French king who knows the situation in your empire and is abreast of the Jesuits' maneuvers would allow you to report to our sovereign at the first sign of a new campaign by the priests. Louis XIV holds considerable influence with the pope and could ask him to rein in the zeal of his religious orders. Many things are simply due to your not being well enough known in our country. Propaganda is rooted in ignorance. Forgive my frankness, it makes me ashamed to say it, but the Jesuits have managed to represent this country as a land of savages, awash in ignorance and brutality. It then redounds to their credit to introduce the light of faith. If I could describe the situation to our king as it truly is, he would understand. I would help you, on both sides, establish relations of mutual esteem, as between great Christian kings, one from the West, the other from the East. I believe that this would dam at its source the stream of intruders who wish to trouble the order of your kingdom and seize both power and immortal souls."

Coming to the end of his tirade, which he had delivered in crescendo, carried on a sudden wave of inspiration and passion, Jean-Baptiste kept his eyes fastened on the king. Motionless, the sovereign considered for a long moment. Then he called in the guard. A tall and very thin young man appeared, a lance in his hand and an engraved sword at his belt.

"Send to town immediately," he said. "Have Murad brought here."

14

A man who has lied much, stolen much, reneged and betrayed much can live to a ripe old age and finish his days in peace only if he has also maintained faith in perhaps only one quarter, but a faith that is constant, impossible to subvert, and all-protective. Such a man was Murad. This Armenian had lived to an improbable age such as we see only among the peoples of the Caucasus, whose arithmetic, as it happens, is excellent, but who end up becoming confused and lost about the age of their hoary elders. Murad's long life was divided into only two periods: his childhood, spent in a village near Lake Van up till the moment he arrived in Ethiopia with his merchant father; and, starting at the age of fifteen, a period of constant and unshakable service under four successive Abyssinian kings. He had seen all of Ethiopia's recent history: the Jesuits' mission, their expulsion, the anarchy that followed, Fasiladas's resumption of control, and the accomplishments of his son and of his grandson, Iyasu. For his knowledge of languages, his skill at diplomacy, his rapid judgment of men, he became the chosen emissary of the neguses, particularly to India and the Dutch in Bali. To his lasting glory, he had returned from his most recent mission with an enormous bronze bell that the Batavians had given him in sign of their appreciation.

Jean-Baptiste had met Murad several times since arriving in Gondar. On their first encounter he had had occasion to treat Murad for an illness that his great age might reasonably have protected him from, but that his undiminished sexual vigor led him to contract, as he put it, "for the twenty-fourth time." Poncet's medication had been effective, and the old man was proceeding toward a twenty-fifth incidence when, one night in the company of a young houri, a stroke deprived him of the use of half his body. Thanks to Jean-Baptiste's care, life had slowly returned to the afflicted side, but one of Murad's hands was still clumsy and his lips drooped. His mind was unaffected, and Poncet was relieved that the king was supplementing his own judgment with that of a man who had always looked on the young doctor with unbiased approval.

The old man arrived after an hour. He had the highly disgruntled look of a man roused from bed during the early hours of his sleep. Jean-Baptiste knew that Murad slept little and poorly, but he also had an inkling that the show of displeasure was only a feint. It allowed the old man to hide his satisfaction at still being consulted and, as the wily merchant that he was, to set a high price on his efforts and the compensation he might reasonably expect for his sacrifice.

The king laid out for him the entire business of Jean-Baptiste's embassy, though without any mention of its romantic dimension. He questioned Murad on the aptness of such an undertaking and on the means of accomplishing it.

The old man listened, sitting on a chair inlaid with mother-of-pearl, that formed part of the monarch's hunting equipage. He sat at an angle, leaning on one elbow, his eyes half closed. Jean-Baptiste had the sensation that behind the lowered lids, the old man's eyes, still piercing though whitened by cataracts, were darting back and forth between himself and the king, paying special attention to himself. The young man allowed his eagerness to show, dropping any pretense that the subject the negus was describing was of anything but the highest importance to him. After allowing the king's words to steep in silence for a time, Murad spoke, his voice somewhat broken by illness:

"Your Majesty, this is an excellent idea. But as Herodotus said, the lyre can be, depending on one's use of it, either a musical instrument or a bow—in other words, a weapon. Similarly your enterprise may engender widely differing results, depending on how it is conducted."

This was Murad's usual way of speaking. He never gave his opinion without taking cover behind a maxim from the Greek philosophers, whether actual or invented, just as a warrior hides behind his shield to approach the man he plans to strike. The king waited to hear the rest.

"First," said Murad with an expression of extreme weariness, "Your Majesty must set nothing down in writing. The road between here and the Western capitals is long, and the danger of your letter's falling into the wrong hands and being misused is far too great. Even in this country, think of the capital the priests might make of it if they learned that you were soliciting an embassy from the Frankish king. Or if the letter went astray during the journey, the Turks would be alerted of your intentions and Sire Poncet revealed as your creature. And finally there is the Frankish court to consider. You know the Jesuits, their skill at casuistry, their devious and perfidious minds. A single word, perfectly harmless in your estimation, may be twisted by them into a call for their presence, or an act of allegiance to Rome, or any number of things. In short, set nothing down in writing."

"How am I to proceed, then?" said the king, who had listened to these words standing, his hands behind his back.

"As your father and grandfather did. And as you have often done yourself."

"By sending a messenger to accompany Sire Poncet," said the sovereign. "I have considered such a course, but who would it be? You, Murad?"

"Your Majesty asks this only as a matter of form, but I am flattered and I thank you. No, you know that death has half struck me down. Such was my resignation when it came that I bowed my head and death missed me. Nonetheless, I expect to be struck again before long. And I hope it will be for the last time."

"Then who?" asked the king. "Hajji Ali is apt only among Mahometans. He could not manage such a mission."

Poncet was relieved that he would not be traveling again with the extortionate Hajji Ali. He looked at Maître Juremi. From the back of the tent where he sat in silence, Maître Juremi called him to his side.

"Maillet wants young Abyssinian nobles, remember?" said the Protestant in a low voice.

"There is not the slightest chance of it. But I'll ask."

Jean-Baptiste returned to the king's side.

"What would Your Majesty say to the inclusion of several young men of good family? They might draw great benefit from the voyage and could study in France, learning our language and in turn teaching yours to our scholars—"

"Have you lost your senses?" said Iyasu. "No Abyssinian Christian can leave this country without being massacred by our Muslim neighbors. And don't forget that the matter is to remain a secret."

Poncet assented readily to these arguments. At least he could honestly say that he had tried.

Once again there was a period of silent thought.

"Demetrius?" said the king suddenly, looking at his interpreter.

"No, no, he is too useful here," Murad objected.

He had rushed his answer ever so slightly, whereas he normally wore an air of weary detachment. Jean-Baptiste understood that the old man had a candidate in mind and was pointing the emperor gradually toward him.

Murad allowed the names of two or three others to be proposed, who were eliminated out of hand. Finally, after a studied silence, the Armenian diffidently cleared his throat.

"There is always our nephew. . . ."

"What nephew is this? I am aware that your sister has several children, but I thought they were all girls."

"She has a son as well. Like me, he is named Murad. I realize this is not very convenient. Let us call him Murad the Younger, if you like, although he is almost forty years old. He was raised in Aleppo. Your Majesty is perhaps aware that my brother-in-law traded in that region for some time. His wife, my sister, returned here fifteen years ago. I believe she found herself increasingly in disagreement with her husband. At any rate, the father kept the son, as is the custom among us. Alas, it was not for the purpose of making him into anything, despite the boy's excellent qualities. He became, if Your Majesty can credit it, a cook."

"And this, Murad, is the man you would send to call on a great king?"

"Your Majesty well knows that the best envoys are the humblest, because they pass unnoticed. The only thing that counts, really, is quickness of thought, and my nephew is not by any means slow. He was no ordinary cook, as it happens, but worked for an important Christian merchant. He learned languages, the rudiments of French among them, I believe. When he returned here last year I was surprised to see how well he did. I won't say any more about him, Your Majesty, as you will have the chance to see him for yourself. He left two days ago to fish on Lake Tana. It is his great passion, and, after all, he does cook fish so well. . . . I will send for him and bring him to you tomorrow."

"Very well," said Iyasu without enthusiasm. "I will receive him."

He could see that his old messenger was set on having a member of his family appointed to the mission, which he judged lucrative. That was the rule. The king's counselors did nothing for him, he well knew, unless it also profited themselves. But they were also too well treated to prejudice the king's interests even slightly in pursuit of their own. Every undertaking was like a boat, ballasted on one side by the profit to the man commissioning it and on the other to the man executing it. Thus balanced, it was unsinkable.

"The envoy is a problem," went on Murad, "that we are well on the way to settling. But has Your Majesty decided on the terms of the message the envoy is to carry?"

"Certainly," said the king, confident once more. On this topic he needed only the old man's sanction, not his advice. "He will carry my greetings to the king, not those of a subject or a vassal, but the blessing that one king may confer on another, equal to equal. From what I know of this Louis, he is powerful. I wish him to maintain his power and to extend his dominion over men. I wish him health as well, for I understand that he is already old. I wish him joy in love. In expressing these wishes, the messenger is to make clear the parity of our situations. He will say that he is the envoy of a descendant of King Solomon and the Queen of Sheba through Menelik, their son, King of Kings of Abyssinia, emperor of Upper Ethiopia and of great kingdoms, seigneuries, and countries, king of Shoa, of Cafate, of Fatiguar, of Angote, etc., all titles and honors that I myself will make certain the emissary knows without omission before I allow him to leave. Then he will tell King Louis that we want no more clerics from Rome to come troubling our peace. He will let the king know that we were not hostile to them on principle, that we even welcomed them at first with open arms, but that they abused our hospitality and our trust. Let him send us artisans and workmen if he likes, because those of his country are very skillful and will embellish our capital, as the painter Brancaleone embellished our churches in former times to the great glory of the reigning negus. Finally, he will say that it would please me for his loyal subject, Sire Jean-Baptiste, son of Poncet, to be placed at my court as his ambassador, that he might inform the French king of developments in my country while keeping me informed of events in his. That is my message. It is not the address of a petitioner, but of a sovereign who sends greetings to a brother and an equal. There will be no mention of religion, as it is understood that we both believe in Christ—a fact that should unite and not divide us. Besides, I can make nothing of the theological quarrels on this subject and am convinced they are no business of a king's."

"And what presents will you send?" asked Murad.

"Presents? Are they of any use in these circumstances?"

"Your Majesty, you have told us yourself that you would like to speak to him as an equal. What does a great prince do when he sends greetings to another prince on his own lands? He offers him presents as the best way of displaying his own magnificence and showing that he expects nothing himself."

"You are right, Murad," said the king. "Prepare offerings of the kind we would give to princes of our world. And it is your task, Poncet, to tell us what would be particularly appreciated in this West of which we know so little."

With these words, the king dismissed his visitors. Murad returned to his bed groaning, to hide the pleasure he felt at having negotiated so profitable an arrangement.

Two days later, Murad the Younger appeared. He met in secret with the king, with only his uncle in attendance. He then came to introduce himself to Poncet and Maître Juremi. He was a large, big-bellied man, and his cheeks were extraordinarily red, as though he had been slapped hard and the marks had stayed. He was dressed in the Kurdish or Persian fashion, his long shirt draping a pair of baggy trousers that were visible only at the tapered ankles. A wide cloth belt was wrapped around his waist. On his shaved head he wore a yellow silk turban. All these fabrics were spotted with grease. It was not that the man was unclean, but that, being greedy, he snatched and gobbled at his food and spilled grease over himself as fast as he could change his clothes. The care that Murad the Younger took over his personal appearance never survived the onslaught of a meal. He stopped for nothing, not even to unfold his napkin.

This defect in his dress spoke against him. Yet he had an attractive face, and the long-ago harmony of his childhood features had been preserved almost intact in the layering of his facial fat. Wrinkles had made no inroads into his plumped flesh, and even his beard, though he left it to grow, took the form of two sparse tufts on either side of the dimple in his chin. The Franks saw one advantage to him from the outset: looking as he did, Murad the Younger could go anywhere without attracting attention. What he spoke was not French exactly but the inimitable lingua franca of Levantine merchants. It would certainly be possible to imagine a better ambassador, but this one would at least be an honest traveling companion, a man of discretion, and a good cook.

Jean-Baptiste's overriding thought in any case was to leave as soon as possible. They had overcome all the major obstacles in their path, and the hardships of the return trip scarcely worried him. He was in Cairo already and thought of Alix constantly. His memory of her, kept in a watertight compartment of his mind, was intact. During the trip he had been careful not to think of her too often, not wanting to fall into despair at being so far away. But now her image was clearly visible in his mind, as close as the moment when he would see her again and announce the great news of his embassy. Jean-Baptiste dreamed of all this as he prepared for the return journey. The problems, uncertainties, and many thousand things to do and steps to take kept him from doubting even for a moment that she was waiting for his return as impatiently as he. In the early stages of love, whatever slows its progress feeds it, and whatever opposes it gives it courage. More contrary circumstances than the forced separation of these two lovers only days after they met can hardly be conceived. Paradoxically, nothing could have worked better to strengthen their feelings and push uncertainty aside.

Spurred on by the prospect of returning home, Jean-Baptiste and Maître Juremi managed to finish their preparations and collect their caravan by the time the emperor was set to leave on campaign. Other than themselves and

Murad the Younger, whom the king had provided with a large number of spare outfits including several ceremonial costumes—two trunks' worth in all—there were ten Abyssinian slaves. The six men and four women, all of them black-skinned, half naked, and with their hair braided around cowrie shells and wooden beads, had been captured in the southern provinces. Murad the Younger carried a very succinct letter, drafted by his uncle and signed by the emperor, sealed with many seals of state, but addressed to no one in particular and stating simply that the Armenian was an official envoy of the negus, with no further details of his mission. He conscientiously learned the message he was to deliver to the king of France by heart. The slaves would serve the travelers during the voyage and, at journey's end, be presented to Louis, son of XIV, as Murad insisted on saying. There were other presents as well, including five horses and two young elephants, hobbled and attached to each other by a heavy chain. There were also three trunks filled with civet musk, tobacco, and gold dust.

The French physicians needed two horses to carry all that they had accumulated during their stay—gold, jewels, hides, elephant tusks, and other presents that their patients, the emperor chief among them, had begged them to accept in payment. On a small donkey they also packed a double leather sack, as voluminous as it was light, filled with the dried plants, roots, and seeds they had collected during their stay. They left Demetrius several beakers of the potion for the king along with directions for medicating him, for although he was perfectly cured for the moment, it was highly likely that the illness would return.

They now knew so many people in the city that it took them three whole days to take their leave. Jean-Baptiste, his thoughts on his beloved, declined all offers of carnal pleasure as courteously as possible, and there were many during these final evenings. Maître Juremi did duty for both.

The last day finally arrived. The dry season was coming to an end and heavy clouds rolled across the skies at night. The travelers held a last conversation with the king in the guardroom at the top of the palace where they had met the first time, and the sovereign was moved to tears, embracing them like brothers. He said he would ask God every day to protect them and bring them back soon.

"Here," he said, giving each a gold chain with a gold medal half a hand's breadth across stamped with the image of the Lion of Judah. "I know you don't believe in it, but there is a little more in these than their material substance."

The king put the chain around Jean-Baptiste's neck with his own hands and embraced him, then did the same for Maître Juremi, and promptly disappeared.

That same day they saw him once more, but from a distance, at a public audience. As far as the priests and princes were concerned, the travelers were not allowed to see the king in private—though that they did so was probably common knowledge.

The two Franks were led into the palace courtyard, where the throne had been brought. Only a few steps from the sovereign, the four lions moaned in their cages. As always, the emperor was immobile and spoke only through his official "mouth." Poncet and Maître Juremi prostrated themselves at full length on the ground. The rough flagstone they pressed their faces against had an almost familiar taste, entirely different from its cold severity on their first arrival. This soil, or stone, rather—though the difference hardly counted in a land where the basalt so closely underlay the sky—was also partly theirs from now on. As the audience lasted a good while and the priests thought best to keep them prostrate for a long time, each of them noticed on rising that the other had moistened the ground slightly but perceptibly with his tears.

A detachment of thirty mounted soldiers escorted them from the city and remained with them as far as Axum, five days' journey away. There they were joined by Murad the Younger and the remainder of their caravan, including the elephants. A simple escort of seven men continued on with them as far as the empire's border. Then they made tracks for the Red Sea coast.

3

The Letter of Credence

I

Diplomacy is an art requiring such calm, such constant dignity, such majestic deportment, that it is hardly compatible with effort, haste—or, in a word, work. A sensible diplomat, Monsieur de Maillet never performed his duty so well as during those moments when, having actually nothing to do, he could devote himself to it wholly. He then managed to raise this nothing to a state of governmental grace, shrouded as it should be in secrecy and perfumed with disdain toward anyone who might have the gall to request an accounting of his time. Since the departure of the mission for Abyssinia, and after the unpleasantness of the clergymen's intrigues, the consul had finally resumed the ordinary course of his service to the state. He read the gazettes, which reached him after some delay, kept abreast of new postings among his fellow diplomats, and sought the direction in which he might point his own legitimate ambition. Finally, he paid visits to a considerable number of Turkish and Arab personages, according to an order determined long before his time. As he had nothing to say to them, and cared to hear nothing from them in return, the conversations often had the fine, incised quality of Eastern carvings, where a thousand fretwork passages attract and charm the eye, without offering a single shape, figure, or symbol: nothing.

This harmonious existence was brutally interrupted in the early days of May 1700, some eight months after Poncet and Hajji Ali set out. It all occurred within two short weeks. First, the pouch arrived from Alexandria with a letter from the comte de Pontchartrain. The consul shut himself in his office to read it undisturbed. It began with the standard forms of greeting and passed on to matters of minor interest. Then the minister turned to the topic of Ethiopia, and Monsieur de Maillet was surprised to discover the following lines:

> As to the business of your emissaries to Abyssinia, I am afraid that the good Jesuits who reported the king's intentions to you may have confused them to

> some extent with their own, though the two are not identical. It is true that, within my own hearing, His Majesty has expressed pleasure at the prospect of Abyssinia's entering the fold of the Holy Catholic Church, through the meritorious efforts of its servitors in the Society of Jesus. But he has not wished to receive a deputation from the king of Abyssinia here at Versailles. Having conferred with His Majesty again today, I can assure you that he would take no pleasure in welcoming such an embassy, as it could not fail to irritate the Ottoman sultan, with whom, given the present state of Europe, it is more important than ever to maintain good relations. It appears from your letter that you have little confidence in the safe return of your mission. If, however, your emissaries should return to Cairo, and if they chance to be accompanied by envoys from the king of Ethiopia, it is my express recommendation that you detain these plenipotentiaries from making the journey to Versailles. Keep them for some time at your side, receive their expressions of homage, and then send them back to their master with a great cargo of compliments, and nothing else.

These new instructions presaged trouble. Monsieur de Maillet wore a somber expression at meals and kept himself in constant consultation with Monsieur Macé during the subsequent days. The secretary, who had been vegetating in his cubbyhole, was pleased to be called on. There was another dramatic turn of events the following week. An Arab horseman arrived in the colony at a full gallop, his red cape fluttering in the wind, leaped from the saddle in front of the consulate and announced that he had a missive for the representative of France. The consul received it from the messenger's own hands, as stipulated on the envelope. After a bout of questioning, Monsieur de Maillet learned that the courier had come from Jidda on the Arabian Peninsula in three stages. Payment was to be made on arrival. Monsieur de Maillet left his secretary to haggle over the price.

The new letter precipitated the diplomat into a greater state of agitation than the first, and the operation of the entire house was thrown into a fluster. The well-oiled machine that was the consul's mind, so adept at grinding idleness to a fine powder, creaked and groaned at the seeds of perturbation now cast at it by the handful. Madame de Maillet was concerned that her husband might be endangering his health again.

The most worried of all was certainly Alix, starved as she was for news. During these long months she had traversed every stage of emotion, from hope, to worry, to pessimism, to dark forebodings. She was now approaching the shores of fatal resignation.

The arrival of the two couriers had raised Alix's impatience and curiosity to fever pitch. But Monsieur de Maillet had resolved not to divulge the cause of his preoccupation to his family. He remembered all too well the domestic disorder that had resulted from his overconfidence at the time of the mission's departure for Abyssinia. At the first question on the part of those around him the consul therefore muttered that there were complications and shut up as tight as an oyster.

Despite their best efforts, which included listening at doors, Alix and Françoise were unable to find out anything more. They were reduced to drawing up hypotheses. The one that occurred most naturally to Alix, being anxious and in love, was that something terrible had happened to Jean-Baptiste's mission. She had despaired of learning any news when Françoise at last came up with an idea.

"Since the consul is not being forthcoming," she said, "the only thing for it is to conduct a search."

"Enter his office?" said Alix. "No, that's impossible!"

As bold as the young woman had become under Françoise's tutelage, the idea of so marked a transgression terrified her.

"It is not so difficult!" said Françoise. "At night he leaves all his papers spread out on his desk, and the door is not locked. The little Nubian who closes the shutters told me so."

"You are forgetting that the watchman sleeps in the antechamber, and that it's the only passage into the office."

"Did you know," said Françoise slyly, "that Maître Juremi was afraid the drink we doled out to Father Gaboriau when you first came to their house might not make him doze off completely?"

"So?"

"He left another flask with me. Just a few drops from it, poured into any liquid, and the poor man would drift off into a sleep so deep and irresistible that we could stand next to him and talk without even lowering our voices. We never had to use it with the priest. But I still have the flask."

The next morning, the sentry had to be waked up by pouring a jug of cold water down his shirt. Monsieur de Maillet grumbled about the drunkenness of native servants. But he noticed nothing else.

Yet at eleven o'clock the night before, after making sure that the guard was asleep, Alix had crept into her father's office while Françoise kept watch at the door. On the tooled red leather of the desktop, Alix recognized the comte de Pontchartrain's letter. Its wax seals and the count's crest deeply engraved in the heavy, watermarked paper were unmistakable. Alix picked it up carefully, attempting to inscribe in her memory the exact position of the sheet before moving it. She set it aside, opting not to decipher it, as it seemed to her that the essential lay elsewhere. Sure enough, she discovered another smaller letter underneath it.

As much as the first letter stood out from all the other correspondence by its majesty, the other did so by its poverty of aspect—the paper wrinkled, weather-stained, and covered with the marks of dirty fingers. Alix picked it up cautiously. It had been sent from Jidda and was in Jean-Baptiste's handwriting. Alix pressed it to her heart. She held it there for a moment, not daring to read it. The long wait had made the young woman so sensitive that in clasping the piece of paper that Jean-Baptiste had once held, she felt the same thrill as if she had put her hand on his. Finally, she steeled herself to read it. It was a short note, clearly written under difficult conditions, and with a bamboo point that made blots on many of the letters. The lines angled upward to the right.

> Excellency:
> I am presently on the return journey to Cairo. The mission to Abyssinia was fully successful, although I regret to say that Father de Brèvedent died before reaching the capital of Ethiopia. I am bringing an ambassador from the Negus with me. He is at this moment crossing the Red Sea, having been detained for some time at Massawa. The King of Kings has entrusted us with presents for the French sovereign. We bring ten Abyssinian slaves, horses, two young elephants, and much more. We have still to work our way up to Port Said, once our party has reassembled and we have found a ship to take us there. If all goes well, we will arrive in Cairo in a month. I pray Your Excellency . . .

"In a month!" said Alix.

She looked at the date scrawled at the top of the page and made a rapid calculation. The letter had been written exactly twenty-nine days earlier.

She set Jean-Baptiste's letter back on the desk and put the minister's on top of it, no longer needing to read it as she had already learned what she wanted to know.

2

From the rise where they had pitched their camp, Jean-Baptiste and his companions could see the entire city of Suez. It was no more than an agglomeration of low Arab dwellings, punctuated by a few Ottoman structures and the ocher mass of the customs house with its Roman tile roof. Long, two-trunked palm trees hoisted their frayed green standards to flutter in the wind from the gulf. The triangular sails of the coastal traders scored long marks on the finger of blue sea extending between the folds of the desert. The travelers had reached the flat coast of Egypt, leaving the escarpments of the Sinai Peninsula behind.

Suez is the melancholy place where the dream of water ends. The swell that starts in the Indian Ocean and rolls up the extended arm of the Red Sea breaks against its sands, while the Mediterranean, stiff and immobile, makes no answer to the Red Sea's call. Countless caravans, everywhere visible by their silhouettes or their tracks, extend their threads across the belt of sand separating these bodies of water.

It was the end of the rainy season. The last dark rainsqualls were unhurriedly gathering to drop their dense, cool shadow on the earth. The small band of travelers watched from camp, sitting by a brushwood fire the slaves had made for them by scouring the surrounding area far and wide for sticks. Day was fading rapidly, the colors making gorgeous combinations, the shadows scooping out the terrain and heightening the contrasts. Before this magnificence, the travelers felt all the poverty of their condition, hardly daring to look at each other. The only one who seemed not to suffer from their present state was Murad, whose sole preoccupation at that hour was the quality of their grub. Again and again he raised the lid of the pot simmering over the fire to check the color of the stew.

Of the proud procession that had left Gondar, little remained. Murad's horses had died the moment they came down from the high uplands, stung by insects they were unused to. To obtain other horses the Armenian had had to send a message back to the emperor. Five new horses soon arrived, which just as quickly died. This seemed highly suspect to the two Franks, whose mounts had never had the least sickness. Irritated by the delay, Poncet had gone on ahead with Maître Juremi, taking sail for Jidda, from where he could send a message to the consul. Finally, having sacrificed much of the contents of the chests—which Poncet suspected him of having sold very profitably in Massawa—Murad loaded what was left onto the donkeys and the two mules. Such was his equipage at that time. The elephants had not survived much longer. One of them had died of the heat along the coast. The other, seemingly the sturdier of the two, had been loaded onto a small trading scow, taking up the entire deck. Ten men were needed to haul him aboard with chains. Murad was proud to see him floating that way over the water. Along with the rest of his company, Murad then boarded a dhow that was to sail in convoy with the elephant. What went through the animal's head is a mystery, but hardly had the two vessels cast off when the young elephant, seeing himself surrounded by water, was seized with panic. Working his ears and trumpeting horribly, he managed to break two of his ties and trample the deck to pieces, while the crew scurried ineffectually to stop him. The scow capsized, and the sea closed over both the elephant and the boat, which were still held together by two chains. Five of the sailors also drowned in the accident.

So Murad arrived without any elephants. All he brought was the ears of the one that had died on land, which he had cleverly thought to have cut off and placed in a tightly nailed wooden crate. They were large, handsome ears, as befitted an African elephant. Jean-Baptiste praised the Armenian for his presence of mind in saving a token of the emperor's magnificent gifts. At least they would have something to show the skeptics. Murad accepted Jean-Baptiste's compliments modestly. In his own mind, the point of saving the ears had been entirely different. He had heard that this part of the elephant, dried and suitably seasoned, offered an unparalleled delicacy.

The slaves fared hardly any better. The na'ib of Massawa, a native prince who reigned over his bit of island thanks to a firman from the Turkish sultan, was perfectly ready to respect the wishes of the negus, who asked that the travelers be allowed to pass undisturbed. The na'ib was too much beholden to his powerful neighbor to think of crossing him. But there was no mention of the slaves in the King of King's message, and the na'ib therefore decided to keep the four women for his own use. One of Murad's remaining men died on the elephant's scow. Four reached Jidda. The sherif of Mecca, whose intended gifts the Armenian had sold at Massawa on the pretext of lightening his animals' loads, considered the civet and two sacks of gold dust that the travelers offered him too slight a recompense. Casting eyes on the two most muscular Abyssinian slaves, he declared them his property. Poncet resisted, and the sherif agreed to take only one of them. It was therefore in the company of the three survivors, an adult with a club foot and two children of eleven and fourteen, that they took their dinner that night on the heights above Suez.

The two Franks hardly improved the tableau. They still had their horses, it was true, and most of their baggage, but Poncet had been seriously ill in Arabia and on the trip up the Red Sea. Earlier, in Massawa, it was Maître Juremi who had been sick. After a year of traveling, they were gaunt, wasted from fever, and suffering from sores on their legs which they had acquired on shipboard, and which the salt spray had swollen and the sand was now irritating even further. Their only hope of restoring dignity to the returning expedition lay in the set of clothes they had managed to buy in Jidda: new trousers, cotton shirts with lace collars, and red vests. Some corsairs had recently taken the clothes as booty off a European prize ship and had agreed to trade them to the travelers for an immoderate quantity of gold. These fineries had been carefully folded away in a leather sack. The question now was to decide how they were to be used, and, more generally, how the expedition's imminent arrival in Cairo was to be staged.

"We are three days' journey from Cairo," said Jean-Baptiste. "We will travel together for two of them. At our last camp, Juremi, you will leave your horse with us, take a mule, and head north. You will reach the Nile at Benha in two days' time and arrive a day later in Cairo by the Alexandria road—since Alexandria is where you are supposed to have gone."

Although this man had shared all the hardships of the voyage, there would be little glory for him on his return. But Poncet knew that Maître Juremi had tacitly accepted this humble role when he joined the trip, a role the old soldier was accustomed to.

"And will the two of us stay together?" Murad asked Jean-Baptiste, somewhat anxiously.

"For two days only. You'll then wait at the place where Juremi leaves us. I'll go on ahead."

"What?" said Murad. "Stay alone? In the middle of the desert?"

"You won't be alone," grumbled Maître Juremi. "You'll have the slaves."

"Some consolation. Have you looked at them?"

"We will stop in a safe place, near a caravan halt," said Poncet sharply. "And I will pay someone to guard you."

"So, you will go first . . ." said Murad without conviction.

"I'll spread the word of your arrival. The next day, in the middle of the afternoon, you make your appearance, as nobly as you can. One of the slaves, the oldest one—and we should wrap some strips of felt around his feet to hide his lameness—will follow you on the other mule. The two children will bring up the rear on the donkeys."

Murad nodded.

"How many clean outfits do you still have in your trunks?" said Poncet.

"One."

"Then keep it in reserve. Change into it after your arrival, for official audiences. When you meet those who come to greet you at the entrance to the city, simply ask them to excuse the appearance of a man who has made a long, difficult, and dangerous voyage."

They agreed on a few more details as night fell, then turned in and slept around the fire wrapped in their hides. Jean-Baptiste felt a tremendous elation. His body sent him a thousand signals of tiredness and pain. He also felt the gaze of all the stars under which he had slept for the past year but which he was soon to be separated from. The thought of Cairo nearby, the sensation of it almost, filled his head. A traveler doesn't grow impatient at the start of a journey, when everything should discourage him. And he holds fast in the middle of the voyage. But on the point of returning home he asks, Why the delays? Why are the minutes passing so slowly? Especially when so few stood in the way of his finding peace, of finally knowing.

Jean-Baptiste had nurtured the idea of his return for long months. He thought of Alix, of her love, and of their reunion at long last. All of a sudden he realized how much the entire edifice he had built stone by stone to raise himself to where he could keep the woman he loved in view no matter how great the distance between them, this patchwork tower of fragile hopes, mended recollections, snippets of sights and sounds pulled from the jumble of a few far-off days, how much all of this rested on quicksand, on the crazy gamble that someone who hardly knew him could wait for him and love him practically without having seen him. This being with whom he had walked so far and for so long—was it anything other than his own desire? All that night, resting uncomfortably on the sharp stones of the desert, Jean-Baptiste asked himself not only whether Alix loved him but whether she had in fact ever existed.

In the end, he decided to leave this last camp in the middle of the night. Everything had gone as planned the previous day. Maître Juremi, grumbling as usual, had set off in the direction of Alexandria. Murad was reassured because they had made camp at a very busy caravan halt, and besides, two janissaries had decided to spend the night there. They all retired early, and Murad was soon snoring loudly. Jean-Baptiste, for his part, knew that he would never fall asleep. He saddled his horse quietly, left his donkey and all his gear to follow with the rest of the party, which would reach the city on the next day, slipped on his clean shirt, trousers, and suit, and set off alone. A big white moon sat up in the west, lighting the trail as brightly as a winter sun. The day had been burning hot, and pockets of warm air subsisted along the road, which the trotting rider slipped on and off like so many silken coats. The horse's hoofbeats echoed like the sounds of an enormous heart beating under the desert's surface.

The world was still steeped in darkness as Jean-Baptiste passed under the ruins of a Ptolemaic temple. He felt no call to meditate on the brevity of time, taken as he was with experiencing the opposite, the eternity of every second and the unending slowness of his last moments away from home. He arrived in Cairo with the dawn: the sentinels slept and the gate was shut. At the sight of a well-dressed and unarmed Frank, the guards allowed him to pass without asking any questions. The city was still asleep, except for its beggars, already stirring at this hour like gray shadows. A cool breeze sprang up with the sun, and the swallows swooped and chattered overhead.

The old watchman of the Frankish colony almost fired his musket at Poncet on first seeing him ride up, then recognized him and let off whoops of joy. Jean-Baptiste hushed him energetically.

At last he turned onto the main street and saw the consulate halfway down it, flying the fleur-de-lis on a white field. His horse, lathered from the long run, walked on unguided. He had stopped urging it on and rested the reins on his pommel. Jean-Baptiste looked up at Alix's window: it was open but the curtains were drawn. There was nothing now between herself and him but this thin barrier of printed cotton, whose blue motifs he could see in reverse. No desert separated them, no mountain, no wild beast. Once again they were divided only by the frail, powerful screen that men set up in front of one another when there is any question of loving, helping, or sharing. The horse stopped without Jean-Baptiste's even noticing.

A clinking sound in the garden—probably a watchman come to see what the stranger wanted—roused Jean-Baptiste from his daydream. He urged his horse to a walk, turned down the first street, and, with forgotten familiarity, retraced the path to his house. He dismounted, hitched his horse to a ringbolt in an archway, and walked up to his door. The key was hidden as usual in a hole in the wall under a plaster chip. He entered. The ground floor was still in darkness, but it was broad daylight above in his own part of the house. Nothing had changed. He had ranged across worlds, lost the trace of his own passage, spoken to beings so inaccessible they belonged practically to myth, and in the process nearly died by assassination, drowning, and hunger. And all during his long absence, which seemed as foreign to reality as a dream, the fuchsia had continued to open its purple droplets, an agave was brandishing its life's flower on the end of a long scaly shaft, the araucaria had turned red, and the orange trees formed fruit. The slow loyalty of his plants had dug a tunnel under his agitated life, a passage through which the past flowed intact into the present.

Jean-Baptiste also could see how much the natural development had been controlled, guided, and held in check by loving human hands. Nothing was overturned. The objects were all in the places he remembered having put them, aside from a few chairs scattered on the terrace. But for the furious living mass to have preserved its vigor and order, its fecundity and moderation, he knew what constant attentions must have been lavished on it. This peace and gentleness were the equilibrium struck between the opposing violence of the plants and the intelligence that cultivated them. From his first glance he understood that he hadn't been abandoned.

With this reassurance, he felt a vast fatigue flood in on him. He went to his hammock and lay down fully dressed, his spurs still attached to his boots. The tension of the journey, the constant state of alertness, the vigilance of an entire year fell away from him all at once. The barrier he had raised against exhaustion, battered by an ocean of weariness and holding by only a few fibers, now broke. He closed his eyes and went to sleep.

Jean-Baptiste awoke from a violent dream. Standing among the plants, one hand shutting off her scream, her eyes wide with fear, was Françoise. She recognized him and her face changed.

"Oh! I am so sorry to have screamed, Monsieur Jean-Baptiste. Monsieur Jean-Baptiste! It's you! How could I have known? Lord! How you have changed!"

She approached the hammock, took the young man's hand, and kissed it.

"Lord! You are so thin! And that beard that makes your cheeks even hollower! And that long hair!"

She went on looking at him with tears in her eyes. He was too moved to say a word.

"What beautiful clothes!" she said, touching the damasked cloth of his red coat.

The ship captured by the corsairs must have been of great value. Jean-Baptiste, who had not paid much attention to the matter in Jidda, realized he was dressed like a gentleman.

"Are you hungry?" asked Françoise, remembering herself. "Thirsty? Wait, I'll get something from my place."

"No," said Jean-Baptiste, "don't bother. Later, later. Just tell me, where is she?"

"Ah! Monsieur Jean-Baptiste, what a pleasure to hear you ask. It means you haven't forgotten her. I was afraid, because of your long trip. I was always telling her to wait and to hope. But so many things can happen along the way, and hearts can change."

Jean-Baptiste sat straight up and hung his legs outside the cradle of cloth.

"Change? Not mine in any case. But tell me, where is she? What . . . what are her thoughts?"

"Her thoughts are of loving you, and she has thought nothing else since the day you left."

"Ah! Françoise!" said Jean-Baptiste, taking the servant into his arms, or rather throwing himself into hers as though she were his mother.

Then he stepped back, holding Françoise's big hands in his own.

"Does she come here?"

"Every day."

"When?"

"Well . . ." said Françoise looking out the window at the climbing sun, "around now."

Jean-Baptiste jumped to the ground, his expression anxious.

"She mustn't . . ." he said. "Go to her. Keep her from coming. Tell her I am back. But . . . she can't see me like this. Is Manuel still here?"

Manuel was an old servant who lived on the same courtyard and whose master had settled a small pension on him before returning to France. Poncet and his partner gave him work from time to time. Manuel was still an active man, though completely deaf.

"He is at home," said Françoise.

"Call him. Tell him to prepare a basin of water for me and some soap. I also want him to cut my hair and beard. You, Françoise, must nurse me."

"Are you wounded?"

"Thanks to heaven, I am sound inside, but my outer envelope is somewhat tattered."

Françoise set to her task immediately. Jean-Baptiste's mind, in the meantime, had been working.

"I must present myself at the consulate in a short while. But once I am known to be back, she can no longer come to visit here. How will we see each other?"

"Don't worry. Many things have happened while you were away. I now work for Madame de Maillet. I come and go at the consulate as I please, as I have kept my room here. We will make arrangements."

"Françoise!" said Jean-Baptiste, kissing her hands.

She pretended to set off at a run. Reaching the first step of the staircase, she turned and spoke in as natural a voice as she could find. She might have been inquiring on a purely formal point.

"Your partner, Maître Juremi, is not with you?"

"No," said Jean-Baptiste, failing to read anything into the question. "You know he went to Alexandria."

"Come, you don't have to play that game with me. I know perfectly well that he joined your expedition."

When, on the point of leaving Cairo, Maître Juremi had given Françoise her instructions, he had also confided his secret plan to her, and the poor woman had taken it as much more than a simple confidence. She had guarded the secret preciously, even from Alix, as something—in fact, the only thing—she had ever shared with this man.

"Well, go on believing what everyone else believes. He went to Alexandria. But," Poncet went on, "something tells me that he will be here in two days."

3

Jean-Baptiste was wrong to think that nothing had changed in his absence. This he was to discover on entering the consulate. After considering the matter at length, the consul had actually moved his desk from one end of the great reception hall to the other. It now occupied a place beneath the portrait of the king, at the back of the room and no longer near the window as before. The consul gained in majesty what he lost in fresh air. Coiffed in a tall, dark peruke, wearing a navy-blue doublet with gold buttonholes that opened onto a silk vest with foliar designs, and sweating more than ever but bearing up under the hardship with his usual courage, the consul received Poncet toward four o'clock in the afternoon.

Seated behind the great leather-covered surface of his desk, on which sat nothing but an ornate bronze inkstand, Monsieur de Maillet listened to his visitor's descriptions without inviting him to sit down. Jean-Baptiste, clean and shaven, his hair trimmed, but still very tired, stayed on his feet, like a chesspiece on the black and white squares tiling the floor. This was one of the little tactics the diplomat used to shorten conversations. The other was to exhibit a bad temper, as he did now.

The consul wanted to make clear that the apothecary's mission had ended, and that the man should expect nothing beyond the brief congratulations he had received on first being shown in. The message Poncet had posted from Jidda, which had arrived a week earlier, had punctured any surprise his arrival might have caused. The paramount concern now, and the consul's only concern, was to welcome the negus's plenipotentiary. The druggist must understand that though he had been momentarily useful in delivering their message, the matter would now pass into the hands of diplomats, who moved in a world that a simple peddler of nostrums could hardly aspire to without ridicule. Monsieur de Maillet asked questions relevant to giving the Ethiopian embassy a proper welcome. He asked the envoy's name, the number in his retinue, the direction from which he was traveling, and the hour at which he would be likely to arrive. As to inviting the young man to tell his adventures on the journey, he took good care to avoid it. At the traveler's first overtures in this direction, the consul made it plain that these were details that a man with his obligations could hardly be expected to attend to. For the consul to have given an indulgent hearing to these incidents of travel would have been highly impolitic. The man was sure to try to turn them to his advantage, constituting as they did his only title to glory.

Jean-Baptiste was extremely tired. The flood of emotions he had felt on entering the consulate, and the hope (disappointed, as it turned out) of encountering Alix, had sapped him of any energy he might have used to feed his insolence. The welcome he had met with was entirely in keeping with what he knew to expect from the consul. Yet in the depths of his heart, he had hoped that perhaps . . . He felt a profound dejection settling over him.

"May I have the consul's permission to retire?" asked Jean-Baptiste, already taking a step toward the door.

"Thank you," said Monsieur de Maillet, who knew the proper recompense for merit. "Goodbye, Monsieur Poncet."

The young man went out. Macé, who had been present at the interview in a dark corner of the room, now approached the consul's desk and, bending forward, spoke in a low, hurried voice.

"Excellency, it might not be inappropriate for this man to accompany the delegation that goes to meet the embassy."

"Him?" asked Monsieur de Maillet. "And in what capacity?"

"It seems to me . . . that the negus's envoy and this apothecary know each other. At the very least, our first contact with him would be made easier. And the ambassador might well ask where his traveling companion was. . . ."

"You are right," said the consul. "He can still be useful. Go see if he is still in the street and inform him that he is to be present."

Monsieur Macé trotted to the door, leaving in his wake the fresh odor of jasmine that the laundress had managed to infuse into his clothes in place of his natural secretions.

He crossed the hall and flew out onto the landing. There, unexpectedly, he bumped into Poncet, whom he had thought to find farther along the road. He sensed that Françoise, who carried a wicker basket under her arm, had been in conversation with the apothecary. As soon as she saw the secretary, however, she entered the house as though proceeding in from the garden without interruption. Monsieur Macé, who never forgot anything, particularly anything he could not explain, filed his impression in a drawer marked "Suspicions," which occupied a remote but well-defined area of his mind. He addressed Jean-Baptiste as though he had noticed nothing.

"Prepare yourself to join the delegation that will set out to greet the ambassador tomorrow morning. We haven't decided on the time yet, but we will send you word by the soldier on duty."

Monsieur Macé then hesitated and continued in a lower voice, as though dispensing entirely personal advice, "And try to wear suitable clothes. We are dealing here with the ambassador plenipotentiary to a king."

Jean-Baptiste looked at him thunderstruck. A voice in his head told him to laugh out loud in the man's face, while another told him to grab the clown by his lace ruff and dash his head against the wall. But he was hardly listening. A sense of sadness and pointlessness filled him that only sleep could wash away. He turned on his heels and went home without meeting anyone.

Françoise had only had time to slip a few words to him at the door to the consulate:

"She won't see you today."

Jean-Baptiste ruminated these words and, once he reached home, sank into a deep despair. It was the kind that is caused not by a dramatic event, but instead by the distressing realization that everything around you is bearable only because of the presence or anticipated presence of a single being. If that being should somehow fail you, then the world, which for the moment is still livable, would all turn to rubble and the people in it all become venomous traitors and buffoons.

Alix, still in her bedroom, was hardly calmer. The return of Jean-Baptiste, so long anticipated and so often imagined, now seemed to her, as such things do, an entirely unexpected turn of events and one that caught her unawares. She was relieved that Françoise had reached her just as she was preparing to leave the consulate for her daily botanizing. She had narrowly avoided a surprise encounter whose many difficulties she could now clearly envision.

She would therefore be seeing Jean-Baptiste a little later. Her thoughts were still too muddled for her to think of any plan. Françoise would take care of everything. Alix had only to make herself ready. Yes, yes, the young girl thought, all I have to do is get ready. Françoise went out. She sat down at her dressing table. Then her strength failed her.

All the sure pride in her own beauty that had matured over the past year ebbed away. She found her face puffy, her complexion insipid, and the color of her hair atrocious. It had been Jean-Baptiste's gaze that had first made her aware of her physical assets, and now they were all melting away as she prepared to come once more under his scrutiny. She had lived in a dream, with the sweet certainty that she loved and was loved in return. Under normal circumstances, these imaginary bonds are interwoven with real ones. They reinforce each other naturally, and the canvas is made up in equal parts of truths and imaginings, actions and inventions, memories and desires. But here, because of their unusual separation, love had woven only its immaterial part, delicate and beautifully colored, but likely to fall to dust like a butterfly's wing at the first touch.

Françoise came back up to Alix's room expecting to find her ready.

"Well, what's the matter with you?" she said. "Hurry and get ready."

"I don't want to."

"Come, come, what is it?"

"Look, there, on the side of my nose."

Françoise came closer, squinting.

"Lord, I don't see a thing."

"You are kind, Françoise, but there is no point in lying to me. I have a huge pimple, I feel it, it's in plain sight."

Then, in definite tones:

"I don't want to appear looking like this."

"Jean-Baptiste will be here at any moment. It seems to me that it's a question of catching a glimpse of him. He is coming for your sake. All he wants is to see that you are still here, that you are waiting for him. It's nothing you need go to any great lengths for. Let him see you. You will get to see him. Both of you will be reassured as to your feelings, and you can spend a longer time together in the days ahead."

"No, Françoise, this pimple is too hideous. I don't want him to see me this way."

As a woman of experience, Françoise sensed that it was useless to insist any further. Alix was not so vain as to be truly concerned about the pimple. It was just a symptom of the constraints that beset those who are in love. There are times when lovers can run through space or through dreams quickly and freely to find each other or to flee. But there are times also when a small movement, even the least gesture of a hand or arm when love is first unfolding, takes more effort than it would take a galley slave to break his chains. There was nothing to do but wait. Françoise went to let the young man know, crossing him in the hall. Alix, alone in her room, sank her teeth into her knuckles.

~

The Frankish colony in Cairo brought together all the nations of Europe: natives of France, Italy, and England, as well as other countries. It counted several hundred persons all told, most of them merchants. Of the nations represented, only two had consulates: England and France. But the English delegation, habitually pared down, lacked a consul at the moment, and France held the dominant position.

The consulate of France wielded power directly over the French, who came under its administrative care, and indirectly over the citizens of other nations. France protected them in some cases because they were Christians belonging to small, defenseless communities, such as the Maronites. In other cases, where a country had no legation in Cairo, France assumed a governmental role toward its citizens.

Consular authority was not well accepted for all that. The merchants who peopled the European colonies of the Levant submitted to it with ill grace. They had no choice. Submission to consular authority was the condition under which the Turks allowed them to live and practice trade on Islamic soil. To provide a counterweight to the consul's power, and to increase their chances of a hearing, the merchants elected a deputy whom the consular authorities had the obligation to hear in any matter concerning Frenchmen. In the past, consuls had sometimes chosen to pit their strength against the deputy's and had come off very much the worse for it. When he arrived to take up his duties, Monsieur de Maillet had been coldly received by the community. The preceding consuls had been drawn from the colony itself, whereas his appointment came from Versailles. From the outset, therefore, Monsieur de Maillet had bent all his efforts on winning the deputy's personal favor. At the time the man in question was a certain Brelot, a corpulent merchant who took part in the silk trade in Cairo, having begun life in the French silk town of Lyons. Rich and extremely frugal with respect to the necessities—his children were said to wear clothes at home so full of holes a beggar would have rejected them—he was also extremely prodigal when it came to luxuries. No display of wealth was too costly if he might hope to rise by it in the estimation of the one gentleman then residing in Cairo, namely the consul.

It was entirely natural, therefore, for Monsieur de Maillet to turn first to

Brelot in drawing up the detachment that would set out the following day to greet the Ethiopian ambassador. Among the instruments of his growing glory, Brelot owned an elegant English cabriolet, bought from a banker in Damietta. The poor Englishman had gone bankrupt and, with tears in his eyes, had relinquished his chaise for the price of his passage on the galley to Marseilles.

Brelot was called in for consultations at the consulate several times during the afternoon. By evening, the list of those included in the detachment was complete. The rumor of an important arrival made its way around the colony. Some reported that Poncet had returned. Several merchants came to prowl around the consulate on trifling pretexts. Monsieur Macé was instructed to tell them that Monsieur de Maillet was expecting the arrival of an important personage on the following day, that they were asked to stay home and not make any distraction in the streets, and finally that a detachment would ride out to meet the plenipotentiary but only those on the list would be allowed to join it.

The next morning Jean-Baptiste woke up in an excellent mood, reinvigorated by a night of deep sleep. He reexamined the events of the previous day, deciding that it was probably for the best not to have seen Alix precipitately, and that the news Françoise had brought him was excellent. As to the consul's reception of him, it was just what he had expected, and his plan took it into account. He had now to go humbly with the delegation to greet Ambassador Murad, then guide the Armenian along the path he had outlined for him previously. He put on his good red suit over a shirt of fine lace, dusted off a felt hat he had left in his closet, buckled his sword to his side, and went to saddle his horse.

By the time he arrived at the consulate, the detachment had assembled. At its head was Monsieur Fléhaut, the chancellor to the French consulate. Jean-Baptiste had never seen the man perform any but the humble tasks of keeping accounts and sending letters, yet he belonged to the same diplomatic caste as Monsieur de Maillet, though on a much inferior level. He wore an embroidered suit of clothes and a large plumed hat. He had never looked so fine in his life. On his right was Monsieur Frisetti, the consulate's first dragoman. He practiced in town and made his living from commercial translations. The consul sometimes gave him particularly delicate interpreting assignments and had accredited him to translate all the official documents that passed between himself and the Ottoman powers. On Monsieur Fléhaut's left, riding a horse caparisoned for a king, pranced Brelot. It had taken several men to hoist him into the saddle, as he was stiff from gout, but he cut a fine figure there under a large brown peruke and in a suit of his richest silk. Behind him came the cabriolet, empty but for the coachman. Brelot would have the honor of a place in the carriage beside the ambassador on the return journey. Finally, riding two abreast on horses of lesser quality, came four merchants, whose selection had been the subject of lengthy negotiations. Two of them were Venetian and had won the privilege of taking part in the convoy by offering their mansion as lodging for the Abyssinian minister. In all discussions of protocol, one point had invariably been settled without argument: Poncet would draw up the rear. He took his place there willingly. The little troop set off at ten o'clock. No sooner had they encountered the emissary's caravan than the procession would return to the colony with him, making a pass under the consulate's balcony. Monsieur de Maillet would salute the emissary from there, forbidden from any closer contact until the diplomat was installed and the instruments of accreditation had been duly exchanged. The ambassador would be led on to the "District of Venice," as the Italian quarter of the Frankish colony was known.

The cortege crossed Old Cairo, keeping along the ramparts so as not to attract too much attention from the Turks. They were always suspicious of such shows of pomp when they did not know the reason for them. The troop emerged through the Gate of the Cat into the outlying districts and soon found itself traveling in the desert. They stopped a quarter league from the city walls at the site of the temple through which Poncet had ridden the day before by moonlight. The day was hot, and a wind from the desert raised a haze of dust that stung their eyes. Without scattering, the members of the detachment spaced themselves out so that each might enjoy a bit of shade. The sight was rather odd. From the desert rose gigantic Greek columns, eroded by the wind, while behind them, sitting their mounts stiffly, a group of motionless horsemen sweated into their rich clothes and freshly curled perukes. Some continually scanned the horizon. Others distracted themselves by counting the gleaming black pellets dropped by the sheep that a turbaned old herdsman was desultorily tending.

Poncet, anxious that he might face difficult questions as the wait dragged on, offered to scout the road ahead. He urged his horse on, galloped for an hour, and returned at a slow trot without having seen anything.

The afternoon was now well along. He found the dignitaries dismounted, in their shirtsleeves, parched with thirst, and ready to direct their anger at him.

"I don't understand," he said. "Something serious must have happened."

He could see that the others were now beginning to doubt even the existence of an ambassador. While they worried because they didn't know the man, Poncet, who did, had other reasons to be concerned for Murad's fate.

"It is almost four o'clock," said Jean-Baptiste. "I propose that we go home. We will send two janissaries back to keep watch, and they will let us know if the envoy arrives during the night."

Without waiting for a response, which could hardly be good-natured in the circumstances, he gave his horse the spurs and fled toward Cairo.

4

The two Arab sentinels guarding the Gate of the Cat on that particular day were cheerful old men, their bodies seamed with glorious scars. The aga of the janissaries had marked his gratitude for their military valor by naming them to this peaceful post, where they would finish out their lives. Cairo at this time had more to fear from riots than invasions. The guardians at its gates were mainly responsible for closing them at night to keep out hyenas and other animals from the desert. During the day, seated cross-legged on a rug in the shade of the vaulted gate, the two old men played checkers and sipped tea, which was brought to them by a little girl with bare feet from a neighboring bazaar. Toward nine o'clock in the morning, they noticed in the midst of the crowd entering the city a man wearing baggy trousers and a high flannel waistband in the Kurdish style. He was a fleshy man and weighed heavily on the back of his poor mule. The animal had come to a halt in the middle of the ramp leading up to the gate and refused to move another inch. The man bestirred himself to flog the mule with a limp branch, already broken in several places and hardly likely to make much impression on the beast. Three black slaves—Nubians, one would have said, though with different features—pushed at the mule's crupper, but the animal arched stubbornly against them, and the end result of all their efforts was only to keep the beast from sitting down altogether. Farther along, peacefully tied together, three donkeys with pack saddles and another mule grazed on the tiny blades of grass that grew between the stones of the parapet.

In the end, the man got down from his unwilling mount, walked toward the sentinels, and stopped in front of them, winded at having gone ten steps on foot.

"Ah! Dear friends, brothers!" he said, panting. "Can you help me get this mule to walk this far? It's a rotten animal that has never in its life passed through the gates of a city. It's scared now and won't listen to reason."

The man spoke Arabic with a Syrian accent.

"Where are you from, then?" asked one of the sentinels. "Don't they have gates in your cities?"

"I come from Van, in Anatolia, and we have plenty of gates there. But my mule and I are two different things. I bought this mule from peasants in Arabia Felix."

"Hah! Then it's a mule that doesn't know how to read!" said the old man, roaring with laughter.

The second old man, uncertain of what was funny about this remark, was nonetheless won over by his companion's hilarity. And the traveler, seeing them both laugh, thought it would be a good idea to laugh as well and shook so heartily that he almost lost his silk turban.

"And where are you going with this animal that doesn't know how to read?" asked the first old man, loud enough so that the group of onlookers gathered around them could all share in the joke.

"To the consul of the Franks," said the traveler.

"Oh! You want to know if your mule can maybe read Latin!" said the other old man, setting off another round of laughter that the man with the mule joined in with happily.

Two or three more variations on this theme were played out before calm returned. The sentinels wiped the tears from their crinkled eyes. They felt sympathy for this jolly stranger who had given them an opportunity for a laugh without seeming in the least to take offense.

"What's your name, brother?" asked one of the guards.

"Murad, my friend."

"Right, then, Murad. Look, we're not going to pull on your mule. I know these animals. It wouldn't do any good. We can do much better than that. We are going to give you some advice, some good advice, yes?"

"I'm all ears," said Murad, somewhat disappointed.

"If you went on through this gate, you would have to cross the entire city. There are many archways over small streets and your mule that doesn't know how to read would take them for gateways. So the best thing is to turn right around. At the bottom of the ramp is a prickly pear, do you see it?"

"I see it."

"Turn right immediately beyond it and follow the little path that goes around the city. You'll see other gates at a distance. Count six of them, and on the seventh go toward it. It's not a gateway like this one, it's a large ironwork grille, and it won't scare your mule. Go in there, and a hundred yards beyond it on the left you'll find the Frankish quarter."

Murad thanked the two old guards warmly and followed their suggestion, this time with the full cooperation of his mule.

The little crowd dispersed slowly from under the arched Gate of the Cat. An hour later, while the sentries were still laughing about it, they saw a crew of Frankish riders pass by at a smart trot. The men wore colored jackets and perukes, and in the midst of their sumptuously harnessed horses was a varnished black cabriolet. They hurtled down the ramp and drew away from the city rapidly.

~

For the gardener at the consulate to enter the main building was entirely exceptional. He was an old Copt, a native of Cairo, and a devoted servant. He could be heard at nightfall pottering on into the late hours, gliding quietly through the alleys, a brass watering can in hand, making no noise beyond the murmur of water falling like rain onto dry leaves. But on this day, the gardener had no choice. The consulate was empty: Monsieur de Maillet's coachman, the night and day watchmen, and two menservants had followed the delegation that had gone to meet the embassy. There was no one left but himself, Gabriel, the old gardener, and as he found no one to whom he could pass on his message, he went through door after door until, more and more hesitant, he reached the office of the consul himself. Monsieur de Maillet had placed his peruke and his damasked jacket on a wooden rack. He was pacing back and forth in a lace shirt and silk trousers, mopping his brow with a handkerchief. Monsieur Macé was huddled on a chair, waiting for an order or a word of conversation. It was he who first noticed the gardener's hesitant entrance.

"And what does this one want?" asked the consul when he noticed him in turn.

Monsieur Macé questioned the old man in Arabic, which was his only language.

"He says there is a man here to see you, Your Excellency."

"A man!" said the consul with a malicious smile. "How strange! And why not a pumpkin or a marmoset? Tell this simpleton that he is to take care of our flowering borders to the exclusion of all else. And that I don't want to see him here again. If a man asks for me, let him simply say that I am busy."

After hearing the consul's answer translated, the old man's face took an offended look.

"He says that he will go tell them that. But he doubts whether it will make them go away from his windows."

"Tell *them*?" said the consul. "And how many are they?"

"Four," said the old man, "with donkeys and mules carrying packs."

"And what do they look like? Is it a caravan?" asked Monsieur de Maillet.

"Yes, if you like," said the gardener. "It's a caravan, but it looks like nothing I have ever seen in these parts."

"And why did the guard at the entrance to the colony let them come in?"

"Probably because the man said to him the same thing he said to me."

"And what was that?"

"Just that he was the negus of Abyssinia's ambassador," said the gardener with a smirk of respect.

Monsieur Macé turned pale and translated the old man's words.

"Good Lord!" said Monsieur de Maillet.

The diplomats remained speechless for a time, then, taking great precautions, advanced toward the window. They looked out, one after the other, and drew back violently.

"Can it be possible?" they said together.

They looked again. Below, under the plane trees of the central street, a miserable retinue had halted: three donkeys, their coats bald in patches, their withers ulcerated and pecked at by small birds, and two mules that the lowest water carrier in Cairo would not have wanted. These poor animals carried bulky loads that were tied directly to their backs with sisal ropes, wound with strips of cloth where they chafed most. Three black men waited dumbly on their feet, their cotton shirts the color of the desert. Sitting on the ground against a tree, Murad had taken off one of his shoes and was scratching fiercely at the sole of his foot.

"Macé," said the consul finally—born to command others, he took it upon himself never to be unnerved by the unexpected. "Go downstairs and express the consulate's respects to him. Explain the situation and take him to the District of Venice, to the house that has been prepared for him."

The secretary went out, preceded by the gardener, who had already disappeared. Monsieur de Maillet remained alone. He cast a glance toward the king and was suddenly filled with immense respect for his sovereign's genius and for that of Pontchartrain, his minister, remembering the latter's recent letter to him with tears of gratitude.

In the meantime Monsieur Macé had reached Murad, who was still scratching his foot. He coughed to draw attention to himself.

"Ah, we have company," said the Armenian, putting his shoe back on and standing up.

He held out his hand to Monsieur Macé, the same one with which he had just been scrabbling at his toes.

"I am Murad, the ambassador from Ethiopia."

"Your Grace, you are most welcome," said the secretary, folding at the waist in a low bow that obviated the need for a handshake.

"Come, come, get up," said Murad solicitously. "You are going to hurt yourself. Tell me now, are you really the consul?"

"No, Your Grace," answered Monsieur Macé, his hat pressed to his heart, one leg extended slightly to the rear, his head bowed. "His Excellency the consul has sent me to welcome Your Grace and convey his respects. His Excellency the consul also presents his apology to Your Grace. An official delegation was sent out to meet your convoy, but it must not have found you."

"It's because of this confounded mule," said Murad, addressing a kick at the animal, which failed even to make it flinch. "It wouldn't listen to reason. I had to go the long way around and come in through a grille. Well! At least we have arrived. The road was a long one, believe me. Where is Poncet?"

"He is with the delegation."

"With the delegation! But then how am I to manage? I don't know this city at all. No one is going to want to give me lodging."

"Give you lodging? Your Grace, it has all been prepared. You have only to follow me."

"Really? Now, that's good news. And will you give me to eat as well?"

"To eat, to drink, anything Your Grace may desire," said Monsieur Macé, more and more astonished.

"God is most great. Well then, I'll follow you. You three, get over here! They are Abyssinians, normally a hardworking people, but I seem to have been given the three laziest ones. Come along, come along."

They set the mules and donkeys in motion and crossed the whole colony. Monsieur Macé was congratulating himself on the fact that the consul had forbidden traffic in the streets that day. The fewer witnesses, the less he would have to worry that a figure from his past would emerge one day to ruin his career by saying: "Oh yes, Macé, I remember seeing him lead the ambassador of Ethiopia's two donkeys."

Murad stopped along the way to relieve himself against a plane tree, the noises he made in his throat betraying the pleasure this gave him.

They arrived finally at the Venetians' house. The ground floor was assigned to the embassy. It was a wooden house with an overhanging second floor supported by an elegant set of triangular braces. Between it and the street was a small but well-maintained garden. A low box hedge had been trimmed to represent the arms of the Republic of Venice, the effect being of an escutcheon with a raised design, green on green, in the middle of the lawn. Murad insisted that all the animals be let into the garden and instructed the Abyssinians to let them wander there freely once they had been unloaded.

The Armenian took off his shoes to enter the house and threw himself down on the first sofa, swearing that he would never rise again.

Monsieur Macé excused himself, as he explained, so as to have refreshments sent.

"And some grub!" Murad yelled after him before he could quite disappear from view.

The secretary described the ambassador's bizarre behavior to the consul on his return. Monsieur de Maillet told him that a diplomat who allows himself to feel surprise while in a foreign land is like a knight who raises his visor in the middle of a battle.

"After all," said the consul nobly, "we should show him some indulgence. Look where he comes from."

A second list had been drawn up the day before with the names of all the merchants who had not had the good fortune to be chosen for the welcoming delegation but who had been marked out for other honors, namely that of bringing the ambassador refreshments.

"Must I . . . despite the . . ." asked Monsieur Macé.

"Naturally," said the consul. "Tell the first of these gentlemen to perform his office."

All afternoon long, a succession of worthy merchants filed through the Venetians' house, with a procession of valets carrying baskets of fruit, plates of cake, and trays of desserts. This was the price they paid for the honor of approaching the Ethiopian ambassador. All the merchants rushed to the consulate afterward to tell Monsieur de Maillet that they would not be caught doing it again. It surpassed all belief that the loutish character who had received them was the minister of a king. Not placing any blame on the consul, they accused Poncet of having foisted an impostor on them. Brelot's delegation returned just as these deplorable scenes were occurring, all of its members furious at Poncet. When they learned what had happened, they stopped accusing the apothecary of making them wait for a nonexistent envoy but immediately joined the chorus of grievances leveled by the refreshment-bearers. Taking advantage of the reigning confusion, Jean-Baptiste slipped out of the consulate.

"Silence, sirs," said the consul in a loud voice, finally managing to make himself heard. "I now ask you to retire, and I thank you for your help."

Another chorus of protests arose. The consul stopped them with a gesture.

"This man is the envoy of a great king, but a king who has been cut off from civilization for many centuries. That is why we must show our indulgence and why his arrival remains, despite everything, a great occasion. The envoy in any case counts for less than the message he carries. Tomorrow we will know what the king of Abyssinia has to say to us."

On leaving the consulate, Poncet had gone straight to the District of Venice to see Murad. He found the Venetians' drawing room cleared of all its furniture, which had been stacked by the Armenian's orders along the outside walls. What had been the merchants' reception room now contained nothing but rugs and the cushions from the armchairs scattered on the ground. Murad sat cross-legged under the great glass-bead chandelier, surrounded by a considerable number of silver platters, crystal bowls, and valuable pitchers.

Jean-Baptiste asked him to tell the story of the mule's behavior and the reason he had arrived by an unexpected route. He listened to Murad's version of how the colony received him. The Armenian considered all the merchants to have shown him great impudence. After asking him to make himself at home and offering him presents, they had then had the effrontery to regulate how he might use this property. Nothing was to their liking, neither the mules in the garden, nor the furniture that had been removed, nor the coffee brewed Abyssinian-style (it is their one great pleasure) over a small fire most properly lit on the front-hall tiles.

After laughing heartily at this tale, which only increased Murad's indignation, Jean-Baptiste told him to change nothing in his behavior. He then gave him very precise instructions as to what to say and do the following day when someone from the consulate called and asked for his letters of credence.

Then Jean-Baptiste hurried home. He was expecting word from Alix in one form or another and had been anxious all day (it was all he could think of) at not having seen her the day before.

He climbed his stairs in the dark, lit a candle, and discovered, as he had expected, a message folded in four under the candlestick. It was a note from Françoise, summoning him to meet them in the garden at the end of the colony's main street when the chapel bells struck two.

5

Alix stood waiting for the appointed hour in her darkened room. There was only a sliver of moon, often obscured by heavy clouds. On so dark a night Françoise had thought it safe to walk through the streets as far as the park. At least they would be at some distance from the consulate and its spies. In the early part of the night, when the young woman still had plenty of time for deliberation, she had told herself that she wouldn't go to this rendezvous, that it was a foolish idea, that she was risking her honor. Then as the hours passed she pushed these thoughts away from her, just as you might push a thief against a wall who had started off attacking you. To herself she said: Don't I love him with all my heart?

From then on she was more certain that she would keep the appointment than she had been before that she would break it. It was not the old arguments of her upbringing that came into her mind now but her new convictions, which she had acquired herself over the course of the past year. In her conversations with Françoise during these long months she had discovered the dignity of true love, which was governed not by interest but by passion. And as to honor, there was always the example of her mother, who had so successfully guarded hers—what was she now if not the slave of a man who had taken her as his possession? These dangerous thoughts passed through Alix's mind as she dressed, but it would be wrong to think that she was laboring under Françoise's influence in this. When the two slipped out of the house by the service entrance and blended their shadows with those of the street, Alix felt a shiver of joy. It was not just the thought of what she was doing that caused it, but the intimate awareness that action, present action, danger (which might be a form of sacrifice), fulfilled in her what was most authentic and least warped by civilization—what might simply be called her true character.

Waiting for the rendezvous, Jean-Baptiste reflected that he had always had easy, passing love affairs, in which the first moment—which was also often the last—took the form of a contest. The participants, each of them coldly lucid, sought either to conquer or resist, and the whole game came down to nothing more than hiding for as long as possible what one truly thought. This time each knew deep down and in advance what the other felt. There was no question of conquest or abandonment. What had to be done was to bring into the world, into the air where words resonate and gestures unfold, the love that had already been conceived and that had lived inside them for so long. He felt that the responsibility to do this made him awkward.

As the two muffled strokes of the clock reverberated in the dark, both lovers were heading toward their rendezvous. Alix and Françoise were arriving from the gate's left, while Jean-Baptiste, who had hidden in the back of the garden, was approaching from inside. Both felt that they were living through a fleeting and irreparable moment, one that was precious not because of the commitment it implied, which in any case had been made long ago, but simply because it would never happen again. Each was determined to make the moment last as long as possible, to fix it in their memories the way you fasten on the features of a person you know you will never see again. In short, they were determined not to hurry their meeting. And yet, the moment they saw their shadows approach one another, the moment they were alone together, their resolve abandoned them. Their separation had been long, the dark and deserted meeting place added to their anxiety, and desire drew them on: they embraced immediately and covered each other silently with kisses.

"How happy I am!" they said, one after the other.

They tasted each other's mouths and touched each other anxiously, as though to make meticulously sure that the other was there, in the flesh, at the same time taking pleasure in it.

Both were at the stage of love where everything else disappears, and they needed few words. It was enough for them to be near one another. But Françoise, who was keeping watch by the grille, came to tell them they had not much time. These words brought them back to reality, and to an awareness of all the obstacles in their path.

"How will you persuade my father?" said Alix, looking at her lover, whose thin silhouette was all she could see in the dark. "He is talking more and more about marrying me off."

"For the moment," said Jean-Baptiste, "we must tell him nothing and let him suspect nothing. Let us go on seeing each other, as I can no longer live without holding you in my arms, now that we have finally come together. But let no one know anything until I have put my plan into action. I will go to Versailles."

"What?" said Alix, huddling against him. "You have barely gotten here! Do you already want to leave?"

"Give it some thought and you will see that it is the only solution. The king wanted an embassy. Well, I will bring him one. He alone can give me the reward I want. I'll return a gentleman and your father will be able to refuse me nothing."

Alix was ready to believe anything the man she loved might tell her. The plan displeased her because it meant that they would again be separated, but she agreed that it was the best plan possible and swore that she would help Jean-Baptiste with every means at her disposal.

"The one way you can help me is by not forgetting me."

She gave an indignant protest, which was muffled by a long kiss.

In the end Françoise returned and begged them to separate, as it would soon be time for the janissaries to come by on their rounds. They parted, came back with quick steps to embrace once more, and finally set off each in a different direction through the hot night. The palm trees, shaken by the wind, crackled above them.

~

Murad had confidence in Jean-Baptiste. Had not the negus himself shown affection for this stranger? He therefore willingly agreed to do whatever the physician asked. What made this all the easier was that the other residents of the Frankish colony did not appeal to him at all. These overly rich and overly amiable merchants reminded him of his old master in Aleppo, who always simpered kind words and acted with great hypocrisy. He had often had the urge to throw the carefully prepared food in his employer's face. Now he could afford to do so. Too bad if those on the receiving end had done nothing to him.

"What do you mean, my letter of credence?" said Murad haughtily to Monsieur Macé, when the secretary came to ask for it. "Who do you take me for? I am the envoy of the king. The King of Kings, what's more."

He looked at his small, chubby hand, his little finger adorned by a copper ring, and went on:

"His Majesty expressly recommended that I give his letters to no one but the king of France in person. I must go to Versailles to deliver them."

Monsieur Macé insisted, but the Armenian refused to be budged and in the end dismissed the Frenchman rudely. The secretary returned terrified to the consulate and narrated his interview to Monsieur de Maillet with every expression of regret.

"Hah! So that's how it is!" said the diplomat. "He doesn't want to show his letters! But what customs does he hold to? We will allow that he sits on the ground and insults the entire colony. But he must at the very least agree to present himself according to the rules."

"Perhaps to you . . ." suggested Monsieur Macé.

The consul froze and fixed his poor secretary with a baleful glare.

"No doubt you imagine that I, who represent the king of France, may address a man who does not show the courtesy of presenting his credentials?"

"No, clearly," said Monsieur Macé, capitulating.

"Good," said the consul. "We will send another delegation to reason with him."

"No merchant will consent to go back there."

"Then you will go yourself," said Monsieur de Maillet. "And you can tell him that if he does not produce his letter of credence before tomorrow he will be shown out of the colony. He can help himself to whatever lodgings he can find in the old quarters of Cairo."

Macé went to deliver the message and was thrown out on his ear. Murad had pushed rudeness to the point of sending a greasy piece of baklava flying at his head, after taking a bite of it first.

"This little comedy has gone on long enough," said Monsieur de Maillet with calm and resolution. "I know just how to get to the bottom of this business of the letter. And believe me, if it turns out he hasn't got one, I will have good cause, given his coarse behavior, to turn him out onto the street: him, his animals, his slaves, and his rags."

So saying, the consul asked for his carriage to be drawn up and for the pasha to be informed of his impending visit.

He returned from his audience highly pleased with himself and slept excellently that night. The following morning, however, at the moment he was entering his office, Father Plantain was announced.

This Jesuit had arrived in Cairo shortly after Father de Brèvedent left for Ethiopia. The stroke that had laid Father Gaboriau low had allowed the newcomer to appear openly, and within a few weeks Father Plantain became the official representative of the Society of Jesus in this station of the Levant.

He was a man of some forty years of age, and owed his strong build to the fact that his family had worked for centuries in the cattle industry in the Charolles region of France. He had long, slender hands that he clasped and unclasped slowly, all the while looking tenderly at them, perhaps because they alone did not betray his cowherd's origins. His head seemed almost flattened beneath the big stone of his rounded, gray cranium, which bulged outward over his eyes. A high forehead, ordinarily a sign of intelligence, gave him instead a somewhat dull expression, as though its weight pressed down on his face and on his whole self. Given his physical makeup, he could easily have become a stone carver or a musician. He had a good head for studies, however, and entered the novitiate. Since his arrival in Cairo he had given the consul many proofs of his suspicious disposition and his tendency to engage in intrigues. At first Monsieur de Maillet had thought the priest was simple and straightforward. When he discovered a touch of duplicity in him, he realized his error and ever after attributed no end of slyness to the Jesuit.

"What a pleasure to see you, Father!" said the consul, as the black-robed man appeared in his doorway. The diplomat armed himself at the same moment with all the caution a man uses to pick up a venomous animal on the end of a stick.

Father Plantain was not in the least obsequious: his deviousness was hidden under an almost military bluffness. He barked out his greeting of "Excellence!" loudly and stood to attention. Monsieur de Maillet took him by the arm and led him to an armchair.

"I received your note, Excellency," said the Jesuit. "Thank you. What excellent news! We had already known for a week, thanks to you, that poor Father de Brèvedent did not survive the journey. Aside from this misfortune, all is well. Our ambassador has arrived!"

The consul had informed the representative of the Society of Jesus that the Abyssinian mission had returned. He had not, however, invited him to join the delegation that went to meet the caravan—which in retrospect might well seem a kindness.

"It appears," said the priest, "but I would like you to confirm it, that they came back with three natives of Abyssinia?"

"So I hear," said the consul.

"Do you mean you have not seen them either?"

"Only a glimpse."

Monsieur de Maillet had no intention of broaching the question of letters of credence with this troublemaker.

"They have only just arrived, don't forget," said Monsieur de Maillet innocently.

The man in black shook his head several times, which, given the weight he seemed to carry, made the gesture painful to witness.

"Three Abyssinians at the Louis-le-Grand School in the seats reserved for students from the East," said the Jesuit, his eyes shining. "That will be a great stroke for us."

The consul gave a weak smile.

"Were you aware, Excellence," the priest went on, leaning forward, "that the Capuchins have captured seven of them, apparently, in the late war between Ethiopia and the king of Sennar? Think of it! And they are going straight to Rome . . ."

He leaned toward the consul, lowering his voice even further.

". . . if the Turks allow them to embark."

Accompanying these words with a smile, the priest left no doubt that he intended to intervene in the course of events.

"We will have the same difficulty," started the consul, regretting it immediately, "in sending the three Abyssinians who have come to us out of the country."

"Ah, Excellence," said the Jesuit, drawing himself up majestically, "what the king of France wants carries some weight here all the same. The Turks listen to us, I believe. Of course, I am speaking out of turn. You are the diplomat and must know these things better than I."

Monsieur de Maillet admired the perfidy of this seemingly rock-solid man, who hissed insinuations like an old laundress. He resolved to take matters in hand somewhat.

"Diplomatic matters are, as you suggest, Father, highly complex. And if I may put it so bluntly, they are perhaps even more so than you imagine. The main concern is for everything to be done in a regular and orderly way. You serve the Christian faith, you are used to the transmission of movement through the ether, to the lightning descent of the Holy Ghost into a man's soul. We, on the other hand, work at the surface of the earth. Politics deals with the movement of men. It mustn't be hurried."

The Jesuit understood nothing of this little speech. He looked at the consul from his deeply shadowed orbits, as his father might have looked in years gone by at a fat and handsome animal that he believed to be treacherous. He was convinced the consul was keeping something important from him. The conversation lasted another ten minutes, during which he learned nothing further.

The Jesuit hesitated in the street on the way out, then headed to Poncet's house. He knocked at the door, but Jean-Baptiste was not in. He then went to the Venetians' house. An old Turk, stretched out behind the garden door, told Father Plantain that His Grace the ambassador of Ethiopia was seeing no one.

The Jesuit went home in great perplexity.

~

As night fell, Maître Juremi returned discreetly to the colony, staying in the dark shadows of the trees as he passed in front of the consulate. At home he found Poncet as delighted to see him as if they had last seen each other two months earlier.

"And here I imagined you were being given a hero's welcome and would be telling your exploits to a gaggle of admiring ladies!" said the Protestant when Jean-Baptiste had finished telling him about the events of the preceding days.

"That shows how well you know the colony. They are afraid, they spy on each other. I am unwelcome wherever I go. The only ones who want to see me are the ones I want to avoid, like the Jesuit who came by this afternoon and let the neighbors know he wanted to talk to me. Believe me, the journey hasn't ended. I have felt lonelier here in the last two days than when we were crossing the desert."

"What about Murad?"

"I was getting to him. He has been given princely quarters, but the consul has not yet agreed to meet him. He wants to see his letters of accreditation. I have made Murad promise not to give in. He is going to say no more than that his mission is to proceed to Versailles."

"And . . . your girl?"

"I don't know when I'll be able to see her again. Last night, though . . . Have you eaten?"

"Not yet."

"Then let's go to Yusuf's, across from the mosque of Hasan. We can talk in peace there."

The two set out happily on foot toward the old quarter of Cairo.

~

Poncet and his partner returned home toward midnight. Just as they reached their door, a shadow leaped out at them from the dark arcade. Maître Juremi drew his sword.

"Mercy!" said the shadow. "It's me."

"Murad! What are you doing here at this time of night?"

They pushed him into the house. Poncet lit a candle. The Armenian was in a lather and breathing heavily.

"I had just gone to bed," said Murad, panting, "only a short while ago, when twenty men entered my house."

"Twenty men? Who were they, soldiers? merchants?"

"Soldiers. Turks. Complete madmen. They jumped on me and held me at bay with a big sword, right at my neck, here."

He showed the plump skin hanging under his chin.

"And then?"

"Then they searched everything, rummaged through everything, opened everything. And when the house had been turned topsy-turvy they told me to wait on the pasha tomorrow morning."

"What did they want?" asked Poncet.

"What did they take?" asked Maître Juremi.

"Nothing."

"What, nothing?"

"Nothing. Not gold, not presents, not clothes."

"They didn't take anything?"

"Only the negus's letter," said Murad, lowering his eyes.

6

During Poncet's long absence, Husayn, the pasha of Cairo and Poncet's faithful patient, had taken a bad fall from a horse and broken his leg. The charlatans who were called in to treat him managed by their treatment to mangle the skin and reopen the break. What neither riots, nor poisons, nor debauchery had accomplished was brought to pass by a stumble over a marker stone. Husayn died in horrible pain.

The man sent by the Sublime Porte to replace him was entirely different. His name was Mehmet Bey, and he was a pure warrior. He had served in Hungary at the forefront of the Turkish assault and had come away with a great hatred of Christians. Nonetheless, he knew the Franks well enough to distinguish one nation from another, something few Turks took the trouble to do. His preference, if the word can be used, was for the French, against whom he had never fought directly and who had concluded various secret alliances with the Sublime Porte against the Hapsburgs. As age gained on him, Mehmet Bey had fallen into the hands of the imams and muftis. These saintly men skillfully made themselves the pasha's spiritual directors, in the hope that this scrupulous but ignorant Muslim would prove less conciliatory than his predecessor toward Islam's enemies.

When Murad, having been summoned, appeared before the pasha, Mehmet Bey at first gave vent to a violent fit of rage. The Armenian, terrified even at the thought of this interview, had sought to give himself composure by arriving at the citadel on his mule. As it happened, the right to enter the citadel mounted was limited to Christian ambassadors, in view of the concessions between their nations and the Sublime Porte in Constantinople. The guards roughly made Murad dismount and dragged him before the pasha.

"Just who do you take yourself for?" asked Mehmet Bey, standing imperiously in the red uniform of the Turks, a gold-fringed turban encircling his head. "And in the first place, bow down! Do you intend not to honor the sultan?"

"I . . . I honor him and I pay respectful homage to him," said Murad, trembling, on his knees, his nose pressed to the stone floor.

"Besides," said Mehmet Bey, walking around the man who lay prostrate before him, "aren't you a Turk? You speak our language and seem to share our customs—with the exception of respect, which you are sorely lacking. You wouldn't be an apostate, would you?"

"No, no," said Murad, who, his nose still to the ground, imparted to his backside the movement of denial he would have made with his head had he been standing. "I am Armenian. My religion comes to me from my father, and the Turkish sultan, the Grand Signor, in his merciful wisdom, has allowed me to retain it."

Mehmet Bey hated nothing so much as the Christians of the East.

"The sultan shows great kindness to you Christians, who stab us in the back while we are fighting the Frankish dogs! But that's the way of the world. . . ."

He walked back, lost in thought, to the carpeted and cushion-strewn dais where he ordinarily held audiences and sat down.

"Get up—show me your traitor's face."

Murad straightened up but stayed on his knees. His fat head was red and swollen from being held down for so long. The pasha signaled to one of his guards, who approached him bearing a silver tray. From it the pasha took the negus's letter.

"Not only do you live on the soil of the Prophet without recognizing his word, but what's more, as far as I can see, you are in league with the Abyssinians, who fend off Islam adamantly and even do battle with it."

Murad attempted, once the blood had returned to his stomach, to gather his wits and remember what Poncet had advised him to say.

"I am a merchant, Your Excellency," he whimpered. "I make a living any way I can. It was chance that took me to the Red Sea. For a time I was in the service of the na'ib of Massawa. He is a good Muslim. He never had occasion to complain of me—you need only ask him. One day he gave me a message for the king of Ethiopia—"

"Why should he have messages carried to that jackal?"

"In the past, Your Excellency, the Abyssinians have cut off his water and his food. The na'ib has no choice but to treat with his neighbors, whose land lies in the mountains above him."

Mehmet Bey squinted his eyes slightly, a sign that Murad's words had penetrated to a deep layer of his mind, somewhat below the thick slab of his certitudes, in an area where there sometimes shimmered (the more seldom the better, as far as he was concerned) that irritating thing called an idea.

"Then do you believe the negus can truly stop the waters from flowing into our countries? And if so, why has he never done it when he hates us so heartily?"

"He has done it with Massawa, which is a peninsula. For a time he deprived it of everything."

"But what about us, here in Egypt, who live off the water of the Nile?"

"Excellency, from everything I know, the negus lacks neither the means nor the motivation to deprive the Muslims of their life-giving water. But consider this, that if he diverts the upper course of the Nile, changing its westward flow, let us say, to an eastward one, he will not only cause Egypt's ruin but . . ."

"But what?"

". . . but at the same time bring prosperity to the Somalis, who are as Muslim as yourselves."

The pasha registered these words. They traveled through the dark regions of his mind until at last he burst out laughing, and his laugh was docilely echoed by the guards posted around the great hall.

"The water that God sends to earth," said the pasha, "is destined to nourish those who believe in him and follow his Prophet. If your master thinks he has power because the rain falls first on his pathetic mountains, he is wrong. And was it to bring that message that he sent you here to me?"

"No, Your Excellency."

"I shouldn't think so, or you would at least have come to see me. But you have not thought it necessary since your arrival here, despite being a subject of the sultan, to pay your respects to him, or rather, to me."

"I fully planned to, Excellency, but time . . ."

"Don't lie. The truth is obvious. The negus has sent you to make an alliance with the Franks, an alliance that is necessarily against us. I imagine this is once more the handiwork of those Catholic priests who are constantly abusing our hospitality."

The muftis, recognizable by their black robes and white turbans, were clustered at one end of the audience hall, from which there now arose whisperings and little exclamations of agreement. They were pleased with the pasha's firmness.

"Excellency, the negus has sent me to make certain purchases—"

"What?" said Mehmet Bey in a thunderous voice. "More lies! Take care that I do not give you a whipping that will cure you of these treacherous manners. It is something I should have done long ago, to you and all your kind."

Murad prostrated himself as before.

"Have pity, Excellency!"

"Let me inform you once and for all that I know everything. You have openly and repeatedly said that you are the negus's envoy to King Louis XIV. And the letter I hold, uncovered by my soldiers at your lodgings, officially states that the Abyssinian king has invested you with a mission. What mission is that?"

"It is true that His Highness the king of Abyssinia wants me to go to France."

"No doubt to reach a perfidious agreement with that nation and attack us from the rear while we are waging war on Europe?"

"No, Your Excellency," said Murad, straightening up, as he was almost choking.

"Then why?"

"Simply to thank His Highness the king of France for having saved his life."

"Saved his life!"

"Yes, Your Excellency. It is a simple matter. The negus was gravely ill and, finding no remedy at home, asked for help from the French. The French consul, after informing the royal council, sent the negus a Frankish physician, who cured him. By way of thanks, the emperor of Abyssinia has asked me to bring this King Louis a few presents and convey his gratitude to him."

"Where is this Frankish doctor? Did he stay in Abyssinia?"

"No, Your Excellency, he returned here with me. He is at this very moment in Cairo."

Mehmet Bey knew nothing of this business. But he had heard tell of this physician in his predecessor's entourage. Now it happened that there was a limit to the pasha's blind faith in the doctors of Islam, notably as to their wisdom relating to matters of bodily health. On the battlefield, Mehmet Bey had several times observed the ascendancy of the Christians over the Moors in the realm of medicine. Besides, most of those who practiced medicine were totally irreligious, which never seemed to keep them from practicing their art successfully. He concluded that it was best to moderate his religious principles where this subject was concerned. And as he had been suffering more and more intensely from gout over the last two years, he had a keen interest in the matter of this Frankish doctor. He asked Murad several questions about the negus's illness, which the Armenian was unwilling to answer directly, and also on the techniques used by Poncet. While continuing to deal with Murad severely, the pasha seemed somewhat mollified by the reason he had given for his journey. In the end he dismissed him.

"Don't forget, Envoy, that you are here on sufferance from me. At any moment I can summon you to appear here and give you my orders. The message you carry gives you no special rights, and certainly does not license your insolence. Now go back to the Franks. But let me not learn that you have been plotting with their priests, do you hear?"

"Your Excellency," said Murad after a last genuflection, "I understand everything. You will never have a more devoted servant than myself."

"Pray God I will," said the pasha.

The Armenian saluted and began to leave the hall, bowing and walking backward. Suddenly he stopped.

"Your Excellency! My letter!"

"You may retrieve it at the French consulate, since you pretend to be a diplomat and the negus has charged you with a mission to the French."

Murad could see that this answer would lead to complications ahead, but he was so happy to get away with his head still on his shoulders that he left almost at a run, forgetting his mule.

~

That same afternoon, the emissary from the King of Kings made his appearance at the consulate of France, Monsieur de Maillet having sent word that he was now prepared to see him.

When Murad emerged from his audience with the pasha he was thoroughly rattled. The insouciance he had felt on his arrival in Cairo was gone. Despite Poncet's advice to stay firm, the Armenian abandoned the tone of easy familiarity he had first used with the Franks. Surprising the consul no end, Murad entered his office and fell to his knees, just as he had done at the pasha's. Monsieur Macé lifted him to his feet. The consul pretended to notice nothing, summoning the same courtesy he would have shown to a duchess if a wind had momentarily lifted her skirts.

"Dear sir," said the consul when both of them were comfortably seated, "the Turkish pasha, alarmed at the rumors that have circulated about you since your arrival, thought it wise to make certain of your identity. Believe me when I say I had nothing to do with this breach of conduct. I abhor all forms of violence. But it is our fate to live in a foreign land, and the Turks have accorded themselves certain rights. One upshot of this business is that, as the pasha chose to deliver the letter seized at your house into my hands, I now have in my possession the papers I have vainly entreated you to show me since your arrival. What might have been rather unpleasant for you has at least had one fortunate consequence, in that I now know beyond the shadow of a doubt that you are the accredited envoy of the negus, as proved by this document, conveyed and authenticated by that sovereign's seal. I therefore have the honor of offering you my respects and of recognizing you before me as the messenger of the emperor of Abyssinia."

Murad bowed his head courteously, then cast a quick glance around him, as though fearful, on the heels of such good news, of being visited with some unexpected humiliation.

"The letter of credence," went on Monsieur de Maillet, "while it establishes your legitimacy unequivocally, makes no mention of the negus's wish to have you visit the court at Versailles. Let us, if you will, agree to the following: during your stay in Cairo we will defray your expenses and those of your household, which I believe numbers three persons?"

Murad nodded.

"I will put at your disposal the sum of five Abukel sequins per month, which will be paid from consular funds. When you judge that your mission has reached its goal, we will give you every assistance in returning to Abyssinia."

"But," said Murad timidly, remembering Poncet's advice, "I am also the bearer, aside from my letter of credence, of a personal message for your king."

"I have already told you," said the consul, in the gentle tones one uses with a sick man who won't take his syrup, "the letter says nothing about your having to carry the message yourself."

"And yet . . ." said Murad weakly.

"Dear sir," said the consul acerbically, "the matter is entirely simple. Let us not add complications to it. You have a message for the king: very well, then pass it on to me. If it is written, I will send it, but nothing of the kind was found by the pasha during the course of his search, as far as I know. If it is a spoken message, I will echo it faithfully in an official dispatch. If the message is to be accompanied with presents, we will have them sent to France on our ships and they will arrive at their destination safely."

"But the king told me to be sure and go myself."

"Listen," said the consul. "You needn't answer immediately. Give it your thought. I understand that you need time to accustom yourself to this town, and to your mission here."

More than anything, Monsieur de Maillet believed that Murad would realize with time just how precarious his position was and see where his best interest lay. A further argument then occurred to the consul.

"The negus will not count it against you that you have not delivered his message yourself. The truth is that the case is very simple: the Turks formally oppose your leaving this country for Europe. Thanks to our good relations, they will accept your presence here at the legation, but they will never allow you to board a ship for France. Do I make myself clear?"

Murad agreed that nothing could be more so. He was actually relieved at the news, surprising himself. At heart he had no wish to beat against the wind and tide to visit this King Louis XIV, whose portrait lowered at him from above the consul and made him seem even more terrible than the pasha. He ended his conversation with Monsieur de Maillet joyfully and returned, sweating under the three-o'clock sun, to report on the surprising news to Poncet.

~

Because of some undetermined quirk in the climate, the quills from geese raised in Egypt are worthless. Instead of being firm and standing up to paper the way goose quills do in Europe, they are exceedingly pliant and become even softer when they are dipped in ink. Monsieur de Maillet therefore had his quills sent to him from France. The employees of the consulate were obliged to make do with the local product, while he reserved the good quills for his own correspondence, in those rare cases where he wrote himself. On that night, he had resolved to write Monsieur de Pontchartrain in his own hand. True, he suffered from a recurrent pain in his wrist, but he was not to be deterred from setting down his thoughts to the minister himself. His tall, slanted script shone under the light of the torch.

> I have represented to the emissary of the negus that the Turks were opposed to his embarking for France. Strictly speaking, this is not precisely true. The pasha of Cairo lacks the authority to prohibit a mission of this kind, if we should genuinely endorse it. Yet it is true enough that an Abyssinian embassy could not fail to displease the Sublime Porte at this time, with consequent ill effects on our continued good relations. My statement is therefore indirectly true, and the Turks do indeed make such a journey impossible. I will hold to this line, and I have good reason to believe that the person here representing the King of Kings will raise no objection to it.
>
> Allow me, though, to pursue my logic a bit further. It would be a great shame, I believe, if the Abyssinian initiative, so well begun, should not lead to a development that signally advances our interests. I propose to this end that we remove the business from the Jesuits' hands and that we prosecute it according to our own lights. What was the Jesuits' interest in this matter? To convert the country. They were prevented from doing so by the untimely death of Father de Brèvedent. But they would consider the voyage a success if they could return to France with the

three Abyssinians who have traveled this far with the emissary Murad. After being properly educated in the good fathers' schools, these natives could be sent back to their country and have a much greater chance of converting their countrymen than a foreigner ever would have. This is what concerns the Society of Jesus. In my opinion, they should be fully gratified in this matter. Buoyed by their success and absorbed in the task of preparing their new Abyssinian protégés (and future emissaries), the Jesuit fathers will no longer be interested, at least for the time being, in an embassy to the negus. We will have satisfied them and recovered a space of time when we may maneuver independently. I propose to use this opportunity to send our own embassy to the negus as quickly as possible, one that will travel with the emissary Murad—of whom we will rid ourselves at the same stroke—and one that will finally be worthy of the name.

The principal merit of the mission by our envoy Poncet was to show that the voyage was possible, and indeed that it was less dangerous than one might think. By sending a true embassy, we will not be dependent again on the whims of an apothecary, and we need no longer fear that our entire mission will be compromised by hidden priests more or less skillfully concealed in its bosom. Such an embassy, conducted by a true diplomat, might begin to establish political relations with the king of Ethiopia on a solid basis. It might at the same time develop commercial ties, and highly promising ones, in the name of the French East India Company. We know that gold is abundant in this country, and that its natural resources are largely unexploited. In fact it represents a stage, still entirely free of competition, toward the farthest reaches of the Orient.

Who can be trusted to lead such an important mission, you might well ask. Although I do not know him yet, it appears to me that the chevalier Le Noir du Roule, whose arrival you announced to me in your latest dispatch and who will fulfill the responsibilities of vice-consul at Damietta under my orders, has all the requisite qualities for such an undertaking.

I am aware of the tender regard for my family that has led you to honor me with the choice of Monsieur Le Noir du Roule. I hope to show you by my suggestion that I do not place my interests as a father above those of the king. I venture to hope, in fact, that the two will coincide and that Monsieur Le Noir du Roule, resplendent with the glory and fortune I propose to put in his way, will be all the better fitted afterward to honor my family by joining my daughter in matrimony.

7

When Jean-Baptiste heard Murad's news, he realized that the game was up. An alliance between the consul and the pasha, whether due to a simple convergence of interests or a genuine agreement, destroyed any further chances of proceeding with the embassy as far as Versailles. If Murad agreed to deliver his message to the consul, the diplomat would twist it to his purposes first before passing it on to the king. And there was not the slightest chance of his advancing Poncet's interests, despising him as he did.

All the effort, the endless days of travel, and the hardship had come to nothing. Jean-Baptiste was on the point of sinking into despair when two pieces of good news reached him one after the other. Without changing the outlook for his future in any way, they offered him the prospect of immediate happiness.

As he was discussing the matter with Maître Juremi in the cool shade of the terrace and concluding as he turned the question in every direction that the journey to Versailles was definitely compromised, a guard from the consulate arrived to hand him a note from Monsieur de Maillet. The consul was inviting "Sieur Poncet" to dine on the following day in honor of the arrival of "His Excellency the Representative of His Majesty the King of Abyssinia." A list of the guests was attached. The only thing that interested Jean-Baptiste was to read: "The Hon. Consul of France, Madame de Maillet, and daughter."

Not long after, Françoise appeared at the window of her house, leaped onto the terrace, and described a plan to Jean-Baptiste that he was to follow in every detail if he wanted to see Alix alone after the ceremonial dinner. Having accomplished her errand, Françoise busied herself wandering through the apothecaries' house in order, as she said, to see that they were missing nothing. She pushed her investigation as far as the ground floor, where Maître Juremi had gone back to preparing his concoctions. He acknowledged her with a grunt, and the poor woman climbed back upstairs hurriedly, passing Poncet in a state of emotion, and disappearing by the same way she had come.

The next day Poncet hid in his house, waiting dolefully for the hours to pass before dinner. At noon he slipped out to visit Murad. He explained in detail the behavior the envoy was to follow that night at the consulate. Jean-Baptiste was concerned that Murad's first social appearance would give the consul further cause to prevent him from going on to the French court. Then he went home, telling Maître Juremi, whom he found in a surlier mood than ever, to greet any callers. A lively curiosity about Poncet was building among the merchants, as each wanted to be the first to hear the story of his travels. And as the apothecary had not yet told his story to anyone, the value that was set on it increased day by day. Father Plantain also came by three times. Maître Juremi stood blocking the door, and the Jesuit shifted this way and that to catch a glimpse over the Protestant's shoulder of the mysteries contained in the house. Father Plantain complained bitterly that Murad was also seeing no one, and that he would like all the same to hear the story of Father de Brèvedent's death. Maître Juremi restrained himself from tossing the Jesuit bodily into the street and listened to his jeremiad politely, though without budging an inch.

Dinner time arrived at last. Jean-Baptiste dressed with care. The clothes he had bought from the corsairs, though somewhat more elegant than necessary in the normal course of affairs, were perfectly suited to tonight's event. Maître Juremi declared that his friend looked magnificent. Poncet read a certain sadness in his companion's eyes, not at being left out of the celebration, for which he had little inclination anyway, but at being reduced to clandestineness, as though all the work, danger, and also successes of their months of travel were inadmissible and guilty facts, to be hidden as he hid the simple and innocent faith he loyally held to.

As he walked toward the consulate, Poncet reflected that he owed it to Maître Juremi to restore his good name and judged that he could do so most effectively from France. Here was another reason to lead an embassy to Versailles. The chance of it, however, was growing ever more remote.

Monsieur de Maillet had ordered up a dinner in the grand style. He wanted to welcome the envoy of the negus and also compensate him for his disappointed hopes. The guards, in janissary costumes, stood at attention on the steps before the main entrance holding their curved swords aloft to make an arch for the arriving guests. A lavish profusion of candles in the chandeliers illuminated the entrance hall and the grand reception room, giving a brilliant gleam to the gold of the picture frames, the polish on the parquet, the scagliola flooring, and even the lackeys' copper buttons. The women plunged delightedly into this artificial light, knowing that it flattered them, causing their eyes and jewels to sparkle while bathing their features in a dazzling blur. The ladies of the colony, for the most part worthy wives of merchants, had often led chaotic lives in the world before settling into their present conditions. The first and generally longest period of their careers might have been minding a shop's till, or even treading the boards of a traveling cabaret. When their adventurer husbands had at last found their fortunes in Cairo, they were able suddenly to satisfy their bottomless desire for respectability. They bought jewels from Jewish merchants who smuggled them in illicitly, and they gave the latest Paris fashions to be copied by twelve-year-old Arab seamstresses, whom they then failed to pay. These baubles and accouterments came to adorn their bodies late, when work and concupiscence had largely worn the bloom off. But it is the characteristic of luxury, and the reason it is so desirable, that it transfers to the owner some of the qualities of the object owned. The goutish fellow who parades about town in a stylish cabriolet takes on the very ease of his horses, and the woman whose youth has fled becomes for an evening as new, as brilliant, and as refreshing to the eye as the organdy in which she is swathed and which she brushes shamelessly against the legs of men.

Among the last to arrive, Jean-Baptiste paid his respects to the consul, who was greeting his guests in the entrance hall, then plunged into the sea of taffetas, pearls, and glittering stones to find the only woman who held any merit in his eyes. On this grand occasion, all the rooms on the ground floor had been opened: the reception hall, still displaying its majestic portrait of the Sun King but with the consul's desk removed, and another room behind it that was ordinarily shut for reasons of economy but where the tables had been set up for tonight's dinner. Alix was not there. Jean-Baptiste finally discovered her in a room he had not known existed. It was a small music room, where the women often retired in the evening. Near the window, which opened onto the rear of the garden, a green spinet decorated with an Arcadian scene stood against the wall. Alix was standing by a small mantelpiece with a pier glass above it, so that when he entered Jean-Baptiste had the startling experience of seeing her simultaneously head-on and from the back. The room was small and they had the impression of being suddenly thrust face to face, which disconcerted them both. But the scene around them was too animated, too filled with laughter, exclamations, and noisy greetings, for such a detail to be seen by anyone else.

An attentive observer might have noticed, however, that though Alix had taken the greatest care in her clothes and coiffure, she had not until then deployed her charms; but now, as she became animated, they shone resplendently. It was as though a fan had opened, or a peacock spread its tail, or a butterfly its wing. The gust of wind she had been waiting for had arrived, and she opened to it, as though taking on beauty, and it carried her like a sail. Jean-Baptiste, his heart in his throat, stood still for an instant, then took two steps forward. Immediately, like a soldier who discovers that he is the target of every bullet, he was surrounded by five or six women who had heard of the young man's exploits and had been begging their husbands daily to invite him to their houses. Seeing him enter, strikingly handsome in his red vest with silver braid, his hair flowing freely, cravatless, they conflated their interest in his story with the physical thrill they experienced on seeing him, at a time when the armor of their rich adornment nourished in them the secret illusion that they were still irresistible.

Jean-Baptiste, on the verge of sinking under the onslaught, was rescued by a general movement that carried everyone out of the little music room and into the ceremonial hall: the ambassador had been announced. In fact it was a false alert. The consul had sent his carriage for Murad, but the Armenian had been unready and had decided, somewhat absurdly, to send the carriage back at the appointed time in case the consul should need it. He had therefore ordered his three slaves to go ahead with the conveyance, instructing them to say that he would arrive shortly on foot. When the carriage rolled to a stop in front of the consulate, the consul himself rushed to open the door and, under his guests' unwavering gaze, discovered to his confusion that it contained three natives, their legs bare, their bodies draped in simple cotton cloth, their eyes wide with terror. Murad trotted up to the door some ten minutes later. The guard at first rudely prevented him from entering, not having recognized him in the dark.

These contretemps delayed dinner somewhat and prolonged the pleasure of the guests, most of whom had never been honored by such a show of official pomp. At last the guests took their seats around two long tables. Ambassador Murad sat at the first table opposite the consul. The second was presided over by Sieur Brelot, the colonial deputy, whom Monsieur de Maillet hoped in this way to mollify after the ridicule he had met in heading the delegation that had missed Murad's arrival. The place across from him was given to Frisetti, the first dragoman at the consulate. Poncet was at this second table, between two women he immediately found distressing, and the secretary Macé was his first male neighbor to the right.

Jean-Baptiste scanned the room to see where Alix would be seated. He felt a pang of disappointment at first, but she had gone to the wrong place and in the end seated herself to Frisetti's right, almost directly across from her lover. It was the first time since their earliest meetings that they had been close to each other in public. Under the bright lights, they almost had the illusion of being master and mistress of the house.

Jean-Baptiste avoided looking in Alix's direction too often, for his feelings were so strong he was afraid they could be read on his face. Once all the guests had taken their seats, the general hubbub fell. The diners turned to one side and the other to make courteous remarks, and the conversation took off immediately.

"And now, dear Monsieur Poncet, you are surely going to tell us of your adventures on the way to Abyssinia?"

The question came from Monsieur Macé himself and met with general enthusiasm around the table.

"You must ask me questions," said Jean-Baptiste. "Abyssinia is at a great distance, and each day there occurred incidents that could all by themselves supply a chapter in a book."

"Begin with the journey itself. Was it all that dangerous to get there?" said Macé.

To all appearances, the secretary's question was prompted by genuine curiosity, but the truth was that, as always, he was following orders. The consul, busily planning to send a new embassy, this time an official one, had decided to learn just what dangers it would face. Murad was of little help in providing information. The best plan was therefore to get Poncet to tell the story of his travels. But the consul was not willing to ask him directly, nor did he wish to give the apothecary a sense of his own importance by seeming to take an interest in him.

In planning the dinner, Monsieur de Maillet had the idea of flattering Poncet and beginning the process of shriving him in public, without appearing to pay him any particular attention. Monsieur Macé was given instructions to make him talk as much as possible, while inscribing everything he said in his prodigious memory, and to guide the direction of the narrative with judicious questions. Feeling Alix's eyes on him, Jean-Baptiste took flight. He cared not a straw for the absurd bourgeois seated all around the table. It was to the woman he loved and to her alone that he agreed to give an impassioned account of the dangers, sufferings, and joys he had met, that she might share them, if only after the fact.

Macé had great difficulty channeling the traveler's narrative toward practical matters. Poncet was constantly digressing onto details that struck the secretary as superfluous. For instance, he launched into an endless description of the coffee ritual in Abyssinia. The ladies took a vivid interest in these subjects and overruled Macé when he tried to get back to the king of Sennar or the condition of the trail as far as Lake Tana. Soon he gave it up as hopeless and left Poncet to answer laughingly the most unfruitful questions.

Toward dessert, the buxom spouse of a merchant, flushed with drink, was emboldened to join the conversation and address Jean-Baptiste loudly in a voice that betrayed her early training as a fishwife.

"Sir, they say that Abyssinian women are extremely beautiful. Have you not brought a woman back with you?"

Everyone looked at Poncet.

"A woman?" he said, lowering his eyes.

There was a general pause. Jean-Baptiste raised his eyes and looked at Alix for a brief instant, all the force of their love passing between them in that glance.

"In truth, Madame," he said, without paying the least attention to the woman who had asked the question, "it was to find a woman that I undertook the journey. And I believe I have found her."

These words were spoken so seriously that an awkward silence followed, lasting several seconds.

"He is having us on!" said a man's voice finally.

There was a sudden release of tension, and several people laughed.

"You are joking, are you not?" said Jean-Baptiste's neighbor, leaning toward him.

"Naturally."

There was a general "Ah!" and the conversation picked up again with all its former animation. But Monsieur Macé, who could not look at Mademoiselle de Maillet without thrilling at her beauty though he had strictly forbidden himself to do so, had observed the glance she exchanged with Jean-Baptiste and interpreted it correctly. He looked hard at them afterward and kept note of his observations, filing them away for later use.

Dinner came to an end. The guests rose to take coffee in the reception room under the portrait of the King Louis XIV. Those who had eaten at Poncet's table were joyous and brimming with amusing anecdotes; those who had been seated at the first table were grim-faced and indignant. In quiet tones they retailed the scandalous behavior of the emperor of Abyssinia's plenipotentiary. Not only had the ambassador eaten uncouthly and with his hands, but he had asked question after question on the price of poultry, the methods used to prepare it, and the quantity of butter that went into the sauces, until it began to seem as though they were sharing dinner with a cook. Flushed with wine, he had gone so far as to wipe his fingers on the skirts of the woman next to him. Any doubt as to the meaning of his behavior was dispelled when, after swallowing a ball of sherbet, he pretended to deposit a frozen kiss on the neck of his other dinner partner, the wife of the colony's richest banker. Things might have taken an unpleasant turn had not Monsieur de Maillet, the final arbiter of good taste in the colony and the model on whom each regulated his behavior, engaged the company's attention in a new direction by pretending to choke.

While these stories were making the rounds, and the guests who had witnessed the disturbing scenes at one table were exchanging their grievances for the piquant tales of those at the other, Alix went to find her mother and told her that she had a violent migraine. Madame de Maillet knew the efforts her daughter had made in preparing for this dinner after initially refusing to take part in it. She kissed her on the forehead and wished her good night. Jean-Baptiste, however, had more difficulty in making his getaway. Twenty women pursued him and he promised nineteen that he would come to dinner, greatly delighting them though also diluting somewhat the value of his favors. The twentieth judged it wiser to ask for nothing, which immediately aroused the jealousy of the others.

Jean-Baptiste went to pay his respects to the consul, who congratulated him on his eloquence and verve, which all the guests at his table had commented on. The physician asked if he might accompany Murad home, saying that the Abyssinian envoy was in the habit of retiring early. The consul readily agreed, glad to be rid of this unfailing source of embarrassment. He offered his carriage but did not insist: the Armenian, who had collapsed into an armchair in a deserted corner of the drawing room, his tunic stained with food and his hands greasy from picking with his fingers, was capable of causing untold damage to the new blue satin bolsters of the conveyance. Poncet said the walk would do them good and dragged the ambassador off, as the man bowed on all sides and offered incoherent grunts. At the foot of the entrance stairs they were joined by the three Abyssinians, who had been fed in the kitchen.

"Bring torches for the honorable ambassador!" commanded Monsieur de Maillet.

"It might be better to cast no more light on the scene than necessary," Jean-Baptiste suggested.

The consul saw the justice of this and allowed them to leave in darkness, like a small tribe on the retreat.

Once in the street, they walked together for two hundred yards. Poncet then gave Murad's arm to the strongest of the Abyssinians, who spoke

Arabic, and directed him to conduct the ambassador home to the Venetians' house. Jean-Baptiste, for his part, turned left, walked around the spacious grounds of the consulate, and entered a small street lined with windowless walls on either side. One of them walled off the kitchen yard of the legation and had a door through which deliveries were made. There he found Françoise waiting for him.

8

Poncet followed Françoise up a narrow back stair that smelled of damp. He next made his way alone into a dark dressing room, then into a bedroom whose windows were wide open to the starry night. A light north wind carried the smell of silt from the delta down to the city. From the ground floor could be heard the confused noise of the dinner guests, many of whom were still lingering below, laughing loudly. The guttering candle on the nightstand cast its yellow glow on Alix, who stood waiting for him. Jean-Baptiste walked toward her slowly and took her in his arms. She had not changed her clothes, and Jean-Baptiste felt beneath his fingers and lips the very hair, jewels, fabrics, and face that had been so recently imprinted in his mind, and to which he restored the color, harmony, and brilliance they had worn under the great chandeliers of the drawing rooms. In brief, the two lovers were alive to each other and finally able to realize the joy of reaching for what they wanted at the instant they wanted it. They had faced too many setbacks up to this point for them to accept the slightest barrier to their pleasure now. They lost themselves in long and voluptuous kisses, while from below came the sound of cheering, of the kind you might hear rising from the darkened hall at the end of an opera when the handsome couple find themselves reunited on stage.

Beside them was a bed, and their privacy was complete. But it would be to misunderstand them to believe they could have given in, at this stage of their love, to their full desire for one another. They still sagely nourished the hope that they would one day have the right to love each other, and they waited against that time to remove all limits to their bliss.

"My love, my love," Alix murmured, continuing to cover Jean-Baptiste's face with kisses, "how happy I am. I love you and want to stay like this always."

It may have been the thought of this impossible stretch of time that made her start and draw back a bit from Jean-Baptiste. She looked at him, her deep eyes glistening with tears, and spoke to him gravely:

"Tell me, when are you leaving for Versailles? And more important, when will you come back to take me away with you?"

"Ah!" said Jean-Baptiste, turning his face slightly away.

"What is it?"

"It has all grown so complicated. Your father won't hear of a journey to France, claiming that the Turks are against it. Of course, we haven't exactly helped things: you have seen Murad."

"Do you mean . . . that all our hopes have been for nothing?"

"No!" said Jean-Baptiste, squeezing her hands. "It just will be more difficult and take longer than I had hoped."

Jean-Baptiste did not want simply to admit that their cause was lost. He did not know where to turn for hope, yet at that moment, standing before Alix, he felt that to give up would be more hateful and more unacceptable than defeat.

From the front steps of the consulate almost directly below came the sounds of couples starting to leave in large numbers. They said goodbye noisily, and their thanks were endless.

"Listen," Alix said. "We don't have much time. As soon as the last carriage drives up for its passengers, you will have to go."

Saying this, she kissed him again, then went on:

"You should know that some urgency has entered into it now."

"What do you mean?"

"My father . . . Ah! I didn't want you to know. There is no point in complicating things."

"Go ahead, tell me."

"My father has constantly been mentioning, these last three days, the arrival of a man who is being sent to him from France. He is a diplomat and is to take a consular position in Rosetta or Damietta, I forget."

"Well?"

"Well, my father has talked about this man several times, describing his eminent birth, his career, his future, all the while looking at me significantly. He hasn't said anything yet, but my mother has already told me that my father has been plotting to get me married for some time. He asked the minister, our relative, to send out to him a man of the kind he was looking for, a gentleman."

"And . . . what do you think of all this?" Poncet said.

"I think, love, that I want you and you alone and that I have already taken a dislike to this stranger."

"When is he expected to arrive?"

"I understand that he is on his way even now."

Jean-Baptiste frowned.

"Listen," he said, pulling himself together. "Things may take a while for us to arrange. And this man could arrive here before I have what I would need to approach your father. In the meantime, don't agree to anything, and don't commit yourself to anything. Resist, find a thousand excuses, pretend to be sick. If you need them, I can send you potions through Françoise that will make you cough, vomit, turn pale, or even make you thoroughly ill, if necessary. But whatever you do, don't commit yourself to anything."

"The only commitment I have ever made, from the bottom of my heart, is to be yours always. Don't worry. I'll do what you ask me to do. And anyway, I know my father. He might refuse me something that I want, but he would never force me to do his bidding. If we come to loggerheads there will be a standoff and it will last a long time."

They kissed again, still hearing a few voices from downstairs as the last carriages were drawn up. Everything they had to say to each other could pass through Françoise. The only message they could not charge her with was this satiety of the senses, this dialogue of hands and lips, this conversation of two bodies searching for and answering to each other in the whisperings of velvet and silk.

From the dark of the dressing room, Françoise called softly that it was time and that someone might come up at any moment. They took leave of each other with tears in their eyes. Alix waited for the last sound of steps to die away in the stairway before she slid back the bolt of her bedroom door and lay down slowly on her bed, fully dressed.

~

Poncet arrived home to find Maître Juremi seated on the terrace, a lantern at his feet. He was drinking from a small glass of tangerine liquor, distilled long before during times when his alembic was not otherwise in use.

"Well," Juremi said, "here's our lover."

Jean-Baptiste sat down across from his friend without a word.

"Ah! Ah! It looks as though we've had some bad news. Drink this to warm your belly."

Maître Juremi handed his friend a small glass, which Poncet set down untouched on the balustrade.

"You're letting yourself go, my friend," said Juremi, getting to his feet.

He was in a lively mood, despite the late hour. It looked as though he had spent a quiet evening and had been awaiting his friend's return to bestir himself. He paced across the terrace in long strides.

"What is it? She won't have any part of you?"

"She will," said Poncet stupidly, his mind elsewhere.

Maître Juremi pounced on this little bone and started to gnaw on it noisily. He explained to Jean-Baptiste that this was the essential point, that he was extremely lucky, that the obstacles would all fall away, since his feelings were reciprocated.

"Get up and fight! That's all you have to do. Look at the state you're in."

"We won't be going to Versailles," said Jean-Baptiste gloomily. "The king won't knight me, and I won't marry her."

"And the night will never end, the water will never fill the fountains again, and the hyenas will finally devour us all. Come, come! Show some spirit, you old pessimist."

Maître Juremi crossed the terrace with his heavy step, entered Poncet's room, unhooked two swords and the chest protectors, and returned toward his friend.

"Here, en garde, as in the old days. See if you aren't your old self again within five minutes."

Jean-Baptiste had no desire to get up out of his chair. In the still air around him hung the last droplets of scent Alix had attached to his skin and clothes. Yet in a deep corner of his heart he felt he had abandoned his friend that night and wanted to make up for it, even if only a little. He rose to his feet, pulled on the leather plastron, and assumed the en garde position. Maître Juremi touched within a few seconds. Again they placed themselves en garde. Poncet, still not himself, parried weakly a few times in quinte and septime. Maître Juremi lunged and touched once more.

"Come, come! Do I have to run you through from stem to stern to purge you of your ill humors?"

The sound of foils irritates a man at some deep layer where his warrior spirit slumbers. There has never been a case where the first tickling of the swords has not aroused a man's combative spirit even when his mind was utterly engaged elsewhere, and made his muscles tense and his eyes glisten. By the third bout, Poncet was almost himself. Maître Juremi touched again but not so cleanly. They next had a long and evenly matched passage at arms, full of gambits, surprises, muffled cries, and reverses. At last, Jean-Baptiste touched and at the same moment gave out a horrible yell.

"The Jesuits!"

Maître Juremi, speechless, lowered his sword and looked around him in bewilderment.

"What Jesuits? Where?"

Jean-Baptiste moved away, leaned against the guardrail, and, keeping pace with his thoughts, traced with his sword hand in the air the letters of an imaginary proclamation.

"The Je-su-its. The Jesuits! Of course. They are the only ones who can help us in this."

"What the devil are you talking about?"

"Of the journey to Versailles. They are the only ones, do you hear? Hah! Why didn't I think of it sooner? Yes, the only ones who can bring the consul around and help us win our way to the king himself are the ones who transmitted the king's orders in the first place. Just because we've learned to distrust them we shouldn't forget their power."

"But," said Maître Juremi gravely, "you forget that we made a solemn promise in Abyssinia that the Jesuits would never come back. If we want to go to Versailles, it is only to make sure the king hears an account that directly contradicts what the good fathers have been feeding him. They are the last people we want joining us on the journey."

"You are right. But the upshot of your intransigence is that we will not go to Versailles and the Jesuits' version will be the only one heard at court."

"It is better for them to propound that version alone, without our concurrence."

"No!" Poncet said. "If we join the Jesuits to go to Versailles, it will not be to concur with their account but to contradict it solemnly once we are before the king. We will be using them and that's all."

"You haven't yet gone over to their opinions, but you have already adopted their methods, it seems."

"And how do you fight, unless it is with the same weapons as your antagonist? If I attack you with a sword, do you defend yourself with a spoon?"

"To ape your opponent's faults is already to concede a victory to him."

"Then the best is to remain pure and die."

"Yes, it is better to die than to betray oneself. But," said Maître Juremi, glowering from his great height, "it is possible to stay pure and win."

"We are losing sight of the issue," said Jean-Baptiste with some asperity. "How are we to get the negus's message to Versailles? That is the question, the real question. And what I am telling you is that the only ones who can accomplish this miracle for us are the Jesuits."

Maître Juremi turned around, took three steps toward the wall, then faced his friend again.

"Jean-Baptiste, you are confusing everything. This journey matters to you for personal reasons. And now you are ready to break your word to satisfy your most egotistical desires."

"Don't!" said Poncet, striking the metal of the balustrade with the pommel of his sword.

"Am I wrong?" asked Maître Juremi, still standing at the edge of the shadow.

"You are right and you are wrong. Yes, I want to go and plead my cause at Versailles. No, I will not betray the king of Abyssinia. I will devote the same energy to each of these missions and accomplish them both."

Maître Juremi took a step backward to cloak himself in shadow. Poncet knew this effacement signaled a grudging acceptance.

"Leave it to me," said Jean-Baptiste in a calmer voice. "All I ask is that you remain neutral and have faith in me. I alone will speak to the Jesuits, I alone will take the risk of bringing them into our plans, I alone will take the risk of disavowing them finally before the king."

"In my religion," said Maître Juremi, emerging from the darkness, "we preach by example alone. I will not try to convert you by force, or even by persuasion. Personally, I won't go to the Jesuits, and I am too wary of them to believe that they can be duped. But I won't keep you from following your plan . . . and I hope you will succeed."

Jean-Baptiste, pleased with his idea and satisfied that his friend would not oppose it, walked toward Maître Juremi, who took a step forward also. They seized their glasses and toasted to their cordial disagreement, while Vega looked down on them and the dogs of Cairo barked noisily.

~

Following his dinner at the consulate, Murad developed a raging headache that he blamed on the food, though it was more likely due to drink. He had sampled large quantities of every beverage and even indulged in mixtures that his neighbors at table found scandalous, for instance champagne, Burgundy, and absinthe in a single glass.

On top of everything, the Ethiopian slave who shaved his head every morning with a glass shard—Murad had a great distaste for the metal in razors—had scratched his scalp. A drop of dried blood was visible under his turban. Poncet arrived toward nine o'clock and informed Murad that he had sent for the Jesuits' spokesman and that the priest would be arriving soon. Murad, who had not forgotten the emperor's words, was at first indignant. After Poncet explained his plan he felt reassured and returned to an enumeration of his digestive complaints.

Father Plantain arrived a bit before the stated hour. He stood in front of

Murad and Poncet and, at a gesture from the ambassador, sank onto the carpet with all the grace of an ox going down under the poleax. Murad very civilly offered him coffee and cakes, which the Jesuit accepted. These were shortly brought in by the three Ethiopian slaves in procession.

As soon as he saw them, Father Plantain straightened up onto his knees.

"My God! How beautiful they are!"

In the lead was the eldest of the three, dragging his clubfoot, while behind came the older child, hideously cross-eyed, and the younger, who had lost all his hair to ringworm.

"You think so?" Murad said, looking at the sad cortège.

"I see their souls," said the priest, his eyes wet.

He was looking at them, in point of fact, with the beatific respect of a shepherd in a grotto to whom the Virgin has been kind enough to appear.

"Well then," Poncet said, "how fortunate a gesture on the part of the negus. These three servants are among the gifts he intended for King Louis XIV."

Father Plantain did not take his eyes off the Abyssinians until they had hobbled back into the kitchen.

"You say these are *among* the gifts the emperor has for the king of France. Are there others?"

"Ah, Father, there certainly are," said Jean-Baptiste, "and very sizable ones."

The priest had difficulty imagining what present could surpass the one he had just seen. Poncet, allowing his curiosity to build, reached slowly into his pocket and removed a letter.

"This message fortunately escaped the attention of the pasha's police."

"A message! A message from the emperor?"

"Written by his own scribe under his dictation and authenticated by his seal."

Murad followed the discussion between the two men. On hearing Poncet speak of a letter from the negus, he turned his head toward him so abruptly that he reactivated his headache. He just had time to see the apothecary's conspiratorial wink before he stretched out on the cushions, begging Father Plantain to excuse him. The priest was already holding out his hand to Poncet for the letter.

"Alas," said Poncet, putting the paper back in his pocket, "the king expressly asked that this message be delivered to no one but Louis XIV in person. If the other was opened, at least it was only a credential letter. This one, though, will be seen by no one. I have sworn it."

"And . . . what does it say?" asked the Jesuit, tormented by curiosity.

"Father, the letter and its import are all one, and both are for the king."

"Yes, but setting the details aside, what is the spirit of it?"

"Entirely favorable. So much I am able to tell you. The negus pays his respects to the king of France and shows himself well disposed in all matters of religion."

"Good, very good," the Jesuit said. "And does he go so far as to admit the two natures of Christ?"

Poncet raised his eyebrows with the air of someone who knows a great deal and has no cause for worry, but cannot say anything. Father Plantain aped an expression of pleasure to show that he understood.

"And . . . the other presents?" he asked.

"They are here: gold, civet musk, spices, silk sashes, and the contents of a case we are allowed to open only in the presence of the king."

"Excellent . . . excellent! Your mission has been a great success."

"Father de Brèvedent, alas, was not able to see its outcome. But we have been faithful to his memory, believe me, and we could not have accomplished our mission more fully had he still been among us."

"So I see! The orders of the king's confessor, Father de La Chaise, could not have been more aptly carried out. You must certainly give the king an account of these magnificent results."

"I have also thought so," said Poncet bowing. "Alas, you know that it is impossible."

"Yes, the Turks . . ."

"The Turks, Father, are an easy target."

"What do you mean?"

Poncet clapped his hands for the slaves to come and fill their cups. He wanted them to file past the Jesuit one more time to bring the priest to a pitch of excitement. As soon as they were gone, Father Plantain resumed his questions.

"You were saying something about the Turks," he said, trying to recover his bearings.

"No, Father, it is you who were speaking about them. I was simply expressing my doubts."

"What, you do not believe the pasha would forbid you to travel to France?"

"I do not know Mehmet Bey," Poncet said, "but I was his predecessor's doctor for several years. However fanatical they may be—and I hear that this one truly is—the Ottomans never go beyond a certain limit with us."

"What do you mean?"

"I mean that a Turk would never order a house in the colony searched without the consul's prior consent."

"You think . . ."

". . . that the Turkish pasha and Monsieur de Maillet have formed a strange alliance against us in this business."

The Jesuit was at first dumbstruck. Then, his nostrils tickled by the aroma of intrigue, he assumed an even more confounded expression, his eyes motionless at the back of their cavern of eyebrow and bone, his lips compressed.

"Your accusation is an extremely serious one, Monsieur Poncet. You would have me believe that there is a plan afoot to thwart the king's will."

"You seem to think, Father, that the king has only one will. I fear that there are several wills expressed in his neighborhood, one by those whose concern is with the king's salvation, and another by those who direct his politics."

Father Plantain sank into deep reflection.

"For our part," said Poncet, "we obeyed the orders brought by Father Versau and scrupulously performed what the king expected of us. I believe it crucial for maintaining the links we have established to carry our account back to the king, and also for the negus's ambassador to confirm that his message reached Louis XIV and that he returns with an answer. But this certainly conflicts with the interests of those who are more concerned to preserve our alliance with the Turks than to see France fulfill its Christian destiny."

The Jesuit rose laboriously to his feet.

"I will soon get to the bottom of this," he said.

He took his leave of Poncet, advised him not to wake Murad, who had been snoring for several minutes past, and set off at a brisk pace. He had the delighted look of a man who is preparing to plunge into sin, the better to do battle with it.

9

Poncet heard nothing more for three days, three long days during which he avoided going out because those who were so eager to claim him for dinner seemed to have lookouts on every corner. It was the hot season. The wind off the Nile carried a miasmic tide up from the delta. Poncet put the word out that he was sick, and before long he genuinely was. He felt a fever running all through his body and occasional spasms of pain in his knees and elbows. A leaden torpor kept him lying in his hammock all day, absorbed in disjointed dreams that evaporated on awakening, leaving a residue of sadness. Françoise, who came to see him every day, told him laughingly that he was lovesick, and Poncet was perfectly ready to believe it, yet he made no improvement. On the second day, Françoise brought him a note from Alix, which he read and reread a hundred times. It was nothing, a few tender words, and not very compromising ones in case they should be intercepted—but she had written them. He looked at the lines. They blurred, and the arabesques became a revelation of her gestures, of her hand that had made them, and of her entire body as she guided her pen. On the third day there was another note: it too contained tender words, and toward the end Alix included a brief digression, one that must have cost her an effort as it departed from the preoccupying subject of their love.

> I am not sure if you have noticed it, but our dear Françoise is consumed by a passion she has not been able to declare. She is in love with your friend Juremi. His appearance is so formidable that I sympathize entirely with her hesitation. As you know him well, you might perhaps sound him out."

Maître Juremi, whose travels to Abyssinia were unknown to all, came and went freely in the colony and the town. He had resumed calling on patients, although he treated no one himself. Poncet's clients begged him for fresh supplies of old prescriptions, so the Protestant was kept busy bringing jujube paste to cold sufferers and calomel to the constipated. He also kept an eye on Murad, who seemed content to stay quiet for the moment.

When Maître Juremi returned on the third evening, Jean-Baptiste asked him to keep him company. He knew his friend to be reticent in matters of the heart, and thus he approached the subject slowly. With his illness licensing him to a certain melancholy, Poncet brought up the past in nostalgic tones. They had been friends for years and traveled together extensively, yet there was still much that Jean-Baptiste did not know about Maître Juremi's life.

"Didn't you tell me once that you had been married?" Jean-Baptiste said in the course of remembering some other detail.

"Yes," said the master-at-arms gloomily.

"And are you still married?"

"Possibly."

"What? You don't know?"

The Protestant disliked making confidences. Jean-Baptiste insisted.

"All the same, there is something incredible about being married and not knowing it."

"Oh, I know. But life . . ."

"Come! Tell me all about it. It will provide me some diversion, which I sorely need."

"It is a very simple business, but I'm afraid you won't find in it the gaiety you are looking for. My father was a blacksmith in the outskirts of Uzès, as I have told you before. Our family was originally from Italy. Sometime during the last century, my ancestors converted to the Reformed Church. I never took any notice of this until I was eighteen years old. For one thing, there were only Protestants living around us. I learned my father's trade, and he planned to take me into the business. At the age of twenty-five I married a local girl. Her name was Marine. You can't imagine what those times were like. It was all twenty-five years ago! People from my region used to get along, they used to help each other and hold wonderful celebrations on the slightest pretext, even though we had very little. Protestants like to get together, maybe because there aren't that many of them—it reassures them to be part of a crowd. And there was a fine crowd outside the church on the morning Marine and I were married. There was wine, and there were fiddlers. Then a week later, without exaggeration, a week later the king revoked the Edict of Nantes, which allowed Protestants to profess their religion in France. We all knew that something terrible was coming. Louvois, the king's minister of war, sent his dragoons to be quartered in the area. There was an assembly of our people in the mountains, and even more gathered there than had come to our wedding the week before. All the heads of families were present, wearing sheepskin coats and large black hats and carrying their Bibles. They decided that all the young men between twenty and thirty-five would go abroad the moment things took a turn for the worse."

"You left a week after your marriage?"

"Nine days exactly. The decision wasn't motivated by pity. The community didn't want to protect the weak but to distance our fighting force from the enemy: we left women, children, and the elderly behind. Only young men, the ones who could fight, were taken out of harm's way. So that's what happened. I crossed the mountains and gorges of the Causses region, hiding along the way, and reached Aquitaine, where I found work on fishing boats. Then I made my way to the United Provinces, under the stadtholder William. I fought in his armies in England. Then I came back to the Holy Roman Emperor's lands, where you met me as a master-at-arms in Venice."

"And your wife?"

"I know nothing of her fate," said the Protestant, lowering his eyes.

"Did you love her?"

"She is my wife."

"All the same!" Poncet said. "Nine days!"

"But an oath taken before God is binding for all eternity."

"And what if she is dead?"

"Then I am free."

"Were you never tempted . . ."

"Of course I have been tempted," Maître Juremi said, shaking his head. "And I have often given in to the flesh, as you know. But taking a wife is something else. And we don't have that convenient institution confession. No, on that score I have never broken my oath."

"What was your village in the Gard called?"

"Soubeyran."

They spoke no more about it. That night, Poncet wrote Alix a note telling her that Maître Juremi might not be free, but that if he himself ever reached France he would look into it. He advised her to say nothing to Françoise.

~

On the fourth day, having made his investigation, Father Plantain presented himself at the consulate.

"Your Excellence," the Jesuit said in more military tones than ever, "I received urgent news from Constantinople this morning."

Monsieur de Maillet pricked up his ears.

"I believe you are acquainted with Father Versau?" the priest continued.

"He was in Cairo last year."

"Precisely, after many misfortunes, a shipwreck and so on."

"I remember it very well."

"Then you also remember that it was he who was responsible for making the king's wishes known to you with regard to the Abyssinian mission?"

"Certainly."

"I wrote to give him an account of that embassy's return."

"The word you used the first time was more accurate—it was a mission, not an embassy."

"As you like, but it changes nothing. My letter went out by express messenger not long after the pasha ordered a search of the premises now occupied by the negus's envoy. I naturally mentioned this incident, as well as the Turkish official's refusal to allow the Ethiopian ambassador to proceed to Versailles."

"What of it?" said Monsieur de Maillet, growing slightly pale.

"Father Versau has just written to convey his outrage to me. Although I presented the affair to him in the most innocuous terms, he has taken the bit between his teeth. He writes that the pasha has no right to intervene as he did and even less to oppose the journey of His Grace Murad and Sieur Poncet to France. The original mission traveled to Abyssinia by the king's wish, and by that same wish the negus's answer is to be conveyed to Louis XIV."

The consul twiddled nervously with a curl that fell onto his neck.

"Therefore," said the Jesuit, as though pronouncing sentence, "Father Versau has asked me to provide him with every detail of this business so that he may write a memorandum of protest to Monsieur de Ferriol, who is, I believe—"

"Yes, yes . . . the French ambassador to the Ottoman court."

Monsieur de Ferriol, as the man to whom all the consulates in the Levant reported, was Monsieur de Maillet's immediate superior.

"And what would be the point of this memorandum?" the consul asked.

"It would allow the ambassador, over whom Father Versau holds great sway, I believe, to apprise the sultan of this business. In a case such as this, when one of the pashas oversteps his authority, the Grand Signor designates a qadi to travel to the place in question, make an investigation, and determine the appropriate sanctions. The Turkish governors are not allowed to act like satraps. When they abuse their power, they are punished accordingly."

Monsieur de Maillet, who could foresee the future as well as anyone, knew what enormous storm clouds these words portended, and at no great distance.

"No, no, no," he said. "Father Versau must not go to any trouble—"

"What? And let the Turks trample underfoot the agreements that have bound us together for more than a century? If we allow this, the concessions will mean nothing at all and Christians in this country will suffer the bloodiest forms of persecution."

"You are right, Father, but this concerns a local matter, and the solution to it must be found right here. Let us not bring Constantinople into this."

"Alas, it is done already," said Father Plantain haughtily. "And I say all the better, as the pasha seems to understand nothing but force."

"You do not know him very well."

"And I would want it no other way."

"Of course, he is a Turk, and a soldier to boot. He is somewhat violent. He gets carried away. But he is willing to listen to reason."

"Good. Then he will listen to reason from the sultan."

"Listen," said Monsieur de Maillet, rising to his feet, "let me try to reach an agreement with him. Do not write immediately to Father Versau. I will lodge a protest with the pasha personally."

"Then we will call on him together."

"Together!"

"Yes, because it is I who in some sense represent the aggrieved party. The mission was entrusted to our order, and this Turk is preventing us from carrying it out."

"But you know that he is a strong Muslim. He will not look on us with the same complaisance if I am alone or in your company."

"Then let us deal directly with the sultan. He at least does not look on us unfavorably. My letter is ready in any case. All that is still missing is the details, which you can supply me. I will send it tomorrow."

Monsieur de Maillet was perspiring freely. He could see no way out of the dilemma, and, like a man faced with two forms of torture, he chose the one he imagined to be the least painful.

"So be it, then. Let us go see the pasha."

"In that case, we must go immediately, as the packet to Constantinople cannot wait."

The consul agreed to this last requirement and sent word announcing his visit to the Citadel. The guard came back within a half hour saying that an audience could be granted if it occurred without delay. Accordingly, Monsieur de Maillet and Father Plantain, with Monsieur Macé as interpreter, set off in the consul's carriage. The Jesuit was at a high pitch of excitement, though he avoided showing it. The consul looked out the window, biting on his sleeve.

From the moment the delegation entered his presence, Mehmet Bey sensed that some serious business was afoot. He cut short the ceremonial greetings and asked the consul to explain the reason for his visit.

"The matter is the following," said Monsieur de Maillet, greatly embarrassed, in a voice he intended to be both firm and conciliatory but that was rather hesitant and false. "I have come before Your Greatness to lodge a protest."

Mehmet Bey made no response. He looked at the Jesuit, then at the consul, sensing that there were to be awkward consequences to his alliance with the diplomat, which he had already begun to regret. Monsieur Macé translated. The consul continued:

"According to treaties signed by both our nations, all Christians live here under the protection of the king of France."

The pasha closed and opened his eyes slowly, like a panther.

"You cannot therefore intrude on the residence of a Christian without prior consent from the French consul, nor can you restrict the movements of a person who, being so entitled, might wish to journey to the side of the king of France, his lawful protector."

So saying, Monsieur de Maillet shut his eyes, as though not to see the fuse he had just lit burn its way to the powder.

"To whom are you referring?" the pasha asked angrily at last.

"To that Armenian who arrived from Abyssinia with a Frankish doctor from the colony."

"And what do they have to do with this man here?" the pasha asked, motioning toward Father Plantain.

The consul was dripping with sweat. He even thought he might be on the point of fainting. Standing in the middle of the big room, he felt the walls spinning dangerously around him.

"Nothing," he said. "Father Plantain must leave soon for Constantinople. He will give an account of this audience to our ambassador if the results are unfavorable."

Mehmet Bey set his hands down on the cushions beside him as though to make his stance firmer.

"I do not understand your Frankish ways. What have you come to learn that you do not know already? You protest? But about what? I took those letters only because you asked me to, and I turned them over to you. As to the Armenian, he is free. Take him wherever you like. He is a Christian and his fate is no concern of mine. But I have a warning for you: if you have tales to tell in Constantinople, I may add a word or two of my own. I find that the Frankish ecclesiastics are present here in great numbers and highly active given that the city offers so few Catholics to minister to. We know they spend their time hatching plots, and the sultan will surely be interested to hear some of them in detail. Has my explanation proved satisfactory?"

"Your Greatness has entirely convinced us," said Monsieur de Maillet, who, without taking the risk of leaning forward, inclined his head as politely as he could.

They withdrew.

On their return, the carriage was filled with a heavy silence, contrasting with the noise and animation of the streets. The consul had hoped against hope that the pasha, standing by their complicity, would act out their little comedy to the end and take all the blame on himself. It was a risky strategy, and it had failed. Father Plantain, for his part, had just seen the results of his investigations confirmed: it was the diplomat who had cooked up the whole thing. The priest made every effort to continue looking furious, but inside he was bubbling over with delight, as there was little that Monsieur de Maillet could now refuse him. It was true that he had not achieved his victory without the pasha's firing a warning shot across his own bow, but this did not worry him. When they reached the consulate, Monsieur de Maillet closed the door of his office behind them, sat down, and removed his periwig without bothering to ask the priest's leave.

"I grant that I owe you an explanation. The truth is, it is not the pasha who stands opposed to Sieur Murad's voyage but our own minister, Monsieur de Pontchartrain. I have formal proof of it here."

He struck the top of his desk with his forefinger.

"Reasons of politics, I imagine?" the Jesuit said.

"No, no, no!" the consul said in the high-pitched voice of the teacher who is constantly having to correct the same fault in his pupil. "This is not a question of politics but of common sense, Father, even of seemliness. Have you taken a good look at this Murad? He carries himself like the lowliest of porters, insults the modesty of ladies, gets drunk at table, wipes his hands on the drapes . . . Tell me honestly, can you for a moment imagine him at Versailles? Can you see him before the king?"

He pointed at the portrait above them.

"The king of the most refined court on earth. No, one must be reasonable, and the minister's instructions could not have been clearer: take stock of who you are dealing with and judge whether the thing is possible. Well, I will tell you: it is not."

"So it is a question of the man concerned. You are not against it in principle?"

"No."

"Then Poncet and I will go to Versailles."

The consul thought for a moment, examining Father Plantain. It displeased him that the Jesuits were once more taking part in this business. They could influence the king in such a way as to compromise his own initiative. But this was the lesser of two evils. If the Jesuit was allowed to inflame opinions in Constantinople, a terrible scandal would ensue. There was also the chance that the consul could get his own enterprise under way before the Jesuit and Poncet ever returned from France.

"The idea is an excellent one," said Monsieur de Maillet finally. "Fléhaut, my chancellor, will accompany you."

"And you will use your influence with the pasha to ensure that the three Abyssinians may embark with us?"

"I promise to do so."

"Then let us set all this down immediately in writing, if you please, so that Versailles may know to expect us. The same courier who leaves tomorrow for Constantinople can carry the dispatch as far as Alexandria. It will reach Marseilles on the royal galley by the thirtieth and be in Paris by the start of next month."

"Certainly. But at the same time you must write to Father Versau telling him to do nothing on his end, because everything has been settled from here."

"I will do so within the hour, Excellency."

This resembled a treaty. At least it was diplomacy. The consul had the feeling that he was at last returning to his calling, after the hours of haggling that had carried such a strong odor of trade. Despite his defeat, he was breathing easily once more.

10

It is not surprising that men should look to the sky as a guide to their destinies. The movements of the heavenly bodies have a suddenness and regularity that make them closely resemble the course of human events. Once the consul had been found out, everything changed, as at the moment during the night when Pegasus sinks on one side while Orion, followed by the Pleiades and all the rest, rises on the other.

Jean-Baptiste instantly recovered from the illness he didn't have. He plunged into preparations for the journey, whose departure was set for four days away. All the necessary arrangements were quickly made: Murad would stay on alone at the Venetians' house, and the consul would continue to provide for his incidental expenses until the envoys returned. Then Murad would be advised to return to Ethiopia, possibly bearing an answer from the king of France.

A tally was made of the presents going to Versailles. When they left Gondar, the travelers had felt rich and heavily laden. The expenses of the trip, however, along with the rapacity of the Turkish customs and the deterioration of certain stuffs, had reduced this fortune considerably. Poncet and his partner, aside from the jewels the emperor had given them, each had a sack of gold dust. Jean-Baptiste, concerned with the success of the journey to France, was inclined to include his sack with the presents for the king, if the remainder proved insufficient. And Murad's load was a meager one. There were the three Abyssinians, of course. Poncet was not enthusiastic at the idea of bringing them, knowing all too well the vigilance of the Muslims. But the Jesuit was determined and there was no arguing that the other presents were pitiful and inadequate. They consisted mainly of four pounds of civet musk, an evil-smelling mixture they were advised to exchange for tobacco, which they did, though at a loss. There was also a sash made of silk and embroidered with gold thread. At Gondar, against a tunic of white muslin, it would have drawn universal admiration; in Cairo, and even more in Versailles, it would seem to European eyes no more than an ugly rag. And finally all the livestock, the mares and elephants, had died along the way. The only thing left was the crate containing the ears of the pachyderm. Poncet verified with Murad that these had been well packed, and Murad guaranteed it hand on heart. The knacker who had hauled away the elephant's carcass, knowing the use Murad intended for the animal's ears, had practically pickled them. They would emerge from their crate as soft and supple as if still attached to the living beast.

After a stormy private interview with the pasha, during which he had to offer embarrassing explanations and reiterate the most humiliating apologies, the consul informed Father Plantain that he had obtained the necessary authorization for the Abyssinians to embark for France. The only precaution was to make sure the muftis of Alexandria heard nothing of it. Fanatic as they were, they opposed the departure of any Africans for Christian lands.

The time came for farewells. Monsieur de Maillet put the best face on it and invited the travelers—Poncet, Father Plantain, and the chancellor Fléhaut—to dinner at the consulate. Jean-Baptiste appeared completely recovered. The consul took care to stay on good terms with him, since he might now cause problems for the consul in high places. It was a working dinner, and the women were not included. They joined the men only at coffee, served in the small music room Jean-Baptiste had discovered during the gala reception. Neither Monsieur de Maillet nor his wife had any inkling of the pleasure and confusion they were arousing in the hearts of the two lovers, whom they brought together in a room so small that they brushed against each other a dozen times with every appearance of doing so accidentally. At her father's urging, Mademoiselle de Maillet took her place at the spinet and played a few melodies. For plucked strings to produce their effect, hearts must be properly attuned, and those of most of the listeners in the room that night were not, except for the hearts of the two young people, who were so soon to be separated. Just as acid etches the surface of a copper plate in certain places and not others where it is coated with wax, so the notes of the spinet did not trouble the conversation between the Jesuit and Monsieur de Maillet, nor Monsieur Macé's obsequious attentiveness, nor Fléhaut's timid vanity, but it scored deeply the tender hearts of Alix and Jean-Baptiste, for whom a more invisible or delicious torture could not have been imagined.

They managed to contain their emotion well enough, but they emerged from it so hungry for each other that they were driven to commit a grave indiscretion.

Poncet had barely returned home when he saw Françoise arriving in great haste. She brought the message that Alix would wait for him in the garden, as on the last occasion, shortly after midnight. There was a moon, though, and they would be seen. The danger was much greater. When Jean-Baptiste objected, Françoise replied that they were well aware of the moon. Where did courage lie, Jean-Baptiste wondered—in deciding for both of them to cancel the plan in the name of safety, or in choosing the path of boldness and pleasure? Their love was strewn with so many obstacles already that reasonableness was bound to be interpreted as a mark of indifference or cooling. This was something Jean-Baptiste could not afford. He answered that he would be there.

At the appointed hour, he was already hiding in the square when he saw in the distance the forms of the two women hurrying toward him, far too brightly lit by the moon. As they arrived at the grille, Jean-Baptiste suddenly noticed another shadow that seemed to slip from one plane tree to another. Alix came up to her lover and embraced him. He held her against his chest, but cautioned her to be quiet. He kept his eyes on the dark place where he had seen the moving form disappear. He saw it again gliding between two trees toward the garden.

"You have been followed," Jean-Baptiste whispered to Alix.

These words brought terror to her heart. Françoise, waiting by the gate, had also seen the shadow, and she approached the couple. She heard Jean-Baptiste's warning.

Perhaps in response to a vague premonition, Poncet had put a dagger in his belt when he went out. He now grasped its hilt and quickly formed a plan, which he passed on to the two women.

"I will confront your pursuer and unmask him. Both of you hurry back to the consulate, but be careful to stay hidden and not run. Do you have the key to the back door?"

"Yes," said Françoise.

"Then make a detour around to the back, and, most important, once you are home, pretend to be sound asleep. Things might—"

"Go!" said Françoise. "Don't worry about the rest."

Jean-Baptiste kissed Alix quickly, not neglecting to concentrate his full attention on the taste, the softness, the look in her eyes, so that he could fix them in his deepest memory. After tomorrow it would be the only thing to sustain him for many long months. Then he tore himself away from her and ran to the side of the garden where the shadow was darkest. He worked his way around the grille and emerged through a wooden gate. Slowly he eased his way to the edge of the broad street and hid behind the trunk of a plane tree. He could clearly see the silvery figure of the two women scurrying down the small street that bordered the consulate. As the shadow of their pursuer crossed the street and disappeared once again behind a tree, Poncet had just time to see that it was a man, dressed in the Frankish fashion, of medium height, and apparently unarmed. In order to catch him, he realized, he would have to come out of hiding. The best would be to approach him from behind, for the man was probably looking toward the two fleeing women. Poncet quickly covered the ground between himself and two more trees. He was now behind the same tree where the man had been hiding just before he crossed the road. Jean-Baptiste should therefore be exactly across from the man and arriving in the opposite direction from where he was looking.

Poncet waited a moment, then sprang across the street, grabbed the figure as it moved through the darkness, immobilized the man, and stuck his dagger to his throat. There was no fighting to speak of. Coming into contact with each other in the dark, the two had fallen to the ground and rolled, with Jean-Baptiste easily gaining the upper hand. His adversary was neither strong nor skilled at fighting, and he allowed himself to be dragged into the light, the dagger still at his neck.

"Help! Help! Guards, guards! I am being attacked!"

The man Poncet held at his mercy started to shriek.

"Macé!" said Jean-Baptiste.

The other shouted all the louder. The consulate was not far away, and clinking sounds could be heard from the direction of the entrance, presumably the guard taking up their arms. Lights appeared in the windows, and three men came out onto the street. Macé was still shouting, and Poncet knew that if the first shrieks had been prompted by fear, these were intended to attract his rescuers and cause his assailant's capture. As he continued to shout, Macé looked at Jean-Baptiste and, despite his precarious position and the knife at his throat, smiled at him with sarcasm and contempt.

Do you really think, he seemed to be saying, that it is you who are holding me?

The guards were approaching on the run. Jean-Baptiste let go of his prisoner and took to his heels. The three sentries let out exclamations of surprise when they discovered Macé sitting on the ground rubbing his throat. He ordered them not to pursue his assailant.

The rest of the night passed in customary quiet. There were three people, however, who did not sleep. Jean-Baptiste lay awake wondering whether Alix had made it back in time, not knowing that she had returned without incident and gone to bed immediately. No one had even thought to check if she was in her room. She, for her part, had heard the first sounds of the brawl and a man's scream, and was desperately afraid for Jean-Baptiste. And finally there was Monsieur Macé, lying fully dressed on his narrow iron bed, wondering what course to take the following day. The consul would know he had been attacked, and he would have to say who had done it. The idea of denouncing Poncet was particularly sweet to him. If he had been watching Alix and her maidservant at all, it was, given his earlier observations, in order to trip up Poncet. But how could he explain the attempt on his life? Why would Poncet have attacked him? He would simply have to talk about the lovers' assignation. That was the crux in any case, and the consul would not feel personally concerned until he understood that his daughter had been hurrying toward dishonor. But how could Macé make such a serious accusation stick when he had no proof? Poncet was sly enough to turn the whole thing around and accuse him, Macé, and possibly even find a way to compromise him. There was no time to wait and surprise the lovers on another occasion, since Poncet was leaving for Versailles the next day. Finally, toward five o'clock in the morning, Macé determined on a course of action and fell asleep relieved.

Jean-Baptiste, who had hardly slept either, rose at dawn and went over his luggage one more time, particularly the contents of the medicine chest he always brought on his travels. Then he went to call on the Jesuit. Father Plantain was just finishing his mass, and Jean-Baptiste paced in front of the oratory until it was over. The two then went to the consulate to say their farewells, for Poncet wanted as much as anything to arrive before being called there by the consul and to avoid going alone.

Monsieur de Maillet received them in his office after a half hour, in his dressing gown and wigless. With a tight-lipped smile, he wished them good luck in their mission and prayed the Jesuit to convey his greetings to the comte de Pontchartrain, should he have the honor of meeting him. He asked them to take good care of the chancellor Fléhaut, who had little experience of travel. Finally, he asked Father Plantain if he might have a word alone with Sieur Poncet.

The consul rose and motioned the apothecary to follow him to the other end of the long room. The low morning sun sent shafts of dust-filled light angling through the darkness and enveloped the two men in pallid veils, against the amaranthine background of the wall hangings.

"I am told that you attacked my secretary during the night!" said the consul in a near whisper.

"He was following me. I did not know who he might be."

"He followed you in order to expose you. Apparently you were robbing a young lady of her honor."

"Is it his duty to protect the virtue of the colony?"

"It is not yours to compromise it."

The consul had answered in quite loud tones. He looked toward the Jesuit, who had not moved and who, ten paces away, continued to look lovingly at his hands.

"Believe me, if any family should bring a complaint before me, even while you are away, I will impose sanctions and send word to France to have them executed."

Good, thought Jean-Baptiste, he knows nothing. He bowed respectfully.

"I have also been told," went on the consul, now slightly embarrassed, "that you have lost all sense of proportion in this domain to the extent of going so far as . . . as to seek an interview, dealings with . . . my own daughter."

"Oh, sir, with your daughter it is an entirely different matter."

"And what matter might that be, pray tell?"

Jean-Baptiste was decidedly driven at each departure to perform a feat of boldness and insolence toward the consul, which he dedicated to his beloved. Both times it was done unpremeditatedly, on a sudden dare or gamble: the first time, before leaving Cairo for Ethiopia, he had arranged for her to take care of his house, and this time, he was almost horrified to hear himself say in the same whispered voice in which the conversation had been held:

"Well, with her it is quite simply love."

The consul stiffened as though stabbed in the back by an assassin's dagger.

"I love her," Jean-Baptiste continued without lowering his eyes, "and I am foolish enough to believe that she too—"

"Be quiet! And drop these ideas immediately," said the consul sternly.

"These are not ideas—"

"Enough, I say! I have long known that you harbored such designs but hoped you would not persist in nurturing these absurd dreams."

"I nurture them and they nurture me."

"Well then, dream on. But do not take it any farther. I have other plans for my daughter."

"Before you put them to her, you should know that I intend to ask you for her hand."

Monsieur de Maillet laughed loudly and spasmodically two or three times, the sound echoing around the large room, then resumed the whispering tone of their conversation.

"In truth, it is a declaration very much as one might expect—spoken before an open window, ten minutes before departing on a voyage, by a lowly apothecary."

He held a fixed smile on his face, the look of bemused contempt one might cast on the contortions of a clown.

"This is not a declaration," said Jean-Baptiste firmly, "it is a warning. I will return here with the king's favor and a noble rank to measure yours. Then, and then only, will I make a formal declaration. But there is to be no question between now and then of other commitments being made for her."

Speaking these words gave Jean-Baptiste relief and pleasure, as insolence and vengefulness always do. At the same time, he knew himself guilty of a terrible misstep. It was unpardonable to reveal himself to an adversary he had not yet beaten, to show himself to the other in all the ease of victory while his opponent still had the time to deal him a telling blow. As a man gains experience and maturity, he is able to recognize such blunders immediately. And as he pays for his clearsightedness with a nostalgia for the time when he might still commit them, the impulse to punish such transgressions harshly is all the stronger.

"I will pay due attention, you can be sure, to this warning," said Monsieur de Maillet with an evil smile. Then he beckoned Jean-Baptiste to join the Jesuit.

~

They left that afternoon, all three travelers riding in a four-horse carriage rented for the occasion by the consulate. Behind them, in a calèche whose blue top had been lowered completely to hide them, rode the three Abyssinians, who sat shoulder to shoulder on the seat behind an old Arab coachman. The procession assembled in front of Murad's house, where the packages were loaded on. The Armenian said a tearful goodbye to Poncet, though he was in fact quite happy not to be making the dangerous journey himself, as he had grown used to his sinecure in Cairo and was delighted to be extending his stay.

Maître Juremi and Jean-Baptiste parted as usual with no other show of emotion than a brotherly embrace. This time, Jean-Baptiste was certain that his Protestant friend would not stir from Cairo. It was far less dangerous for him to go exploring Abyssinia than to prowl around Versailles as a political emigrant in the vicinity of the king and the Jesuits. Maître Juremi promised to keep an eye on Murad and to send any news he could of Alix; and as he was on the point of climbing into the carriage, Jean-Baptiste took his friend aside. Whether one likes it or not, a journey delivers one into the hands of an uncertain fate. He would never forgive himself if, wanting to behave too well, he had kept two people apart.

"Be gentle with Françoise. I think she loves you."

Neither was in the habit of making this sort of confidence. The large man looked at Jean-Baptiste awkwardly, lowered his eyes, and would have had the greatest trouble hiding his confusion had they not again been swept up in the bustle of departure.

"Poncet, what is keeping you? We are late," said the Jesuit.

Maître Juremi ran from one side to the other to make sure the carriage doors were properly shut, then watched the delegation draw away.

The carriages passed in front of the consulate, where the only person to appear was Madame Fléhaut, a thin figure in a gray woolen dress who waved to her husband, then clapped her hands to her mouth to stifle a cry. For a second time, Jean-Baptiste was going away in order to bring himself closer to the woman he loved, and he was still confident.

4

The King's Ear

I

They reached Alexandria without noteworthy incident, the Jesuit watching over the three Abyssinians and anticipating their every wish. Although they never said a word, the three did seem to wonder why this man had suddenly become their slave without their having correspondingly become his master. As to Chancellor Fléhaut, he never opened his mouth during their daily stages but suffered a thousand deaths whenever a meal was delayed past the usual time.

It was in Alexandria that they encountered their first mishap. The two carriages arrived at the port at nightfall and pulled up in front of an ancient lazaretto converted into a hotel by a Frenchman named Rigot. This was one of Monsieur de Maillet's picked men, who reported back to him in exchange for his protection. He greeted the travelers, served them dinner, and lodged them in two separate pavilions, attending them himself. Unfortunately, the coachman of the Abyssinians' chaise, an old Arab from Alexandria, decided he would rather spend the night at his own house. On the way home he met a cousin, by chance one of the most fanatical muftis in this working-class district, and mentioned the Abyssinians and their Frankish escort. His cousin carried off this interesting bit of news under his burnoose.

The following day the royal galley was to sail. The port was bustling to an extraordinary degree: a crowd of porters, their loads balanced on their heads, climbed up and down the gangplanks, and shouts echoed back and forth between the boat deck and the jetty, while the sound of voices could be heard from the dark lower deck reserved for the oarsmen. The sunlight beat down vertically, making everything shimmer: the whitewashed walls of the port buildings, the crates of fruit, even the coarse cloth of the sacks being hoisted into the air by wooden cranes. The carriage bearing Jean-Baptiste, Father Plantain, and Fléhaut slowly made its way through the press. Children grabbed the spokes of the carriage's large wooden wheels and held on through an entire revolution. Sometimes the carriage would stop and one of the children would end up with his head down, laughing. Behind them came the Abyssinians' cabriolet, its top glowing ultramarine in the sunlight. Because of the crowd, the second carriage fell some distance behind, and the Jesuit, glued to the rear window of the first carriage, uttered small noises of worry and consternation. The convoy was still some fifty yards from the ship when events unexpectedly took a violent turn. A fat Egyptian in an ample beige robe and lace skullcap made his way toward the cabriolet, which was barely moving, and abruptly folded back the blue top. There in the sunlight appeared the three Abyssinians, huddled together in terror. At the same moment, another man materialized on the step next to the coachman and ordered him to stop, which the old Arab did all the more readily as he recognized his cousin. The cousin then began to call out in the loud voice of a muezzin until all the Muslims in the port stopped their work to listen. He harangued the crowd vehemently, pointing to the three Abyssinians, who had by now wrapped themselves in their muslin veils. From time to time, the haranguer shook an accusatory fist in the direction of the first carriage.

"I am going back there," said Father Plantain, grabbing the door handle.

Jean-Baptiste stopped him.

"Step outside the carriage and you are a dead man," he said.

Then, speaking through the opening to the carriage driver, Poncet ordered him to get the horses moving at all costs. The coachman, a German from the Frankish colony, understood the situation quickly enough. He whipped up his team and, with the four horses prancing and rearing, forced a passage through the shouting crowd. The carriage soon came to a halt near the boat. Poncet ran on board, pushing the trembling Fléhaut ahead of him and firmly pulling the Jesuit behind, while the priest still looked for a way to rescue the Abyssinians. At the gangway, they fell upon the captain, who was waiting for them with the chief qadi. This old cleric was inclined to execute the pasha's orders, the travelers had discovered the previous evening, as long as enough hard coin was used to stiffen his sense of resolve. But the qadi had warned them that it was forbidden for African Christians to embark from Alexandria, even if the caliph's representative had authorized it. It would be a delicate matter to board the Abyssinians, as even the lowliest Muslim could effectively oppose it. Now that the irreparable had occurred, the dignitary raised his palms to the skies and said there was nothing he could do.

The cabriolet had disappeared from view. A seething mass of humanity had assaulted it. Father Plantain wrung his hands, his face contorted with pain.

Jean-Baptiste meanwhile lost no time in enlisting the help of two sailors to bring the baggage on board. As the last trunks were being hoisted in the air, the crowd was turning from the cabriolet and setting off with the three Abyssinians in its midst. Of those unfortunates nothing could be seen but an occasional flap of white cotton. The mufti who had led the attack then turned his vociferations on the other carriage, and a portion of the throng began to approach it. Poncet waved to the German that he was free to go. The driver cracked his whip, urging the horses into a gallop, and disappeared in a confusion of yells, burst watermelons, and spilled flour. Furious at his escape, the crowd began to point at the ship. Several bare-chested men leaped onto the dock lines and tried to climb hand over hand onto the boat.

The three Franks were ushered by the chief mate into a dark room in the poop and barricaded inside. Meanwhile the captain and the rest of the crew held off the crowd, as thousands of voices on the pier clamored for the robbers of Africans to be delivered to the Prophet's vengeance.

In the end the gathering dispersed and the galley was able to cast off. Once at sea, the captain came aft to release the travelers himself and present his respects.

"What happened to the Abyssinians?" asked Father Plantain, more desperate for news of them than if they had been his own children.

"By this time," said the captain politely, "they are probably all Turks. Muhammad has gained three followers. This may be highly unfortunate for them, but let us rejoice all the same, as the king of France very nearly lost three subjects."

The captain's name was de Hooch, and he had been born into a Flemish family in Dieppe. Smiling, he took hold of Poncet and the Jesuit familiarly by the arm and steered them, along with Fléhaut, to his cabin. But all this seaman's good humor was unable to dispel the persistent melancholy that settled over the three passengers for the duration of the crossing.

It was October. At the mouth of the harbor they met a spanking sea breeze, and the galley slaves were able to lay off their oars. Aside from the oarsmen, who were segregated from the rest of the boat, the crew consisted entirely of military men with very little to say for themselves. The moment the Egyptian coastline sank out of view, Fléhaut shut himself in his cabin and refused all nourishment, until he reached a state of near inanition. Poncet sent him medication mixed with his soup—actually, he added nothing to the food. The chancellor thanked the doctor for his good care, not suspecting that he owed his recovery more to the cook.

The Jesuit was no better company. He prayed for hours on end in the bow, and the cabin boy who swabbed the deck left the area around him untouched so as not to disturb him. Jean-Baptiste guessed that Plantain was asking God's forgiveness for the business with the Abyssinian slaves. It took him two days to realize that the priest was mostly terrified and was invoking God with an eye more to the future than the past. He only wanted not to drown.

The one man with whom Jean-Baptiste held free and pleasant conversation was Captain de Hooch, a seaman's son and a proud soldier who had fought valiantly during the Dutch wars. As second in command of a vessel, he had taken part in the great victory of Beachy Head, where he had fought under the comte de Tourville. De Hooch had a genuine affection for Louis XIV. He had seen him only once and from a great distance, but he knew many stories about him—stories of the king's childhood during the Fronde, which had touched hearts all over France, stories of his glory, his battles, his marriage, and his alliances. There were also stories of his amorous escapades and portraits of his mistresses and his bastard offspring. In the five years he had been traveling in the East, de Hooch had missed many of the more recent episodes. In fact, he was most expansive on the early days of Louis's reign, which had passed into legend, and on the one war he had seen firsthand. If Poncet had lived the last few years in Europe, he would have realized that de Hooch knew no more about the king than was common knowledge to every Frenchman. But there, with the green-and-purple swell surrounding them and the light piercing through the clouds obliquely, the life of Louis XIV as told by the seaman took on the aspect of a Greek epic. Thanks to the thousand intimate or glorious events in the king's life that the captain recounted in detail, Jean-Baptiste had the feeling he was entering into this demigod's intimacy, as a shepherd in Ovid's poem imagines during his siesta that he is speaking on familiar terms with Zeus. Whereas Jean-Baptiste's compatriots had grown fascinated with the Sun King little by little over time, he was immersed in the royal lore all at once, like those adults who are baptized in front of their own children. In short, he was becoming a Frenchman once again.

The ship put into Agrigento for five days. One night the captain, Father Plantain, and Poncet set out into the hills to have supper at an inn. It was warm enough to sit on the terrace looking down over the port, but the trellis was continually shaken by sharp gusts of autumn wind. When they returned to their ship, they discovered that the tobacco intended for the king had been stolen. Fléhaut, who slept in the cabin next to the storeroom, had heard nothing—unless it was that his wife had advised him never to point the finger at anyone. The captain questioned the men on watch, who agreed that they had seen children sliding along the dock lines. Punishment was meted out here and there, but King Louis XIV's tobacco was nonetheless smoked, in all likelihood, somewhere in the green-and-gray mountains ringing the port.

They left one morning at five. This time the winds were against them, and the ship crashed against the waves, which spewed up yellow foam. As it was raining, the sails could not be raised, and the oarsmen had to put their backs into it hour after hour. Poncet hardly knew which was better: to ask to see the galley slaves so that at least he would have an accurate picture of their plight—horrible, certainly, but bearable all the same—or simply to go on imagining them, their straining bodies chained to the benches two decks below, coloring his every moment of rest with guilt. The galley slaves' torture ended, for a time at least, after two short passages that brought them to the port of Marseilles. From the forecastle Jean-Baptiste watched impatiently as the quays of the old port drew near. Once the ship's lines were safely moored, he said farewell to the captain and jumped lightly ashore.

He might have been lulled during the crossing into believing that the Jesuits would exercise only slight control over him—Father Plantain was a discreet man and in any case preoccupied by his fear of the sea. But once in the port of Marseilles, there was no further doubt possible: five black-robed gentlemen, standing before three carriages of the same color, awaited them on the quay. Only Fléhaut, carried out of his cabin on a stretcher haggard from anorexia and sleeplessness, could plausibly have justified such a funeral cortège. But Father Plantain, once more full of life the moment he set foot on land, accepted the congratulations of his colleagues and settled into one of the carriages. Poncet, who had dressed in his red velvet suit and felt happy and free, was obliged to shut himself in one of the hearses with the others, surrounded by the ash-and-sackcloth faces of his new guardian angels. They proceeded in the direction of the Pharos, where the Jesuits had a residence. Built next to a flat-fronted church on the model of the famous Il Gesù in Rome, it consisted of a gigantic structure of white stone, capped by a flat Roman-tiled roof. Jean-Baptiste was shown into a narrow cell on the third floor, whose window opened onto all Provence: on one side were the houses leading into Marseilles, while on the other was a beautiful countryside of plowed fields and cypress rows, interspersed with woods of pine and chestnut. In the distance, at the farthest horizon, a sinuous white line, the snowy crest of the first tier of Alps, separated the brown, quiet earth from the cloud-tossed and rainswept sky. This time it was Poncet who locked himself in his quarters, leaving the task of making conversation with the Jesuit fathers to the others.

Two days later the travelers set out again in another black carriage, this one poorly sprung and driven by a coachman who, no doubt hideously underpaid, inflicted on his passengers the disgruntlement he lacked the courage to express to his masters. The wretch seemed to make a point of taking every pothole at full speed, and the travelers found themselves more than once thrown into one another's lap. Bruised and unhappy at having seen nothing along the way because they were too busy holding on to whatever they could, the three emissaries arrived in the dark of night at the Château de Simiane, where the Jesuit fathers had arranged for them to stay.

The marquis de Simiane, a large, charming gentleman who spoke in the colorful accents of Provence, had not been expecting them for another two days. Greatly embarrassed by the misunderstanding, he greeted them in his hunting clothes with disarming simplicity and introduced his wife and two sons, who looked astonishingly like their mother: long pointed nose, black hair, and oval face. It was a tender sight to see this worn and afflicted matron supported by these two sturdy young men, seemingly intent on restoring to her by their constant attentions the gift of youth and beauty she had bestowed on them. They dined that night on game, served on blue-and-yellow Moustiers porcelain.

"Look," said their host gaily, "it's so you'll feel more at home!"

And he showed them at the bottom of the heavy, round, high-glazed dishes a design on a Turkish theme. There were Moors hunting ostriches, reading the Koran by a fountain, and riding horseback in a long file.

"You are fortunate," said Father Plantain with no apparent trace of humor, "to find them nowhere hereabouts but at the bottom of your plate."

The next day, Poncet asked the marquis if he might join him hunting. His host's sons accompanied them to make four. The forest was swathed in warm mist, and the golden leaves were dripping. The thick humus, covered at that season with chestnut burrs, muffled their horses' footfalls. An icy wind from the Alps pricked their nostrils and carried them the scent of pine forests and juniper scrublands.

They returned after nightfall, ashamed to have left Madame de Simiane alone till past dinner with two such stiff guests as Fléhaut and Father Plantain. But they were happy with their hunting, exhausted, and joined in friendship as people are who have tasted great pleasures in each other's company and not traded three words.

The hunters changed and had a light supper, the others having already gone to bed. Poncet, dreading the thought of taking to the road again the next day in the same black cage and with the same crows as before, asked Monsieur de Simiane whether he might sell him a horse and the saddle to go with it. That way, he could travel with the carriage but in the open air.

"I understand entirely!" said the marquis. "You have just returned to France. You want to drink it in, to walk in the wind. I myself have never been able to live indoors, and that is why you will not find me at court. You need a horse, my dear friend, and you shall have one tomorrow. Keep your gold. On your return, if God wills it, you will bring this horse back to me, or another, or none at all. You are always welcome here."

The four of them then sat down in large armchairs around the fireplace, and Monsieur de Simiane asked Jean-Baptiste to tell them something about Abyssinia. Poncet elected to describe how the Abyssinians hunted for elephant.

His story was well received, and Monsieur de Simiane entreated him to tell another. In the end, the account of his journey to Abyssinia kept them awake for a good part of the night, and if he had not insisted on going to bed, the others would have listened on until dawn.

The physician saw the success of his stories as a favorable omen. It was the first time he had narrated his travels, and he was heartened at the interest they had elicited. If the king is of a similar mind, I will have no trouble captivating him, he thought.

The next morning Jean-Baptiste left the Château de Simiane riding a spirited chestnut. On the road to Valence, he kept pace with the carriage at a slow trot, now perfectly happy to see its occupants violently jolted. The sky was the varnished blue and gray of a Moustiers plate. Except, thought Jean-Baptiste, that there is not a Turk in sight.

2

After her last nocturnal meeting with Jean-Baptiste, Alix was afraid on his behalf, and Françoise did her best to reassure her the following morning. During the afternoon, the young woman learned through the domestic grapevine that "poor Monsieur Macé," as her mother called him, had been the victim of a nighttime attack. She understood the whole thing and was furious. But she did not direct her anger at "poor Monsieur Macé," for whom she could not have felt more contempt. How destitute of company she had been in former times to allow herself to show any interest at all in such a man! Now that she could judge him, as she believed, more clear-sightedly, but in fact now that she was doing him the crushing injustice of comparing him to Jean-Baptiste, she saw all too plainly his obsequiousness, his lack of spine, and his innate abjectness, which she could not really hold against him. The person who received the full and sudden brunt of her anger was her father. She knew for a certainty that Monsieur Macé had been following orders and spying on her for the consul.

As Alix was not a moderate person, a fact she was only just beginning to realize, she heaped on her father the full complement of all her other ill humors as well. She privately put the blame on him for her new separation from Jean-Baptiste. The first time, her lover had contracted to travel to Abyssinia before she had come to know him. That was no one's fault. But this time, Jean-Baptiste had left because of her father. It was his intransigence, his fixed ideas, and his indifference to the lives of others—his daughter's in particular—that had put difficulties in the way of her marriage. She also reproached the consul for spoiling her last moments with Jean-Baptiste by having her followed. Again and again she pictured the humiliating moment when she and Françoise, their hearts racing, had set off tottering in their narrow pumps to escape the wretched spy. It was a hunting scene. Yes, her father treated her like a game animal to be tracked and pursued. And this reflected the actual balance of power: she and Jean-Baptiste were like rabbits in a cornfield, having to hide, flee, and outwit the dogs on their trail.

Starting from this scene, which had cracked her heart open like a nut, Alix reviewed her whole childhood and what had passed for her education. It had been neither more nor less than what was generally provided for girls at that time. As a child she had been placed in the unassuming hands of a governess whose main concern was to see that she held still on the rare occasions during the week when she was brought into her mother's presence. Then Alix had gone to convent school. The one in which she grew up did not, like some others, open onto the world at large through the brilliance and originality of its boarders. Instead, she had been stuck in a hole in the backcountry. The only hope held out to these secluded children was to pass as soon as possible into another relation of dependency, in the household of a husband they had not chosen. And as if to prepare them for this fate, which society dictated from start to finish, they were taught to wear ceremonial dresses stuffed with horsehair cushions and hooped with iron. In the consular residence in Cairo, Alix had no society around her to make her consider these customs as normal. She only followed them out of habit—but the habit broke, along with her high heels, on the night when she became the quarry in a hunt. She was made keenly aware of what was natural, as well as of the web of contrivance in which she was enmeshed.

During her lover's first voyage she had prevaricated to her father, carefully hiding her feelings from him. She had been sorry to do so, and the respect she had felt toward her parents had in no way been diminished. This time it was different. Convinced that her father had treated her shabbily, she felt a strong inclination to rebel. No concept of fair game would mar her tactics. She would defend herself with whatever paltry weapons she had and would even try to acquire new and more powerful ones.

She waited for the summons from her father.

He called her into his office two days after Poncet's departure. The consul had no natural suspicion toward his daughter for, being too egotistical to take much interest in those around him, he attributed no hostility to them or in fact any capacity for independent thought. Monsieur de Maillet had not directed his secretary to stalk the young woman. But Monsieur Macé's insinuations and Poncet's insolent propositions had prompted him to seek out his daughter and put her on her guard.

"Have you taken any notice," he said without a trace of animosity, "of that apothecary, Sieur Poncet?" The gentleness with which he invariably addressed his daughter convinced him he must love her.

"Certainly, Father. It was you who introduced us," said Alix evenly.

If he thinks to make the partridge take flight at the hunter's first step, she thought, he is wrong.

"He is gone, and I hope we will never see him again. But I would ask you to answer a question, as I would like to take certain measures in case he should ever try to return to these parts. Has he ever made improper advances to you?"

Alix smoothed a fold of her blue-and-black dress from her lap as though sweeping away a nuisance. In case he should ever try to return? she thought. My father will try to keep him from returning. . . . But if the king rewards him, Jean-Baptiste will overcome that too. . . .

"You are hesitating?" said the consul.

"I am thinking back. But really, Father, I can think of nothing of the kind. I have only seen the man a few times, and he has always conducted himself with the utmost propriety."

He doesn't believe me, she thought to herself. Deny, deny, deny.

"You are quite sure you never let slip an equivocal statement, something a crass individual might have taken as a cue to trespass on your modesty?"

"Me, Father?" she said, opening wide her blue eyes.

She knew herself well enough to know that her irises could expand to a rock pool, a lake, through whose limpid water the stones of her heart seemed to be palpitating.

If he doesn't know, she thought, he'll see nothing in my eyes but the purity of an innocent. If he does, he'll see a dagger.

Monsieur de Maillet stretched, walked up to Alix, and took her hand in his and patted it the way one might pat a small animal.

"Of course," he said. "My questions are too crude. But I try as best I can to protect you, and this individual said certain things of which I was afraid you might hear some echo."

"What things, Father?" she said, withdrawing her hand from his.

"Nothing. The words of a drunkard. The man is a scoundrel, as, alas, are most of the adventurers who fetch up in this colony. That is why I prevent you as much as possible from seeing anyone."

"Thank you, Father," said Alix, reassured that she had weathered the first assault and believing that the time had come for a counterattack. "Owing to you, my virtue has never been endangered in the least. Unfortunately . . ."

"Yes?"

". . . I am deeply bored here."

"I know," said Monsieur Macé.

He moved away, then abruptly spun on his heels and walked back to his daughter.

"I had not planned to announce the news yet, but so be it. I have made arrangements so that in a short time, yes, a very short time, you will no longer be bored."

"How, Father?"

"You will be getting married."

Lovers have no sense. For a moment she thought her father was going to tell her that Jean-Baptiste . . .

"This is troubling news to you, and I can understand," said the consul. "But consider that we are going about it none too early."

Alix curtsied docilely to show that she was at her father's orders.

"And might I know for whom you intend me?" asked Alix humbly.

"Someone you are to meet shortly. I will not say that he is traveling from France entirely for your sake, but it is almost true. The man is exceedingly wellborn, and our cousin Pontchartrain has personally spoken for him, a fact not to be sneezed at."

Alix curtsied again and asked no further questions. This seemed both to surprise and to relieve her father. He had not feared a refusal—his authority was too great for that. But there might have been alarm, and questions, and a show of emotion that, while not posing an obstacle, could have introduced complications. One always imagines a young girl's heart to be more complex than it is, he thought, but when one has brought a child up correctly, it is all very simple. Monsieur de Maillet looked fondly at Alix as the irreproachable product of order and family harmony.

"Father," she said, "I look forward to seeing the man you have spoken of, and have little doubt that I shall discover in him the virtues so strongly recommended to you."

Monsieur de Maillet smiled affectionately.

"Nonetheless," the young lady went on, "I don't imagine my marriage will take place tomorrow, and in the meantime I should like you to grant me a favor."

"Say on," said the consul.

"It is this: the climate of Cairo is stifling me. Look how pale I have become. I believe that even to attract the consideration of a fiancé—"

"What's that? You look absolutely radiant to me."

"Yes, because I have painted my face. And it is not every day that one learns of one's impending nuptials. Naturally my cheeks have color at this moment. But believe me, Father, I am wasting away."

"We will be in Cairo for several more years, and you will have to get used to it," said Monsieur de Maillet in peremptory tones. "If you marry the man we have settled on, it is possible that you will be following him to other parts. But I warn you, he is a diplomat destined for service in the Levant, and you may find yourself one day in even worse conditions. Can you imagine being shut up in a legation in Damascus or Baghdad? You have no idea what those cities are like! At least here you have the breeze from the Nile."

"Precisely, Father. That is exactly what I want. I am not pining for the social life of Cairo. I only need contact with nature, some fresh air. You have a country house a league from Giza. Allow me to spend a few days there with my mother and a few servants."

"That house is unhealthful," the consul retorted. "There are poisonous mosquitoes on the river and you would get fever."

"In the summer. But in the winter it is healthy. Your predecessor reportedly spent two months there every year."

In truth, said the consul to himself, the most important thing is that she raise no objection to the marriage. She deserves a reward on that account. Best not to foment rebellion where for the moment there is nothing but goodwill.

"I do not want your mother to leave Cairo. The consulate cannot spare her for long."

This was an odd but genuine tribute. While he had said "the consulate," he clearly was thinking of the consul.

"Then I will go with servants only," said Alix.

"Which servants? That laundress who is always at your side and about whom I hear bad reports?"

Monsieur Macé's bile has spilled over onto her as well, thought Alix.

"What has she ever done wrong, Father?" she said, using her large eyes once again, training them steadily on the consul's face.

"In any case," he said, looking away, "two women cannot stay there alone. You will need two guards from the consulate, and I will ask the aga for a few janissaries to put at the far end of the park."

"Oh! Then I have your permission!"

"For the sake of your complexion," he said gruffly. "And on condition that you return the moment I call for you, as the man I have spoken of will not be long."

Alix agreed to this condition and went off, happy to have conducted herself creditably in battle.

Monsieur de Maillet gave the orders as promised, then, as he too felt satisfied with the interview, spent the rest of the morning writing three letters to persons of his acquaintance, one of them being the minister Pontchartrain, whom he set on his guard against Poncet. He described the man for what he was: a drunkard, an inventor of stories that contained not a shred of truth, a man driven by ambition and a taste for debauchery. The consul harbored grave doubts about Poncet's stories of having traveled to Abyssinia, suggesting that the mythomaniac had probably never gone beyond Sennar. The arguments Monsieur de Maillet was able to marshal in support were fairly slender, but Providence so willed it that he received additional ones in the days to come.

As had also happened after the first mission's departure, the large, bearded friar known as Brother Pasquale, the Capuchin superior, came to call on the consul to vent his grievances. He had learned of Father Plantain's departure for Versailles with the Abyssinians and was protesting what he called "France's bias toward a particular order of ecclesiastics." Monsieur de Maillet replied amiably that he favored no one and was at Brother Pasquale's disposition to support the efforts of his order, to the extent that he was able, in any other matter.

"Your offer comes at a good time," said the Italian priest. "We are planning an expedition to Abyssinia soon."

"Another one!"

"For the moment, we are staying in Sennar, and no one has gone any farther," said the priest. With a sly smile he added, "Even your protégé."

"My protégé?"

"Yes. Signor Poncet!"

The consul showed the liveliest interest. He asked Brother Pasquale to repeat what he had said. The priest confirmed that according to the most trustworthy information of his brothers in Sennar, Poncet had traveled only some ten leagues beyond the border after fleeing from the town, that he had stayed in an Abyssinian village serving as a customs post but not been allowed to proceed any farther, that he had waited there several months, that he had even married a native woman according to the customs of the country, an easy thing to do, and that he had returned full of stories about an emperor he had never met.

Monsieur de Maillet, overjoyed at these words, asked the Capuchin why he had not come to tell him earlier. The other replied insolently that if it pleased the French to make themselves ridiculous by treating a former Armenian cook as an ambassador, he had no call to interfere. But he explained that he had sent a full account to Rome and that all the Capuchins knew the truth, even those in Paris.

"What you are telling me is of the highest importance," said the consul gravely. "Can you obtain the report by the fathers in Sennar? Is it in writing?"

"I have at the monastery a long letter from the superior at Sennar."

"I appeal to you to give me a copy of the letter. There is still time to stop the whole business."

The Capuchin said nothing but waited significantly. The consul, having swallowed the hook, started to work his way up the line.

"It is agreed and you have my word. I will do everything I can to help the mission you are planning."

"Word of honor?"

"Word of honor."

"Good. The letter will be in your hands tonight," said Brother Pasquale, who had what he had come for. "I will return in a few days to tell you of our plan and how you may help us."

So saying, the Italian left the consul as abruptly as he had arrived. But Monsieur de Maillet was starting to appreciate the man's rough frankness, in such marked contrast to the polite underhandedness of the Ignatians.

It took a brief week for a band of servants to prepare the house at Giza. They opened all the windows and brought fresh air into every recess. Next they fumigated all the rooms against fever. And finally they furnished it with new crockery and put fresh sheets on the beds, which they had brought down with them in two carts.

The day after the house was ready, Alix arrived with Françoise. Alix's mother had preferred to stay in Cairo, as expected. The three servants who accompanied them were entirely devoted to the two women—and there were many more who might have been chosen, since the entire household took sides against the consul, whose avarice and contempt for his inferiors made him disliked. As for the little garrison of Turks supplied by the aga of the janissaries, it stayed at a considerable distance from the house and was allowed to watch over the property only from outside.

Mademoiselle de Maillet arrived in a calèche at three o'clock in the afternoon, wearing a plain blue doublet and a black velvet dress and with her curls tied by a single ribbon. She had heard the house described but had never actually seen it. It appeared before her on a raised embankment that was surrounded on either side by water during the flood season. The building itself was a Moorish palace with wooden arcades in the form of pointed arcs, the windows protected by lattices of openwork cedar. Crowning the house was an octagonal tower with a roof in the shape of an Ottoman helmet. All that was missing was the Islamic crescent on top: such an emblem had once perched there, but when the ruling pasha offered the residence to the French consul some fifty years before, he had seen to it that the symbol was removed.

The structure was on a hillock overlooking the riverbank, raised out of reach of the Nile's regular floods. The alluvial fields that surrounded it on three sides were left untended by the consul, despite their evident fertility. A rich grassland had grown up there, leaving the house surrounded by what seemed a large area of unbroken lawn. The fourth side, which sloped down to the river, was planted with large trees; their close canopy prevented other plants from growing and created a carpet of dried leaves that ran through the shade down to the reeds along the river. The white sails of the feluccas plying the Nile seemed to keep their distance from the property, as though the prohibition against drawing too near were passed by word of mouth among the boatmen. A wooden pier, to which an old and useless boat was moored, advanced some twenty yards out into the water.

Alix made a tour of the house, stopping at the wooden terrace of the drawing room to breathe in deeply the sour breeze off the river. But she did not indulge herself in this pleasure for long.

"Come," she said to Françoise. "Let's not waste a second in starting our program."

3

November was cold. Jean-Baptiste, who warmed his hands as best he could on the withers of his horse, arrived at the post houses frozen. He arranged with his companions to gallop ahead at his own pace and meet them at the gates of each large city. Finally he was traveling with the sense of being free and independent. He went into the villages, talked to the peasants, listened to the old men idling in the squares. In Lyons he bought himself a postilion's cape and a broad felt hat with a red plume, and learned as well that the king of Spain had died.

After three more days of travel, carriage and horseman met up at Fontainebleau, arriving at the Jesuits' residence in the dead of night. Gusts of wind continually extinguished the carriage's copper lanterns. It started to rain, and the black trees lining the road on either side whipped to and fro in the wind. Jean-Baptiste laughed, opening his mouth to bite at the cold rain. He realized he had missed this weather during his years in tropical climes. The next day they reached Paris, passed the tax collector's booth at the southern gates, and descended toward the Bièvre, as around them black shadows hurried to reach shelter before the rain started again.

They were lodged in an outbuilding of the Louis-le-Grand school. Fléhaut, who had family in the nearby village of Auteuil, left them the first day.

"He is going to give his report to Pontchartrain," said Father Plantain spitefully as the diplomat drove off in a chaise.

The great news of the day was that Louis XIV had accepted the terms of the king of Spain's will. Having no children of his own, the Spanish monarch had willed his crown to Louis's grandson, the duc d'Anjou. Now that his scion was to occupy the throne in Madrid, the king of France would virtually rule both kingdoms, effectively becoming the most powerful man in Europe, hence the entire world. War was inevitable. The Jesuits discussed these great events with satisfaction—Father Plantain supposing that the greatest king in Christendom could afford less than ever to neglect his role as the protector of the Catholic missions, particularly in the Orient and perforce in Abyssinia. Nothing occurred but that Father Plantain connected it to what had become the great business of his life: to bring within the pale of the Holy Roman and Apostolic Church a country that he did not know and that asked nothing of him.

Jean-Baptiste had never been to Paris before. On the first night, he made his way down to the Seine and let his horse drink at the edge of the quay, among the rowboats and the wash houses. The next day he took a tour on foot. At first he stayed in the large open spaces where new construction was underway: he passed the Invalides, walked along the quays as far as the Pont Neuf, then made a wide arc on the northern boulevards as far as the Bastille. He noticed that the fashion in clothes had changed greatly since he had left the country. The French in Cairo were far behind in this respect, and his best suit of clothes looked sad compared to what people were wearing in the capital. The following day he went to the rue Saint-Jacques and bought himself a coat of green velvet with silver braid, a silk vest, black trousers, and stockings. In this garb, he felt the courage to enter the city proper, that is, to pass through the narrow streets of the central district where one could so easily overhear the insolent comments of other passers-by and shopkeepers. He looked well, carried a sword, and had lively eyes. No one murmured a word against him.

Jean-Baptiste was determined that he would find lodgings in town at his own expense. The Jesuits had brought him and were making arrangements for the royal audience—that was enough. He did not want to be in their debt beyond that. Yet he was not rich, and the prices in the capital were high.

My bag of gold dust, thought Jean-Baptiste, will find a better use buying me independence than going to form a present for the king. His Majesty might even consider it insulting to receive so small a sum.

He brought the gold to a money changer and found that, though it came from a great distance, it was worth no more on that account. The banker looked at him suspiciously and, after a long pause, gave him what seemed a remarkably light bag of écus. It's better than nothing, Jean-Baptiste thought, and more than enough to pay for good lodgings.

Setting out to find a room, he first strolled around the Ile de la Cité, then by the Hôtel de Ville, and he finally discovered what he was looking for near the Church of Saint Eustache. It was a tavern whose sign had caught his eye and that seemed perfectly adapted to his circumstances. Painted on an iron sheet was the figure of a large African in a loincloth carrying a spear. Jean-Baptiste entered the establishment, which was called Le

Beau Noir. The innkeeper was a tall, hollow-cheeked, gray-faced man who seemed to take better care of his clients, luckily, than of himself. The sound of laughter and animated voices came from the main room facing the street.

"I bought the store from a dyer," the man explained, smiling broadly. "He chose that unusual sign, and I decided to keep it."

Jean-Baptiste asked if there was a room free and what it might cost. The only one left was hardly more than a cubbyhole, and expensive at that, but it had its own fireplace, and the innkeeper assured Jean-Baptiste he would carry up as much wood as his guest cared to burn. The young man, who had been cold from dusk to dawn and whose nostalgia for the sensation was wearing thin, accepted the terms and paid for four days in advance. He returned to the Jesuits' residence to pick up his portmanteau and medicine chest and announced that he was moving out, asking only that they take care of his horse. Father Plantain tried in vain to keep him from going, but Poncet promised to pass by the school each morning to gather any news and be ready in case they were called for their audience with the king. He returned to Le Beau Noir, ate a hearty dinner, and warmed his insides with a very creditable Burgundy wine. The innkeeper, curious, came up to make conversation. Jean-Baptiste told him that he had come from Cairo and practiced the art of healing with medicinal plants.

"A doctor, then!" said the tavern-keeper, bowing respectfully.

"More or less," said Poncet, concerned not to provoke any licensed physicians.

"Oh! More, sir, unmistakably more. I know those ruffians from the School of Medicine. They assassinate us and rob us into the bargain. I am much more likely to believe in the secrets of plants, especially when they come from the East."

Jean-Baptiste took care to say nothing further or prevent the man from talking. As he was going upstairs, he heard the innkeeper spreading the news of his profession from table to table, as respectful glances were cast his way.

Let's hope this brings clients, he thought, because at the rate money goes in this city my whole sack of gold dust will soon have melted away. And who knows how long we will be staying here?

The Jesuits, in the meantime, had not sat on their hands. The great events in Spain had put the court in turmoil and taken the king's full attention. But the priests bided their time and took the opportunity to promote the Ethiopian cause among their own ranks. The Society of Jesus accounted for the spiritual directors of most of the prominent figures in France, starting with the king. Thus they were able to spread word of the myth-shrouded Abyssinian mission in a hundred important houses and announce the arrival in Paris of the hero of this journey of exploration. Several dinners were given for the faithful, but Poncet always refused to attend on the grounds that he was saving the first hearing of his story for the king himself. Father Plantain reproached him feebly for his behavior, but in reality the priest was highly honored to go alone to these prestigious houses, where he spoke before a rapt audience of rich and titled men, beautiful women, and, in brief, a whole dazzling society that his horse-trader ancestors would have been enormously proud to see him frequent. If there is one thing that priests are generally good at, it is making much of a mystery. From the bits and pieces that he knew about the voyage of Poncet and Father de Brèvedent, Father Plantain wove an edifying account, one that was even more fascinating for its gaps, and that ended on a triumphant note as it dealt with nothing less than the return to the true faith of an entire noble people. Poncet, remaining invisible, took on a mythical stature as the stories were told and retold within aristocratic circles.

While this was going on, Jean-Baptiste was playing cards with his fellow diners at Le Beau Noir, his feet wedged against the central fireplace. Or he went out when the sun shone for walks in the Tuileries gardens and came back to water the hibiscus seeds he had planted in a window box. The very day after moving in, he received his first visit from a patient. It was the son of a serving girl, whom the innkeeper, Monsieur Raoul, brought to his room personally. The child had a violent throat infection. Jean-Baptiste gave him some medication and took no payment. Two days later, the patient was on his feet, as would have happened had nature taken its course unaided, but the doctor was skillful enough to turn this to his credit. His reputation quickly spread, and he began to draw some profit from it.

Thus, during his first week in the capital, Jean-Baptiste developed two widely different reputations. He was hailed as an ambassador among the nobility who did not know him, and as a healer in the poor quarter of the city where he spent his days. In fact, he acquired even a third reputation, though he was unaware of it and it would have displeased him. Because of the delay in obtaining a royal audience, the letters written by Monsieur de Maillet and the Capuchins had caught up with the travelers and begun to undermine their credibility. The comte de Pontchartrain was warned against them in the strongest terms, and a number of clergymen whose links were to Rome rather than to the Jesuits began to whisper that the whole business of an embassy was a fiction and Poncet an impostor.

Father Plantain considered that this odious campaign should be defused, though it did not as yet amount to much. It would be impolitic to wait for their audience with the king, which might not occur for some time. His Majesty was preparing for his grandson's departure to Spain, and probably force-feeding him a few elementary notions of government. Father Plantain therefore summoned Poncet to his quarters at the school, and the physician appeared one morning between two visits to patients, his cheeks pink with the cold.

"Dear friend," said Father Plantain unctuously, "certain jealous parties—we know them well in our order and are accustomed to their hate-filled criticism—have had the gall to suggest that your voyage to Abyssinia was entirely invented. We must show them wrong, immediately and incontrovertibly. If you would have the kindness, now that we have arrived, to hand me the letter given to you by the negus, I will have it translated and authenticated immediately. We will then have it published by the gazettes, which for once will serve to spread the truth of our cause."

The bustle of Paris had distracted Jean-Baptiste to the point where, as he walked to his meeting on the rue Saint-Jacques watching the fast cabriolets trot past, the squadrons of gray musketeers, the calèches with smart ladies, he had entirely forgotten his mission with the Jesuits, especially the letter he was supposed to be carrying. In fact it was no more than a scrap of paper he had scribbled on himself, using a poker and a drop of candlewax for a seal.

"The negus's letter?" he said, his eyes a blank. Then he remembered. "Oh! Of course. Please forgive me, the cold has made my mind sluggish. Well, Father, it's impossible."

"And why is that?"

"I lost it."

Lightning might have struck the room and split the ceiling in two, and it would not have left Father Plantain more dumbfounded.

"You say that . . . so calmly! Lost. But do you realize what this means?"

Then, taking hold of himself, the black-robed man said in a loud voice: "Come, you must find it! It simply cannot be. Look everywhere. Go back to Marseilles if you have to, with your eyes glued to the ground."

"No," said Poncet, who wanted to close the lid on his little story, "it would do no good, I assure you. I lost it on the boat."

"Let us send a courier to Marseilles. The galley is very probably still there, or else we can send a frigate to intercept it."

Jean-Baptiste shook his head.

"It is useless, I tell you."

He pulled up a chair and sat down on it sideways, one elbow resting along the back, with the ease of a man holding forth at a tavern. This was the story he told.

"We had just rounded Sardinia. I remember very clearly that you were on the forecastle as usual, Father. You were praying, I think. No, you were reading your missal, that's right. The surface of the sea was streaked with the wakes of large fish, at least three feet long. It almost seemed as if they were following us. I went to the kitchens and got some crusts of bread to throw them to see if I could make them alter their course."

"And?" asked the Jesuit, growing morose.

"It worked! They altered their course! They drew a beeline for the bread, and—"

"The devil with your fish!" said Father Plantain. "What about the letter?"

"It fell from my pocket."

"Onto the deck?"

"No, into the water."

The clergyman put a hand on the oak table to steady himself.

"And would you believe it," said Poncet with animation, "I saw three of those monsters pounce on the paper all at once and tear it to shreds."

The Jesuit put his hand to his heart. He was hardly breathing.

"What has happened?" asked Jean-Baptiste. "Are you feeling ill?"

He sat the Jesuit down on his chair and rang for a servant to bring a glass of rum.

Father Plantain soon recovered from his fit, being of solid timber. But the priest who came to help Plantain signaled Poncet to leave, as the mere sight of him was causing his patient paroxysms of anger.

Jean-Baptiste left with a grim expression, but no sooner had he turned the corner at the Hôtel de Conti than he burst into laughter in the street.

Up to this point, Jean-Baptiste had recruited his patients from among the flotsam and jetsam that washed up at Le Beau Noir. Its few rooms were rented out to petty merchants and to foreigners traveling on unknown business, and the tavern was frequented by coachmen, soldiers, and workmen from the nearby Halles, whom Monsieur Raoul greeted familiarly. The night Jean-Baptiste came back from his meeting with Plantain, the innkeeper was waiting for him. He wanted to take him to the house of a mysterious patient, and his voice, when he spoke of him, was hushed with respect.

The man lived on the same street, almost across from the tavern. The high stone front of his house contrasted with the tipsy half-timbered construction of Le Beau Noir and the hovels on either side.

"A half century ago," said the innkeeper, "in the days before the king outlawed dueling, the house I am taking you to was the greatest center of fencing in all Paris."

"Ah! I should have brought my sword."

"These days, there is nothing to worry about," said Monsieur Raoul, halting to give Poncet a little more information before they reached the door. "The house was sold to a very honorable bourgeois, who was for a long time a magistrate in parliament. His wife died twenty years ago during an epidemic. They say it made him an atheist, but I don't believe it. What is certain is that he raised his two children very well. They are grown now and only come here rarely. His daughter is married to a foreigner and lives abroad; his son serves in a regiment in the East Indies. The man lives alone, but being of a cheerful disposition he quite likes to entertain at home as well as to go out. In the past six months, though, he has often been ill. The bouts are sometimes so intense that he howls with pain. We used to hear him even at the inn, until he changed his bedroom to the other side of the house so as not to alarm the passersby. The doctors have bled both him and his purse indecently. They are well on the way to murdering him and taking his fortune. You can be sure that they will proceed in the right order and ruin him first. He has only a maidservant to look after him. Luckily, she is a saintly woman and sees to his welfare. I spoke to him about you. Last night he had a terrible fit. This morning the maid came to say that he would like you to treat him."

Having said this, Monsieur Raoul walked up to the doorway and pulled on an iron chain. Far off, they could hear a bell ringing through empty hallways. A moment later, the maidservant appeared. Her face was all wrinkled, but her eyes sparkled with youth. She wore an apron tied around her waist and a simple batiste headdress.

"He's come to see your master, Françoise," said the innkeeper.

Jean-Baptiste felt a shock at the sound of her name, and the thought of Alix went through him like a dagger. He recovered in a moment. The servant led them down long, dark hallways lined with oak chests. Despite their emptiness, it was possible to imagine the halls once filled with family life and the shrieks of children. They climbed a creaky staircase and entered a bedroom hung with damson-patterned crimson velvet.

The man lay on a bed of linen sheets waiting for them. Tall, his face round, his hair short and gray, he forced a weak smile onto his face, which was contorted with pain.

Poncet asked the innkeeper and the maidservant to step outside. He examined the patient, who showed him where the pain was by pointing, so intense was his effort not to cry out. Jean-Baptiste questioned him at length, telling him to indicate yes or no with his head. Finally, when he had formed an idea of his illness, Jean-Baptiste left with the promise to return the following morning.

He spent the better part of the night preparing a potion, which he administered to his patient the next day. But the pain did not go away, and he worked again all afternoon and brought a new medication, which had no more effect than the first. The following night he directed his search in a different direction, sorry that Maître Juremi was not there to help confect the preparation. Finally, on the following morning, he brought the patient a third remedy, based on the gum of the cistus shrub. This produced a calming effect within less than an hour. The easing of the pain could be seen in the patient's face, which relaxed almost under their eyes. The relief brought sleep in its wake. That night, he called Jean-Baptiste back. When the young man arrived, he found his patient dressed and sitting up.

"Please take a seat," said the man amiably. "And allow me to introduce myself. My name, which is unlikely to be known to you, is Robert du Sangray."

4

Among the servants who accompanied Alix to Giza was Michel, a grizzled Copt from Luxor, who had been a groom and riding master at the consulate for more than twenty years under successive families of French diplomats. He showed Alix that brand of fearful admiration the Egyptians have for their master when that master is a woman and a charming one at that. At first he did not understand what she wanted. When she asked him for riding lessons, he assumed she wanted simply to sit sidesaddle on a horse and turn circles at the end of a longe. For this he chose a square of grass below the house large enough to form an outdoor riding ring. On the second day he prepared to repeat the exercise, but Alix informed him that she wished to progress more rapidly. With a snap of his whip, he brought the horse to a gentle trot. Preparing for the third session, the old groom was just starting to reattach the longe when Alix went up to him, faced him squarely, and with a firmness that was slightly frightening in so young a girl, explained herself to him in plain terms.

"Michel, we have not got much time. My father may call me back to Cairo any day. Meanwhile, I want to learn to ride. Is that clear? Let's forget the sidesaddle and the longe. Give me a man's saddle and a pair of spurs. I am wearing corduroy trousers that can stand up to anything. Teach me all the different paces, how to jump, and what I need to know to ride fast and go anywhere."

The old man was surprised, but he carried out her orders. He was worried, though, for you cannot learn to ride without falling. What if she fell and broke a bone through some fault of his? He didn't like the consul, but he was afraid of him. Alix swept away this last obstacle by saying that in the event of an accident she would take full responsibility and say that she had ridden the horse out all on her own.

Reassured, Michel entered into it with a will. Within a week, his fear had turned to pride. His young pupil had acquired excellent reflexes and the start of a good seat. Thanks to her natural grace and an unsuspected intrepidity, she controlled her horse with firm but supple authority.

Soon she was riding out on walks. Going alone was her only recourse, as they had brought only the one bridle and saddle. Besides, for all that he gave advice to riders, the old gentleman no longer rode himself because of rheumatism. As a precaution, the janissaries camping at the entrance to the property were alerted about Alix's rides. Each morning they saw a rider come out and cut across the fields, crossing the canals on the red earth dams built by the peasants. They thought it was a man, for the simple reason that Alix hid her hair under a wide-brimmed hat and wore a loose shirt that hid her figure.

The exercise from riding should have been enough to wear her out completely, yet the young lady did not stop there. At her request, Maître Juremi joined them by boat the day after their arrival. He drew up to the pier at nightfall and, unaided, hauled a long wooden chest up to the house. It gave a metallic clink each time it struck the ground. He took a number of buttoned foils from it, two leather chest protectors, and a pair of fencing masks.

That very night, Alix took her first fencing lesson on the wooden terrace looking out over the Nile. With Maître Juremi there was no need to draw a fine point. He understood what she wanted and treated her with the same sternness as a man.

Alix next asked him to teach Françoise as well. That way, if he was obliged to leave, the two women could continue their training together. Alix smiled inwardly at the confusion that reigned over this second lesson. Françoise exaggerated her beginner's awkwardness, but Maître Juremi, who had no such alibi, twice allowed himself to be touched out of distraction.

When all was done, Alix lighted the fencing master to his upstairs room herself. Françoise surely wanted to confide her feelings to her young friend, but the girl collapsed on her bed drunk with fatigue and fell asleep.

The days passed to the sustained rhythm of physical exercise. Once, having warned the janissaries that the servants planned to hunt down a roving dog, they passed an evening in pistol practice. Alix learned to load the weapon and fired off a dozen shots without trembling.

The evenings weighed more heavily on them. The three dined together on the terrace, with Alix having to bear the brunt of the conversation, so embarrassed were the other two at finding themselves face to face. The long silences that settled over their meals were filled with the croaking of the thousand frogs that lived in the reeds along the riverbank.

The girl was amused to see this man and this woman, both of whom had considerable experience of the world, and both of whom were naturally of somewhat cheerful disposition, thrown into such disarray by love. She thought long and hard about the implication for herself.

Yet the atmosphere of these evenings started to grow burdensome. Alix hoped that something would happen, although she did not dare say anything to Françoise. One night, returning from an outing, light-headed from having ridden at a full gallop, the young woman had the impression that the situation had finally changed. After dinner, a particularly quiet one, Maître Juremi spoke out, his deep voice filling the darkness.

"Mademoiselle, I beg your pardon, but I left the care of our plants in the hands of a neighbor. You know better than anyone how much those plants mean to us. I would like your permission to return to Cairo tomorrow morning."

"But our lessons . . ." said Alix, immediately regretting her selfishness.

"One shouldn't hurry. You have learned the basics. Improvement will now come with practice. I will leave the foils and other gear with you, and you may practice with Françoise. In truth, you no longer really need me."

Françoise, her lower lip trembling, looked at Maître Juremi desperately. She rose, and maintained her composure by taking the coffee tray and disappearing into the kitchen. The master-at-arms left the table in turn, bowing gravely to Alix, and walked in the opposite direction, lantern in hand. She heard his step resounding on the hollow treads of the staircase.

Maître Juremi left at dawn the next day; the two women accompanied him to the pier. The lines were cast off, and the boat floated off with the current. The sun, distorted by the haze, rose square-shaped among the palm trees on the far bank. A sailless felucca slipped by over the water carrying wood, its slender gaff hanging crosswise from the mast like an aerialist's balancing pole. Two large pink wading birds pointed their beaks toward the sun, from a distance looking as though they held the glowing orb and were slowly pulling it from the water. Françoise was crying.

"What happened?" asked Alix, taking her by the arm.

Françoise wiped her eyes, sniffed, and shrugged. She looked at Alix.

"I'm so sorry. I'll feel better in a moment. There. It's under control. How silly we are! At our age!"

"Did you talk to him?" said Alix, settling down on the dock and installing her friend beside her.

"Of course! I'll tell you, though you'll have guessed the whole thing already. You know how he would spend his whole day on this dock pretending to fish so as not to run into me. Yesterday afternoon I went and found

Michel, who always has a flask of your father's marc for his rheumatism. I drank two whole goblets and came down here. Juremi was doing absolutely nothing until he heard me coming, then he started pulling on a line and fussing with the hook. I sat down next to him. He grumbled. I was scared, believe me. Though I don't know how to swim, I would have been less frightened throwing myself into the water. But then he spoke—with that voice of his, you know what it's like. Imagine how uncomfortable I felt. I was about to say something, and suddenly that big drum was reverberating in my ears."

"What did he say?"

The sun was already high. The bank had turned lighter and the river darker. The shorebirds had flown off.

"'Françoise,' he started, and I can't tell you my feelings when I heard him say my name. 'Françoise, I know what you have come to tell me. It is useless to talk. You see, my family accepted terrible suffering rather than give up their faith. Not one of us ever did. It wasn't a question of religion. The truth is that we were incapable of going back on our word. Well, you should know that I have given mine.' He stopped for a moment, set his fishing line aside, and placed his hand on mine. Then he continued: 'If life has released me from my vow, as I may one day learn, then I will be free. And it would be to you that I would then give my word, if you would accept it. For the rest of my life.'"

Françoise burst into tears, and Alix took her in her arms. After a time, the two went up to the house together.

I suppose it means happiness for her, thought Alix. But how dreary lovers are!

She looked back over the brief moments she had spent with Jean-Baptiste, and it seemed that she too must have presented an unusually weak and insipid picture of herself.

At Versailles, she mused, among so many lovely ladies, how will he ever remember me?

The thought, which at any other time would have undone her, only provoked her to gallop faster.

~

The counselor Robert Pomot du Sangray proved to fit the innkeeper's brief description well. He was by nature cheerful and enjoyed the company of others, and his good qualities all came to the fore once his pain receded. Thanks to Jean-Baptiste, he now for the first time had a weapon to ward off the pain. Even a few hours of remission would have made him enormously grateful. But the treatment calmed his symptoms for an extended time, as the passage of several days confirmed, and his gratitude knew no bounds. Du Sangray gave the apothecary a purse of thirty gold écus and assured him he would cover all his expenses for the duration of his stay in Paris, which he hoped would be a long one.

A great kindness can sometimes cancel all debts. The old man's friendship was in Jean-Baptiste's eyes a rich and sufficient payment for his services. He would have felt uncomfortable asking for anything else. He therefore took the purse and announced that he would accept nothing more.

Each afternoon, he came to visit his patient. Du Sangray, who having recovered his freedom of movement, raced all over town and only came home in time for their daily consultation. As a result it was not always entirely clear who was visiting whom. The doctor and his patient would on occasion meet at the door, each arriving from a different side of the street. Their conversation had moved on from the subject of illness and evolved into the free and disorderly exchange common between two friends.

"Now why should you not stay in this house?" the counselor asked at the end of a short week. "Le Beau Noir is a good tavern but an execrable hotel, from all reports."

"It would not be kind to the innkeeper, who brought us together in the first place."

"I will make it right with him. He will go on bringing your meals. And as I am now past needing Françoise's clear broths, I will ask him to include a portion for me. We will stay his good clients, and at this time of year, with the fairs, he will have your room rented within a day."

Jean-Baptiste agreed. The counselor ordered an apartment prepared for his guest. It was light and prettily furnished, with two full-length windows in the front which gave onto the bustling street and offered a view of the faithful coming and going through the porch of the Church of Saint Eustache. The large chimney of Italian marble was unblocked, and Jean-Baptiste, delighted at finally being able to warm himself, held hellfire blazes in it. In the back were a bedchamber, two small rooms, and a wardrobe, to which he had his meager luggage carried: his bag, his medicine chest, and the crate containing the elephant's ears.

"When I bought this town house," said Sangray, coming to check on his guest, "it had been closed for ten years and was literally an object of hatred to its owners."

"There was fighting here, I believe?"

"At the start of the century it was a meeting place for those who called themselves the Refined of Honor. No one casts any doubt on their honor. But their refinement consisted in applying strict rules—which they devised themselves—to the practice of butchery. Imagine, the nominal tenant here, the comte de Montmorency-Boutteville, had engaged in twenty-two duels by the age of twenty-seven! The last took place under the windows of Richelieu's town mansion, for which he was decapitated the same year on Midsummer's Night."

"Glorious memories," said Poncet, moved.

"You think?"

"Yes, I feel that those men truly lived."

"More often they died," said Sangray. "And they made others die. I remember all too well the horrors of the Fronde. I was a child during the uprising, but I will never forget the chaos of those times when might ruled. No, Doctor, I am a man of law, of balance. I feel myself more the jailer of those old ghosts than their preserver."

From the outset Jean-Baptiste felt great trust in this gentle, patient man who considered everything with an open mind. He told him the story of his travels to Abyssinia, and the tale stretched over several lively nights of conversation, with both men sitting in large claw-footed armchairs, their feet stretched toward the bronze firedogs.

Out of these evenings came a resolve to apply themselves to literary tasks. Sangray undertook to finish the work he had started on the varieties of human law, and Jean-Baptiste, at Sangray's behest, decided to put the story of his journey in writing. They set to work the very next day.

But the counselor was more than a man of book learning. Now that his illness had retreated, all of life was there for him to rediscover, and there was no pleasure that he did not embrace. When a ball was announced at the Palais-Royal, he was invited, being a familiar of the duc de Chartres. Sangray was delighted to attend and invited Jean-Baptiste to join him.

They were both the same height, though different in build, and the counselor lent his guest a suit of dress clothes with gold braid and fine lace trim. Monsieur Raoul, the innkeeper, who also rented carriages, sent a coachman and cabriolet for them. They set off in time for supper.

5

The Palais-Royal represented at that time the only remnant of court life still in Paris, the rest having been transported to Versailles, around the king. Although there was pomp and ceremony at the Palais-Royal, it was carried on without the crushing presence of an autocrat, for the duc de Chartres, the king's nephew, showed affection and fellow feeling toward all those around him, and a spirit of freedom reigned. In this atmosphere of genial warmth, the most beautiful plants flourished more unconstrainedly than at Versailles. Beauty, youth, and wit such as are rarely met separately were found conjoined there in a remarkable number of individuals, women in particular. Sangray introduced his companion to the duchesse de Chartres, although not to her husband, the master of the house, who had been called to Versailles earlier that night and had left before they arrived.

During supper and afterward, when the small crowd gathered in the salons, Poncet relaxed his caution somewhat. A group had formed around him in one corner, consisting of a number of lovely women. He had no notion of their identities except for an extremely elderly lady whom the others addressed as Madame la Marquise. Jean-Baptiste's handsome presence and his exotic provenance, along with that special gift women have for sensing a mystery wherever it is concealed and for prying it open with their curiosity, conspired to place him at the center of a group avid for novelty. He fell into the trap all the more readily as speaking was for him the surest way to avoid being overcome by shyness and awe in the presence of such a brilliant court. He allowed himself free rein in describing Abyssinia, and the subject gave rise to a thousand fascinated questions. In the rough and tumble of social conversation, Jean-Baptiste made the mistake of pushing the picturesque a little too far. He explained with a wealth of detail how the Abyssinians traditionally ate live oxen during their most prestigious feasts, the guests at the banquet tearing off hunks of palpitating flesh and sliding their fingers in the incisions along the animals' spines.

The end of his story was greeted with a frosty silence. The ancient marquise cast an outraged glance at him, fluttered her fan weakly, and soared away toward the veranda. The entire company of young women followed her, with a voluptuous whispering of their bird-plumage taffetas.

The young man, alone on the couch, inhaled the scents left in the air around him by their bodies swathed in lace, their bosoms that exhaled musk, pepper, and jasmine, their faces coated with white powder and reddened with Pernambuco wood. He had never seen anything as graceful. Each of these women, from the youngest to the oldest, was madly desirable. They had concentrated the feminine into a nearly pure form, the way a plant can be distilled down to a few drops of liquid that can either cure or kill.

Yet something bothered him. Was it the strictly artificial nature of their graces? After all, this may be appropriate in a palace, he said to himself, in the light of these hundreds of candles, during the few hours after their finery is confected and before it begins to wilt. But if these women found themselves in the other world, the real one, what would they become? Would they wizen like mummies? Only in this air saturated with rice powder can they breathe. And for a man to please, he must follow the same hours, move in the same settings, and show the same manners. Just look at them all.

Jean-Baptiste surveyed, with as little insolence as possible, the twenty-year-old chiefs of staff, the gallant bishops, the gentlemen whom the sight of a naked sword would have horrified. The heart of man has been tamed, his faith, his glory at arms, he told himself, and these delights are nothing but a captivity. Yet he felt troubled when two young beauties eyed him as they passed.

Sangray discovered him lost in thought and sat down next to him.

"Well, my friend, congratulations! I have received favorable reports on you from all sides. And I am being complimented for having brought you."

"You are mocking me. On the contrary, I have been extremely clumsy."

Jean-Baptiste told him about the unfortunate oxen and the outraged departure of his audience.

"It is of no importance. You did no more than provide these ladies with a seemly pretext for flocking to the tartlets that had just appeared on the sideboard. Believe me, they have already forgotten the whole thing, except that they found you charming."

As if to confirm his words, a small group of ladies with several of the marquise's young companions among them passed by and cast gracious smiles in their direction.

"By the way," said the counselor, "I have heard some news relating to your affairs. The young king of Spain leaves Versailles tomorrow. Our sovereign's duties as royal preceptor come to an end. He will be able to resume his audiences, and yours should not be long now."

Throughout the drawing rooms, knots of guests had formed around faro and backgammon tables. Jean-Baptiste and Sangray took the opportunity to slip away, after discreetly thanking their hostess. They rode home in a calèche. Françoise had built roaring fires in the bedrooms. Jean-Baptiste went to sleep holding his right wrist to his face: the duchess had grasped it in a friendly gesture and it still exuded her musky perfume.

The following day Monsieur Raoul arrived with a message for Jean-Baptiste. It was a letter from Father Plantain, who still addressed his mail to Le Beau Noir, as the doctor had not thought it wise to let the Jesuit know that he was now living at the counselor's. The letter read as follows:

> Get ready. We will go to Versailles the day after tomorrow. Our audience is scheduled for Wednesday at four o'clock in the afternoon.
> Father G. Plantain SJ

After lunch Jean-Baptiste went to the Louis-le-Grand school to discuss the details of the audience.

On the way home he made a detour by the Louvre. According to rumor, the cavalry of King Philip V of Spain, lately known as the duc d'Anjou, was rehearsing there for the glorious procession that would set out the following day. On the quay, Jean-Baptiste encountered the king's first and second grooms, superbly plumed and costumed. Behind them came twenty-four pages in satin doublets and hose, gaudily festooned with silver galloons and lace, and mounted on garlanded steeds. Twelve hand-led Spanish horses came next, displaying their beribboned manes, their gold bits, bosses, and stirrups, and their red velvet blankets with gold and silver embroidery. Jean-Baptiste could not make out anything else because a troop of gray-clad musketeers kept the curious from approaching too near the Louvre Palace.

Arriving back at the counselor's, he found his host seated in the salon next to the fire. He joined him there, holding out his own hands to it. It was three o'clock. Françoise served them dinner in front of the fireplace. They spoke about the royal procession and Poncet's upcoming audience.

"How do you plan to go about it?"

"Well, I will tell the truth," said Jean-Baptiste simply.

"Ah! You are starting off poorly. Are you not aware that to a king, the truth is simply what it pleases him to hear?"

"I don't know what it would please the king to hear, but I do know what some would like to tell him, and it is false."

"Whom are you referring to?"

"The Jesuits."

"Are not the Jesuits arranging this audience for you?"

"They are. But this does not preclude our having different views on what to tell the king."

The counselor set down the piece of turkey he was eating with his fingers, drank a long swallow of sparkling wine, and looked at Jean-Baptiste with astonished eyes.

"Are you telling me that you plan to contradict the Jesuits in front of the king? My friend, I am glad to be dining with you, as I fear it may very well be for the last time. But what is your goal, exactly?"

"In fact, I have two."

"Not a good principle."

"But the two form only one in my own mind," Poncet went on heatedly. "I want the king to send me back to Abyssinia as his titled ambassador, and I want him to grant me all the privileges incident to this responsibility, including a title of nobility."

"The way you have put it, it is ambitious but not impossible."

"You see."

"But why do you so want to go back there?"

"It is not that I am so determined to. But the king's favor would allow me to fulfill two vows I have made."

"Sweet Christ! To whom?"

"The first is to a young woman. She was born to a higher rank than myself. I have vowed to marry her. This I can only do if the king ennobles me."

"I understand. These are things one does at your age. The other vow?"

"To the emperor of Abyssinia. I swore to him that the Jesuits would not return to his country, and that if he invited France to send an embassy, I would fill the post myself."

"So you must both ask to be sent there and make the king understand that the Jesuits are not welcome. And it is the Jesuits themselves who have brought you this far!"

"I had no choice. Without them I could never have gone beyond Cairo."

"So I have been telling you."

"But they are unaware of my intentions."

"I can well believe it. So you must contradict them at the very last moment, in the king's presence. Do you realize what you are about to do? And you are laughing!"

"I am laughing because, despite the evidence, I feel confident."

"Your youth makes you brash. Beware. The court is a place of intrigue where little store is set by courage, than which nothing is so easily overcome. They need only be several, stay in the shadows, and strike from behind, and they will succeed."

"No, Counselor," said Jean-Baptiste gently, "I truly don't believe that I am mad. My confidence comes not from being oblivious but on the contrary from all that I have seen. And do you know where? Riding to Paris, yes, traveling across this kingdom, talking to the people in the countryside and in the towns. I found myself saying: 'The man who rules over all this is a great king.'"

"You think?"

"No, wait. He is a great king, because I remember from when I lived in this country the stories the old folks told about the Fronde, that terrible insurrection, and the Wars of Religion, and the great plagues and famines. And this king, following in the footsteps of his father and grandfather, has put an end to all this. He has overpowered the great and brought the nobility into submission. In the countrysides I saw the many châteaux left empty by those nobles who have joined the court, while all who remain are humbly devoted to the king. And as for the church, it has submitted to the king's authority in return for his help in fighting the Protestants. He has built up France's military might, driven back its enemies abroad, and taken command of an unrivaled power."

"You have not forgotten the cost of all this? Europe is united in opposition to us, the people are crushed under the weight of taxes, and the Protestants and Jansenists are hunted like vermin. And there is no voice in politics except the king's own, trust me. I spent thirty years in parliament."

"That is not the point," said Jean-Baptiste, shaking his hand to regain control of the conversational dice. "I am not making historical judgments. I am describing the work of a man who wanted to be a great king and who has become one. And I am saying that another such is the king of Abyssinia."

"You are comparing . . ."

"Yes. The same will, the same determination to subject all else to his authority, the same unrivaled power. Iyasu has accomplished the same thing. If ever two men could understand each other, those two could."

"And you propose to speak in this vein to the king of France?"

"I am certain he will understand me. The Jesuits tell him: 'The Abyssinians wish to revert to the Catholic faith.' I will tell him: 'Your Majesty, accept the friendship of a great king of the East. Send him an embassy, trade with him, buy his gold from him, sell him the output of your manufactories. But do not seek to disturb the structure of his nation by converting it, just as you would never allow your own to be disturbed in such a way.'"

"Jean-Baptiste, you are a madman!" said Sangray, rising to his feet. "I feel too much friendship to let you fall into such a trap, one you have set for yourself."

He took two strides across the room, then came back to the fireplace and faced the young doctor.

"Poncet, what is Abyssinia?"

"A country."

"No. It is nothing. A corner of Africa inhabited by savages. Nothing, do you hear? And what is France? Everything."

"This from you, Counselor? You who have heard my accounts of Abyssinia, you who draw parallels between the customs of different nations and hold that they must not be judged before they are understood, you who have told me to write—"

"To write, yes. But not to speak. And certainly not to the king. What I believe is felt and understood by few. That is why I toss my thoughts into the great river of written words, where my bottle will perhaps be opened by another who thinks as I do and will hear. But for now, one has to acknowledge what everyone thinks, and everyone thinks what the king thinks. If the king ever sought power it was not that he might be compared with others, and certainly not with men whom he considers never to have achieved civilization. I warn you, Poncet, in all friendship—and my affection for you is the affection of a father for a son. When you stand before the king, any comparison you make between his power and that of a native prince, even a Christian one, will be held against you as an insult. You will immediately forfeit any chance of obtaining what you want, or even of leaving this country freely."

Jean-Baptiste was thunderstruck by the force and sincerity of his friend's warning.

"Then what must I do?" he asked dejectedly.

"Write down your ideas. I still maintain it. Later we will plot how to publish them and to which enlightened minds to show them. But for the time being, before the king, do not voice any opposition to the Jesuits. You may exaggerate the dangers and difficulties of the journey if you like, to make them hesitate to undertake it—though nothing will stop them. But if they say that the negus wants to convert, do not contradict them. Accept it. You cannot expect to obtain favors from the king unless you submit to his views. Would you like to be a noble? It is entirely possible, and I can help you. But you must first learn to please. Show the king your devotion to him. Tell him you have spread the news of his greatness to the far ends of the earth, and the kings of the East, dazzled, have asked you to extend their humble respects. Tell him that the true faith is making progress thanks to him, and that you took a Jesuit to that country, who, alas, faltered along the way, but that you hope to lead many more there."

"Lead many more there!" burst out Jean-Baptiste. "I promised the emperor I would keep them from ever returning!"

"Rein in your pride, my young friend. You cannot form a wall against the Jesuits all on your own, not when they have the greatest king of Christendom in their confessional. Too bad for your vow. We are no longer in the time of the Refined of Honor. Some may regret it, but I don't. It has to be recognized. Have you seen all the empty mangers below, all the hollow casks? I implore you: don't make a mistake about the era we live in."

Jean-Baptiste pivoted toward the fire and crossed his arms.

"We shall see," he said between his teeth.

6

In Cairo in the meantime, Monsieur Le Noir du Roule was nowhere to be seen. The consul feared another terrible shipwreck. He imagined his future son-in-law washed up on a beach like poor Father Versau, clinging to a tree trunk. The truth was not so tragic. The young diplomat was simply taking his time along the way. He had himself set down in Civitavecchia, traveled to Rome by coach, and visited the city at his leisure, even forming a liaison or two among the ladies of Roman society. Next he had gone down to Bari and crossed to Corinth. He finally turned up in Alexandria and reached Cairo soon after.

Monsieur de Maillet had decided to lodge du Roule at the consulate, despite his being a subordinate. He wanted to honor his status as a gentleman and, more especially, make him feel part of the family. Having set his mind at rest about his daughter's consent, the consul was now anxious about the intentions of the fiancé. Would he find Alix to his liking? The consul was not the sort of father to be blinded by love for his children. He judged his daughter not according to her appearance but according to convention, and he found her wanting. Had she not, at his summons, returned from Giza the preceding week, her complexion darkened by the sun, going everywhere bareheaded, and looking like a savagess? A man of delicate tastes, acquainted with the salons of Paris, might not want to be compromised by such a woman.

On the day du Roule arrived, Alix appeared in the entrance hall as the traveler's carriage drew into the courtyard, and it was too late to send her upstairs to change. Monsieur de Maillet noted with consternation that her cheeks had not a trace of powder and that her hair was pulled back around a part like the meanest servant's. She wore a too-large dress of her mother's. It not only looked ridiculous but was worn, and its dark burgundy color had been out of fashion even in Cairo for fifteen years. All the servants at the consulate were lined up in the entrance hall behind the Maillets, and it would have been difficult to make a scene in front of so many people. Besides, the new arrival was already opening his carriage door and an Arab footman was setting out the step. The consul had planned to maintain his position on the landing. This was a point of protocol he had discussed the evening before with Monsieur Macé. Yet in the heat of the moment, he found himself rushing down the stairs toward the traveler and greeting him at the foot of his carriage.

Monsieur Le Noir du Roule was a tall man, agreeably built, with a slender waist and a finely turned ankle. It was immediately clear that he carried his graces in the full knowledge of the effect they produced. He never moved an arm without considering in what advantageous light to place it next. It was with the utmost naturalness that he took care to keep his chin high, his heels together, his shoulders well back. Had he been a more supple man, he might have had the figure of a dancer, but there was far too much power in his bearing for him to appear anything but catlike, a large predator whose superior elegance hides superior cruelty.

Alix shuddered when he came near and she saw his face. It was as sharp as a blade. His long, narrow nose extended from a deeply lined forehead, his cheeks were hollow, his lips a thin line, his chin pointed. All the while responding to the consul's polite proposals, Le Noir du Roule cast his eyes deliberately over the assembled company. One of his eyebrows, angled like a chevron, stood higher than the other, while his eyelids, as stationary as a shutter, protected his black eyes. Of all those present, he took most notice of the young woman, looking at her firmly and intently. She understood at once that she would never manage to hide her charms from such a man simply by neglecting her appearance.

The newcomer saluted the ladies in the manner of the court, which seemed strange but was accepted by all as the newest form of custom. Then he entered the building with the consul and Monsieur Macé. They spoke briefly, and the traveler went up to his room. When he came down for dinner he was dressed even more elegantly than before, wearing a sky-blue coat of fine velvet lined in ultramarine and embroidered with gold, and a pale pink vest that matched his breeches. Alone of his kind in the dining room, he still managed to seem the one normal person by virtue of his having recently arrived from Versailles. The others—and the consul most of all—seemed to be dressed in old rags. Alix, who sat at her father's left, had put on an attractive dress, as the disguise she had worn previously had had no other effect than to rile her father. In any case, she sensed that nothing would deflect this man's glance from her—he had detected her beauty as a leopard locates the outline of an antelope in thick brush. Everything in the manner of Le Noir du Roule indicated his sense of having a right to her, but it was not the way she had imagined it. No doubt her father and Pontchartrain had spoken to him about the marriage plans. She had expected that. What she had not anticipated was his quiet, almost savage assurance. He had the look of a libertine who is sure of himself, of his charms, and of his wiles, and who would take her no matter what, even if she were not practically bound and delivered to him already, and perhaps then with even greater pleasure.

Monsieur Le Noir du Roule enlivened the table with his brilliant conversation. He loved the arts, and he described Egypt's monuments, which he had not yet seen, with all the knowledge of an informed reader. His features rotated from expression to expression as he spoke like an automaton. There was no transitional stage between his different faces, and one sometimes followed another rapidly the way the left hand of a guitarist jumps invisibly from one chord to the next. Only his eyelids never moved. Over fruit he looked directly at Alix.

"And you, Mademoiselle, have you ever seen the Sphinx?"

"No," she said sharply.

Just as her father was about to object that she had only just come back from Giza, he heard an exclamation. Alix had risen from table and, after taking a single step, fallen to the ground in a faint.

Françoise and the cook, whom Madame de Maillet rang for, carried the young woman up to her room. Her parents followed, greatly troubled.

"You see," said the consul to his wife as they climbed the staircase, "I was sure that she would catch a fever in that house."

"She doesn't feel hot," said Madame de Maillet.

"Never mind. Sitting all day and exciting her thoughts with novels, she was bound to end by having vapors."

In the drawing room, meanwhile, Monsieur Macé tried to distract the young diplomat, all the while begging him to overlook the incident.

"It is not contagious, is it?" asked Le Noir du Roule, his nose buried in a lace handkerchief.

~

It was December, and Versailles lay dejected and inanimate after the brilliant festivities to mark the departure of the new king. The gardens, strewn with yellow leaves and banked in mists, looked like a network of drainage ditches fanning out into the dark woods. A few frozen shadows could be seen: a handful of gardeners busying themselves around a stump or sweeping the grounds back and forth like plowmen. The palace, under its gray slate roof, raised its lugubrious facade into the path of the damp winds. Behind the paned windows could be seen the feeble light of torches that burned all day. Not a carriage crossed the main courtyard but the horrible groaning of its axles over the limestone paving blocks suggested the passage of a laden cart on its way to the executioner's. And everywhere, from behind wooden palisades, came the sound of workmen's mallets as they labored invisibly in the high reaches of an extensive scaffold system.

Jean-Baptiste, Father Plantain, and Father Fleuriau arrived on the evening before the audience and spent the night in a house built by the Society of Jesus in the town of Versailles, looking on the Cours la Reine. In the end Fléhaut did not join them in Paris. He left word that he would meet them directly at the audience.

"That means he has his orders and Pontchartrain wants him on his side," said Father Plantain.

Supper jarred unpleasantly with the succession of roast capons and *pâtés en croute* that Jean-Baptiste was used to from Le Beau Noir. He had to make do with a thin broth, shredded cabbage, and a nubbin of cheese. Fleuriau, green and gaunt, subjected these trifles to endless mastication and then exclaimed at his satiety as though he had just eaten a feast. A tubercular fire was kept fitfully alive in the fireplace. Poncet had dined in his felt cape, but his teeth were chattering and he asked leave to go and burrow into his bed, taking the precaution to have it thawed first with the warming pan. Absorbed in shivering, he thought of nothing but the particles of heat he might preserve by adopting one position or another. He fell numbly to sleep like an animal that has fallen into icy water.

At eight in the morning, a footman came to pull the curtains, light a fire, and tell him that the fathers were waiting breakfast for him. The meal was as depressing as the previous one, and in addition Poncet, who did not care for chicken broth at that time of day, learned to his displeasure that the house did not stock tea, coffee, or chocolate. He ordered a large glass of malmsey and drank it in one long draft. Meanwhile, Father Plantain announced in lugubrious tones that Father Fleuriau felt ill, would keep to his bed that day, and would therefore not accompany them to the audience. Presumably he was feeling the aftereffects of their copious meal the night before.

At ten o'clock, a carriage sent to them by Father de La Chaise rolled up to the door. The weather was even more overcast than the previous day; a large dull cloud with yellow glints threatened snow and swallowed all the light. The Swiss guards at the castle gate were wrapped in three layers of coats. Although every chimney on the palace roof was smoking, the visitors met no one in the courtyards.

The weather brought comfort to Jean-Baptiste. On a fine day, the brilliance of the gilt and ornaments, the harmony of the gardens, the elegance of the buildings would have weighed on him in their triumphancy. This smoldering den, though, had a certain humbleness. For all the greatness that the king pretended to, he was subject to the power of the seasons and had to protect himself and his litter of nestmates from the rude caprices of the rain and cold. Versailles, in the grip of winter, was no empyrean of luxury and power but a simple shelter of stone and slate where the tribe gathered shivering around tepid fires, waiting with bended backs for winter to move on.

They entered by the grand marble staircase, where lackeys in light livery bustled, their hands blue with cold. The vast flight of stairs was steeped in icy dampness and smelled of wax and sarcophagi, while from above came a muffled echo of voices. The visitors walked upstairs abreast in tight formation, not one of them reaching out to the iron balustrade with its gilded rosettes. On the upper landing they stumbled on a clutch of whispering footmen, but whatever the source of their agitation, it was not the visitors' arrival, which no one seemed to have noticed. Having climbed the last step, the little party looked upward mechanically for the next flight of stairs: it seemed odd to have arrived at the top when there was still so much height between themselves and the ceiling. It was at this moment that Father de La Chaise joined them, stepping from behind a curtain they had not noticed. In a severe cassock, a black taffeta skullcap on his head, the man smiled continually. His fixed expression was at first reassuring, but soon made them worry. From his comportment and his susurrant speech, it was evident that he was familiar with the most minute aspects of greatness. His frail figure against the herculean setting spoke of his ineradicable fragility, and he looked at Poncet worriedly out of the corner of his eye. When Father Plantain explained to him that there was a crate still to be brought from the carriage, Father de La Chaise summoned two lackeys. His signal to them, firm and imperious, gave an indication of the icy depths that underlay the calm surface of his personality. He took Father Plantain aside and, turning toward a large gilt molding, said a few words to him in a low voice.

They followed the king's confessor into the first room, which was the guardroom. Father de La Chaise informed the duty officer, who was pacing with a shouldered musket, that a crate carried by two men would be following them—and it appeared at that same moment.

They next entered the first antechamber, a vast room where the king generally took supper. Bronze wall sconces emitted light, while the windows reflected nothing in the mirror but an orange sky growing ever darker. Nyert, the king's first chamberlain, a small man in a short wig, was waiting for the visitors at the door; they followed him across another room, this one unlit and filled with a gray penumbra. At the opposite side was a double door, far enough ajar to reveal the strong light in the next room, where a chandelier with thirty candles shone. The chamberlain gathered the visitors in formation, then opened the door wide, and presented them to the king.

7

The king's room was devoid of any character, which perhaps explained why Louis XIV wanted to transform it. Too small to be a reception room, especially in comparison with the Galerie des Glaces, onto which it opened through three doors, it was also too vast to be a private office. Within the context of grandeur it was a modest room, while within the context of modesty it would have to be called pretentious. The result was a crying lack of majesty. The king, placed at a moderate distance, was neither exalted against a vast perspective nor made overwhelming as an illustrious person can be in a small space, where his presence devours all the air. He was simply there, no more impressive than a bourgeois in the midst of a small gathering. But he was easily recognizable by his large three-cornered hat with white plumes. The others wore only their perukes.

The chair the sovereign sat on completed the homely image. It was a sort of armchair covered in black leather and edged with gilt tacks, but mounted on a three-wheeled platform. The two large wheels in back made it possible for a pair of Swiss guards to propel him, while the roller in front, attached to a long iron tiller with a handle, allowed him to steer. Nothing betrayed the infirmities of the king's body more strongly than this engine designed to assist it. The illusion of being in the presence of a demigod, an individual made supernatural by power, was quickly dispelled by this three-wheeled contraption.

The king's insistence on appearing grave, impassive, and majestic despite the plainness of his circumstances only made him seem disgruntled, unhappy, and offended. This, at any rate, was Jean-Baptiste's first impression as he entered in the midst of his cluster of clergymen. The king only vaguely resembled his official portraits, particularly the one gracing the consulate in Cairo. Contrasting it with the face in front of him, Jean-Baptiste had the impression that the painter had not set down the sovereign's image but its reflection in the sublime world of Ideas, neglecting the smallpox scars, the red nose, the wattles at his neck. In short, Monsieur de Maillet had been wrong to have the picture restored: by putting splotches on it Nature had made a better likeness than the painter. In the group around the king, Jean-Baptiste noticed Fléhaut, standing on the periphery, and a man with a high periwig and a long, pointed nose beside him but closer to the king, presumably Chancellor Pontchartrain. All of those present, down to the lowest Swiss chair-pusher, imitated the sovereign in wearing an air of importance, which is to say (the two states often resembling each other) that they looked offended, indignant even, at the brazen intrusion of the new arrivals.

The Jesuits bowed humbly but discreetly, in the character of men recognized to have the privilege of submitting fully only to God. Jean-Baptiste, who fleetingly remembered stretching himself out at full length on the floor, made a deep bow. It was unfashionable but sincere, and showed that he felt no compunction about eclipsing himself before the sovereign.

The formalities over, there was a moment of general hesitation. Jean-Baptiste also noticed a palpable tension pervading the room. It reached its greatest concentration in the few feet of space dividing the clergymen and Poncet from the group around the king. There was a hum, an almost audible crackling in the air, as at the approach of the electrical center of a thunderstorm on a summer afternoon.

"Sire," said Father de La Chaise, who alone dared walk forward under the gathering threat, "you know Father Fleuriau, who is responsible for our missions to the East. To his great regret, he is too ill today to appear before you. But I have the great honor of presenting to you Father Plantain, who has the difficult responsibility of representing us in one of the lands under Turkish rule, namely Egypt."

Father Plantain lowered his broad forehead once more and kept his hand pressed to his heart.

"It is from that country," continued the king's confessor, "that the mission for Abyssinia set out, which Your Majesty had the great goodness to conceive and support. The attempt was made to reestablish a foothold in this unfortunate Christian country, which long ago strayed into heresy, and where several of our brothers, alas, were massacred at the start of the century. You are aware, Sire, of the arduous efforts of our order to lift peoples from the error and ignorance that would otherwise damn them for all eternity. Father Plantain, with your permission, will render an account of the mission you desired."

The king coughed a bit into the palm of his hand, raising the sleeve of his green doublet. Jean-Baptiste noticed, although the gesture was rapid and almost imperceptible, that the king took the opportunity to wipe a droplet of spittle from the right corner of his mouth with the lace of his sleeve. His mouth drooped to that side and did not close completely.

"Speak, Father," said the king. "We take a great interest in this matter."

"Sire," said Father Plantain, reddening to the top of his head, "it is my painful duty to report first that the courageous missionary who carried the hopes of our order into these distant lands is no longer of this world. He was called back to God in the course of his severe journey. His sacrifice has fortunately not been in vain. The emperor of Abyssinia welcomed the remainder of the mission with great goodwill. He announced that he is well disposed toward the Catholic faith and sincerely hopes that he may join it. Moreover, he expressed his most humble submission to Your Majesty, whom he recognizes as the greatest Christian sovereign in the world. He dispatched an envoy to Cairo to present his respects, a man who might properly be called an ambassador, though the position is unknown among his people."

"Why is that man not here?" said Louis XIV.

"Sire, we heartily desired it. But Your Majesty knows what obstacles the Turks put in the way of a person traveling to Europe who is not native to it. Fortunately, the ambassador did not arrive alone. He was accompanied by Sieur Poncet, whom you see here."

Father Plantain turned toward Jean-Baptiste. The tension in the air, which had dissipated somewhat during the previous moments, resumed its former intensity, and Jean-Baptiste realized that he was its focus.

"Sieur Poncet practices the trade of apothecary in the stations of the Levant. At present, he resides in Cairo. Our missionary, the late Father de Brèvedent, whom I mentioned to Your Majesty earlier, made the journey to Abyssinia with him. The emperor was ill. He had requested the attendance of a European medical practitioner. It was through Sieur Poncet that the mission gained access to the negus, as the Abyssinian sovereign is known. And it was also with him that the negus's envoy traveled on the return voyage."

So saying, Father Plantain stepped back, turning to Jean-Baptiste. Louis XIV in turn cast his eye on the doctor, as did all the king's entourage. The moment had come.

Jean-Baptiste stepped forward slightly, gave another brief bow, and began.

"Sire, in the absence of the ambassador dispatched by the emperor of the Abyssinians to Your Majesty's side, it falls on me to convey the message that that sovereign wanted to have heard in this court. I would add that the emperor greatly hoped Your Majesty would return an answer, and I am at your entire disposal to carry it back to him, though I should risk my life once again to do so."

"What is the message you have been given?" asked the king.

"Sire, I will answer you at once. But if it please Your Majesty, I would like to say first that the king of the Abyssinians did not send me forth empty-handed. His kingdom is rich, its soil full of metals and gems, its forests of animals inconceivable even to the most fertile imagination. The negus wished the king of France to receive, in token of his friendship . . ."

A murmur arose among those present. The king's eye never wavered.

". . . and admiration," Jean-Baptiste added quickly, "the handsomest specimens of these riches."

"Well," said Louis XIV, "where are the presents?"

His eye rested on the crate, sitting at the feet of the two footmen.

"Ah, Sire. The emperor gave us sacks of gold dust that it took five mules to carry. Next came civet and incense to load the backs of another four mules. Then ambergris and ten sacks of the finest coffee grown in all the world. That was the first load. Behind came five purebred mares of a grace to delight Your Majesty, horses that went surefooted on any terrain. The emperor wanted them saddled and bridled with the best leather. Eight Abyssinian soldiers walked beside them, chosen as the strongest in the negus's guard and the most hardened to conditions on the high plateau."

The Jesuits had imperceptibly drawn back from Jean-Baptiste to look at him as he spoke. He stood straight, his eyes sometimes on the sovereign, sometimes on the audience around him. He spoke in a confident voice, and for a few moments the rumors in the room were stilled. The mules laden with gold, the richly saddled mares, and the procession of young Abyssinians seemed to file through the room at a slow pace from one end to the other, disappearing into the Galerie des Glaces.

"Behind," continued Jean-Baptiste, "closing the march and serving as our rearguard, walked two of the gigantic animals known as elephants, their chains hung with silver bells. Each of their tusks might have furnished the ivory for a life-sized statue of a man."

Pontchartrain leaned toward the sovereign and spoke a word in his ear. This simple motion, interrupting the rapt attention of the assembly, broke the spell.

"In short," the king interrupted, "is all that in the box?"

An ironic murmur rose from the courtiers, and evil smiles were posted on their faces.

"Alas, Sire, in some sense it is."

The growing rumor burst, as when water is tossed on a fire, into a few hissing laughs.

"Yes," repeated Jean-Baptiste, raising his large, earnest eyes toward Louis XIV, "the journey had the better of many things. The climate killed the mares. The Turks confiscated the Abyssinians. The gold, ambergris, and incense were stolen from us."

He took a step toward the crate.

"You may have doubts, Sire. This will prove the truth of my story and give you some idea of the magnificence with which the sovereign of Abyssinia wanted to honor you."

He had earlier provided the footmen with crowbars. Now Jean-Baptiste ordered them with a gesture to open the case. The king signaled the Swiss guards to wheel his chair forward a few steps and, using his tiller, positioned himself crosswise so as to be able to look left at whatever was to appear. As the two footmen worked at the box, an expectant silence settled over the room. The only sounds were the roaring of an enormous log in the fireplace and the screech of the nails as they were pulled from the planks of the crate. Finally, the lid came off. Jean-Baptiste motioned the footmen to step back and set the lid to one side. All that could be seen was a moist linen cloth, brown in color, covering a bulging shape. Jean-Baptiste drew it aside, and the rest all happened very quickly.

He paused for a moment, then seized something with both hands, something as wide as the crate. He straightened up, and the heavy thing unrolled with the force of gravity. It was greenish, fuzzy, and nauseating. The elephant's ear was gummed with mold into an unrecognizable block. As it opened, it exuded a fine, light-colored powder, like flour gone bad, that formed a heavy, pestilential cloud. Disgusting-looking insects, startled by this sudden shock, jumped in every direction with whatever complement of legs, wings, and antennae they had and scuttled off across the floor in terrifying hordes.

Jean-Baptiste was so stunned by the rotted state of the object that, looking around him with a desperate expression, he continued stupidly to wave the supple and fungus-ridden apron before him, as it broadcast its filth into the air.

There was a brief moment of astonishment, followed by tumult in the assembled company.

"The king! The king! Help!" cried out a voice, most likely Pontchartrain's. "Don't let him breathe in any of it!"

The Swiss guards spun the king's chair around and pushed it out through a door that quickly opened into the gallery.

"The guard! The guard! Call the guard!" shouted another voice.

"A doctor!"

The company drew back from Jean-Baptiste, who stood alone under the chandelier in the middle of the room. The others formed four small clusters in the corners.

Someone spoke the word "poison," which evoked such fearful memories among the members of this court that every nose was soon buried in a handkerchief or lace sleeve. The guards burst through the door into the room. Half a dozen of the men threw themselves on Jean-Baptiste, striking at his hands with the butts of their muskets to make him drop the reeking instrument of death. They pulled down a wall hanging, wrapped the crate in it, and threw the whole thing into the fire. The room was meanwhile thoroughly aired, with those in attendance prudently passing into the Galerie des Glaces, where the Jesuits were allowed only after a considerable time.

Father de La Chaise, who desperately wanted to see the king, was finally led into the council room where His Majesty had been moved for safekeeping. Fagon, the king's physician, had discovered no trace of poisoning by volatile substances. As a precautionary measure, however, he recommended a bowl of warm ass's milk. Pontchartrain had gone from the council room by the time the Jesuit arrived. La Chaise threw himself at the sovereign's feet and asked his forgiveness.

"Come," said Louis XIV, "get up, Father. It will prove to have been nothing at all. My Swiss guards were more frightened than I. But as I am their prisoner on this chair . . ."

"Sire, I regret the whole thing enormously."

"Look beforehand at the presents that you bring me," said the king in a gentle, if slightly ironic, tone.

"We should have—"

"Let us close the incident," the king cut in. "Do you know, I had a premonition about it. The man hardly seems trustworthy. From all sides I had heard strong suspicions, and in truth there were many who feared he was an impostor. I listened to you all the same and agreed to receive him."

"Sire, his behavior was execrable, I agree. But we have never had the slightest doubt about the accuracy of his statements."

"You are a saintly man, Father. But I fear you are more adept at unmasking the demon within than the flesh-and-blood rogue who might stand before you."

As the king mentioned the demon within, Father de La Chaise saw him remember with a sudden tremor that he was speaking to his confessor, and an imperceptible shadow of fear clouded the monarch's gaze.

"Your words cause me great pain," said the Jesuit humbly.

"No need for that. I continue to place my trust in you. Know that I admire the work of your order and sustain it more than ever. In the case of China, I have just ordered your mission in Peking to receive our full support."

"A blessed deed," said the Jesuit, bowing.

"And as to Abyssinia, you have asked my help in sending six of your men back there, am I correct?"

"Yes, Sire."

"I grant it you. But do not make a public case of it."

"Thank you, Your Highness."

"As to this supposed traveler," the king went on, "I have taken the measures that should have been taken in the first place. He will be examined by a panel of learned men to see whether he is telling the truth. If they agree that he is not an impostor, then we will hear what he has to say."

"The procedure is a reasonable one, Sire. But I am quite certain that the panel will vouch for the authenticity of the man's journey."

"We shall see," said the king.

"Our fathers may then leave for Abyssinia without delay?"

"Tomorrow, if you like," said the king, picking up a leather folder from the desk to signal the Jesuit that he was free to go.

Father de La Chaise returned through the gallery. The rock-crystal chandeliers held black reflections. Outside the day had grown lighter, the wind having blown the late-afternoon clouds away as the sun set.

Pontchartrain thought it was clever to sabotage our audience, thought the black-robed man as he scurried along. He warned the king against us and alarmed everyone when an incident of little consequence occurred. And in the end he has been defeated. His Majesty, to be forgiven for disappointing us, has granted us everything we could have wished for.

As he approached the door to the guardroom, he thought, This Poncet has served us well, though he behaved like an imbecile. We will have to defend him, because any damage to his reputation will reflect on us. But at least we are no longer dependent on him.

8

The carriages stopped in front of the Church of Saint Eustache shortly after the last stroke of eleven. The darkness in the street was total except near Le Beau Noir, where a pale candlelight filtered through the unwashed windows.

Jean-Baptiste got out, closed the door, and, instead of heading for the cabaret, walked around the chaise to knock on the counselor's door.

"What?" whispered Father Plantain, half-opening the carriage door. "You are no longer staying at the inn?"

"As you see," said Jean-Baptiste, striking the door twice more with the knocker.

Finally the door opened. The counselor himself appeared, carrying a torch. Father Plantain, horrified, concealed himself in the shadows of his carriage and signaled the coachman to whip on the horses. From the second carriage two guards dismounted, enveloped in felt capes and carrying muskets.

"Come in, quickly," whispered Sangray, who had not yet noticed the escort.

"I am not alone," Jean-Baptiste announced, pointing at the two approaching soldiers.

"By order of the king," said one of them to the counselor, "we are not to leave this man's side. Does he live with you?"

"As far as I know," said Sangray.

"Then you will have to make a bit of room for us as well."

The counselor let Jean-Baptiste pass, followed by the guards, then bolted the door. The hallways were frigid, but Sangray, showing little concern for the military men, invited them to set up their camp there for the night. He then entered the drawing room, where Jean-Baptiste was waiting for him by the fireplace. Two large logs crackled merrily on the hearth.

"I expected you back toward seven o'clock," said the counselor in a low voice. "Actually, I was starting to despair of ever seeing you again. I was just thinking I would have to go tomorrow to the Palais-Royal or to Saint-Cloud to try to get news of you."

Jean-Baptiste collapsed into an armchair, his feet and hands outstretched toward the fire, his eyes vacant. He looked more somber than Sangray had ever seen him. At his friend's urging, his expression still absent, the young man narrated the story of his audience with the king right up to the final incident. He then described being taken into custody. The musketeers believed him to be a poisoner, particularly as he had professed himself an apothecary. They very nearly started beating him for a full confession. "Have the present that I brought the king examined," Jean-Baptiste had told them, "and you will see that it is nothing like what you imagine."

At this, the captain of the guards realized that by throwing the crate into the fire they had destroyed the evidence of the crime. He ordered anything left of it to be promptly extracted from the fireplace. The wood of the crate had burned up, but they did manage to find several almost intact pieces of ear under the ashes. A mastiff was brought in to taste a bit of it. The dog swallowed the cooked meat greedily. He even seemed to want seconds, proving that the dish was not unhealthful and was even, when properly prepared, as savory as Murad had always maintained.

At last the Jesuits returned, accompanied by a secretary. They directed the musketeers to release the suspect, though he was to be kept under watch until his examination by a jury of learned men. There had been many formalities to see to. Once the guards were chosen, there was another wait while they made ready. Finally, the two carriages had traveled to Paris from Versailles through the cold, dark night.

"Ah," said Sangray, laughing when he had heard the story. "So it was no more than that!"

Jean-Baptiste shrugged.

"It seems enough to me."

"Yes, as you say, it is enough. But the damage is not so bad. Tell me that part again where you are standing there holding a moldy elephant ear. . . ."

He started to laugh. He did so cautiously at first, so as not to offend his friend. Then the anxiety of the past hours relaxed its grip on Sangray. He lost any moderation and laughed so loudly, so heartily, his whole body wobbling as though shaken by an ocean swell, that the guards stuck their heads in the door and Jean-Baptiste himself was overcome by amusement, and at last by frank hilarity. They regained their composure only after a very long spell, and after many relapses, wiping the tears from their eyes.

"All the same," said Jean-Baptiste, serious once more, "I have lost everything."

"I do not think so," said Sangray, who was unbuttoning his vest to breathe. "In fact, it is the opposite. That elephant's ear saved your life. I saw you headed for summary imprisonment, or the galleys."

"But," said Jean-Baptiste, whom the counselor noticed sliding off once again toward melancholy, "I have failed in everything I set out to do."

"Ah, dear friend, tomorrow is another day. I am in no mood to listen to your laments, which I believe to be highly exaggerated. My advice to you, after this emotionally trying day, is to go no farther tonight than this bout of mad laughter, which has just given us both such delight. Go to bed and think only that you are alive, a fact that should be a source of astonishment and satisfaction to all of us at the end of every day, and the most trying ones in particular."

So saying, he hugged Jean-Baptiste like a father, picked up a chandelier, and led the procession to the bedrooms, where he wished his guest good night.

The following days brought an unrelenting succession of bad news. First, the story of the royal audience spread through the court, and the gazettes in town reveled in it. As no one knew the exact nature of the reeking object Poncet had had the audacity to flourish before the king, the anecdote took on not so much a ridiculous as a sinister aspect, and it seemed that an attempt on the king's life might truly have been made. The vilest rumors circulated about Jean-Baptiste. He was now openly accused of being an impostor, and the scandal was fanned surreptitiously by the Jesuits' enemies. Their object was less to damage the young traveler himself than to harm the reputation of his apparent allies; but as the high-placed Jesuits stood beyond reach, it was he who was dragged through the mud.

Then the trial, which Jean-Baptiste had hoped would be soon, was scheduled for several weeks away. A jury of competent scholars had to be gathered first, and they needed time to go over the case. All indications were that the questioning would begin only after the Feast of the Epiphany.

Finally, the Jesuits informed Jean-Baptiste that the king had granted their request, a fact that took on special color from his being detained in the capital. A mission consisting of six Jesuit fathers, among them a doctor, a botanist, an astronomer, and an architect, would be leaving the very next week. Three of the missionaries came from houses in Provence, two from Palestine, and the last from Asturias. The Society of Jesus would dispatch them directly from their present whereabouts, and they would meet in Alexandria. The missionaries would therefore not gather in Paris, which the fathers considered unfortunate, as they would have to forgo the benefit of Poncet's precious advice. But once they reached Cairo, they could make good the deficiency by calling on Murad, who would accompany them back to Abyssinia.

Jean-Baptiste wanted to object that they could not employ the Armenian without his consent. He quickly realized that he had no way of stopping them.

December was advancing. The winter solstice arrived, along with days so short and dark they hardly seemed to interfere with the nights. Candles were kept burning continuously. Parisians lived chained to their fireplaces. Jean-Baptiste, overwhelmed by the turn his affairs had taken, saw his predicament in the blackest light. He had wanted to honor his promise to the negus, and here he was responsible for the most massive incursion of Jesuits into Abyssinia in a half century. He had encouraged love and hope to grow in Alix's breast, yet he no longer had any hope of rising above his condition and would inevitably cause her disappointment and suffering. It even seemed that he had sunk lower than before, since he now had the unsavory reputation of being an impostor and a pitiable magician.

Sangray tried to cheer him up by telling him that he had seen the duc de Chartres at the Palais-Royal and heard him speak in Jean-Baptiste's defense. The conversation had turned to the supposed attempt Jean-Baptiste had made on the king's life by brandishing an unknown object in his presence, causing it to exhale mephitic vapors. "My uncle took fright over nothing, as usual," said the duke, laughing. "What did he expect to receive from Abyssinia? A Swiss chronometer, no doubt." After hearing this sally, the counselor took the prince aside to inform him that Poncet was his guest. The duke appeared interested in meeting Jean-Baptiste. It was too soon to tell what use such an ally might eventually prove, but at least it gave them a ray of hope.

Jean-Baptiste seemed to take no consolation from this story. He continued to mope by the fireplace in his apartment.

"Then why don't you write?" Sangray said to him finally, with some impatience. "Yes, write, as a man might pace back and forth, not to go anywhere maybe, but so as not to die of the cold. And once you have summoned your memories and told the story of what you saw and did, you will be able to answer your judges all the more firmly."

Jean-Baptiste took this advice. At first he did so without enthusiasm, but gradually he became absorbed in the project of writing his memoirs. Rather than plunging into black thoughts of the city in winter, he relived bright days on the Abyssinian plateau, coursing antelope on horseback, seeing the negus's guard with their gold shields and leopard-skin stoles. He was in Gondar, roaming the spice markets, and he could smell the cinnamon and red peppers. In the soft light of evening, he heard the howling of hyenas. Women passed him casting long, grave glances at him, their eyes at once startlingly white and startlingly black.

He wrote by the fireplace in his apartment from morning till evening. The guards relieved each other at his door, sometimes never seeing him all day. From his meager baggage, he had pulled a white cotton suit such as the Abyssinians wore, with narrow trousers and a muslin veil wrapped togalike over the shoulders and embroidered with a narrow band of color. He had brought these clothes back from Ethiopia without really knowing why, thinking he might offer them to someone as a present. He now took pleasure in wearing them himself in his room. Around his waist he tied the belt that had been intended for the king of France but that the Jesuits had advised him not to give. Dressed as an Abyssinian, Jean-Baptiste felt all the closer to his subject. He completed his costume with the gold chain and pendant that Negus Iyasu had given him at the time of his departure. Holding this object that the distant and improbable monarch had handled, Jean-Baptiste felt curiously moved, for it confirmed the negus's friendship and his very existence at a time when everything conspired to cast doubt. Jean-Baptiste's reverie, which he set down in fluent narrative form, was in harmony with his white-garbed self, and Sangray grew accustomed to seeing his guest in this outfit when they took their meals together.

One day, Monsieur Raoul called Poncet urgently to attend a guest at the inn who was having an apoplectic fit. The chancellor's edict did not prevent Jean-Baptiste from going out as long as he was accompanied by his guard and stayed away from the royal family. The diners in the tavern all rose to their feet as one at the sight of this young man, clad in white and belted in gold, followed by two musketeers. The awestruck crowd thought a prince must have arrived unexpectedly from the Orient, perhaps on a flying carpet, and the king was honoring him with a vigilant escort. The merchants taking supper at the inn were even more astonished to see the brilliant procession embark up the rickety stairs to visit one of their number. Jean-Baptiste, as it happened, could do nothing for the man. On entering the merchant's room, he found him giving the death rattle. The doctor left, and the corpse was carried downstairs shortly afterward. The onlookers discussed the possibilities in lowered tones. Most of them sided with an old winegrower from Chablis who believed that their merchant colleague must have converted to a distant and unknown religion in the course of his travels, and that the apparition all in white was a strange priest, come to give him his last rites.

Having once gone out of the house in this garb, Jean-Baptiste saw no reason not to do so again. Monsieur Raoul received increasing requests for consultations, and he was glad to be able to satisfy them. Jean-Baptiste only agreed to visit the poor and never accepted payment. The truth about him gradually came to be known in the quarter, and people were no longer surprised to see him go by, always in the early afternoon (when he surfaced from his writing), his tall figure wrapped in a white toga, escorted by two soldiers of the king, and looking in an alleyway for some sordid hovel where a child was suffering from disease.

Throughout the sections of Paris where his visits took him, the inhabitants referred to him simply as "the Abyssinian" and greeted him in a friendly spirit whenever they passed him in the street.

9

"In your opinion, what does holy oil look like?"

Monsieur de Maillet, seated in a large armchair, his legs crossed with those of Monsieur Macé, who sat opposite him, had posed the question in a low voice.

"Your Excellency, I would say . . . without knowing precisely . . . I imagine that it looks like oil."

"Very well," said the consul with slight impatience, "but of what kind is it, in what quantity, contained in what sort of flask?"

"Oh, it only takes a very little. A dab on the forehead . . . some on the hands."

"In short, Macé, you are in the same boat as myself," said Monsieur de Maillet, drawing himself up. "You have no idea."

"I will make inquiries," said the secretary, nettled.

"It makes no difference anyway. The Capuchins will find out. Tell me again who is to supply it to them."

"A certain Brother Ibrahim, a Syrian monk. He knows the Coptic patriarch and says he can get the coronation oil from him."

"When?"

"As soon as the Capuchins are ready."

Monsieur de Maillet rose to his feet and put on a heavy cape. December could be cold in Cairo. The desert was not far off, and the devilish houses were built to withstand only the dog days of summer. The consul never took off his wig these days, smoothing down its long ends over his chest to ward off the cold.

"Then the Capuchins' plan, if I understand it, is to bring the emperor of Abyssinia the holy oil for his coronation, though that event took place more than fifteen years ago, correct?"

"Father Pasquale says it makes no difference. The Abyssinians are used to muddling through on their own, being cut off from the world, but not having holy oil has long been a source of regret to them. If someone were to bring them the chrism, they would be very grateful, even fifteen years after the event, and would enthusiastically perform another coronation ceremony."

On concluding his little speech, Monsieur Macé coughed noisily.

"Let us grant it for the sake of argument," said the consul. "What did you say to Father Pasquale to explain why I could not see him?"

"Your Excellency, I claimed that you were indisposed, as you suggested."

"Did he believe you?"

"I doubt it. In any case, he will come back tomorrow. And if Your Excellency will allow me an opinion, he will not give up. He says that you promised to help him with money."

"This is infuriating," said the consul hotly. "I must write to Versailles. I do not have the means to fund the Capuchins' voyage and their delivery of holy oil!"

He shrugged.

"Really! The whole thing is extraordinarily bothersome. The ecclesiastic orders should hold their peace. They are threatening the success of our own embassy, the one led by Le Noir du Roule—the only one, to my way of thinking, worth a sou."

"Perhaps we could join their expedition and ours into a single embassy?"

"Ah! Have you taken complete leave of your senses?" said the consul.

He was about to elaborate on his indignation when a discreet knock was heard at the office door. The secretary hurried to open it and returned with a small parcel.

"It is the mail from Alexandria, Excellency."

Monsieur de Maillet eagerly took the letters from Monsieur Macé, cut the sealed cord that held them together with trembling fingers, and went through the contents: nothing from Pontchartrain, but a brief letter from Fléhaut. The consul opened it impatiently and read it, making frequent exclamations. Fléhaut told the story of Poncet's audience with the king, its outcome, and the upcoming trial. He also announced, with an injunction to secrecy, the arrival of the six Jesuits.

"Damn!" said the consul. "Can it be possible? We thought we had just seen the last of them. Now there are six more coming!"

But the remainder of the letter gave him such pleasure that he could not resist reading it aloud to Monsieur Macé.

"Listen to this: '. . . But the minister has arranged for the Jesuit mission to be entirely independent of the consulate. In addition, Monsieur de Pontchartrain, who cannot find sufficient praise for Your Excellency, has persuaded the king of the advantage of sending our own embassy to further the nation's political and commercial ends. . . .' Such a great man! Such a dear cousin! '. . . The minister appears to find Monsieur Le Noir du Roule suited for this mission, which may therefore leave without delay. The next consular chest will contain the funds necessary to equip this expedition. Signed: Fléhaut.'"

Wrapped in his cape, his wig askew, the consul sank into a chair.

"Macé, things have finally taken a turn in the right direction. An embassy. . . . Go and get me Le Noir du Roule."

"I do not believe he is in," said Monsieur Macé.

"Find him."

That would not be hard. Every afternoon the young diplomat, a passionate gambler, went to the house of a widowed merchant where he held a bank at faro. The man had been rich once, before meeting du Roule. Monsieur Macé tore the young man away from his game with difficulty and brought him before the consul.

"My friend," said the consul cheerfully, "I have excellent news for you."

Really, it had better be good, thought du Roule. He has called me away from a game where I could easily have won a thousand livres. Du Roule bowed politely.

"Please sit down. The news is rather staggering. The minister has named you our ambassador to Abyssinia."

Four or five expressions flitted over the young diplomat's face, triggered by internal springs. As usual it was impossible to tell what he was thinking.

"In truth," he said brightly, "the surprise is overwhelming."

This dandy seemed anything but overwhelmed, his hose spotless despite the muddy street he had crossed to reach the consulate.

"When do I leave?" he asked.

"Ah! Such enthusiasm, such impatience!" said the consul blithely. "Stay a moment, if you please. The money is arriving by the next cash box. Everything must be prepared with care."

"A few days?"

"More. A few weeks. If all goes well, let us say six weeks. Perhaps eight."

"Perfect!" said du Roule.

"We do not want you to set off headlong. We think a great deal of you, dear friend. Improvisation was fine for the adventurers who blazed the trail, but a real embassy will require more substantial means, rich presents, a guard . . ."

They went over the expedition in some detail. It was almost time for supper, which was always eaten early at the consulate. Monsieur de Maillet asked the secretary to leave them alone for a few minutes.

"Are there no personal arrangements you would like to make before your departure?" the consul asked once he was alone with du Roule.

He expected the young diplomat to take advantage of the present circumstances to declare his intentions toward his daughter. At every opportunity, the consul had made frequent and unmistakable allusions to the matter. But either du Roule's upbringing had made him unusually reticent or (as the consul feared) the young woman had failed to please him, having not tried in the slightest to make herself attractive. At any rate nothing had come of it.

"No, Excellency, not that I am aware," said du Roule calmly, his expression one of mild surprise.

~

The chevalier Hector Le Noir du Roule was the third child of a family that applied the law of primogeniture all the more strictly as it had nothing, and had for a very long time had nothing, to divide among its heirs. He was raised negligently in the family castle near Senlis. Everything in it harked back to his ancestors, who looked down grimly from wall after wall. All the expressions of culture enshrined in the castle—arms, nobility, the arts—were paired in the child's mind with a disclaimer, since, though long and lovingly cultivated there, they had led his family to ruin. The young du Roule developed the habit of seeing every ornament and every object of beauty—from a canvas by a great master, to a bronze wall sconce, to a tapestry, to a knightly sword—as a commodity that could be placed against a wall or a piece of furniture to hide a crack, a mousehole, or a mildew stain. The chevalier (for so he was called by the peasantry, his family having no title to bestow on any but the eldest son) was allowed to run freely through the hunting grounds with the little peasant boys. The young nobleman quickly discovered that these young scamps often ate better than he. He soon became adept in both worlds. Outside he was sly, brutal, and mean to the point that it became a weapon, almost a livelihood for him. At the castle he was the epitome of elegance and politeness, thereby earning a bit more food and clothing from the women in the family than he had a right to. He also sought their caresses, for he developed early on a sensual need for soft skin and perfume.

Only his eldest brother had a tutor, but by copying his brother's lessons he learned enough to become secretary to the duc de Vendôme, to whom he was recommended by a cousin of his father. It was through this small door that he entered the wider world, where he continued to belie the grace that brought him such notice in society by the gambling and orgies that he pursued outside of it. By what chain of seduction and baseness, of application to work and dedication to vice, he was appointed by the statesman Torcy to the Ministry of Foreign Affairs it is better not to know. Du Roule had for some time eyed a career in diplomacy. He believed his refinement of manner might count to his advantage there, while the fact of living abroad would give his strong passion for lucre the necessary scope.

He was offered the consulship in Rosetta. Of all the stations in the Levant it was the most poorly paid, but Rosetta was a port and therefore saw a good deal of trafficking. He told himself he could easily round out his salary there. He set off—and no sooner had he arrived than he was offered, on the basis of his impeccable reputation, a wife and an embassy. Two blessings, to all intents and purposes.

But it was best to think things through and not act heedlessly. Mademoiselle de Maillet was a respectable match, and he could certainly drive a bargain over her dowry. Du Roule was in no hurry, however, to be tied down. Abyssinia was of more interest to him, although he knew little about it except that it was reputed to have gold, gems, and spices. Monsieur de Maillet had laid out woolly plans of extending the French East India Company to Abyssinia, having had the misguided notion that he, du Roule, might actually go to work for someone other than himself. This the chevalier was not about to do, as he was seeking to acquire his own fortune and had no intention of being hampered by scruples. He recognized the cynicism in himself and was proud of it. Yet in his own way (much as it would have surprised him to hear it) this realist was a dreamer. There was nothing pragmatic about the fortune he proposed to acquire. He imagined he could carve out a kingdom for himself as the very first Spaniards had done in America or again the Frenchman Pronis in the Mascarene Islands; he would become a king somewhere, at the head of a considerable fortune. And he feared that in those circumstances, Mademoiselle de Maillet would no longer suffice him. He dreamed of princesses, of queens. He therefore had no difficulty in coming to a quick decision: first the trip, then, if there was still call for it, the marriage.

But this plan failed to take into account the strong action of his senses, which Alix had powerfully excited. After a week he told himself: Really, the marriage holds no attraction for me, but I would give anything to take my pleasure with this skittish child.

Unfortunately he was no longer in the countryside, on the hunting grounds of his family castle, and the consul's daughter was no peasant girl that he could tumble at will. He had to marry her first, and this he did not want. Equivocating with the consul to dodge his unspoken offers, du Roule had not renounced finding a way to spend a few voluptuous moments with the daughter before leaving, but without having to make any promises first. He watched her and gradually developed a plan. By the time Monsieur de Maillet confirmed his embassy, du Roule was certain that the young lady nursed a secret passion elsewhere and that the proposed marriage was as unwelcome to her as to himself. This was reassuring to the libertine. The love she felt for another—and Monsieur Macé, whom du Roule had enlisted as an ally, quickly informed him of his name—might drive her to accede to her passions, which he felt were strong and which, as a man of experience, he would skillfully redirect toward himself.

Having stayed several days out of sight after fainting at the table, Alix reappeared. Du Roule followed her everywhere with his eyes. Monsieur de Maillet, delighted, pretended to notice nothing and went on scolding his daughter for being untidy and unwelcoming to their guest. Did Alix give credence to her father's reproaches? Or did she know how much her natural beauty, her loosely gathered hair, her simple dress, and her bursting health—unmistakable despite her feigned indispositions—had stimulated the senses of the young gallant? Did she know how much her shyness and fear betrayed an emotion that du Roule smoldered to follow to its source, namely to convert into desire and voluptuousness?

As he came out of the consul's office freshly invested with his embassy, the chevalier saw Alix going down the stairs. He followed her into the music room, where she quickly picked up a score lying on the spinet.

Du Roule did not even pretend to acknowledge this activity. He walked up to the young woman and planted himself squarely in front of her.

"I have good news for you," he said, bringing his mouth so close that she could feel his breath on her forehead. "I am going to leave."

"But . . . how very unfortunate."

They had never spoken to each other alone before.

"Really? You are sorry to see me go?"

Alix did not answer, but she felt herself in that moment of silence undergoing a rapid and profound transformation. This man close to her, in a drawing room whose door was miles away, her shallow breathing, her redness of face . . . She suddenly saw herself again being stalked in the night, pursued, her heel broken, as the dogs started to bark. Then just as suddenly she remembered her time of freedom in Giza: she felt the easy balance of the foil, the power of her horse, the detonation of the pistols. She drew herself up and faced him.

"What do you want?" she said, looking hard at him with her blue eyes.

"Others want on my behalf," said du Roule. "While I don't want at all. Not any more than you do. We shan't marry."

"You seem well pleased to make the decision."

He came nearer. She did not draw back, and the emotion stirred in her by his nearness was no longer one of fear.

"I am not making a decision," he said. "I know."

"Know what?"

"That I want to stay unattached. And that you no longer are."

"So?"

"So, let us forget about marriage. Go on loving as you do, and let us hold on to . . ."

Her eyes did not waver.

". . . to pleasure," he said, latching on to her lips, which she did not withdraw as quickly as she might.

There were steps in the hallway. Alix coolly sat down at the clavier. Du Roule took a chair at the other end of the small drawing room. Madame de Maillet bustled in and was delighted to find the two lovebirds together, being entirely of her husband's opinion. She invited them to join her at table for supper.

The consul kept the conversation alive during the meal all by himself, giving them the news from the latest gazettes.

"And as for Poncet," he said to his wife, "of course you remember him, dear, that apothecary . . ."

Macé and du Roule glanced at Alix over their spoons.

". . . the tiresome man wanted to see the king. Well, he has seen him. His Majesty was far too keen to be gulled by him. The upstart has been arrested and is now awaiting trial."

There was no movement from Alix, no muttered word or sharp intake of breath to betray her. Alix was back beside the river at Giza, standing en garde by the tall hedge of reeds. The strength she had acquired in those few days had remained well concealed. Since her return, things had gone exactly as though she had never lived those moments of great freedom. She had run away from du Roule, acted the part of a little girl who is ill or timid. All this because she had been waiting for Jean-Baptiste and had sworn not to jeopardize their future. Now she learned that he was being held a prisoner. It was her turn to act, to transform her freedom into transgression, her will into power, so that she might no longer be afraid of anything, either from herself or from others, and could break through all obstacles.

It was a little after midnight when she slipped into the chevalier du Roule's bedchamber, where he was expecting her.

10

The jury of scholars who were to examine Jean-Baptiste was assembled shortly before the new year—earlier than Sangray had expected. It was felt in Versailles that the protracted presence of this foreign prisoner, about whom the most extraordinary stories were being told, was growing to be a problem. The matter was brought before the council of state, and the king himself recommended expedited action. If Poncet was an impostor, it was best to punish him promptly. If he was well and truly the envoy of the negus, then best to minimize what would surely be counted as an affront.

There were four jury members, two from the university and two from the clergy. All four were acknowledged scholars in realms of archaeology and philology so arid that there were none to challenge their learning. Whatever they said had more or less to be taken on faith, so they therefore said little, used as grave a tone as possible, and spat venom on any opinion that was unsanctioned or differed from their own.

To say the jury members were hostile to Poncet would understate the case. The real point, though, was that they wanted to please the king, and Poncet had displeased him. Moreover, the propaganda they had overheard about the supposed traveler had turned their minds against him. For all their eminence, they were susceptible to influence.

Jean-Baptiste was anxious as he went to the first session. Sangray had advised him not to wear his white cotton garb, which would be counted against him as a provocation. He therefore went dressed in conventional woollens, with nothing out of the ordinary. The confrontation took place in a large room at the Sorbonne, decorated with carved and gilded wood paneling. The jury sat on a dais, the professors in academic gowns and the priests in cassocks. The suspect sat below, in front. His guards kept watch over him from either side. Two rows behind sat a sparse gathering of the public, among whom Jean-Baptiste saw Fléhaut (who avoided his gaze),

Father Plantain in company with three other Jesuits, and a number of strangers. As it was winter, the room was cold and the audience prone to cough.

What made everyone uneasy was that the business had all the appearance of a trial without being one. It was an expert appraisal of a person's knowledge. The question was not to discover whether Jean-Baptiste had committed a crime, but whether he had truly performed the journey he claimed to have just returned from. At the same time, what might have been a frank and unalloyed investigation of the truth actually had another dimension. Everyone knew that if Jean-Baptiste was declared a liar, he would then be indicted and pass into the custody of the justice system, where they had other ways of making a person talk.

This ambiguity was patent when the proceedings got under way. The members of the jury asked the "subject" to give his name, birth, and occupation "if he would be so kind." But by his tone, the president of the jury indicated that it would be quite inconceivable for him not to.

"My name is Jean-Baptiste Poncet. My parents are unknown to me. I was born in Grenoble on June 17, 1672. For the past three years or so I have lived in Cairo, where I practice the trade of herbalist."

The president examined the papers in front of him. A court clerk scratched away with his pen on a corner of the dais.

"Now then, you claim to have traveled to Abyssinia?"

"I do not claim it, sir. I affirm it."

"You know that very few Christians today can boast of having returned from such a journey."

"I know it," said Jean-Baptiste. "And I am not boasting about it."

"Yet you went so far as to maintain it before the king," said the other professor, an extremely elderly man, yellow-complexioned, who spoke with the cracked voice of a crone.

"It was the emperor of Ethiopia himself who charged me with this mission."

"We know, we know," the president cut in, as though comforting a madman in the throes of a hallucination, "but let us move on from these general propositions. Be so kind as to answer the specific questions we will be asking you. Father Juillet would like to begin, I believe."

"Sir," said the priest, a fairly young man with a bony face and deep lines on either side of his mouth, "what is the name of the city where the emperor of Ethiopia lives?"

"Gondar, Father."

"Could you spell it?"

Poncet spelled the name out. At the priest's request, he gave a fairly detailed description of the city. The four men listened intently, exchanging glances from time to time, and responding to the suspect's words with expressions of sarcasm.

"Do you know Don Alvarez?"

"No," said Jean-Baptiste, searching his mind. "Where might I have met him?"

"Don Alvarez is dead," said the president with a contemptuous smile. "He was a celebrated Jesuit, a great and veridical scholar. He left an account of life among the Abyssinians, having spent ten years in Ethiopia."

"I would be very pleased to read it," said Poncet.

"You would indeed do well to," said the yellow academic. "You would learn that the capital of Ethiopia is called Axum and not—as you said—Gondar."

"And you would also know," the young clergyman said, "that there are no other cities in that country, where everyone lives on the land and tills the soil, and where the sovereign himself travels from camp to camp."

"Ah, I beg your pardon," said Poncet, "but his account is not current. The country is full of towns and even cities. Gondar was created after the Jesuits' departure because the emperor wanted a stable court and mistrusted the people of Axum. Fundamentally he followed the same course as our kings of France. During the time of Francis I, the court was constantly moving from site to site, then it settled in Paris, and finally at Versailles. This last move is so recent that a messenger who returned from France ten years ago would have made no mention of that town."

"Your explanations are of great interest," said the academic. "We can form a better idea of how, by embroidering on the history of our own country, you managed to construct a picture of the country you claim to have traveled to."

Jean-Baptiste started to protest. The president interrupted their dispute and asked another question. From this brief exchange, the general tone and spirit of the inquiry can be gauged. There is no point in reporting it in detail, especially as the interrogation lasted more than two hours.

The suspect returned home flanked by his guards as night fell. Sangray was waiting impatiently for him. A capon from Le Beau Noir lay steaming on the table.

"Well?" asked the counselor.

"They do not believe a word I say. Everything they know comes from the Jesuits, who left Abyssinia sixty years ago. On the basis of the Jesuits' claim that nothing has changed in that country since the Queen of Sheba, those dolts insist that a half century is nothing and that anything that does not appear in their books must be an invention."

Jean-Baptiste gave his friend a succinct account of the day's session.

"They also asked me if I was familiar with the Abyssinians' religion. I said that I knew nothing about it. One of them asked me: 'According to this people's priests, how many natures does Christ have?' I told them that I had been questioned there in exactly the same terms. 'If such is the case and you answered in conformity with our religion,' the president objected, 'they would certainly have put you to death.' 'No,' I told him, 'I gave them no specific answer, and for an excellent reason: I do not know the answer. I admitted my weakness in theology and asked to be excused for it. My ignorance is what saved me in that country. It would be very strange if it convicted me in this one."

"Good! Excellent! You fought like a lion," said Sangray.

"Like a lion at the bottom of a pit being pricked with poisoned lances on all sides. Do you know that they are also questioning Murad's legitimacy, on the basis that his name is not Abyssinian but Turkish? Of course! He is Armenian. 'Then he is Armenian and the negus employs him as a diplomat,' says that ignoramus of a priest. 'Since when do kings choose their ambassadors from hostile nations?' I tried to explain it to him. He would not hear any of my arguments."

"You must not despair," said Sangray. "Hold firm to your arguments. Obtain a judgment that is moderate, even if unfavorable. We are working for you behind the scenes. In fact, I have some excellent news: the duc de Chartres kindly agreed to read the manuscript you gave me three days ago. News should reach me on that front at the beginning of next week. He has little influence over the king, but he has a genius for inflaming public opinion on behalf of a good cause."

"I think the fire burning at the foot of the stake is already hot enough," said Jean-Baptiste bitterly.

The next day was Sunday. The questioning was to resume on Wednesday. Sangray came to see Jean-Baptiste at ten o'clock.

"You know how little I relish the role of spiritual adviser," he said in a low voice, "but your two guardian angels surely file a regular report on you. The fact that you live with me already counts against you. Don't compound the damage by not going to mass."

Jean-Baptiste heeded his host's advice and led his little squadron to the eleven-o'clock service at the Church of Saint Eustache. He was too ignorant of the mass to hear it as anything but a gentle noise, relieved by the canticles and graced by the beautiful mauve-colored vaults that shone in the weak December light. The atmosphere brought him back to his childhood. He thought of his mother, whom he claimed not to have known but who was in fact a poor servant girl whose masters had refused her permission to raise her own bastard. Whose bastard was he, when it came to that? He had never known. But when a child does not know his parentage, his eyes always turn toward the castle. He believes himself the offspring of a king or a duke, never of a miserable wretch. Or if it is a wretch, it has to be the most fearful wretch of all, the prince of cutthroats, the most generous, the most intrepid, the most invincible of bandits. Our Father which art in heaven? The words truly suggested no image to Jean-Baptiste. They implied a Unique Being, while what he imagined was a plethora of characters who changed at every shift in his development. The heavens are empty for fatherless children, or else overfilled, which comes to the same thing.

From his infancy until the age of twelve, he had been brought up by his gentle grandmother, who lived in the country and earned her living by weaving baskets. All the female figures in the church glowed for him with a radiance they borrowed from this common source. If he had been asked to worship a goddess instead of a god, he would have found the energy to become pope. Would anyone have been the better for it? he wondered, smiling to himself.

As the service progressed around him, Jean-Baptiste sat, stood, or kneeled as was required. The chairs squealed on the cold stone floor at every change of position. During communion, an altar boy standing at the priest's side rang a little bell, the shrill sound reverberating in the cold air like a knell. Jean-Baptiste, on his knees, could see the mist coming from his mouth. He tilted his head and was suddenly struck by one of those revelations that you feel even before you formulate them and that leave you changed forever after.

I am kneeling, he thought, his eyes widening as though before a great discovery. Yes! Ever since I undertook this mission to Ethiopia I have been on my knees. Or maybe it is since I saw Alix for the first time. At any rate it is the same thing. I was a free man. I had never submitted to any authority placed over me. The first time I saw the consul it was he who came to visit me. I sat perched in a tree and I did him the favor of listening to his petition. And now, I am on my knees. . . .

In the meantime, the congregation had risen to their feet at a signal from the priest. Behind him Jean-Baptiste heard the clanking of the musketeers as they stood also. Jean-Baptiste followed suit.

And now I am standing, but it is because I have been ordered to. Whether sitting or standing, I am always on my knees, that is, submissive. I am waiting for the consul to be kind enough to give me his daughter. I am waiting for the king to make me a nobleman. I am waiting for these professors to pass judgment on me. And since they are going to convict me, since the king is going to do nothing to help me, since the consul is going to refuse me his daughter, I am on my knees not before people who love me but before the most malevolent authority. The worst is that I don't even believe in it. I don't think it is an honor to be named a nobleman by a king who grants such favors in order to keep others in submission. I don't believe this religion is worth more or less than any other. And though I believe in a man's right to believe in it if he wants, I deny the church's authority to impose on men's minds, mine in particular. And yet I am kneeling.

The priest had given the benediction and the congregation were filing out hurriedly, their hands deep in the folds of their coats. They looked in passing at the young man lost in thought whom two musketeers seemed to be waiting for.

And all this, went on Jean-Baptiste, because I knelt before the consul. It all derives from that, clearly and unmistakably. That was my downfall. That was the precise moment when I renounced my freedom. I acted as though it were legitimate for a father to dispose of his daughter's wishes. I claimed to love a woman and at the same time acted in denial of her existence and her freedom. I put Alix's life and mine into the hands of that despicable man, her father. *I am on my knees!*

"No," said one of the musketeers timidly.

Jean-Baptiste realized, blushing, that he had spoken the last words out loud.

"Come, sirs," he said, recovering himself. "One must always bow before the will of God."

Then he swept out with his retinue.

As innocuous as it seemed, this episode was to have a profound effect on Jean-Baptiste. From the germ planted here, a new pattern would manifest itself in a few hours that would alter the course of all his future actions.

"Freedom is not a thing to be asked for but to be taken," he said to Sangray that night.

As of the next day, he undertook to put this declaration into practice.

An event that had happened three days earlier now took on great importance. Jean-Baptiste had continued his visits to the sick even as the time approached for his trial. In fact, these were his only outings. The guards went with him as far as the entrance to the rooms where he would be treating the ill but did not come in. Monsieur Raoul served in some sense as his secretary, as cases were referred to him and he evaluated them for urgency and seriousness. On that particular day, three days before the hearing, Monsieur Raoul gave Jean-Baptiste an address recommending that he act with extreme prudence. His face had a strange expression as he spoke.

In the dark, dirty hovel to which the doctor found his way, four people were living: a woman of indeterminate age, dressed in rags, two children with unkempt hair, who huddled in a corner, and the patient. The man's name was Mortier, and at first he pretended he had collided with a cart. But it did not take Jean-Baptiste long to make him admit that the double wound in his calf had been caused by an arrow. He was just coming into the city by the Meaux gates with a load of grain when the archers on watch saw him. Jean-Baptiste assured the smuggler that he would not speak to a soul about it. Then he applied strong tinctures to the wound, wrapped it in a bandage, and gave the patient a strong dose of ipecac. The bone had not been affected. All that was needed was to bring the infection under control. The next day, the patient sweated copiously, and by the second day he was able to eat again.

11

At Jean-Baptiste's second confrontation with the jury, the participants arrived in radically different frames of mind than at the first. The learned men, though unanimous in believing that the supposed traveler had answered their questions badly, were nonetheless aware of the strength of his arguments and the weakness of any proofs they might bring to challenge him. They had taken advantage of the days between sessions to immerse themselves in study and prepare a more rigorous set of questions. Jean-Baptiste, on the other hand, taking delight in his new resolution, arrived at the hearing smiling broadly. The walk there had cheered him up. He had enjoyed a pleasant discussion with his guards, two young men from Picardy who were more or less cousins and had arranged with their commander always to draw duty together.

The session started with a question from the priest who had not opened his mouth the first time. He was a large man, very nearsighted, who held the paper on which he had written his text close to his nose, then looked around the room with mist-filled eyes. He wanted to know the kinds of food the Abyssinians ate. Setting aside its complicated phrasing, the question was simple enough, even silly. Jean-Baptiste answered with polite offhandedness. There followed a number of detailed questions that showed how carefully the scholars had combed over the scant accounts that were available to them. The hall was practically asleep. The atmosphere livened up at a question on the structural laws of the kingdom.

"Primogeniture is the rule there," said Jean-Baptiste, "as it is here. The king's brothers, cousins, and nephews, who might spearhead a rebellion, are neutralized. But rather than allowing them to spend themselves in debauchery, as is the custom elsewhere, in Abyssinia they are imprisoned on top of a mountain."

"And where, pray tell, do the king's brothers spend themselves in debauchery?" asked the president.

The allusion to the duc d'Orléans was too obvious to need further elaboration. Jean-Baptiste smiled.

"Why . . . among the Aztecs, I suppose."

The jurors looked at each other in perplexity. Such gross provocation was highly distasteful, but what a windfall for them! If it continued, they could leave the shifting ground of science and philology to pursue an indictment on the much solider one of provocation against the government. The entire question could be settled in police court. This needed following up.

"Speak to us a bit more on the subject of the king of Abyssinia, if you please," asked one of the professors with a sly smile.

"I have said so much about him already. Truly, I cannot recall another thing."

"Consider thoroughly. How does he live? What is remarkable in his surroundings?"

"I have already described it for you, I believe. The throne, the palace . . . Ah, there is an anecdote. It has just come back to me. The king's windows at the palace look out on two courtyards. One of them contains lions."

"You have told us that."

"Yes. But what you do not realize is that from the second courtyard comes an incessant wailing. The sound never stops. On occasion it grows louder, and you distinctly hear sobs and cries. One day I asked if these noises were made by prisoners, by those captured in war. I was told that on the contrary, the wailers were favored servants of the king, who were generously paid. Their work consisted in producing the music Abyssinians consider that a sovereign should always hear: the sound of his people suffering and calling on him for help."

"Well?" said the president. "What do you conclude from this?"

"Conclude for yourselves," said Jean-Baptiste. "It is not my business to say whether certain kings would or would not be well advised to let the suffering of their people reach their ears."

"Aha!" said the president, glancing elatedly at his colleagues. "Has the clerk noted these words? Perfect!"

Nothing so warms a courtier's heart as the sight of a proud man defying what they must bow and scrape to. They may then watch as power turns pitiless and rationalize their own cowardice on the grounds that defeat was a foregone conclusion.

"Oh, I know," said Jean-Baptiste, who was entering into the spirit of the proceedings. "Here is another, since you take such an interest in the negus. At night, one of the king's noblemen sleeps across the threshold of his bedroom door. In the morning, it is he who wakes the king by lashing the ground with his whip. Why a whip? Because in the days when the negus still traveled with his household through the bush, establishing a new encampment almost every day, it happened that wild animals, predators, hyenas often, would slip in among the tents at night, sometimes even reaching the entrance of the king's tent. The whiplashes served to drive off any ferocious beasts that might have tried to come near him during the night. When the kings built palaces and developed the habit of sleeping there, they kept this custom as though they were still in the jungle and surrounded by dangerous wild animals. Frankly, sirs, do you not find this an excellent example and one that could well be copied elsewhere?"

"Driving the hyenas out of the palace, is it! Whipping the courtiers, for example, at the king's levee, do I read you right?" said the president. "Of course. May it please the clerk to take note. Your stories are truly excellent. What a pity that you did not delight us with these pearls earlier."

The jury were now relaxed and smiling openly. The audience was silent.

"Perhaps you would provide us with a few more details?" said the president hungrily.

"A last one," said Poncet smiling. "I was present during my stay at many executions. There is one punishment I would like to describe to you. They take the prisoner and roll him up from head to toe in a white muslin sheet. Then he is doused in warm, liquid wax. The wax is absorbed by the cloth before coagulating, turning the man into a large, living candle. Then all you have to do is light the thing. It burns like a torch. The man's shrieks can hardly be heard because the roar of the fire is so loud."

The jury members looked at Jean-Baptiste in terror. The clerk's pen was arrested in midair.

"When it is all over, one is left with the black shape of the charred corpse. Here is where it pays to be attentive. If you look carefully, turning the corpse this way and that, you can often find, under a crust of still-white cloth, the prisoner's two intact eyes, preserved by his tears."

Jean-Baptiste rose.

"You have heard enough," he said. "I can think of nothing further to tell you at this stage. Judge me as you see fit. I have only one wish: that you advocate a similar punishment for me, one that would destroy my body but leave me my two eyes, which have served me so well. Goodbye, sirs, and thank you for having listened to the story of my travels."

The silent and icy air rang with the sound of Jean-Baptiste's boots. The two Picards followed him. They crossed the room, climbed the wooden stairs to the great door, and swept out.

~

"My friend, you acted wrongly," said Sangray. "We might have been able to arrange everything. For one thing, the duc de Chartres is absolutely taken with your recollections. To show you how great a store he sets by them, he is determined to meet you. He offers you these ten thousand livres and asks if he might be allowed to publish your account. You see how wrong it was to provoke the judges."

The counselor was standing in front of Jean-Baptiste. As usual, the old man wore no peruke, and his large head was framed by a short tousle of gray hair. He held the doctor tightly, his arms extended.

"Ah, you were wrong and you were right. I understand so well. If you only knew! Here, add this to the duke's gold, I pray you. It comes from me."

He put a large velvet purse in Jean-Baptiste's hands.

"And now, lose no time. You wanted to make a sensation. I would have advised you against it, because everything happens fast here. La Reynie is no longer their chief but the police are more powerful now than ever. Even before the jury makes a report the king will know everything."

"I intend to make my play tonight."

"Good. Just tell me what I can do to help."

Jean-Baptiste told him.

"Alas!" said the counselor. "The duc de Chartres will be inconsolable at not meeting you. He had so many questions he wanted to ask."

Then Sangray embraced his young friend with tears in his eyes.

"And I am losing a son," he said.

"You are not losing him, you are saving him."

"That is some consolation. But confess that although you may escape from your judges, the penalty on me is severe."

This farewell moved the young man deeply. Monsieur Raoul arrived with a pheasant and went to find a bottle of burgundy, leaving the two men to commune for the last time over these two constituents of their evening ritual.

At nine o'clock, Jean-Baptiste retired to his rooms. The two Picard policemen bowed their heads to him respectfully. A half hour later the whole house was asleep.

~

The back of the townhouse in which Sangray lived gave onto a small paved courtyard. In it were a well and two stables, surrounded by a wall some six feet high. Jean-Baptiste's bedroom looked out on the back of the house through a mullioned window. As chance would have it, the roof of the stables was joined to the main building by a wide gutter that passed just below this window. The clock on the Church of Saint Eustache struck ten just as Jean-Baptiste climbed out onto his window ledge in his warmest clothes, wrapped in a greatcoat, and slid down onto the roof of the stable. He carried a sack over his shoulder. Cautiously he made his way along the slate roof edge, leaped onto the wall, then let himself down into the neighboring courtyard, landing silently on a small pile of loose dirt.

It was dark and intensely cold. The stars shone in a sky of black ice.

Jean-Baptiste walked a cautious step or two before a hand grabbed him.

"Mortier?" he asked, startled.

"Shh! Follow me."

The smuggler was not yet entirely recovered, but he was no longer feverish, the wound was clean, and it was healing behind the protection of a good bandage. This was not his first scrape, and though still limping he would in any case have returned to his escapades. No one knew Paris better than he. In an exchange of confidences, Poncet had revealed his secret to Mortier, who was only too happy to do a favor for the man who had saved his life.

They threaded their way through a maze of streets and courtyards. The winter wind had blown out most of the streetlamps, but Mortier knew where there were dogs and what garden gates were left on the latch and could be used as passageways. He knew the route of the night watch and was afraid of nothing, with the exception of informers—who were responsible, as he firmly believed, for his earlier mishap. He looked out over the streets the way a sailor looks at the sea to gauge the danger of the waves and current. In a half hour they had reached the boulevard du Temple, which was lit by large copper lanterns hung from posts.

"Be careful," Mortier whispered. "There is a guard post fifty yards away. Make your way to the edge of the shadow, and if you hear shouting, run for it."

Mortier limped across the wide, well-lit expanse of the boulevard first. When he had disappeared into the shadows across the way, Jean-Baptiste bounded across the street and joined him unnoticed. On the far side were gardens planted with tall trees, among which were a few houses. They cautiously avoided the guard dogs lurking behind certain of the hedges. Soon they left these enclosures and, climbing toward Charonne, entered the pure and empty countryside. They made their way along sunken paths, followed foot trails through the woods, and leaped over narrow streams carpeted on either side with dead leaves.

The moon was still down and no light came from the sky. They found themselves on a wide track where, from time to time, they heard a cow startle heavily from her sleep as they approached a fence. Shortly before reaching the village of Charonne, they cut off toward the right. From the moist air and the rustling of the leaves, Jean-Baptiste could tell that they were passing through a forest. They heard a horse snort in a clearing. Mortier made a signal, and someone in the darkness whistled.

"Is that you, rogue?"

"None other, scoundrel."

A man's reedy, wavering voice, presumably an old man's, came out of the darkness close by.

"Have you brought the beast?"

"Beast yourself, haven't you got ears? Put your hand there. Does that feel like a partridge?"

"You old wag. Hand me the bridle. There you go, Doctor, the horse is all saddled."

Jean-Baptiste adjusted his stirrup leathers by feel, then swung up into the saddle. Mortier went over the route to the post stage where he would get a new mount. When the smuggler refused to accept any money, Jean-Baptiste did not insist but slipped a purse into the man's coat unnoticed.

They shook hands in silence, then each thanked the other with a full heart. Poncet touched his spurs to his horse's flanks and joined the road. At the first crossroads, he turned south, not deviating again. It was so dark at first that he was obliged to stay at a trot, but then a sliver of moon rose in the sky, enough to reveal the terrain ahead. The horse had a pleasant canter, long and smooth. Jean-Baptiste had never been so close to imprisonment: they would seek him and pursue him, because he had disobeyed the greatest of kings. Yet never had he felt so free and confident as on this cold night, lashed by tree branches, his eyes streaming with tears.

5

The Burning Bush

I

What mattered to Alix more than anything was her inner purity, the generous integrity of her feelings, and her capacity to love fully and faithfully. A healthy pride made her believe that the maintenance of these virtues depended on her will alone and would be unaffected by any occurrences to her body. It was in her heart, fierce and intact, that her true maidenhood resided.

To preserve it there was no need to make herself a slave to the material virginity that society upheld only because it feared the freedom of its youth. On the contrary, she thought indignantly, it was to protect that laughable sanctuary that she had up till now had to hobble herself in long-trained dresses, wear iron corsets, lower her eyes in front of strangers, and finally run in the night like a startled quarry.

Now that she had acquired sureness, strength, and skill at Giza, she had still to come out of herself and cast off this last mooring. She would have infinitely preferred for Jean-Baptiste to lead her across this threshold. But since this was impossible, since she needed on the contrary to bend all her energies to finding and rescuing him without delay, she would use any man she could. The chevalier du Roule believed that he had won her over and would possess her. He served pitifully to implement what she herself had wanted. The libertine was horrified despite his long experience—or perhaps because of it—at Alix's coldness and determination during the night he spent with her, yet he remained lucid enough to gauge the terrible consequences of this encounter.

In the first place, he fell into a hopeless adoration of this beautiful and shameless girl, who accomplished everything with a seductive mixture of naturalness, nobility, ardor, and detachment. Next he believed that his victory entitled him to certain rights, among them the right to tussle with her again at his discretion, but he discovered on the contrary that he was at her mercy: on the second night, to his mortification, she turned him away. That was when he started to be afraid. He could not understand what motivated this daring young woman; he despised himself and imagined simply that she was impulsive, sensual, and capable of the wildest acts—even revealing their relations publicly. Du Roule realized that his appetite for pleasure had led him astray. Yet so strong was the impression Alix had made on him that though he feared the worst, he regretted nothing. He continued on the following nights to beg for her favors, and she continued coldly to refuse him. He found himself alone on the landing, imploring her to relent, crazed with desire, never again to taste what Alix had allowed him in their one encounter to know briefly and to long for eternally.

She confessed the entire episode to Françoise, who, in her capacity as a laundress, erased every trace of the incident. Had she been told of it beforehand, Françoise would most likely have tried to stop her. Now it was too late to moan and wail. Alix explained her plans and Françoise raised a thousand objections, as there were countless obstacles in the path the young woman proposed to take. But in the end, the servant had to grudgingly admire Alix's strength and enthusiasm in choosing the path of freedom. She gave in and promised to help the young woman in every way.

On the fourth night that he came to scratch at Mademoiselle de Maillet's door like a cat or a dog, terrified at the scandal he was courting, du Roule was stunned to notice that the bolt was not drawn. He opened the door and walked in. Alix stood facing him. She wore a batiste shirt, corduroy knee breeches, and boots, the outfit she had worn at Giza to exercise her horse. She looked so fierce that the chevalier did not dare kiss her, which he was dying to do.

"Would you please lock the door?" she said.

He obeyed. She pointed to a small chair in front of the narrow walnut desk where she had so often dreamed. He sat down carefully, as the chair seemed fragile.

"Sir," she said, "you have nothing to gain by coming every night to my door. I will not open it to you again, and someone might see you."

"But what have I done?" he asked lamely. "How have I displeased you?"

"The issue is not with you. I can confirm that you acquitted yourself ably of your task."

"Ably! Task! Oh, you are making fun of me," said du Roule, genuinely saddened.

"Not at all. It is a question of seeing things as they are, or rather as they were. You had a job to do and you performed it adroitly. I thank you for it."

"Mademoiselle, you humiliate me."

For all that his life had known its share of debauchery, it was the first time du Roule had ever found himself so completely in the power of a woman he had only planned to bed. He was prepared to throw himself at her feet and beg if it seemed likely to do any good. Instead he tried not to debase himself any further, for her haughty demeanor indicated that the one thing she wanted from him was a bit of dignity.

"Consider if you would," she said, "that our interests are entirely at variance. You wish to avoid scandal, while I seek it."

Du Roule appeared terrified, as though certain that she was preparing to denounce him.

"But do not be afraid. I am as determined to protect your precious reputation as to sully my own."

Du Roule could make no sense of the situation. All he understood was that he had lost his manly energy, and that this woman had somehow fed off it.

"Please speak more clearly," he said in a weak voice.

"All right. We are going to get along, and I am sure you will perform what I ask of you as zealously as last time. Tomorrow you will ask my father for my hand in marriage."

Du Roule leaped from his chair with a bellow that he quickly suppressed.

"Oh, Mademoiselle, there is nothing I pray for more earnestly."

This was true. At first he had thought the marriage not in his best interest. But since the fateful night of Alix's visit, everything had changed. He would have paid any price to bring about their union and find his pleasure with her again. In this he was blind, as what fueled his passion was Alix's freedom. Yet at this moment, he was entirely his own dupe.

"Make no mistake," she said severely. "Neither you nor I have the slightest intention of seeing this marriage take place."

"And why not?" he whined.

"You said it yourself, back when my father was offering me to you. If your mind seems to have changed, it is only because your senses clamor for another taste of what they have sampled. My refusal may irritate you, but you are a man of too much experience to confuse your emotions with your appetites."

"No, no, believe me," said du Roule, on the verge of tears.

"Let us waste no more time on this. I will take you at your word as to your feelings, which are no concern of mine. On my side at least, there is no question of marriage. I simply want you to put the matter to my father. If you insist on refusing, I will reveal everything."

Du Roule sat down heavily on the chair, puzzled.

"Then why do you want me to make your father such a request? I don't understand."

Alix went to the door and softly pulled back the bolt.

"It will not be the first time, dear sir, that you have done something without understanding why. Then we agree? I will expect you to ask for my hand tomorrow. Otherwise, it will be my turn to speak, and the consequences will be much more serious."

"Are you really sending me away?" asked du Roule.

This woman put him in a state of utter confusion, both because of her beauty and because of the memory of the pleasure she had given him.

She pulled the door open wide.

Du Roule glanced with terror out onto the dark landing. He rose meekly and went out, turning back at the door for a look, perhaps a kiss, a last gesture of repentance or surrender such as women sometimes make at the height of their cruelty. But Alix just shut the door in his face.

The next afternoon she went walking into the public garden at the end of the street. She had only recently been allowed to go there, and only if she wore a mantilla and promised to speak to no one. Françoise joined her. Seeing them, more than one merchant envied the consul for being a father and du Roule, who was known and approved of on all sides, for being his future son-in-law.

The winter had not been a cold one. But sometimes, as this afternoon, the east wind drove in the cold from Arabia Petrea, and seasoned it with a slightly salt humidity from the hollows of Suez.

"Have you seen Maître Juremi?" said Alix from under her veil.

"Yes, but I had to go back there twice," answered Françoise. "He is always in consultation. As far as possible, he is trying to take his partner's place."

"Has he agreed to what we asked him?"

Alix coolly embellished this conspiratorial conversation with gestures appropriate to a leisurely walk, pointing out a flower or a bird in the distance.

"He will do anything you ask him to," said Françoise. "And the idea of seeing Jean-Baptiste again . . ."

"You didn't hide that it was dangerous?"

"No, he understands this sort of thing perfectly, but the man is drawn to danger."

"Did he . . . talk to you?" asked Alix.

Françoise looked up into the air and gave a silent laugh that showed off her pretty teeth.

"What could he say to me? We were actually both delighted to hold a conversation dictated by events, one that allowed us to talk without compromising ourselves. You know, we have gone over everything. . . . At our age, luckily, the passage of time is not so painful. We are waiting for each other, that's all."

"I can understand," said Alix, "but I resent it a bit all the same. When you have the good luck not to be separated . . ."

The conversation left them both saddened. They walked on a few steps in silence. Then Alix came back to practical topics, and together they worked out all the details.

Barely had they returned to the consulate when a guard came to tell Mademoiselle de Maillet that His Excellency the consul wished to see her immediately. She entered the large drawing room on the ground floor. Her father stood waiting for her in a scarlet suit with black lining, wearing his tallest periwig, with ribbons in his stockings, and she thought to herself that he looked like a large perfumed doll. He came waddling toward her on his square-heeled shoes. Here it comes, she thought, he is going to take both my hands in his. There, didn't I say so?

"My dear daughter . . ." the consul started, his voice repressing a tremor.

Lacking the courage to finish his sentence, he embraced her. He took a handkerchief from his pocket, dabbed at his face, then resumed.

"I have great and good news to tell you—the very greatest, I believe, a woman ever receives in the course of her life."

"I am all ears, Father," said Alix.

"Well then, the gentleman you see here has asked me for your hand in marriage."

Du Roule was in the room, but somewhat in the shadows and standing in front of a hanging of the same color as his doublet, like a chameleon. Alix, who had not noticed him on entering, now turned her head toward him. He looked like the martyred Saint Denis, still on his feet after his beheading. He had the martyr's bloodless face and the closed eyes of a man who prefers to hear catastrophe coming than to see it fall on him. Alix felt a great pity for du Roule.

"Father," she said calmly, "I wish to speak to you alone."

Few orders have ever been executed so quickly. Du Roule, who had been waiting for the signal, vanished. Monsieur de Maillet turned to his daughter once they were alone, afraid of a last show of willfulness.

"Your emotions have been stirred. Mine as well. Let us try to keep things at their simplest and not disturb the beauty of what is truly mysterious. Now, what did you have to tell me that your future spouse could not hear?"

"Father, you have asked me to keep things simple, and I will. That man will never be my husband."

"Merciful heavens!" said Monsieur de Maillet, starting into the air. "And why not?"

"Because I will never marry."

"Is that so!" said the consul with asperity. "And what new caprice is this?"

"It is not a caprice, it is an impossibility."

"Might I know why?"

"If you wish, father."

"If I wish indeed! It seems to me I have a right to know what is preventing you."

Alix took a long breath, like an athlete before starting an event.

"I will never marry because I am dishonored."

"Dishonored?" said the consul impatiently. "What do you mean?"

"Just that. I am no longer as nature made me, or in the proper state for a woman to meet her husband."

A rafter could have fallen on Monsieur de Maillet's head and he would not have reeled more visibly. He took a step backward and steadied himself on the table.

"Daughter, this is a jest . . ."

Alix went on pitilessly, never lowering her eyes.

"I am at your disposal in case you might wish for a priest, a midwife, or whoever else to verify what I have said and draw up an official report."

Monsieur de Maillet felt a great urge to slap his daughter, and only her implacable gaze prevented him. He contained himself and made a wide circuit of the room, stamping his feet heavily at every step. Passing in front of the king's portrait, he lowered his eyes. Then, struck by an idea, he turned back toward Alix.

"You are not going to tell me," he said, looking at her through narrowed eyes, "that it has to do with that apothecary, that charlatan, that . . . Poncet!"

"No, Father, it is not he."

"Who, then?" said the consul, banging the oak table with the palm of his hand.

"No one you know," she said modestly.

"How can that be? You never leave here. And every visitor to the consulate is announced to me. No, no, you are protecting him, but it can only be Poncet."

"I give you my word."

"Or what is left of it," said the consul with gritted teeth. "Who is it, then?"

"A Turk."

"My God!" said the consul, pierced by this last arrow.

"What difference does it make?" Alix argued calmly. "The fact of it is what counts. It hardly matters who is responsible."

"All the same! A Turk!"

The consul distractedly removed his wig and began to pace back and forth with it dangling to the floor, like a hunter dragging the limp body of a hare.

"And where did you come into contact with this accursed man?"

"In Giza."

"I knew it! I never wanted you to go there. And that servant woman was your accomplice, or even your go-between?"

"Françoise knew nothing about it. She had gone to market with Michel, the groom, to buy some fresh eggs. The man came by the river. He was a fisherman. He took me on the terrace."

"Without your consent? An act of violence? Ah! I will ask the pasha to make reparations, there will be search parties, he will be found."

"No, Father. I consented to it. It may have been the sun, or the quiet of the place, which is quite seductive. When the boy appeared, I suddenly wanted—"

"Enough!" interrupted Monsieur de Maillet. "I do not care to hear any more. Horrors! Damnation! My only daughter, my only hope, my only heir!"

The consul was truly disturbed, though less at the thought of his lost child than at the memory of his endless ruminations, filled with visions of happiness and prosperity, in which she had played a central role.

"Pontchartrain . . . a worthy party . . . almost an ambassador . . ."

He was talking to himself, sitting crosswise on a chair, his cheek pressed against its high back.

"And why did you not tell me this earlier and spare us going to all this trouble?" he exclaimed.

"You had already gone to the trouble," said Alix. "Then, too, Father, I put off telling you because I wanted to spend as much time as possible with you and Mother. As soon as you were aware of my condition—"

"Your condition! You are not going to tell me that you are expecting!"

"Luckily, I have proof that I am not."

"At least that is one less worry."

"As I was saying: when you became aware of my altered situation, let's call it, everything would change. I would then have to submit to your will and bury myself for the rest of my days in some dark convent in the French provinces."

"Precisely! There is, alas, no alternative."

"I know it well, Father," said Alix, allowing a few tears to roll down her cheeks and stain her face. "Let us proceed as quickly as possible. I could not bear the shame of being in your presence for long. It would kill me."

"And it would kill me to continue seeing you," said the consul impatiently.

Already he had moved on to another thought: the chevalier du Roule would have to be advised.

"Arrange your hair and apply some color to your cheeks. I am going to call the young man."

Alix quickly pulled herself together. Du Roule entered, his head hunched between his shoulders, casting fearful glances in every direction like a hunted roebuck.

"Alas, dear sir," said the consul in stately tones, "I have consulted my daughter. And while you are the one man on earth she would accept with the greatest joy, you have a rival against whom it is useless to struggle. Unbeknownst to me, my daughter had made the vow to dedicate her life to Him. I am, of course, speaking of God Himself. My daughter, Alix, has been called to a spiritual life, and I am powerless to stay her."

"Ah," said du Roule, with timid surprise.

He cast a glance at the young woman, for a terrifying moment seeing superimposed images of the carnal beauty he remembered and the unlikely nun the consul had just described.

"Ah well," said the consul sadly, "God disposes, and He sometimes calls the best of us. So be it. While you make final preparations for your embassy, my daughter will take the road to Alexandria. She will embark for France and her convent on the next royal ship."

2

There are certain landscapes whose fate is to remain poor, overrun with brush and thornscrub, yet where human activity has managed by dint of perseverance to bring a miraculous measure of harmony, even prosperity. The landscape here was just the opposite. Nature had endowed it with a dark, well-aerated soil where anything might grow uncoaxed. Above was a clement sky, shared agreeably between sunshine and rain. It was dotted with hills from which clear streams cascaded, their slopes not so steep as to hinder agriculture and even benefiting it. Yet it seemed that men had done everything in their power to ruin these gifts, feuding with each other and unleashing a fratricidal war that led to famine and decimated the weak. The countryside ran wild with briars, which spilled over onto the paths, so that the horseman advancing through it had to be careful not to lose his way. Neglect had reduced even the widest roads to trails through the scrub. Every other house was in ruins. And in the woods, one had to arm oneself against feral dogs that seemed to attack men less from instinct than to settle a grudge.

The horseman rode as far as a village perched on a hilltop. From a distance it seemed quite large and possibly prosperous.

As he got closer he saw that nothing was left of it but tumbledown barns, burned thatch roofs, and the hulks of houses. A few old women, as thin as rails and dressed in gray, herded their skeletal goats through the ruins. The horseman stopped at the village square, where mounds of stones lay at the foot of crumbled walls and grass grew everywhere.

"Hey there!" he called to a young herder. "Come over here."

The child lifted a smudged face toward the man, stared mistrustfully at him, and took to his heels barefoot across the sharp stones. The traveler then noticed an old man, practically concealed beside a well whose carved rim was gone. The horseman alighted and wrapped his reins around the trunk of a walnut tree rooted in a pile of rubble. His coat was powdery with dust from the road. His eyes were hollow, his cheeks covered with a week's stubble, his gait as uncertain as a seaman's who has not stood on solid ground for some time. He walked up to the old man, who raised his eyes to him.

"Can you tell me whether this is the village they call Soubeyran?" said the exhausted horseman, who was none other than Jean-Baptiste.

He had lost his hat somewhere while riding at a gallop, and his forehead and hair were all matted with sweat and grit.

"There aren't many to give this place a name at all," said the old man.

His voice was clear and soft, with a slight catch in it, like an adolescent's.

"But you are right," he went on. "This is what is left of Soubeyran."

"Where are all the people who used to live here?" asked Jean-Baptiste, looking around him.

A northeast wind had been blowing for the past several days, as cold and sharp as a knifeblade. It had stripped the sky of its clouds and left a vivid blue above the charred stones of the village.

"If you know the answer and are trying to entrap me," said the old man, "then you might as well take me with you right away, or kill me here, as I am certainly one of the people you are looking for. But if you are as ignorant as you claim, then you must come from a long way off."

"I come from a long way off."

"And if you have traveled here, it must be you have some interest in the place or know someone from around here. In which case you must be concerned that I am going to give you bad news."

"I am looking for a woman."

"If you were looking for a man, I would stop you right away. There are only two of us here, if you still want to count me as being among the living. But there are a few women left. What is her name?"

"Marine."

The old man straightened up.

"Do you know her family name?"

"She was married barely a week. Her husband fled. His name is Juremi."

"Ah! Juremi! Sure. A strapping lad. He was the second son of my nearest neighbor, over there, behind the barns. Is he alive?"

"He is my business partner and friend. He lives in Cairo."

"In Cairo. In Egypt, the land of the Bible. Great God! What luck! You have no idea how much good news can mean at my age. I will go on thinking of it when you are gone. Truly I am glad that he is still alive!"

"And his wife?" persisted Jean-Baptiste.

"Oh! Don't torment him with any of that. What's past is past. Let him live and be happy."

"But you don't understand," said Jean-Baptiste, resting a knee on the ground and bringing his face close to the old man's. "He is the one who sent me. He has stayed faithful to her all these years, and if you want him to be happy, then he has to know."

"Yes," said the old man thoughtfully. "That's just like him. That's him all over. The rest of his family were all the same way. And maybe the whole village was like that, come to think of it. That's why they didn't spare us."

He lifted his eyes, and there was a whitish veil over them.

"She died the very day after he left."

The silence in this empty countryside had the weight of granite. Even the wind gestured noiselessly above the stones.

"How did it happen?" asked Jean-Baptiste.

"My friend," said the old man gently, looking off into space, "too few of us have survived for our memory to be of any use. This little corner of the earth was no doubt chosen as a place that would see many horrors, many vile deeds. Why tell the story of it? So that infamy will cling to future generations? No, we have buried the memory of our butchers in the same ditch with our dead. It is to love, to peace, and to joy that we must raise monuments, for they cannot survive without us."

"But this woman, this very young woman that Juremi had just married . . ."

"Well, she loved him. Neither time nor men were to corrupt her passion. She died calling his name."

The old man picked up a stick that had been worn smooth where his fingers had rubbed it and stood up painfully. He wrapped his worn greatcoat around his narrow body.

"Will you stay for a bit?" he asked.

"No, I must leave immediately. In fact . . ."

Jean-Baptiste gave the old man his arm, judging that he wanted to accompany him.

". . . if anyone asks, you haven't seen me."

"Are you one of us?"

"No, but we share the same enemies."

"Be careful!" said the old man, inspecting the strong and handsome young man beside him, evidently thinking of all those who had been cut down in the same vigor of youth. "Where have you come from? Your horse looks spent."

"This one comes from Tournon, on the Rhône River. I am afraid it won't go much farther. I have worn out six others since leaving Paris."

"Paris!" said the old man, surprised. "And where are you planning to go?"

"To Sète, by tonight."

"All the post houses in this area are watched by the dragoons," said the old man.

Then he turned and called in a voice that echoed through the ruins:

"Daniel!"

The soot-faced child that Jean-Baptiste had seen earlier showed his head above a nearby wall.

"Come here," said the man.

He turned to the traveler.

"Take this boy behind you in the saddle. He will guide you through the brush to a small encampment of our men—if they are still there, which I think they are. There is activity all through the mountains now, and I am ready to predict that some great events are in the offing. When you find them, say that you have come from Soubeyran and that Jean sent you. That's me."

Jean-Baptiste mounted and lifted the child into the saddle behind him.

"This may take you somewhat out of your way," said the old man, "but you won't regret it. They will give you a fresh horse and you will be in Sète by tomorrow morning."

"Thank you," said Jean-Baptiste.

He put his hand into one of the saddlebags where he kept a purse.

"May I offer you a little help?" he asked timidly.

The old man saw his gesture and stopped him.

"You will need it more than I do. Under every one of these houses are buried coins that the dragoons never found. If they ever saw us with money they would come back."

"Farewell then, Jean. I will carry your greetings to Juremi," said Jean-Baptiste, moved.

He dug his spurs into his horse's flanks. The poor animal, intent on the clematis bush in which it had buried its head up to the neck, did not respond. Finally, it set off, stepping carefully among the ruins that rose in silent vigil over the dead.

"Take a look below," Jean called out as Jean-Baptiste and the child rode off. "Do you see the monument they have raised? A cross! To commemorate their victory. . . . Can you believe it?"

But the horseman was already out of earshot.

Continuing down the road past Soubeyran, they entered a damp and shadowy gorge. A steep path, at times obliterated under leaves and moss, ran alongside the stream. The afternoon was drawing late and the shadows under the canopy growing darker. They kept climbing, hearing nothing but the cracking of twigs under the horse's hooves. When a last outcrop of rock, covered with green lichens, rose directly in front of them, the boy pointed to the right. He communicated entirely in gestures. At his cry, Jean-Baptiste started, not having heard his voice before. It sounded like an animal's cry, wordless, the two-part screech of a tawny owl, which the boy repeated three times. They continued on, passing under the enormous split trunk of an ancient chestnut tree. As they did so, there was a slight rustling of leaves and five men appeared, as though sprung from the rocks and trees. They were dark, hunched, and scowling like devils. They leveled their crossbows and pikes at the rider.

"I was sent by Jean, from Soubeyran," said Jean-Baptiste calmly.

He did not know which of these faces, concealed behind hats and beards, he should be addressing.

"It's true!" said the child.

"Dismount!" ordered one of the men softly.

Jean-Baptiste swung down from the saddle and, once on the ground, raised his hands. The man who had spoken walked up to the horse and looked at its baggage.

"You will find a pistol in the left saddlebag, a dagger in my satchel, and my sword, which you see. But I am a friend and have no intention of using any of them."

The man grunted, signaled one of the men to hold the horse's bridle, and walked up to Jean-Baptiste, taking a blindfold from his pocket and tying it over Jean-Baptiste's eyes. They continued on up the path, the boy still in the saddle, holding firmly to the pommel, while Jean-Baptiste walked blind, guiding himself with a hand on the shoulder of one of the brigands. They walked in this way for about an hour, before the blindfold was removed. Jean-Baptiste found himself in a dark place with rocks and grottoes all around. Night had fallen, and the encampment they had reached was lit by small fires, seven or eight in all. Shadowy figures busied themselves around blackened cookpots, which hung from improvised tripods. A man sitting on the far side of the little fire near Jean-Baptiste invited him to take a seat across from him.

"So," the man said, "you have come from Soubeyran? Are you one of us?"

As he spoke he snapped chestnut twigs into pieces and threw them one by one into the crackling fire. He had a long bony face and bright eyes. From hunger, fatigue, and the habit of enduring terror and inflicting it in return, the faces in this area all had a common aspect. It was as though these men lived in such harsh conditions that, while they were able to survive as a species, they no longer had the luxury of being individuals.

Jean-Baptiste explained what had brought him, and though his story was a long one, he told only the briefest part of it concerning Juremi and his present return to Cairo.

"My name is Catinat," the man said. "At least, that is how I am known here. This Juremi is older than I am and I don't know him. But I think I heard of him long ago. It's lucky that he is still alive. Our fathers had no choice: if they wanted to save their lives they had to leave for distant places. We have chosen to do battle here. Times are changing. The king is old, the country is muttering against him and falling apart. It is not the time to make alliances outside the country but to struggle for our freedom right here."

One of the rebels, dark as night, brought each of them a wooden bowl filled with watery gruel.

Blowing on their portions, they spoke of Cairo and Versailles. Catinat explained that he had been living in the forest for two years and was avid for news of the world. It was clear that his struggle was intended not to destroy the world but to provide a place in it for every man. His brutish life was in the service of a human ideal.

"I must be in Sète tomorrow morning," said Jean-Baptiste, mindful of his situation and worried by his long detour.

"Are you planning to board ship there?"

"Yes," said Jean-Baptiste. "I'll take a fishing scow to Genoa."

"Won't the king's couriers have alerted the local authorities about you? They must be looking for you."

"I doubt the couriers could have traveled any faster than I did. And my flight was unlikely to have been discovered immediately. I still have twenty-four hours."

"Hmm. That's a risky plan. Boats don't leave from there every day. Suppose the orders came while you were still there, trying to bribe the sailors. You'd be denounced immediately."

"I know," said Jean-Baptiste gravely. "I have had all the time in the world to think about it since leaving Paris. But I have no choice."

Catinat finished drinking his gruel and scraped the bottom of his bowl with his fingers.

"My advice is to get a few hours' sleep. Look at yourself. You haven't been resting properly, and a man does no good in such a state. Go into one of those grottoes, roll yourself up in a sheepskin, and get some sleep. We break camp at four o'clock. Between now and then I may manage to arrange something for you."

After the warm soup and the rest by the fire, Jean-Baptiste felt a great wave of drowsiness overtake him. He had slept for only a few hours since his departure, and even then he had stayed on the alert and shut only one eye. He decided to take Catinat's advice. As soon as he had lain down, and in spite of the horrific smell of the untanned sheepskin, he fell into a deep sleep.

Catinat shook him awake at four o'clock as he had promised. He set some clothes down by Jean-Baptiste and told him to change into them. Still drowsy and only half conscious, the traveler shed his old clothes and slipped on a satin doublet with embroidered sleeves that fit him nicely and a pair of fine boots that were only slightly too large. Over this he put on an ample wool cape and a three-cornered hat. In this resplendent costume Jean-Baptiste went to join the group of men standing around the nearest fire, among whom he recognized Catinat. Morning prayer was short but heartfelt, and all joined in with bared heads. Afterward they each received another bowl of last night's soup, though somewhat watered down. Catinat invited Poncet to take a seat next to him.

"Three days ago, our men brought down a young nobleman on the Uzès road. He was foolhardy enough to be traveling without an escort. They made clean work of it, and there is not a trace of blood on your clothes. Here are his papers."

He handed Jean-Baptiste a small red portfolio on which were inscribed the letters H.V. in gold.

"He was one of the young adventurers who join the armies that harass us. There is no one worse. Under the guise of safeguarding their religion, they come here to pillage and attach a fortune to their names, which they received without one. You were lucky on the way here not to be taken for one of them. It's true that you were plastered with mud, while they generally take pains with their clothes. These gentlemen put on their finery to murder us, doing us a great honor."

Jean-Baptiste opened the leather envelope. It contained the dead man's papers. His name was Hughes de Vaudesorgues. He had belonged to the household of the prince de Conti, who had recommended him to the governor general of Nîmes. He was the same age as Poncet, give or take a few months.

"You can keep your horse," said Catinat. "We have only cart horses and they would be out of keeping with your new station in life. But with these documents no one will disturb you. Go to the first stage east of Uzès and change your horse as though you had just traveled a short distance. Your double never went that way and they won't have any reason to suspect you. Then go on to Marseilles. The port is a big one. You will surely find a boat there and no one will notice you. It is relatively common for these little heroes, once they have heard our bullets whistling around their ears, to turn tail and ship for the Levant to try their fortunes there."

A pale day was dawning, the light sliding along the naked branches. The men trampled out the fires, slung their packs over their shoulders, and fell into rank, weapons in hand. Jean-Baptiste walked alongside them, leading his horse by the reins, until they reached a sort of natural terrace, a flat, rocky promontory from which one looked down on the humped back of the great dark forest and, in the distance, the pastel line of the valley. They took their separate ways from there, after a long embrace between Poncet and Catinat. Jean-Baptiste mounted his horse and looked for a last time in the blue daylight at this bearded, miserable, shivering company, which was the very image of human dignity. He noticed that most of the partisans had put on a loose cotton shirt over their shabby clothes, presumably to help them recognize each other. They raised their pikes and swords in a salute to the departing Jean-Baptiste. As he made his way down the path, their eyes followed this figure that they had killed the day before and brought back to life today.

3

Brother Pasquale and a young novice freshly arrived from Italy, Bartolomeo, were waiting in the courtyard. It would have been improper for them to venture any farther. The bearded Capuchin paced in a circle around a date palm that poked up alone and rather ridiculously, he thought, in the dead center of this paved courtyard with its high crenellated walls. Really, he thought, this is like a prison; and all the more so as the windows on the side toward the Coptic church were fitted with wrought-iron grilles. Whenever he passed in front of the partly opened door, the sound of psalms sung by deep voices came to his ears and the familiar smell of incense tickled his fat nose.

Inside the basilica, the atmosphere was distinctly different. Thanks to the wooden shutters drawn across each window and a complicated system of hangings, screens, and partitions, the holy of holies was bathed in complete darkness. Only the dim scarlet glow of the lamps cut across the peaceful assembly of men and objects, parsimoniously revealing a detail here and there and ferreting out with the cunning of a thief the gold, ivory, and gems distributed in the shadow. Ibrahim, the Syrian monk, was helping the patriarch and a few chosen priests perform the lengthy task of blessing the coronation oil. After many preliminaries and a series of interminable orisons, the patriarch removed an alabaster amphora from the tabernacle. Now the benediction proper could begin. Finally a portion was decanted into an earthenware cruet with a small handle and sealed in with a cork stopper. The business came to a halt as night was falling. Walking in procession, the patriarch carried the cruet to the entryway, where an ancient Coptic priest opened the door for them, his head shaking incessantly. Brother Pasquale, furious at having been made to wait so long, nonetheless put on a good face for the Coptic bishop. With an expression of the most humble submission, he received the precious vessel and a rolled and sealed parchment attesting to its authenticity. He kneeled smartly.

"Within three days, Monsignor, this holy oil will be traveling toward Abyssinia," he said in Arabic.

The patriarch made a last sign of the cross over the flagon. Ibrahim exchanged a meaning look with the Capuchin. Brother Pasquale bowed and, with Bartolomeo in tow, slowly crossed the courtyard and exited at last into the tumult of the city.

The Coptic sanctuary gave onto a narrow street bordered by tall houses. In front of almost every house were stands set out by small merchants, lit by oil lamps. The street was still crowded, and passersby bumped into each other in the dark.

"Take the cruet," said Brother Pasquale to the novice. "Your eyes are better than mine."

The young brother took the precious bottle with an expression of terror. A big boy with fat cheeks from the Istrian Peninsula, his vocation for the priesthood was by no means firm. But his father, whom he feared, had wanted to dedicate one of his offspring to God and had chosen him because he was the greediest of his children and the costliest to feed. Since then Bartolomeo had served the Lord loyally, like a soldier who fights bravely because the daily ration is plentiful.

"Did you see, boy, that scoundrel of a patriarch, how he parades in his big gold-embroidered gown!" grumbled the Capuchin, who walked in front and took the opportunity, his hands being free, to throw himself into the crowd and ram his shoulders at random into those around him. "That wretch, if I hadn't started off by giving him half the consul's sequins . . ."

Bartolomeo ran to keep up, staying close to his elder's heels.

"Listen to me," said Brother Pasquale. "You are young, Bartolomeo. You must learn that these Copts are worthless. Completely worthless. If you judge them on the basis of their vestments, their vermilion censers, you might believe they have some wealth and substance. But that's false. The pasha owns it all. He allows them the use of it, but they themselves are as poor as beggars."

"Aren't we also poor?" asked the young Capuchin, panting. He had been surprised to learn, on being accepted into the monkhood, that they took a vow to beg for their food.

"Yes, but we have the pope, don't you see?" said Pasquale. "Of course we are poor, but for us it is a weapon, our special place in the world. We are the scouts. Behind us come the cavalry, the guns, a great army. While the Copts have nothing behind them but the swords of the Muslims ready to cut off their heads. And in spite of that, they put on airs and make us wait for four long hours while they putter over their benedictions."

They had turned down an even narrower street. The darkness was total, but at least there was no one out walking. It was a short cut that allowed them to avoid the citadel and make it back to the monastery as quickly as possible.

"Wait for me, Father," said Bartolomeo. "I can't see a thing."

"Just put one foot in front of another, you great lummox. Didn't they teach you anything in seminary?"

Brother Bartolomeo did his best, but he suddenly stopped, gave a stifled cry, and started chattering with fright.

"Good heavens! Oh my God! What have I done? I'm ruined! Have mercy on me! Lord spare me! Oh my God, my God . . ."

Brother Pasquale retraced his steps in the darkness.

"What's the matter with you now?"

"Have pity on me, for Christ's sake!" said the novice, kneeling on the uneven ground. "I dropped the cruet."

"Broken?"

"Alas, yes. I am ruined."

Brother Pasquale swore in his native patois, terrifying Bartolomeo even further with his incomprehensible oaths.

"Was there ever a clumsier oaf?" he ended, more irritated than angry.

The boy was still on his knees, crying.

"And you're still wasting time crying over it! Come on, it's not so serious, and I am foolish enough to forgive you for it. I warn you, though, I'll be utterly furious if you also make us late for dinner."

"But," said Bartolomeo, whom the mention of the evening meal had reinvigorated as he dried his tears, "what will you do about the holy cruet?"

"That's perfectly simple. Tomorrow morning you'll go to the Arab grocer across the street from the monastery and buy two sequins' worth of agave oil."

"And we'll take it to be blessed by the patriarch."

"Blessed!" said Brother Pasquale, grabbing the seminarian's ear and twisting it. "Was there ever anyone so stupid! Blessed! Have you turned to idolatry?"

"No! No!" whimpered Bartolomeo.

"Well? And what are they worth, the blessings of Monophysites, I ask you? If we go along with them it is only to penetrate into Abyssinia. But they are the ones we have to convert. Not the other way around, either, understand? We have the parchment to authenticate the chrism, and the grocer's oil will do the job every bit as well."

So saying, Brother Pasquale swept the ground with his sandal to scatter the shards of the cruet. Then he resumed his progress without taking further notice of Bartolomeo, who followed along moaning and holding a hand to his ear.

~

Anyone but Murad would have died of boredom after Jean-Baptiste left. He lived secluded in his house at the end of the Frankish colony, and while he lived grandly at the expense of the French consulate, his Abyssinian slaves had been taken from him, he was avoided by both the Egyptians and the European merchants, and the only visitor he received was Maître Juremi. Through the latter, he was able to hire an Arab serving woman. Known as Khadija, she was a very old woman, practically blind, a childless widow forced to work in order to survive. On the second day of her employment at Murad's, Khadija felt a plump hand slide under her ample linen skirts. Her astonishment at such an unlikely breach of propriety lasted several seconds, then she turned on the intruder and slapped him resoundingly in the face, spat at him, and fired off a string of curses. Order was restored, and she continued her work without further interruptions. Murad developed a holy terror of the old matron as a result of this episode. As to Khadija, she must at some level have been grateful for this outrage. At any rate she displayed a touching devotion to the man ever afterward, presumably because he had seen her as an object of desire, and she was never to abandon Murad.

The Armenian had no other company during these long weeks. He was seen trolling the narrow streets of Cairo, usually in vain, after pleasures that might fall within his means. As winter came on, he stayed indoors, staring out the window and fingering a string of wooden beads. From time to time Maître Juremi brought him a few dates. He would suck on them for hours until he had softened the pit, which he would swallow in the end with a sigh of regret.

He belonged to the disparate group of Cairo residents who were waiting for news of Poncet.

One day, to his astonishment, he saw the three Abyssinians returning. He had heard of their misfortune in the port of Alexandria and never thought to see them again. But the poor devils, once they made their profession to Muhammad, had been abandoned to their fate by the same crowd that had shown such vehement concern for their souls. After they had wandered for several days begging for their food, the eldest slave had convinced the two others that they should make their way back to Cairo and find Murad. Their former master at least spoke their language and treated them honestly. They set off in an orderly and silent procession that no one thought to disturb because they visibly observed the five daily prayers, and they reached Cairo by small stages. They then resumed their old place in the household—although the serving woman insisted on staying on—and it was there that Maître Juremi discovered them, much to his surprise.

"I thought I heard that they were forced to become Turks," he said to Murad.

"That's right."

"The poor brutes must be awfully upset."

"Not really. It's the second time they have become Muslims."

"How can that be?"

"Don't forget that they were prisoners of the negus. They were captured in the south of Abyssinia, where there are pagan tribes. Those peoples worship cows, trees, and mountains. When an army invades from the outside, they always end up adopting the religion of the more powerful invader. These fellows were subjects of Sennar first. The king of Sennar persuaded them to pray to Allah, and then they were captured by our emperor and took to following Jesus. So now they are back to where they were after the first conversion. But at bottom, I am sure they continue to worship their mountains or some other thing we don't know about."

Maître Juremi looked at the three Abyssinians. They were happy to be back. They squatted near the door, still, serious, inscrutable. They were living proof that perfect subservience is the most unstoppable form of rebellion.

A few days later, Monsieur de Maillet received news of Poncet's disgrace and the trial that was soon to take place, and he informed Murad that he would stop subsidizing him any further at the end of the month. Monsieur Macé came to notify the Armenian of this decision and added a few remarks whose insolence was designed to leave Murad in no doubt that his best interest lay in returning home, if that expression held any meaning for a man of his character.

Murad fled straight to Maître Juremi's house, where he sobbed and said he was lost. His first thought was to get himself hired as a cook by one of the merchants in the colony. He had worked in that capacity in Aleppo—why should he not do so in Cairo too?

Maître Juremi explained to him that it would be a poor way to honor the mission he had received from the emperor. Besides, if there was any chance of saving Jean-Baptiste it lay in maintaining the truth of his story insofar as possible. He had claimed to bring back an ambassador, and therefore it was best that the man not be found meddling with sauces.

In fact, Juremi was in no position to give Murad wise counsel. He himself was not entirely certain of what had happened in Versailles. And

Françoise had informed him of another disturbing turn of events, namely the imminent departure of du Roule's large and official embassy. Poor Juremi no longer knew what to do. He defended Poncet but with the underlying conviction that his friend had already lost his wager. He encouraged Murad to remain a worthy messenger of the negus, yet he could see that the consulate no longer gave the Armenian any credit and was launching its own mission. In short, he was in a state of great and painful indecision.

Through it all, he kept up his apothecary's practice and continued to fill the prescriptions written out by Jean-Baptiste. He had even secretly become druggist to the new pasha, the terrible Mehmet Bey, who received him against the will of the muftis.

Another troubling element was that Françoise was constantly being thrown in his path as the messenger between himself and the consulate. He found his feelings toward her growing more and more tender, though he still did not know whether he could honestly express them. When Françoise finally told him Alix's plan to go to France on the pretext of entering a convent, and when she further asked him for help in freeing the young woman along the way and accompanying her while she went to find and rescue Poncet, Juremi felt, despite the many foreseeable dangers, as though the sun were finally rising.

At last he would be able to fight, to move, to know. Nothing suited a man of his stripe worse than this life of inactivity and concealment. He shined his boots, cleaned his sword and pistols lovingly, and sang with joy.

The new plan left one person out, and that was Murad. After Juremi had preached patience to him, he brusquely changed his mind and advised him, as the consul had, to return to Abyssinia. He even proposed to give Murad the means to do so, that is, to buy him some pack animals and provide a small amount of money.

That is where things stood, and Murad had not yet decided what course to take, when two strangers came one morning to his door.

They were both Franks whom no one in the colony had ever seen before. They said they had arrived the previous day.

"Are you His Grace Sieur Murad, ambassador of Ethiopia?" said the taller of the two visitors, a man of about forty, thin, and with an extraordinarily expressionless face, even when he talked.

"None other," said Murad drawing himself up. It had been a long time now since anyone had addressed him with such pleasant respect. "And how may I help you?"

"We have come from Palestine, from Jerusalem in fact," said the slight man impassively. "My name is Hubert de Monehaut and this is my colleague, Grégoire Riffaut. We are men of science. He is a geographer and I am an architect."

The other visitor, younger than the first, nodded in agreement. There was nothing remarkable about him except his extraordinarily pale, almost white eyes, which he opened wide and directed at Murad like two porcelain saucers.

"We heard tell that a plenipotentiary from the Abyssinian court had taken up residence in Cairo. We have come in the hope of obtaining a favor from Your Grace."

"I will do everything in my power," said Murad, whose vanity was tickled, and who assumed, if truth be told, the very posture of stiff back and twisted neck that he had observed in Monsieur de Maillet during his audiences.

"Thank you in advance, Your Grace, thank you," said the first visitor, and he bowed deeply, as did the man with the china eyes, after a slight delay.

"We are members of an expedition brought together under the auspices of the Spanish Royal Academy of Sciences," said the spokesman. "Four more scientists will join us before the end of the week. They are traveling here from Europe and have already sent word of their arrival in Alexandria. All six of us plan to go to the country that you represent, Abyssinia. We would like to ask Your Grace the favor of providing us an introduction to your sovereign."

Murad squeezed the wooden beads of his little chaplet in his left hand. Lord, he thought, thou hast delivered me.

"Sirs, it will give me great pleasure to help you in your mission," he announced gravely, "on condition that you tell me your purpose. You are perhaps unaware that the negus, my master, has placed severe restrictions on foreigners entering his kingdom."

"We know, Your Grace. But our purpose is simply to go as men avid for knowledge. The geographer, for instance, might want to discover the course of the main rivers; the doctor, and there is a doctor in our number, might plan to describe the major illnesses. Each of us seeks to satisfy the curiosity naturally elicited in our minds by a new land."

"You are not going to look for gold, are you?" asked Murad sharply.

"In truth, Your Grace, this voyage will cost us more than we will make by it, at least in ready money. No, gold is something that we have already."

That strikes a pleasant chord! thought Murad.

"Sirs," he said, "I will do more than announce your arrival to the negus."

"Better, Your Grace?"

"Yes, I will accompany you to him."

"Is it possible?" asked Monehaut.

"It so happens that you have come to me on the very eve of my departure. Yes, tomorrow I must begin the road back to my master."

"Tomorrow! But we can never be ready in time."

"Alas!" said Murad majestically. "I cannot wait."

"It will take us a week to assemble our colleagues and collect all the material we will need for the expedition."

"Sirs, I would be entirely ready to set back my departure, but, believe me, it is impossible."

"Might I ask you the reason? Perhaps we might—"

"Oh, sirs, the reason is very simple. The emperor allotted me a certain sum to accomplish my mission, and that sum is now exhausted. There can be no question of my accepting even a small amount of money from a foreign power. The French consul offered to come to my assistance, but I refused on my honor as a diplomat. Hence I must leave."

"We understand," said the impassive visitor. "But in the event that Your Grace should do us the service of waiting a bit, it would be incumbent on us, as the party responsible for the extension of your stay, to subsidize the costs. You might say it was simply a question of allowing us to reimburse you for a debt we are contracting toward you."

"In that case," said Murad, "there would be no difficulty."

The slight man, acting with remarkable speed, discretion, and tact, reached into his clothing and removed a leather purse, which he set down at the ambassador's feet.

It was agreed that this payment would be followed by other installments in the event of further delays, but the scientists promised not to draw out their preparations longer than a week.

"There is one last thing, Your Grace," said Monsieur de Monehaut. "We would like it if the consul were not informed of our preparations and even kept entirely in the dark about our plan. Spain and France are friendly at the moment, but tomorrow . . ."

"Have no fear," said Murad.

The two men bowed and thanked him again a thousand times. As soon as they had left, Murad snatched up the purse. He counted twelve Abukel écus, which made him leap for joy.

That night, he spent six of them, indulging himself riotously at a caravanserai.

4

The chevalier Le Noir du Roule was deeply distraught over the events in the consulate. He was at first paralyzed by the fear of being embroiled in a scandal. Then when he saw that he had emerged unscathed, his terror ebbed away like the tide, although he discovered with astonishment that his desire for Alix was as strong as ever. He even had the foolhardiness and effrontery to start scratching at the door of the future nun again to beg for her favors. He no longer went out, his mind being totally occupied with the consul's daughter. He tried to place himself in her path, but in vain, as she remained cloistered in her room. In short—the symptoms were familiar to him, he having often jeered at his friends for showing them—he was in love. His weakness appalled him. He believed that every failing was forgivable but that one, since it made you idiotically dependent on a person who was most likely not your equal and whose conquest very often did not even serve your interests.

The consul took stock of the rejected suitor's unhappiness and, as he felt strongly to blame for du Roule's disappointment, began showing the chevalier tokens of a boundless friendship. The poor youth seemed even to have lost any taste for his embassy. The consul held himself from making further mention of the plan but continued quietly to assemble the elements of the caravan and arrange the purchase of the offerings for the rulers of the territories to be crossed. He was readying everything for the day when du Roule would emerge from his melancholy, but in the meantime, he received the young man morning and evening in his office and spoke to him in consoling terms.

Nothing confirms a person in his sorrows like sharing them with another. Hearing the consul talk day after day about the great trials that Providence sends to sensitive hearts, du Roule pitied himself more and more. But Monsieur de Maillet's ornate rhetoric belonged to an earlier day. In the end, his near son-in-law grew impatient of hearing the consul's grand and pious references to courtly love—the only sort, the diplomat believed, to which a gentleman is susceptible. Du Roule had a strong inclination to shut the man's trap by telling him that he wished for only two things where his daughter was concerned: to have her again for a whole night and to be the one to leave.

He refrained from expressing these thoughts to his superior, but in articulating them to himself he realized that he might not be so hopelessly in love as he had at first believed. It was in his appetites and in his self-respect that he had primarily suffered hurt. Like a wounded man who, after the first shock of pain, makes a lucid estimate of his own injuries and is heartened to realize that he will live, du Roule began to look at himself more favorably as soon as he was sure that he had not succumbed entirely to love. He bravely decided to pull himself together. The very next day he held a bank at faro at a merchant's house and lost heavily. He ate, drank a great deal, and ended the night between two dancing girls at a house kept filled with young beauties by a Turkish procuress. In brief, he stopped letting himself go.

He was able to see Alix as he would never for a moment have stopped seeing her had his judgment remained unclouded: as a woman who was half mad, and who would do very well in a convent, where she would have the leisure to reflect her whole life long on the brief pleasures he had so kindly shared with her.

Out of caution, du Roule took care that Monsieur de Maillet should not learn all at once of the change in him. He pretended to return to health in small stages, and the consul tried to consolidate his progress by being more solicitous than ever. Dispatches arrived from France that confirmed the minister's interest in du Roule's embassy to Abyssinia. Monsieur de Maillet believed himself entitled to take large advances from the consular chests so that the travelers would lack for nothing. This mission was to make its official character unmistakably clear to all, and to the Ethiopians in particular. Everything about it would be different from the shabby equipage that had earlier accompanied Poncet and his supposed manservant Joseph.

The caravan of du Roule's embassy would consist of twenty-three camels of the finest lineage, richly saddled and harnessed. It was to be led by a Moor named Belac, who was an agent of the king of Sennar. With regret, the consul had agreed to part with Frisetti, the dragoman, who would accompany the expedition as its interpreter. As soon as he was himself again, du Roule requested that the task of choosing all the remaining travelers be left entirely to him. Without telling the consul, he chose as his right-hand man a young Frenchman who had arrived in Cairo the year before and had distinguished himself by the extent and number of his vices. Du Roule had met Rumilhac (for such was his name) at the gaming tables, where the young man had excelled at gulling the relatively tame crowd of Cairene bourgeois. Du Roule, whom nobody could claim to instruct in the art of cheating, easily unmasked the other; but rather than denounce him, he joined in partnership with him. Their twinned reputations, which were already highly flattering, swelled to the point that the pair were considered invincible. Rumilhac was still young enough to have a slender and graceful waist, despite his enormous appetite for drink. But on his cheeks was already collecting a skein of tiny purple veins, the first residue of his excesses.

Du Roule chose two more persons of the same ilk, though somewhat less gaudy in their defects: a former policeman who had left the service for obscure reasons and was vegetating in Cairo, and a jeweler from Arles, probably a fence and a forger who had preferred to live abroad. Though preceded by their unsavory reputations, these two characters shared a common insolence and an excessive dignity of manners. Monsieur de Maillet, who had never met the two before, was not delighted with the choice. He had to concede, however, that the group cut a dashing figure even if their references were dubious. As du Roule said to convince him and to distinguish himself even further, "It is exceptionally rare to find true gentlemen willing to run so many dangers."

To this group of men, each of whom had a name if not a position, were added ten or twelve wretches recruited from the dregs of the colony: deserters, footmen on the lam, and mercenaries of all kinds, whom du Roule counted on using as a battle corps.

The first task faced by the two leaders of the troop was to spend the subsidies from the consulate on the goods the caravan would carry.

Du Roule's position was a simple one, and his partners quickly grasped it: the embassy was their pretext, but trade was their real business. The presents would be kept to a minimum and replaced by merchandise that could be sold or exchanged. They would put their stock to use along the way and amass a fortune that they would exchange in Abyssinia for an even greater one. Of course, conditions there might suggest a more ambitious use for their fortune—to buy an army, forge alliances, or perhaps even seize power, and why not? A healthy friendship developed between the traveling companions, with du Roule as the focus of their admiration. Not one of them doubted, given their chief's immoderate nature and intrepid cynicism, that he was a ruler of the earth and that they were accompanying him to his kingdom.

As to the dangers the expedition faced, the men had formed fairly specific notions. Each was convinced he had survived unequaled perils in his adventure-filled past. To ward off hunger and thirst, all one needed was to be well provisioned. And as to the natives, these old hands in the Levant had formed a simple policy based on their dealings with numerous Nubian, Sudanese and other servants from central Africa: there never was a problem with them that couldn't be solved by a good caning. The men equipped themselves with an abundant supply of swords, pistols, and crossbows, not so much to protect themselves as to sell to the savages, whose innocent predilection for exterminating one another they well knew.

Besides, in any relations with the natives it was primarily the women one had to deal with, as they were bolder than the men and invariably the dominant presence. The expedition therefore bought cheap colored cloth, rattles, and even an item recently brought to Cairo by a Venetian merchant, distorting mirrors, such as were found in fairs in Europe.

While these preparations were in progress, Alix was making her own more modest but no less meticulous ones. She had begged leave of her father to keep to her room, and he had granted it with a sigh of relief. His head stuffed with consoling thoughts from Epictetus, whose works he had spent the last days devouring, Monsieur de Maillet believed himself to have acquired the superb detachment of the Stoics toward pain and shame. But this outlook was still fragile: he had only to walk into a door to start mindlessly raining blows on it with his cane. These were simply aftereffects, however, and as far as he was concerned he no longer had a daughter. Madame de Maillet lacked his resoluteness, and he reproached her for it. Yet Monsieur de Maillet had not told her of the horrible crime to which Alix had confessed. Her mother was therefore only bemoaning her daughter's call to holy orders. What would it have been like if she were also mourning her daughter's lost honor? Alix received the poor woman once a day, at the end of the afternoon, and allowed her to cry to her heart's content, drenching the little armchair covered in pink silk where Alix had once spent hours reading. During the rest of day, she opened her door only to Françoise. Monsieur de Maillet, furious with the confidante and laundress and not at all convinced of her innocence, had forbidden her to accompany his daughter to France. He did, however, allow Françoise to keep his daughter company until her departure.

The two women assembled an unusual trousseau for Alix's novitiate. They agreed that for her departure Alix would wear a tunic-dress of dark beige cloth, which was austere enough for the convent and would dispel any suspicions. Underneath this outer garment, however, she would be wearing corduroy trousers, a loose blouse, and a leather belt for her pistols. In her trunk, under a visible layer of the somber clothing suited to a life of prayer, Alix concealed a pair of supple leather boots that Françoise had had made for her in the Arab quarter. The laundress had used her own foot as a model, since it was exactly the same size as the young woman's. Next to them were a pair of roweled spurs and an ivory-handled dagger. And finally Françoise brought in under her skirts a foil that Maître Juremi had sharpened specially for the occasion. Still to come were the pistols, a supply of powder, and lead shot, which arrived soon after in a basket of white linens.

These preparations took about ten days, as the two women were obliged to proceed with great caution. Finally, Alix was ready. While taking her meals, which the cook brought up on a tray, she looked pensively out the window. When would she set out? What was the boat doing? The year was drawing on. February was ending and warmth was slowly returning to Egypt. The sap was rising. One day, the burning bush in the garden was covered with tiny points of red, then it had flowered all at once, then dropped its petals, tinting the entire lawn. Alix read this as a sign that she would soon be with Jean-Baptiste. She had no more tears to spend on regret and suffering: however deeply she looked into herself, all she saw was impatience.

There were many travelers busying themselves in Cairo at that time, but the first to leave was Murad. He went to pay his respects to Monsieur de Maillet, who received him amiably. The consul's spies had reported the presence in town of six new travelers, and he deduced that these were the Jesuits described to him by Fléhaut. The minister's instructions were to maintain silence on the subject, and Monsieur de Maillet followed them scrupulously. In any case, he wanted his own embassy to remain separate from the religious expeditions. He wished Murad Godspeed and conveyed orally the king of France's greetings to the emperor of Abyssinia, should Murad happen to encounter him.

"Which route will you take in returning to Ethiopia?" the consul asked Murad.

"Your Excellence, we will go to Jidda, then on to Massawa, and from there we will take the road to Gondar."

"Then you have chosen to go by sea."

This was good news. At least they would not be in du Roule's way, and with a little luck they would arrive after him.

Maître Juremi also greeted Murad with warmth on his departure, as it meant he need no longer fear abandoning him in bad straits. Providence had come through at the last moment. The Protestant did not know the men of science who would be accompanying Murad, and although a momentary suspicion of their identity crossed his mind, Maître Juremi made no attempt to elucidate the mystery. He was relieved for the Armenian and too absorbed by the delicate mission Alix had given him to find further complications where there might be none. Murad and his sponsors left for Suez on horseback on a fine, sunny morning. The three Abyssinians once more followed in a carriage.

Two days later, an incident occurred that nearly ruined Alix's plan. A courier from Versailles arrived at the consulate, a sign that a boat had docked in Alexandria shortly before and that her departure was therefore imminent. Beset by last-minute doubts, Alix wanted to know if the latest pouch held any news of Jean-Baptiste. She worried that, being separated, they might somehow act at cross-purposes and complicate matters rather than resolve them.

As usual, Monsieur Macé brought the letters to the consul, who shut himself in his office to read them. He came out for lunch and asked his secretary to join him at table. Hastily, Alix and Françoise agreed that the older woman would take advantage of the hour when the consul went upstairs for his nap after lunch to enter his office and look over the mail. She executed the plan boldly and started to read the first letter. The poor woman, hardly used to making out the scribbles of a minister, spelled out the words haltingly, not always understanding each sentence on the first reading. Time was passing, and still she found nothing about Jean-Baptiste.

Suddenly, she heard voices in the hallway, as though a visitor was being announced. There had been no sound of a carriage drawing up to the front steps, and so the newcomer must have arrived on foot. Françoise dropped the letter she was reading and ran to the little music room. On opening the door, she discovered Madame de Maillet, luckily seated with her back to her, sobbing all alone. Françoise closed the door, at the same time hearing Monsieur Macé's voice approaching. Panicked, she slid behind a wall hanging. The secretary entered, in the company of a man who spoke with a foreign accent.

"Wait here, Father, if you would. Monsieur de Maillet will be with you shortly," said Macé.

Monsieur Macé left the visitor pacing around the room, and Françoise heard the secretary climb the stairs. Soon the consul came down. He spoke in the disgruntled tones of a man deprived of his rest in the tropics.

"Well, Brother Pasquale, what urgent matter has prompted your visit?"

"Ah, Consul, excuse me. I did not know that you were sleeping. Here is my news: we have the oil!"

"The oil?"

"But yes, the oil of the coronation."

"Oh, the oil," said the consul testily. "Well?"

"Well, the patriarch, he was very greedy. We had to give him everything you collected for us."

"That is your own business, Brother. We agreed on a set figure, and I am not going to increase it."

"But, I beg you, Consul, our brothers go tomorrow. They don't even have mules to carry them. On foot! They are going to Abyssinia on foot?"

"Please, Brother, do not insist. I have said it before: it is your own business."

The Capuchin was quiet for a moment. Françoise, in her hiding place, hardly dared breathe.

"When I think of all the camels in the caravan of your ambassador . . ."

"That is beside the point."

"Alas! And yet they will also pass through Sennar. They could take our brothers and the oil."

"Out of the question. The two expeditions must remain separate. Those are the king's orders."

"The king of France, maybe. But not the king of Sennar."

"What do you mean?"

"Nothing! We know the king of Sennar very well, that is all."

There was nothing in these words. Yet all the same, visible in the depths beneath them, as though one peered into limpid water and saw dark shapes on the murky bottom swimming with the deliberate menace of moray eels, something definitely lurked there. Monsieur de Maillet understood right away. He should take no risks. The monks would set out no matter what, and as they had no luggage they would travel fast. They had to be prevented at all costs from mounting a cabal against du Roule before he even reached Sennar.

"All right, what do you need?"

After much going back and forth, the Capuchin extorted a camel, two mules, and a small quantity of gold. He left, thanking the consul with a deep bow.

"We will hardly be the losers by it," said the consul to Monsieur Macé, trying to justify his capitulation. "At least now he is in my debt."

The two then left the office. Françoise waited for the consul to climb back into bed and Monsieur Macé to shut himself up again in his broom closet before she left her hiding place and returned to Alix's room.

5

The embassy's caravan left the week after Murad, and Monsieur de Maillet marked the event with a magnificent show of pomp. The full roster of the colony's dignitaries was convoked to see the du Roule mission off, and as many aspired to that circle who lacked any title to it, the consulate was able to sell the honor dearly and recoup a portion of his outlay. The pasha made difficulties about granting the necessary authorizations for the mission, but the consul had no intention of keeping the departure discreet. He wanted to demonstrate the importance France gave to the enterprise. One cannot always bow down before the Turks, he said, even if they pretend to be masters here.

The chevalier du Roule and his band of haughty crooks looked splendid on their camels. Belac, an able caravan leader, had managed to outfit the beasts to noble effect, even tying chainlets of silver bells around their ankles.

The little caravan was unable to join the large one for Asyut that Poncet had traveled with earlier. It was decided in the end that the travelers were numerous and well-armed enough to travel alone, taking a route that Belac knew well and that would lead them directly to the third cataract on the Nile.

As this brilliant procession headed southward, the consul and the elite of Cairo's Frankish colony watched it grow small in the distance, their hearts full. And meanwhile another convoy was bustling to take its departure from the consulate.

Monsieur de Maillet had wanted his daughter to leave at this time so as to minimize the visibility and scandal of her departure. She therefore set off alone, in a black carriage with no coat of arms, and two guards following on horseback. Madame de Maillet kissed goodbye to the nun she was giving to God, then fell in a dead faint in the vestibule. Françoise, who had to carry her to her room, did not even have the opportunity to watch her friend leave.

The consul had tolerated the presence of the laundress turned chambermaid on condition that she quit his sight the very day Alix left the consulate. That same evening Françoise packed her things and carried them back to her house on foot.

Looking out her window, she saw Maître Juremi on the terrace and joined him there. She described Alix's departure to him, and they consulted on the things they would have to do in the upcoming days. Then there was silence and awkwardness between them.

It was six o'clock at night; the square of sky above the terrace was turning ultramarine. A few stars twinkled, while the orange trees still showed green. It was the moment when glinting light of night and the colors of the day cross and greet each other. The jungle in the house was growing ever denser, as Maître Juremi had hardly given a thought to its upkeep lately. Large leaves, pushed by the multitude of vegetation behind them, pressed up against the glass of the window.

"Your plants are getting away from you," said Françoise.

"What is the difference, since tomorrow . . ."

The idea that they would be leaving Cairo in less than two days never to return set them adrift on a common current of nostalgia. They would be leaving, yes, leaving together, to follow the same road, run the same risks, having done nothing else for the last two years, though never yet so close to each other. Françoise felt Juremi darken at the thought.

"Please," she said, "don't avoid me. It's a fact: we are going to be together. Let us simply be happy that we are. I don't ask for anything else."

They faced each other, close together.

"Jean-Baptiste has disappeared and Alix has just left us," she said. "Oh, Juremi, is it only what we both miss that brings us together?"

He raised his great head, half devoured by its mass of beard, and rested his kind eyes on her. She laid her face against his giant's chest, and he closed his arms around her. When night had fallen wholly, they went into Françoise's house, hoisting themselves in through the window. She had a vast bed, propped up on bricks at two corners, and it creaked around them all night, like a great hull crashing through waves of pleasure, tenderness, and freedom.

In the morning, Maître Juremi returned to his house and started preparing his baggage, or at least that was his plan. But he kept wandering from the ground floor to the one above, looking at the plants that had kept him company for so long, sitting down, getting up again, and circling endlessly. The option of praying was not available to him. Under the circumstances he did not know how to address his God.

Françoise had the good sense not to come and bother him. She knew that they would be leaving together at dawn the next day and she would have him beside her to her heart's content.

At five in the afternoon, it began to grow dark in the shadowy den of the lower floor. While a sleeper is awakened by light, a dreamer is often roused from his private world only by the onset of darkness. Maître Juremi lit an oil lamp and realized with alarm that he had done nothing toward his departure. He found a pair of old saddlebags that had been drying out under a wardrobe since his return from Abyssinia and started to gather all that he would need for the journey ahead.

At seven o'clock, there was a knock on the door. Thinking it was Françoise, Juremi grew annoyed. The knock came again—there was no call for such impatience. He slowed his pace even further, grumbling as he walked toward the door, and opened the rusty peephole.

"What is it?" he said gruffly, peering out through the grille.

He could see a man's outline against the lighter background of the arcade.

"What do you want?" asked Maître Juremi, thinking it was someone who had come for a doctor.

"Open," said the man.

"Ho! Take it easy, friend. In the first place, there is no one here."

The stranger approached the peephole until his mouth was practically against it.

"Don't be an ass. Open up."

Maître Juremi felt his face turn pale.

"Is it . . . you?"

"Hurry. Don't leave me out here where everyone can see me."

In a second, the Protestant had shot back the bolt, opened the door, and let in Jean-Baptiste. They fell into each other's arms, mute with tears.

"Let me look at you," said Maître Juremi finally, holding up the lamp and standing back a pace.

His friend was unrecognizable. The bright black eyes were there, and the overall shape of his face, which, once you knew the truth, allowed you to say: "Yes, perhaps it is he." But everything had changed. His hair was cut short and streaked gray in places. A pointed mustache changed the shape of his nose. An imperial in the style of Louis XIII gave his lower lip a proud and indignant look. In addition, he carried himself with the elegance of a gentleman, wearing a taupe doublet embroidered with pearls, sleeves of fine lace, a silk vest, and a three-cornered hat with white plumes, which he held in his hand.

"Would you have recognized me?" Jean-Baptiste asked, laughing.

"Oh, that laugh is unmistakable," said the Protestant, who crushed his friend in a renewed embrace.

"Let's waste no time," said Jean-Baptiste. "My horse is tied to the ring in front of the arcade. Go take it around the back, to Bennoch's stable."

In the back of their house was a coach yard maintained by the Bennoch trading establishment. Being no longer as prosperous as it had once been, it had plenty of empty space, which the neighbors were free to use. Maître Juremi ran out to stable the horse and he returned with Jean-Baptiste's heavy saddle in the crook of his arm and his portmanteau on the opposite shoulder.

Jean-Baptiste was on the upper floor, among his plants, greeting them one after another by running his hands over their leaves as tenderly as he would have consoled a roomful of orphans.

"They are running wild," he said to Maître Juremi. There was not a trace of reproach in his voice, only the tender irony one might use with a schoolmaster whose students disobeyed him.

"Ah! Damn!" said Maître Juremi, whose little walk had restored him. "They told us you were in Paris and being held for trial. We thought you were practically imprisoned."

"I was. But all that no longer concerns me—it all happened to someone else. The person before you is none other than the chevalier Hughes de Vaudesorgues, of the house of the prince de Conti."

He gave a noble bow and smiled.

"How is Alix?" he asked suddenly in a different voice. Maître Juremi all at once remembered the situation.

"She thought you were in Paris too. She left yesterday morning."

"Left!" said Jean-Baptiste. "But how? Who could have—"

"She left in a carriage guarded by two swordsmen. They are headed for Alexandria, where she will board a ship for France. Once there, she will be taken to a convent."

Jean-Baptiste cried out in surprise and anger. Maître Juremi answered him with vehemence, reproaching him for not having sent any news. They both began to ask each other questions, with neither willing to take the time to answer.

Françoise, hearing the noise, jumped out through her window. The two men heard her footsteps on the terrace and stopped speaking as Jean-Baptiste crept toward the stairway, ready to flee.

"Wait, it's Françoise," said Maître Juremi, blushing to the whites of his eyes.

"I went to Soubeyran. Marine died fifteen years ago," whispered Jean-Baptiste quickly before composing himself to embrace Françoise.

She freely expressed her surprise and joy at his return, but her practical nature reasserted itself almost at once and she asked Jean-Baptiste if he had eaten dinner. In fact, he was famished. They cleared a space for themselves at the table, and while Maître Juremi rummaged in his lair and reemerged with a bottle, Françoise climbed into her rooms to get a boiled cabbage, donkey-meat sausages, and a large half-loaf of bread. Maître Juremi spoke first, while Jean-Baptiste devoured his food.

He told the story of Alix's departure, though he knew only the official version—Françoise had never betrayed her young mistress's secret to him. He then described the plan he proposed to follow, according to which they would leave the following morning at dawn. Jean-Baptiste applauded it, and they drank to the success of the enterprise, which had just received a strong reinforcement. Then it was Jean-Baptiste's turn to depict his adventures in broad strokes: the journey, his audience with the king and the troubles that ensued, his escape, and his meeting with the Protestants. They raised their glasses joyously a second time.

"And Murad?" asked Jean-Baptiste.

"He has just left for Ethiopia. He found some patrons to pay his way. It was the best thing that could have happened."

"Are there six of them?"

"Yes. How did you know?"

"Jesuits," said Jean-Baptiste, biting into his bread. "Sent by the French court. After my disastrous audience, the king gave in to his confessor. He ordered this new mission as a present to him and as a reward for the first."

"Then you were unable to convey the emperor's message?" said Maître Juremi.

"I didn't have time for it, and I don't believe that anyone would have listened anyway."

"Ah, Jean-Baptiste," said the Protestant darkly, "I was sure those Jesuits would win out. You thought you could make an alliance with them."

"I had no choice if I was to go to Versailles."

"And why were you so determined to go there?" asked Maître Juremi, his eyes as terrible as when he argued with his God. "For no reason other than to plead your own case and try for Alix's hand."

"You are stating it too strongly," exclaimed Jean-Baptiste. "I believed I could also serve the emperor, convince the king—"

"Calm down," said Françoise, worried at the noise they were making. "Someone could hear you. This isn't the time for it."

"In any case," said Maître Juremi more softly, "the results are plain to see. In the wake of your mission, there are two caravans mounting an assault on

Abyssinia, and the king of France is paying for them both. We swore that there would be no more Jesuits, and now there are six of them hanging onto Murad's coattails. The emperor wanted you as his ambassador. Instead he is going to get du Roule, by all reports the sorriest nobleman in a country rife with highborn riffraff."

Françoise timidly cleared her throat.

"Excuse me. What I want more than anything is to bring peace between you. But since you are talking about Abyssinia, I should tell you something I heard while at the consulate."

She then described the interview between Monsieur de Maillet and Brother Pasquale.

"That makes three!" said Maître Juremi. "The Capuchins were the only ones missing. And with their coronation oil! Another instance of the Coptic patriarch's disinterested fervor. Morbleu! I am ashamed of what we have done!"

"I too, Juremi," said Jean-Baptiste, lowering his eyes. "And if you will stop lambasting me for a moment I'll tell you that I acted in good faith, that I failed, and that I have thought of nothing else on the whole voyage back."

Maître Juremi mumbled something as he peered into the bottom of his glass.

"You see," went on Jean-Baptiste, "as I traveled here I too worked up a plan. There was no provision in it for Alix's departure, since I knew nothing of it. I want ardently to see her, naturally. But I have other business to look to as well. Now listen carefully to what I'm going to say."

Jean-Baptiste, with his mustache and his little beard, had the fierce aspect of a swashbuckler of the previous century, of a Refined of Honor, as Sangray would have said, of a man who issued challenges and was ready to defend them with his life.

"You will proceed with your planned course of action," he said, "without concerning yourself further about me. But instead of boarding a ship along the coast, you will go east toward Suez and Mount Sinai. Juremi, do you remember the monastery where we spent a month on our first trip to Egypt?"

"Where you doctored the abbot for a fever?"

"Exactly. You will go there and hide. No one will find you as long as you are careful not to be followed. I will join you there when I have finished my business."

Maître Juremi was suddenly filled with remorse.

"Come with us, Jean-Baptiste," he said, "I was only talking about the past. Things are as they are, and it doesn't matter. The Abyssinians will take care of themselves just as they have done for centuries now."

"No, Juremi. The past is shut and done only at our death. I still have some things to do here. No one will be able to say that we didn't keep our word."

Françoise warned him that Cairo was full of spies, and he could be recognized and denounced. Maître Juremi could think of no way to soften his earlier reproaches, now that he could see the impact they seemed to have had. Jean-Baptiste curtly silenced their objections. For more than an hour, he continued to question them about life in the colony since his departure, about the state of their apothecary business, and about du Roule's caravan. He had Maître Juremi give him a full list of the patients he continued to care for.

Finally, the three parted company to rest. At six in the morning, in the first light of dawn, Maître Juremi and Françoise gathered their baggage and readied their horses in the yard where Jean-Baptiste's horse had been stabled since the night before. Françoise was dressed as a man, in boots and a wide-brimmed hat. Maître Juremi cut a similar figure, only taller.

Jean-Baptiste felt a wave of emotion as he wished them goodbye. They had barely found each other again and they were already parting. After waiting a quarter of an hour, he wandered for a last time among his plants gathering a few seeds, which he tucked into the pocket of his suit, slung a small medicine chest that Maître Juremi had left him over his shoulder, and set off, at the supple walk of his chestnut mare, into the old quarters of the city, where he had taken lodgings on his arrival the day before.

6

According to their first plan, Alix and her accomplices would dispose of her guard a short distance before Alexandria, flee toward a port on the Cyrenaican coast, and reach France by sea. Françoise and Maître Juremi were to catch up with her on the third day of her journey, when they would mount an ambush against her escort.

Now that everything had changed and they were all to head east to Suez, their delay in reaching her would cause a serious inconvenience. They would have to retrace their steps partway up the delta, cross to al-Mansura, and then go on to Ismailia. As he galloped alongside Françoise, Maître Juremi thought of the dangers the new plan entailed. But when the sun rose above the horizon to caress the cold mists blanketing the plain of the Nile, the Protestant's hardened spirit, used as it was to solitude, opened itself to the pleasure of the ride. From time to time Françoise looked over at him and smiled, the exercise and the nip in the air along the river bringing color to her cheeks. Her hair was tucked up under hat, and only the down on her neck, whose softness Maître Juremi now knew, was visible. It was a wonder to see these two individuals, both of them tested often by fate, roughened unceremoniously by time and the hardships of life, blossoming with such freshness, tenderness, and charm, like the survivors of a ravaged town who find that they are safe and take their gold plate out of hiding.

As they descended toward the coast, they saw more and more seabirds gliding gray and white over the water. In the villages, they came across old men wearing the tarboosh. The enormous open countryside was overlaid with a network of clay canals and swarmed with fellahs in simple gray shirts, who looked at them with the eyes of pharaohs. Fat oxen grazed among palm trees ruffled by the salt wind. Their own rediscovered youth seemed to feed on the youth of the world itself, whose simple and familiar form they saw everywhere around them.

They made good in a single day the distance that Alix's heavy carriage had traveled in two and stopped for the night in Damanhur. The consul's daughter was to stay with the devout widow of a French merchant named Beulorat who, until his recent death, had served as the consul's correspondent in that small town. Françoise and Maître Juremi made do with a seedy post house run by a Copt. Unable to prove they were married, they were assigned to two straw mattresses separated by a screen of palm matting—an arrangement that saved appearances. After feeding them a copious meal of roast capon and yellow rice, the old Copt bid them good night with a toothless and complicit smile. They walked all over town after dinner with their arms around each other's waists. From a distance, they caught sight of Alix's carriage and the horses of her guard inside the precincts of one of the town's rare stone houses. They returned to their lodging reassured, and Maître Juremi asked the manager to wake them before dawn. They left before the first light of day and made their way to the designated place.

Alix's equipage got under way very slowly. Michel, the consular groom, was at the carriage's reins; he had not been told the entire story, but he knew that something was brewing, and he would not stand in the way of it. He loved Alix as his own daughter and was heartsick to be taking her to the convent. The two guards, on the other hand, took their duties to heart, spelling each other through the night at Alix's door. Both scoundrels were entirely beholden to Monsieur Macé. One, a Frenchman, had been freed from the galleys three years earlier and had lived in Abukir without papers ever since. Captured by the Turks, he owed his rescue to the consular secretary, to whom he gave his unquestioning loyalty. The other was a Cairene of mixed parentage, the issue of an unlegitimated liaison between an Italian and a Copt. He worked as a porter at the loading docks on the Nile. Monsieur Macé had long promised to give him his naturalization papers and, in exchange for this unlikely hope, was able to call on him for any task at hand.

As the carriage was about to leave, a new complication arose. Alix's hostess, the widow Beulorat, decided she would like to join the convoy. She had business in Alexandria and felt she might as well travel in the consular carriage. The guards quickly came around to her view, no doubt persuaded by a few piasters. A place was made for her, and they set off. Alix knew that her friends might erupt onto the scene at any moment and insisted on keeping her bag with the dagger and pistols in it at her feet. But now, rather than having a moment to prepare for the attack, she had to respond to the prattling of this zealot.

"Ah, my girl," said the widow Beulorat in honeyed tones, "refrain from staring out the window in that way! You do yourself injury. This landscape is one you are leaving behind. Think rather of the heavenly beauty you will henceforth be adoring without cease."

"I look forward to the prospect, Madame, if you only knew."

"I know, and it may surprise you to learn that I am full of envy. My life, of course, has been of an entirely different sort. I devoted myself to a husband and children. Yet sometimes I ask myself whether I was not made for the Lord."

"How interesting," said Alix, casting still another glance out the window.

"Isn't it? I believe that a religious life would have provided me the peace that I aspire to with all my being."

In her satin mantle, and with her hair curled in the style of the previous century, the wrinkled old lady assumed virginal airs to express how she would have liked to be God's mistress.

"Do you know that I so devoted myself to Him that my husband was at times jealous?"

"Can it be true?" asked Alix politely.

After a half hour of this painful conversation, as the carriage slowed to round a sharp bend in the road, two explosions clapped off in the humid air. Alix rushed to the window but could see nothing. She pressed her face to the rear port: one of the guards was hit and falling to the ground. Michel stopped the carriage. The other guard spurred on his horse, reached the level of the coachman, and ordered him to whip up the coach. At the same time, Maître Juremi charged on horseback from behind the dry stone wall of a garden and bore down on the guard, his sword drawn. The other unsheathed his sword in turn, and the two began to fight.

The widow Beulorat, whose first reaction was surprise, soon realized that Providence was putting her to a new test. She began to yowl like an animal at bay. Alix, who was following the battle from the window with great interest, turned and told her to keep quiet, but the other screamed all the louder. To her undying astonishment, the young woman turned on her and coolly slapped her twice in the face.

"Will you keep quiet, you old biddy!"

Her hands to her burning cheeks, the widow Beulorat looked on in silence, panting with anxiety at the horrible events unfolding around the carriage. She saw the nun, Christ's betrothed, so prayerful until moments ago, remove her austere dress to reveal a horseman's turn-out. The girl then opened the leather bag on the floor. Kicking off her shoes, she pulled on a pair of high chocolate-brown boots and buckled on a set of spurs. Outside, the sound of clashing blades could still be heard; Maître Juremi had the upper hand, but the other was defending himself with great energy. Suddenly, the tide turned against them—a mounted janissary came galloping around the bend in the road and discovered the stopped carriage. It took him only moments to determine who was the assailant, and he rushed to the aid of Macé's one remaining flunky with all the force of his curved saber. Maître Juremi backed off. Alix could see Françoise behind the low wall, too far away to use her pistol, given the violence and confusion of the melee. Turning back into the carriage, where the pious woman was still moaning, Alix grabbed a pistol she had loaded the night before, cocked the hammer, and adjusted the flint. The combatants were only a few paces away. She waited until only the janissary was in her sights and fired. The Turk's sword arm was upraised, and the bullet penetrated directly into his chest, passing out the other side. He crumpled. Astounded to see his ally thus brutally dispatched, the guard from the consulate stood in his tracks a moment too long and Juremi's sword cut his face in two; a second thrust pierced his heart, and he fell backward off his horse with a dull thud.

Alix gave a cry of joy, but there was not a moment to lose. Françoise pulled the corpses to the side of the road and hid them behind the wall, Michel backed the carriage around so as to hide it among the palm trees, Maître Juremi tied the old coachman up just tightly enough to provide him with an alibi, and Alix gagged the widow Beulorat herself.

"Remember exactly what you saw," she said gravely. "I was abducted by two Turkish brigands. Say anything else and my friends will come back to send you a little closer to heaven."

Then she laughed.

"And if you still want my place at the convent, it's free now."

Then she leaped onto one of the guards' horses, Françoise having just shortened its stirrup leathers, and the three friends galloped off toward the east.

When they had put a sufficient distance behind them, Maître Juremi led them away from the road toward some ruins on the crest of a hillock. They dismounted and let their horses rest. The Protestant described to Alix what had happened in Cairo.

"Jean-Baptiste is back!" she exclaimed.

They talked her out of returning to the city only after a long argument. To know that the man she loved was within a half day's ride but to travel in the opposite direction all the same was torture. Whenever fate sends lovers a sign that their love is under a happy star, they are irresistibly drawn to challenging it all the more boldly. She argued that if Jean-Baptiste had managed to escape from Versailles and elude the king, he would not be frightened because she turned up in Cairo again. Maître Juremi and Françoise preached patience and repeated the instructions that Jean-Baptiste himself had given them. In the end she was persuaded, and they drew up a plan to reach the Sinai Peninsula.

"Let's sleep now in this lonely place and take to the road once more tonight," said Maître Juremi.

They stretched out on the ground and rested fitfully, unable to sleep. At six o'clock in the evening they saddled their horses and set off again. The night was clear and they galloped easily through the delta, the moon scattering a thousand milky reflections across the surface of the river and the canals.

At dawn, they arrived within sight of Ismailia. They reached the town toward eleven o'clock to find it silent and seemingly still asleep, with the shopkeepers' wooden shutters still closed, the windows drawn to, and the doors shut even tighter. Not a soul was in the streets. Maître Juremi was not worried for themselves, as the news of the abduction, which had to travel to Cairo first, could never have arrived here yet. But he, like the two women, felt a dull anxiety at the sight of this dead city, which was neither ravaged nor, in all likelihood, deserted.

As they arrived at the end of a wide street, bordered on either side by the monumental entrance porches of two Ottoman mosques, they suddenly heard a wooden shutter open on the third floor of a house and then saw a young woman appear at a window. She shaded her eyes with her hand and squinted like a blind person. Almost immediately, another window creaked in the house across the way and an old man leaned out over the street, his kaffiyeh askew on his wrinkled head. Other shutters opened out as well, and a shop door yawned.

"Why are you getting up so late?" said Maître Juremi in Arabic to the old man in the window above them.

The man looked around to see who might be addressing him. He too kept his eyes almost closed and was having trouble seeing.

"I'm down here, in the street, halloo!" said Maître Juremi.

"Ah, you must be a stranger!" said the old man.

"Just arrived this morning."

"And you don't know that we've been struck by the plague."

The Protestant now remembered. He had heard in Cairo that there had been plague on the far side of the Isthmus of Suez and that certain cities had been struck in Egypt. As he had had no intention of traveling in that direction at the time, it had slipped from his mind.

"Today is the last day of quarantine," said the old Egyptian. "Did you see many corpses in the streets?"

"Not so far," said Maître Juremi. "And everyone looks very much alive."

Now all the windows were opening. Words were flying back and forth gaily from one to another. The street was full of joyful shouts and ululations. The doors were being unbolted and a crowd of men, women, and children, dazed by the darkness and internment, danced in the street, tripped, and bumped into each other as clumsily as if they were blind, laughing heartily.

The three travelers passed unseen through the tumult. They found fodder for their horses and dried fruits for themselves, which the shopkeepers were only too glad to sell them at excellent prices, having long been deprived of business.

Out of precaution, Maître Juremi repeated several times to the man selling them provisions that they were traveling to Suez, and on leaving the city, they started off in the direction of the gulf. They stopped as they had the day before at some distance from the road in a palm grove at the foot of a small sand dune, this time sleeping soundly. In the cool of night they set off again. Instead of following the road they turned back and cut east toward the desert, following the dusty track leading to Mount Sinai.

Almost immediately they left all vegetation behind. There was nothing around them but the bluish shadows of the desert stones, which started up from their sandy beds like steles. Camels would have been a much better choice for the terrain, but their horses dealt gamely with the sharp pebbles littering the ground, and when they passed a first oasis in the middle of the night they decided not to stop there.

They steered by the stars sprinkling the sky. Maître Juremi looked often at Françoise, but, respecting Alix's sadness and not wanting to bruise her feelings, he kept himself from smiling at his friend too much.

7

Behind the Citadel, where the pasha of Cairo lived, below the high walls of the seraglio, ran a dark street. No opening of any kind, whether door or window, was allowed onto it. In consequence it resembled a sort of canal or ditch snaking between two unbroken walls, with the back of the palace on one side and the blank walls of the town houses on the other. A watch patrolled it day and night, and no one dared venture into the sinister corridor. Yet half way along the alleyway, at its most secluded spot, was a wooden postern studded with iron bolts and lacking a keyhole on its outer face. Through this doorway, which pierced the building's thick walls, one gained access to the palace's courtyards. Successive pashas had put this discreet entrance to different uses over the years, betraying their individual characters. Some, like Husayn, who had fallen off a horse and died shortly after Poncet's mission left for Abyssinia, opened this postern only to let themselves out into the city incognito, so that they might walk there, hear what people had to say, and pursue intrigues in the style of Harun al-Rashid. Others kept it bolted shut and under constant guard: these were the ones who feared most for their lives and often died at the hands of an assassin, for Allah knows men's hidden intentions and always satisfies them. Some, finally, used the postern to introduce persons into the palace whom they might not receive officially. Such was the case with Mehmet Bey. Though surrounded by the prayer, hope, and consolation of all the most conservative muftis and imams in Egypt, he nonetheless moderated his intransigence on occasion to the extent of allowing discreet visits from the outside, the callers always being introduced through the postern.

Possessed of the four wives appointed by Islamic law, on whom he had sired twelve children—counting only the survivors—Mehmet Bey was unfortunately prey to an irrepressible appetite for foreign women. He had developed the taste while on campaign in Europe. In those blessed but already far-off days everything had been simple: he received beautiful infidels as his booty, and no one took offense. He had possessed Frankish women of all shapes and ages, which if truth be told made little difference to him. What he liked was the feeling of being astride the worshipers of another God, whether Catholic, Jewish, Orthodox, or pagan. He did so without renouncing his own faith—far from it. He never felt so humbly useful to the Prophet as when planting his true believer's seed in furrows previously plowed by others and so robbing them of their harvest. The muftis recognized the near-missionary ardor of the pasha and looked the other way. But given the proprieties and the delicate equilibrium of the various faiths in this part of the empire, it was well to gratify his proclivities as discreetly as possible. This is what the little door was for.

In the past months, however, Mehmet Bey's body, led a hard dance during his soldiering days, had caused him such pain that he lost the energy and at last even the desire to have a miscreant brought before him, however beautiful, young, or heretical she might be. For three months the only callers to come through the postern had been doctors, among whom Maître Juremi was the most valued.

He came three times a week, on fixed days, just at nightfall. The sentinels knew this and allowed him to enter on hearing the password "hellebore." That night, he arrived as usual, wrapped in a large coat and wearing a broad-brimmed felt hat. He said the password and entered through the postern. A footman, barefoot and dressed in white, led the physician up a set of marble steps to a small courtyard. Passing under an ogival arcade carved with Moorish motifs, he then ushered him into an octagonal pavilion whose walls were tiled with blue ceramics.

A long chain hung from the cedar roof beams, supporting a lamp with multicolored glass in which four candles burned. The pasha was seated in a corner, on a banquette, his feet stretched toward a brass stove vented to the outdoors by a narrow pipe with three elbows. The footman withdrew.

"Come closer, Doctor," said Mehmet Bey in Arabic.

As the visitor sat down on a wood-and-ivory stool and removed his coat, the Turk drew back in fear and gripped the gem-encrusted knife he wore at his belt.

"Who are you?" he asked.

He was on the point of calling for his guard. Jean-Baptiste stopped him.

"Have no fear, Sire, I have been sent by Maître Juremi himself. I am his partner. Has he never spoken to you about me?"

"Are you the one who doctored the negus of Ethiopia?"

"The very one, Sire."

Jean-Baptiste made a deep bow.

"You were the one I originally wanted to see," said Mehmet Bey. "But your partner said you were in France."

"I have only just returned."

"And why did Juremi not come with you? It would have spared me a terrible fright."

"Sire, he is indisposed himself. He sends his apologies."

The pasha resumed his position next to the stove.

"He took very good care of me. But he was always saying how much he wished you were here, that he was far from being your equal."

"Those are the words of a friend. The truth is that we complement each other. I prescribe and he prepares the drugs with a skill that is foreign to me."

"In that case, examine me and decide on a course of treatment," said the pasha wearily.

Jean-Baptiste began by questioning the old man at length on his pains, the circumstances that caused them, and their exact location. Then he invited him to talk about his life, about what he ate and drank, how he slept, and his taste for women. In this way, Jean-Baptiste acquired a sense of the inner being of the man before him, and in considering the roots of his nature, he sought for any secret correspondence they might have with other roots, other living things, and their leaves or fruits, which might restore his patient to harmony.

"Do you give me any chance of recovering?" asked the pasha.

"It all depends on what you mean by that. If by recovering you mean becoming your twenty-year-old self again, then no, Sire, you will not recover. But if you mean having the calm, the energy, and the happiness that are still appropriate to you at your present age, then I can assure you that you are highly likely to find them again soon."

The Turk was delighted.

"I will have to return to my workshop to prepare the medications," said Jean-Baptiste, "and I will bring them here myself tomorrow."

"Don't be late," said the pasha, showing his impatience. "By the way, Juremi must have told you, but I want to repeat it formally: not a word of all this, especially to the Franks."

"Sire, I would like to ask you the very same favor. No one in the colony is yet aware of my return, particularly the consul. And I am not eager for them to learn of it. In fact, I visit my partner only at night and spend my days in an Arab pension in the old city, where I am staying for the time being."

"Really? How strange," said the pasha. "I thought you went to see your king, and that you had been entrusted with a mission."

"Ah, Sire, it is a painful story," said Jean-Baptiste, in the tones of someone who does not want to burden another with his own misfortune. "And it is a very long story, one so full of surprising turns that it might easily tire you."

"Tell me your story," said the pasha, who, like the legendary Sultan Shahryar, liked nothing better than the suspense of a good tale.

"Well," said Jean-Baptiste, "I went to Abyssinia."

He described his voyage at length and his meeting with the emperor, his words tumbling out in such a lively stream that the pasha, his eyes half closed, took signal pleasure in hearing them. He called for mint tea and cakes to augment his pleasure further.

Jean-Baptiste described how the negus wanted no foreign priests in his country and how he respected the pasha, who regularly authorized the Ethiopian Church to receive its patriarch from Egypt.

"He wants to keep to his mountains in peace," Poncet ended.

"By Allah, he is quite right! I believed him to be less reasonable, and the news you bring is good. But," went on Mehmet Bey, "none of this explains why you are in hiding here."

"I am getting to it, Sire! Afterward, I went to Versailles. . . ."

Jean-Baptiste then began a long description of the court of the Sun King at Versailles, which the pasha listened to blissfully. During his soldiering years in Europe, he had often hoped to be admitted to one of its brilliant capitals. Regrettably, he had spent most of his time bivouacking in the middle of fields, and whenever he had had the good fortune to capture a city it was always after destroying it first. Jean-Baptiste lingered maliciously over his description of the women at Versailles, their hairstyles, their perfumes. The poor old soldier swooned with pleasure.

He was then treated to a flattering account of Jean-Baptiste's audience with the king. There was no mention of a putrefying ear, only of the lively interest the French king took in matters relating to the Levant.

They agreed that he was a great king. Mehmet Bey was sorry Louis was not a Muslim, but suggested in a flight of enthusiasm that he had all the qualities needed to become one.

"This still does not tell me why you are in hiding," the pasha prodded.

The night was drawing on. The servant had twice refilled the stove with fresh logs. The pasha had ordered his water pipe to be lit and shared it with Jean-Baptiste. They were by now fast friends and in the warmth of their exchange no longer marked their differences in station.

"Alas," said Jean-Baptiste, "our great king is but a king, a very weak thing by comparison with God. The Lord in heaven sees all things. . . ."

The Muslim, who lived under the constant surveillance of the deity, looked skyward submissively.

"There is no god but God!" he intoned mechanically.

". . . But earthly sovereigns are limited in what they know."

"This is true."

"They are sometimes unaware of what goes on immediately around them."

Jean-Baptiste took two puffs on the wooden mouthpiece the pasha offered him before going on.

"I am quite sure King Louis XIV would never have allowed the plot I discovered at his court."

"The plot!" said the pasha, growing more and more interested in the doctor's story, despite the late hour.

"That is the only word for it. You want to know why I am hiding: well, it is simply because I would not lend myself to the conspirators' designs."

"What was it about?" asked the pasha, squirming with impatience.

"About you, Sire."

"About me!"

"Yes, about you, Egypt, and Abyssinia. It concerns all that is being hatched by those whom you welcome here and to whom you extend diplomatic protection."

"Speak, by the beard of Muhammad!" said the pasha, who had risen to his feet, and whose burning curiosity gave him an almost menacing air.

"Calm yourself, Sire. I will provide you with every detail, but kindly bear me no ill will, as I myself have been the victim of these machinations."

"Come, come."

"All right, then. My mission to Abyssinia had no further object than to bring the king medical attention. The negus then sent me to Paris to thank the French sovereign, toward whom he felt a debt of gratitude."

"You have already told me this."

"Yes, but in France the fact that the Abyssinians were paying their respects to the French king gave certain people ideas."

"Who?"

"The king's entourage, let us say."

"The priests?"

"Of course, and it comes as no surprise, since they have never renounced their hopes of penetrating Abyssinia. But they are not the only ones or even those who are most deeply implicated in the business."

"You worry me. I can imagine nothing worse than those people."

"Sire, it is simply that you are too straightforward. Other minds are more devious and have devised plans more sinister by far, believe me. May I help myself to more of this excellent Turkish delight?"

"Forget the Turkish delight for a moment and go on."

"This is their idea. Abyssinia is rich. It is full of gold, jewels, and rare woods. Abyssinia is a Christian country, though it diverges enough on a few points of doctrine not to pay its respects to Rome. And Abyssinia is situated on the far side of the Turks, which is to say yourselves, Sire."

"And?"

"And it must therefore be controlled."

"Is that all?"

"Yes, ruled if you like. And how is this to be achieved? By converting it? But this would be insufficient in itself, and the reverse might be more logical: to subdue it first and convert it afterward. That is the plan that was chosen."

"You claim that the Franks want to rule Abyssinia?"

"I do not claim it, I state it as fact. All my descriptions of Ethiopia, which I naively imagined would advance the cause of its pacific king, served only to confirm the plotters in their way of thinking: that a light, well-armed caravan, carrying gold and presents, would be enough to take possession of so backward a country. The Jesuits almost took it by themselves less than a century ago by simply winning over the king. But they had no weapons to turn their victory into conquest. This time the weapons will come first."

The pasha, surrounded by the pillows on the banquette, looked at Jean-Baptiste worriedly.

"You are telling me that the embassy that just left . . ."

". . . was the instrument by which certain people hope to take control of Abyssinia."

"There are hardly twenty of them! No, this is a joke!"

"Sire, I have traveled to that country. It is ravaged by rival interests. Twenty men with money and muskets can raise an army, spread chaos, and place a puppet on the throne, or even one of their own men, just as the Spaniards did in the last century among the Incas in America."

"Hmm!" said the pasha, smiling somewhat indulgently. "And is this your celebrated plot?"

"The very one that earned me threats because I refused to take part in it. And I was forced to leave France secretly and conceal my presence here for the same reason."

"Frankly, my friend, I do not believe you. It may be that you had serious disagreements while you were over there. And it is even possible that someone trotted out such imaginary plans in your hearing. But that is a far cry from saying that the caravan to which I myself gave a safe-conduct is planning to crown its leader as emperor of Abyssinia."

"Sire, your seal was absolutely necessary to them. How could they hope to obtain it unless they presented their operation in a reassuring light? It would have been idiotic to expose their plan all at once. For instance, have you not heard of a mission composed of men of science?"

"Yes, I have heard that a group of scholars is heading toward Suez and will go on from there to Arabia."

"And from there to Abyssinia. Accompanying them is the man whom the emperor of Abyssinia sent with me as his representative."

"That Kurdish dog."

"He is Armenian."

"It is all one," said the pasha. "He went with them? I was not told this."

"And for good reason! You now see that they are not twenty men but closer to thirty. Some carry gold and weapons, others bring the king's messenger and the accumulated knowledge of the West."

The pasha was in that state of indecision and perplexity he found particularly painful. Jean-Baptiste took pity and decided to help him make up his mind by offering a final bit of information.

"There is more."

"More?"

Jean-Baptiste looked the pasha straight in the eyes.

"Yes, Sire. Did you ever ask yourself why a party of Capuchin friars went on ahead of the caravan, planning to wait for them in Sennar, and why they carry a vial of coronation oil given to them by the Coptic patriarch?"

"Coronation oil!" said the pasha with asperity. "And what is that?"

"It is the holy oil that, in the Coptic religion, allows the transfer of power and authority to a new emperor."

"The patriarch did that?"

"The Capuchins are en route, even as we speak."

"Without telling me? By the sword of Ali!"

The pasha, worn out from the long night of talking, accepted Poncet's revelation, coming as it did just before dawn. He rose and walked around the pavilion, where the first rays of sunlight shone through the blue glass of the windows to bathe the tiles along the lower portion of the walls in heavenly light. Suddenly he stopped in front of Jean-Baptiste and thanked him dazedly. He made him promise to return the following evening with the medications and walked away toward a patio where a pool of clear water sparkled. As soon as the doctor had left through the small back door, Mehmet Bey ordered his guard to rouse the Coptic patriarch from bed and bring him immediately before him, along with all the imams, who were to be summoned from their homes.

8

At the same time on the following night, Jean-Baptiste once again entered the seraglio by the postern. He was carrying a small case. The pasha received him in the same room as before and immediately pressed him for the medications. Jean-Baptiste brought out several vials, a snuffbox filled with powder, and a sack containing dried roots. He was obliged to deal firmly with the pasha to keep him from taking all the medicine at once. Maître Juremi had told him the Turk had a great appetite for medication, but he had not expected such ravenousness.

"You have a servant, I believe, who prepares your drugs for you," said Jean-Baptiste. "It might be best to call him in so that he can take charge of these and hear directly from me how to administer them."

The pasha clapped his hands and barked a name at the footman who appeared in the doorway. Shortly afterward, an old servant entered and bowed respectfully to the two men. He was small and skinny, with the sad, narrow face of an abandoned greyhound.

"Here are my new remedies," said the pasha. "Listen carefully, Abdul Majid, to how they are to be used."

Jean-Baptiste explained it all at length and had the servant repeat the whole thing back to him before giving him the case. The pasha insisted on taking his first dose there and then.

"Do not expect to feel relief for several weeks," said Jean-Baptiste.

Yet the simple fact of having taken medicinal potions was having an effect on the pasha. Sated, his mouth puckered from the cinchona bark, he stretched out on the cushions with the contented ease of a young husband. But his brow started to furrow as his mind cleared and he remembered the events of the day.

"I summoned that dog of a patriarch," he began. "You were right about the oil. He confessed to it. But I had to inform him of the meaning of all this. The idiot looked no farther than the gold they paid him. He had wondered why the Capuchins were so concerned to crown an emperor who had been reigning for fifteen years already, but he never saw to the bottom of it. Ah, the poor man. He made endless apologies. We would still be hearing them if my porter had not booted him in the backside, at my request, to send him packing."

The pasha gave a resonant burp, for which he thanked God, then continued.

"I also saw the French consul. I did not have to summon him, as he came to complain that his daughter was abducted two days ago on the road to Alexandria."

Jean-Baptiste assumed a look of surprise.

"Did you know her?" asked the pasha.

"By sight, at the consulate. She was a very beautiful girl."

Jean-Baptiste felt a sudden pang as he spoke of her.

"So I have been told," said the pasha. "It is a terrible shame, that is all I could tell him. They were probably brigands. The road is full of them. Another woman, who was also in the carriage but whom they did not take—probably because she was no longer in her first youth—gave a description of the assailants. Unfortunately it could fit almost anyone: two great big men, wearing turbans, and black mustaches, and swearing by Allah. With the girl behind one of them in the saddle, they took off toward the northwest. They are probably going to smuggle her by boat to Cyprus, and from there she will go on to grace a brothel in the Balkans or elsewhere."

"Poor girl," said Jean-Baptiste automatically.

"Yes, but even had nothing happened to her she would not exactly have had the happiest life."

"Why is that?"

"Her father told me she was going to enter a convent. In all frankness, Doctor, I have a certain respect for you, but you are a Christian and there are things in your world I will never understand. Why lock up all these women for the sole use of God? Do you think He truly wants this? Did He not create the two sexes that they might conjoin? When the consul explained the situation to me, I was greatly tempted to tell him that his daughter, who would live shut away in either case, at least had the opportunity to do some good to those around her now. But let us move on. The upshot is that Monsieur de Maillet was in a state of great agitation. He had almost forgotten his embassy. I say 'almost' because as soon as I asked him for news, he seized on the subject eagerly. Since you opened my eyes, I understand his great enthusiasm for the business much better."

Jean-Baptiste maintained a modest expression. The footman brought in the cakes and tea.

"You may not believe this," the pasha went on, "but I lay down to sleep at noon and was quite unable to. All these goings-on were swirling around in my head. I am going to confess something to you, Doctor. I am a soldier. I like to be shown the enemy and told to strike him. Then I am able to give the best of myself. And thanks to you I see the enemy. That is a great thing in itself. But how am I to strike him? We are not on the field of battle. What can I do? You know how the Sublime Porte is in its dealing with the Franks, always negotiating, pulling strings, playing off one against the other. And now we see what all this leads to."

He spoke without looking at Jean-Baptiste, who waited patiently for the right moment.

"If I make a report to the grand vizier, I know what will happen: he will ask me for proof. And any proof I supply will be judged insufficient. He will ask for more. In the meantime, the days will roll by and they may get as far as pouring that accursed oil on the forehead of du Roule, crowning him emperor."

Jean-Baptiste nodded in acquiescence.

"On the other hand, if I take action against the Franks on my own, the consul will raise a terrible fuss, and there is no telling whether Constantinople will support me! No, I have thought long and hard. The only ones whom I can seize without fear of reprisal are the Capuchins. I am going to sleep on my decision one more night, then in the morning I will send a troop to Sennar to arrest them and bring back the coronation oil and the patriarch's certificate. They are ripe for expulsion, and there is no one to raise a strong objection. But what am I to do about the Frankish caravan? Doctor, you are a man of great wisdom—what do you think?"

This was the moment Jean-Baptiste had been waiting for. He drank two long sips of tea and took his time to formulate a response, or at least he gave that impression, as in fact he had readied his answer long before. And he cast it cautiously in the form of a question.

"Perhaps the king of Sennar might take some action?"

"He would never take the risk of attacking an official Frankish embassy."

"Unless his people were to do it of their own accord. . . ."

"What do you mean?"

"When I was in Sennar, the Capuchins threatened to arouse the populace against me. All it would have taken was for them to paint me as a magician. The people of Sennar are extremely afraid of sorcery and quite ready to believe that white men can bring curses on them. That could explain why a frightened crowd might work itself into a fury against a group of unknown travelers, a hysteria beyond anyone's ability to control, even the king's."

The pasha followed the thread of this idea like a man caught in a swift current who catches hold of a liana and hauls himself in hand over hand toward shore. As soon as he was once more on firm ground, he congratulated himself for having confided in this Frank.

He then asked a series of practical questions. Jean-Baptiste answered them clearly and simply.

"It is almost as though you had prepared your answers beforehand," said the pasha, not suspiciously but with a great deal of admiration.

He called for the narghile and drew on it with a look of utter happiness. Jean-Baptiste waited for the next development. It was announced by a sudden grimace on the pasha's face, which sent smoke down the wrong passage and triggered a paroxysm of coughing.

"What about the scholars? The ones who are traveling with that Kurd?"

"Leave them to me, Sire," said Jean-Baptiste. "I will take care of them."

The pasha started with surprise.

"Give me an escort as far as Jidda," said Jean-Baptiste, "and give me your protection while I am in Egypt in case someone denounces me to the consul. I am officially the chevalier de Vaudesorgues. If you will be my official guarantor, I can go anywhere without fear. I will find the six men, believe me, and they will never reach Abyssinia."

After a long hesitation, the Turk spoke.

"It is out of the question."

Jean-Baptiste started, but kept his eyes on the old warrior.

"I cannot be without a doctor," said the pasha.

The tamarisk logs could be heard crackling in the woodstove as it slowly filled with powdery ash.

"It will take four weeks at most, Sire. I have left you enough medicine to last you three months easily. And if necessary, Maître Juremi can attend to you, although he is sick at the present moment."

"There is talk of plague to the east. The town of Ismailia has been under quarantine. You could fall ill."

"It might happen here too. We are all of us in God's hands," said Jean-Baptiste unctuously.

"It is the truth," sighed the pasha. Then, having weighed the advantages of the mission Poncet was proposing against the alternatives—and in fact none came to mind—he agreed.

Now everything had been resolved, or soon would be. From the soothing effects of the tobacco, the soft cushions, and perhaps also the medications, a tide of fatigue swept over the old Turk's carcass after the rigors of the last two days.

Jean-Baptiste took his leave early. The pasha left orders before going to bed concerning Sennar and the detachment that would accompany his doctor as far as Jidda.

~

The chevalier de Vaudesorgues crossed Cairo in splendid array, sitting his gray Arab mare very straight. He took off his hat and lifted his face toward the highest windows, from where the housewives looked down admiringly at the Frankish noble and his retinue of turbaned janissaries with their swords at their sides. Spring was in the air. The day was warm and the sky full of birds circling over the city. The troop passed through the bazaar, which blared with color from the rugs, copperware, and woven stuffs brought out from the stalls and spilling over into the street, where they were fingered by passersby in long blue and black robes and tarbooshes or veils.

They journeyed the whole way to Suez without a word passing among them, as even the highest-ranking janissary took the man they were accompanying for a very important personage and did not dare break the silence. Jean-Baptiste had little to say to them, for his thoughts were taken up with the task ahead. As soon as his mind came to rest, he thought of Alix, wondering how she had fared in her flight across the desert. Jean-Baptiste had confidence in her, in Juremi, and in Françoise. More than anything, he had confidence in his own destiny.

They finally passed the Bitter Lakes and glimpsed the Serapeum from afar. At the close of the second day, they saw the little port of Suez at the extreme end of its gulf, which was as narrow there as an Italian lake. The bay was dotted with white and gray sails, filled by a steady wind from the northwest.

At the janissaries' request, the harbormaster, a bearded, jovial Lebanese, put a two-masted seagoing felucca at their disposal. Formerly a merchant ship, it had been converted to military use by the addition of two cannons. The crew consisted of Turkish soldiers, which was hardly reassuring given the legendary incompatibility of that people and the sea. Luckily, most of them, including the quartermaster, were Turkified Greeks from the island of Chios. They prayed five times a day and believed in the god of Muhammad, but continued to speak the language of Aristophanes.

The boat sailed smoothly down the gulf, experiencing neither squalls nor calms, and passed Mount Sinai, whose mass could be sensed through the mist.

The waters grew choppier at the mouth of the Gulf of Aqaba. During the day, the wet boards of the gunwale and the coppery complexions of the sailors glistened under a bright sun. The nights were still blustery and cold. They stopped only once along the way and reached Jidda on the fifth day at dawn.

The pasha of Cairo had drawn up a safe-conduct addressed to the sherif of Mecca, and the chevalier was received with every consideration. He was assigned lodgings at an inn run by an Orthodox Christian from Syria named Markos. It was situated under some palm trees at the edge of the sands a short distance from the rest of the town, and it was here that Christians were required to stay.

In the back, the building opened onto a walled garden with flagstone walks lined with orange trees and oleanders planted in a regular quincunx. Jean-Baptiste's hunch had not been wrong. Hardly had he walked into the garden than he saw Murad, seated on a cushion, smoking a water pipe. Across from him, the six scholars were assembled in a silent circle, each holding a book.

Jean-Baptiste, in his role as the chevalier de Vaudesorgues, addressed them a haughty bow, sat down with his back to Murad, and ordered a well-sweetened Turkish coffee. The janissaries had left him, at his request. As he had reached his destination and no longer needed them, they had taken rooms in town. Jidda, an active port on the pilgrimage route, concealed all kinds of pleasures under its austere exterior. Jean-Baptiste gave two sequins to the janissary leader and one to each of the others, an amount equal to two crusadoes, which is to say fifty-six seraphins, the equivalent of 112 pardais, or 2,240 tangas, or again 6,720 barucos, a small coin current on the Red Sea and made not of metal but of shards of Venetian glass. In short, Jean-Baptiste had made them rich. They left for town in a dignified but hurried group, eager to have life requite them of the favor that God, working through this naive European, had bestowed on them.

That night, the guests at the inn all took their dinner in silence in a large whitewashed dining room. The only decoration was an ancient rust-eaten knight's sword, which hung from two nails on the wall. The diners then retired to their rooms, candles in hand, and the creaking of the floor above could be heard. Jean-Baptiste waited until Murad was alone, true to his habit of always leaving the table last and polishing off any food the others had left. He sat down opposite the Armenian.

"Sir," said Jean-Baptiste in Arabic.

Murad squinted nearsightedly and bowed somewhat anxiously in return.

"Ambassador Murad, if I am not mistaken?" said Jean-Baptiste.

"Ah! Now how could you know that?"

The Armenian picked up the candlestick and held it close to his interlocutor's face.

"But . . . it almost looks like . . . is it you, Jean-Baptiste?"

"Hush! I am the chevalier de Vaudesorgues."

"Oh! My apologies," said Murad, disappointed. "I thought—"

"No, you idiot, it is me. Only I don't want you yelling it in front of everyone, especially your new friends."

"They aren't my friends. These gentlemen are traveling in their capacity as eminent men of science. They wish to learn about Abyssinia. Since I had no news of you . . ."

"You did the right thing in leaving Cairo, Murad," said Jean-Baptiste, smiling.

He produced a flask of tinned copper and poured a dram of clear liquid into Murad's empty cup and another into his own, which he fetched from his table.

"Brandy!" said the Armenian. "In Arabia, the land of the prophet! Aren't you afraid?"

They clinked glasses quietly and tipped them to the ceiling.

"Yes," said Jean-Baptiste, "I am afraid. For your sake."

"What do you mean?"

"You are crossing over to Massawa?"

"In two or three days, when the sherif of Mecca has stamped these gentlemen's documents."

"Is it a long time since you have seen the na'ib?"

"Yes, a dear old man."

"He is no longer there."

"Really! It is not the terrible Muhammad anymore?"

"No. Muhammad is dead, and you will be dealing with his nephew, Hasan. He is more terrible still, and his hatred of Frankish clerics is boundless."

"Well, that is nothing to us. The negus himself asked me to bring scholars back with me, if I could find any willing to come."

"Scholars, yes. But Jesuits?"

"What?" said Murad. "What are you saying?"

Jean-Baptiste grabbed the Armenian by the collar and brought his face close to his own.

"I'm saying that you are leading six pure-blooded Jesuits to Massawa. And though you yourself are too guileless to have noticed it, there is every chance that the na'ib won't be so thick. Even if he happens to suspect nothing, the King of Kings will find that you have arrived back with six people who think only of converting him. He made us swear not to bring any more Jesuits into his country, and now you are returning with half a dozen in your baggage."

He let go of Murad, who fell back into his chair, as dazed as if he had just been beaten.

"I am lost," said the Armenian.

He started to sob quietly like a child.

"Stop," said Jean-Baptiste, pouring him another glassful of brandy.

Murad tossed it back in a single gulp and set the glass down, his expression sadder than before.

"Oh! I would have done better to follow my own counsel and find a position in Cairo as a cook. That's the only thing I understand. All your palaver about religion and politics confuses me."

"Listen, Murad. Do what I say and you need have no fear. The emperor will shower his approval on you and you can even become his cook if you like."

Murad sniffed without saying a word and slid his glass down the table. Jean-Baptiste glanced toward the kitchen, then poured him another helping.

"Go down to the port tomorrow morning before dawn," said the doctor softly. "I will give you a sack of gold with which you can hire any felucca with its captain and crew. Cross the Red Sea and go to the na'ib. Warn him that six Jesuits are planning to enter his country, and say that you were fortunately able to escape them. Then go on to Gondar, convey my greetings to the emperor, and tell him that the king of the Franks received his embassy and sends his blessings. Your mission ends there. Then you can go back to your uncle and cousins, and I hope you will be happy for the rest of your days."

"And the Jesuits?" asked Murad, cheered by these words and the three glasses of brandy.

"I will take care of them."

"And . . . you?"

"I am a happy man, my friend. And I hope to be an even happier one soon."

"Your fiancée?"

"I am on my way to join her. Who knows, maybe you will see us someday in Gondar."

They toasted each other twice more. Jean-Baptiste repeated his instructions, going over the smallest details. They parted around midnight, ending with a warm embrace.

9

The following day, Jean-Baptiste kept a close eye on the six guests at the inn. Only toward noon did they notice Murad's absence, as they were accustomed to his late rising. One of them went to knock at his door and came back downstairs highly worried. Murad, following Jean-Baptiste's instructions of the night before, had left word with the innkeeper that he had business in town, and as no foreigner could enter town without special authorization, the six Jesuits suffered patiently. They fanned out in the garden and along the dusty road to the harbor, which they were allowed on for a distance of five hundred yards.

Night fell. The Jesuits held council once again, then ate their dinner in silence. There were no other clients at the inn that night except Poncet. Toward the end of his meal, which he took as quietly as possible, Jean-Baptiste drew his chair up to the scholars' table and asked whether he might offer them mint tea and cakes, he having been indiscreet enough to observe from their scant conversation that they were his compatriots.

"You may," said one of the six dourly.

"Well then," said Jean-Baptiste, lifting his steaming glass, "as we are not allowed to drink a health in any other way here, I raise my tea to you—a drink, come to think of it, very close in color to cognac. To your happiness, good sirs!"

They raised their glasses, none of them with any enthusiasm, though Jean-Baptiste was jovial enough for all seven.

"I have not introduced myself—please pardon me. I am the chevalier Hughes de Vaudesorgues, at your service."

So saying, the sham chevalier raised himself a few inches from his chair and executed a graceful little bow to no one in particular.

"We are scholars," said the oldest of the guests dryly, "sent on voyage to gather information for the Spanish Royal Academy of Sciences."

"And where will your voyage take you?" asked Jean-Baptiste innocently.

The six men looked at each other anxiously.

"To Abyssinia," said their spokesman finally.

The chevalier gave a cry of admiration.

"An unknown land! Gentlemen, I salute your intrepidity."

No one looked less intrepid at that moment than the six unhappy travelers, orphaned of their guide and mistrustful of the loud individual who had accosted them.

"May I ask an indiscreet question, gentlemen?" asked Jean-Baptiste in a low voice.

"If you must."

"All right, do not feel under any obligation to answer me. Are you married?"

An uneasy shudder passed through the six guests. There was a pause, and finally the same man spoke.

"No, Chevalier, we are not."

"Now that is excellent," said Jean-Baptiste. "Truly excellent."

"And might one ask why?" asked one of the travelers, nettled. Seated on the left side of the table, he had been examining the intruder with more dispassion than the others.

"Because there is no longer the slightest doubt in my mind that you are going there to convert the country."

All six listeners uttered simultaneous ejaculations of surprise, then looked in apprehension at the door to the kitchens. Fortunately, no one was there to hear Jean-Baptiste's rash words.

"Explain yourself," said the most talkative of the travelers in a quiet voice.

"Nothing could be simpler. I am going to tell you a little story and you will understand. I heard it from a Capuchin missionary who lived in Sennar and traveled a certain distance into the backcountry toward Abyssinia. But first, ho! Innkeeper! Bring candles! And don't spare the tallow—we pay enough here as it is."

Markos arrived limping. He was entirely at his guests' service as long as they made their requests loudly and clearly, for he was starting to grow deaf. They watched him bring in three new candles, and when he was gone the chevalier resumed his story.

"This missionary, as I was just saying, arrives one day at a village in the savannah—a few huts, tall grasses all around, and some low chairs under a baobab tree where the graybeards hold their palavers. He introduces himself in Arabic, which the natives understand a bit. The chief takes a liking to him. He is accepted by the village and, after waiting two days, he begins to talk about his religion—that is, I suppose, about ours."

The travelers nodded, not in the least reassured.

"The chief takes a great interest in this Jesus who performed so many famous miracles. He clearly enjoys the Capuchin's company and tells him he would like to learn more about his religion. Everything seems to be going well. Then night falls, and the poor monk discovers at bedtime that the chief's daughter is waiting for him in his hut. He says nothing and goes to sleep at the foot of the bed without touching her. The next day, the unhappy girl tells this to her father. 'What,' says the chief, 'you have the gall to refuse my daughter?' The priest has to explain with embarrassment that his religion prohibits all fornication."

The six Jesuits listened, growing more and more uneasy. Jean-Baptiste took his time, calling for more tea before going on.

"Fury on the part of the chief! He vents a terrible anger on his visitor. 'What kind of god is this who could give such a command? If he has men's welfare at heart, how can he oblige those who claim to love him most never to touch a woman in their lives? Your god is simply a criminal. He insults Nature and could never have created it.' That night the chief shuts the Capuchin in with his daughter once again, but this time, all the men in the village are gathered around the hut. The monk is warned that he will not be let out alive unless there is proof that his union with the beautiful virgin has been consummated."

"This is a horrible story, Chevalier," said the leader of the travelers expressionlessly. "Stop, please!"

But the Jesuit put little energy into his protest. In fact, they were all burning with curiosity to know how it would come out.

"I have almost finished," said Jean-Baptiste. "My friend was no saint, or perhaps he became one by his actions. At any rate, he did the deed. The chief searched shamelessly for proof the next morning, then approached the Capuchin, beaming. 'Well done, my friend! I am proud of you and I am once again ready to hear you talk about this Jesus. Now you will be able to convert the entire country, that is, to sow the seeds of as many little Christians as your strength will allow. For the best method of propagating one's religion,' the chief concluded, 'is to make many children and not to steal those of others, which is not nice.'"

A heavy silence settled over the room as Jean-Baptiste finished. Unconcerned, he blew on his tea and sipped at the surface noisily.

"Are you saying," said the boldest and most attentive of the Jesuits at last, "that you attribute to the six of us the intention of inseminating all Abyssinia?"

So saying, he directed an attentive glance at the chevalier, as though trying to bring a blurred and distant memory into relief. His face was not entirely unfamiliar to Jean-Baptiste either. In answering him, Poncet dropped his buffoonery, and the change further chilled his hearers.

"Abyssinia is not the hinterlands of Sennar. It is a proud and ancient Christian land, and we insult it to imagine that it is governed by such primitive beliefs."

He looked deliberately at the circle of men around him.

"No, Fathers, I attribute nothing to you. It is not necessary. I simply know, from a sure source, who you are and what you are going to do."

There was such certainty in his tone that no doubt seemed possible. After their initial consternation, they attacked him on another front.

"Well then, since you know who we are," said the first spokesman, "tell us what possible objection you can have to our plan. Do you oppose the spread of the Gospel?"

"You must be Father de Monehaut, then?" said Jean-Baptiste, who had deduced this from Murad's description of his sponsors.

"That is right."

"Well then, Father, I do have objections, a great many. That country does not need the Gospel. It has known it as long as we have. I am aware that the doctrine they believe in is at variance with Catholic dogma, but the heart of the matter lies elsewhere."

"Where does it lie then?" asked Father de Monehaut softly.

Jean-Baptiste seemed to hesitate for an instant, then went on.

"Time has passed and I have changed a great deal. Last year at this time, I would have launched into an eloquent discourse, drawing on many historical, humanitarian, and religious arguments to persuade you not to interfere with this country. I even went to Versailles intending to discourse in this vein."

"Poncet!" said the Jesuit who had examined him so carefully.

Jean-Baptiste recognized him as one of the priests who had been at the Jesuit residence in Marseilles when he arrived there with Father Plantain.

"Yes. When you saw me last year, Father, I was impatient to be heard and understood. But now it is I who have understood."

"Tell us at least what you have understood," said Father de Monehaut patiently, as if calming a madman.

"That you are a force, very simply."

Smiles of contempt appeared briefly around the room.

"A force in service to force," went on Jean-Baptiste, "taking Christ as your flag, when any other flag would do as well as long as it concealed the essential, which is power."

"And?" said the same priest, showing himself a man used to criticism.

"And only force can stop you. For too long I had the naiveté to believe that you could be convinced."

There was a moment of silence. It was easy to forget that this room, lit by candles, was lost at the edge of the sands on the Arabian Peninsula. Suddenly Jean-Baptiste remembered where he was and realized how easily it might become a prison.

"Don't bother looking for Murad," he said. "He is gone, and I hope that by this time he has even reached his destination. The na'ib of Massawa has been warned of your coming. His grandfather is famous for having sent the tonsures of your predecessors to the emperor of Ethiopia to prove that the door to his country was well guarded. And the grandson has inherited all his ancestor's qualities. He is not a Turk. He obeys the Sublime Porte only from a distance. No intrigue, no lie, and no supplication will move him. If you ever take the risk of crossing the sea, you will never reach Abyssinia."

The six Jesuits looked in horror at this elegant young man in a flame-colored suit and lace trim who was dealing them such a harsh blow.

"What should we do?" asked Father de Monehaut gravely.

"Not go to Cairo, where you will meet with a very poor reception. Nor try to reach Abyssinia by land, as all the local rulers have been warned against you. The one course open is to board a felucca and return to Suez, going on from there to the Holy Land or to France, wherever you like in fact. There is no shortage of nations where you have already made yourselves at home."

Jean-Baptiste rose to his feet and went on somewhat awkwardly, looking at each of them as though with remorse.

"I have respect for every one of you, believe me. If it had been my intent to betray you, I would have gone about it very differently. On the contrary, I am sparing you. But I am being faithful to the word I gave a certain king."

The six Jesuits viewed the reversal of their plans with equanimity, and Poncet found himself more distraught than they. It is because I am a free agent, he thought, and act in full responsibility. Whereas they are not masters of their own wills; they obey. . . .

He bowed politely and walked away, turning back before he reached the door.

"There would be no point in alerting the sherif of Mecca, naturally. He knows nothing of your true identity yet, but if it should come to a general unmasking you would be at a far greater disadvantage than I. Get some rest—it is growing late. Good night, Fathers."

He went upstairs and shut himself in his room.

At five o'clock in the morning, with not a breath of wind to ruffle the glassy water, Jean-Baptiste was gliding out of the harbor in a small hired felucca. Eight oarsmen rowed in unison on a northwest heading, following Cassiopeia.

~

That same week, a troop of Turkish cavalrymen sent by the pasha arrested two Capuchins at the third cataract on the Nile. In the sack that one of them was carrying they found a document addressed to the abun of Abyssinia and a flask of oil. When these were brought back to Cairo and shown to the Coptic patriarch, he identified the letter but swore that he had never seen either the flask or the oil before. Brother Pasquale obstinately refused to admit where the true coronation oil was hidden. The bad faith this evinced, stressed heavily by the pasha in his dispatches to Constantinople, brought about the expulsion of more than half the Capuchin brotherhood to Italy. And the order's Abyssinian mission never recovered from this setback.

~

Du Roule's one worry was to maintain discipline among his followers. He had collected such a brave band of rowdies, so eager for riches and conquest, that he was constantly having to dampen their ardor. These valorous men never showed their mettle more boldly than when an innocent maiden was in the offing. Yet while they remained in Muslim lands, their behavior had to be reined in. In Abyssinia it would be a different story. Besides, the men were quite ready to believe that once there, they would be the ones pursued, such was the reported lustfulness of Ethiopian women.

Well equipped, well armed, and well provisioned, the caravan reached Dongola without the slightest hitch. The king of that city received them with every possible show of goodwill. Du Roule and Rumilhac, however, had to work hard not to explode with laughter during the ceremonial dinner that the ruler gave in their honor, so ridiculous did they consider his somewhat mean and shabby pomp.

"It is a great thing to be a savage or near-savage," said du Roule, "but at least they should enjoy the advantages: freedom and utter naturalness. Here they do no such thing. They are more sticklers for etiquette than the old dukes in our country."

The two often complained to each other about Frisetti, their dragoman. He pretended to take the native ways seriously and showed his disapproval of their behavior. It was really too much! One had to be among the blacks for a man of no birth at all to instruct a pair of noblemen in the art of proper manners.

Finding nothing for which to trade in this town, they set off after a day's rest for Sennar.

They reached the first two oases easily. At the third, Belac, the caravan leader, came worriedly to see du Roule. Three camel drivers had let him know they could not go on and refused to give any reason. The local inhabitants of the oasis showed an inexplicable distrust of the whites, although they were used to seeing white traders pass through and dealt with them familiarly. One of the crew, a young giant from Dalmatia, had unfortunately let his hands roam somewhat too intimately over a girl of twelve or so, a snot-nosed, barefoot minx whose honor the natives felt called on to defend with exaggerated zeal. Du Roule managed to smooth feelings by giving the putative victim a necklace of Venetian glass shards and her father a pair of old shoes. But the savages still did not seem satisfied. The whole business was definitely disagreeable and showed the tribe's ill will, at least so Rumilhac thought, toward visitors of unusual generosity.

They left the oasis hoping for a better reception in the next. In fact, they met with worse, and things deteriorated further all the way to Sennar, where they were confronted on arrival by a silent, hostile crowd. Luckily, the king made up for the cold reception of his people by his extraordinary show of concern. He invited the travelers to dine with him on the very first day. Despite their disgust for spicy, greasy foods, du Roule, Rumilhac, and two other supposed dignitaries honored his table with their presence, although Frisetti pretended illness to stay and oversee the establishment of their camp. The Franks, following a custom known and tolerated by all, kept small flasks in their pockets from which they sharpened their drinks. By the end of the dinner, they were gloriously drunk and under the impression that the king knew nothing of the cause of their good spirits, which was to suppose him blinder than he was. The sovereign graciously appeared not to notice, even when the former policeman slipped his hand under the tunic of one of the servants, entirely forgetting what he was likely to find under a long robe in this country. They went back to their caravan afterward and found camp set up next to one of the gates of the city. They went to sleep like happy men, dreaming of glory and wealth.

The following day, the hostility around them was more palpable than ever.

Two of the men were pelted with stones as they walked around town, and none of the transactions they tried to effect in the marketplace was accepted, as though anything that came from the Europeans brought bad luck.

Du Roule decided to press their advantage with the only people willing to treat them with decent respect, namely the king and his court. In addition to the gifts he had presented to the sovereign the night before, du Roule sent word that he would be honored to entertain the queen and her high-ranking ladies with an attraction he had brought from Europe. The following day, a dozen women from court came to test the waters, the queen preferring not to appear the first day.

Rumilhac exploded with laughter at the sight of these heavy Nubian ladies waddling along in their colored veils, their faces freely uncovered.

"What frumps!" he said in French to du Roule, smiling all the while to the guests. "Please come in, ladies. Look, there is the royal favorite, the celebrated La Vallière."

He pointed to an enormous, limping woman with two short braids on the top of her head.

"And here is the lovely Françoise d'Aubigné. Do come in, Madame la Marquise."

It was an old woman with a disgruntled face. After ushering them into the great tent in the center of camp, du Roule revealed the promised attraction: the distorting mirrors from Venice.

The ladies were in the center of the tent and the mirrors were hung all around the walls. When the cloths covering the mirrors were removed, the ladies stayed in their group without moving, and the Frenchmen believed they had not yet seen their reflections. Du Roule and Rumilhac, laying hold of one after another of the ladies and continuing to joke in French, tried to bring them closer to their reflected images.

"This lady can never have seen herself so slender. Look, my pretty! You have the appearance of a camelopard: all legs and the head of a goat."

"Come closer and look at your friend. How serious she looks! Wider than she is tall, as the gentlemen in these parts seem to prefer them."

But Frisetti, the dragoman, who understood what the ladies were murmuring, was not laughing. He could see that they were shocked and amazed by these images. They saw themselves, but abominably deformed, as though transported into the bodies of demons. Appearance, in a land where Islam builds on and incorporates magic, is far too serious to be counted only an illusion. What was revealed to them while du Roule snickered was their own fate, as if hell's gates had opened momentarily to show them the eternal torment they were condemned to.

The first of the ladies to shriek gave the signal to all the others. They scattered from the tent with their veils hiked up for running and made their way, wild-eyed and panting, through the canyonlike streets up to the palace, their cries echoing behind them.

Du Roule, grasping the situation at long last, gave the order to prepare arms and take defensive positions. After ten minutes of fraught silence, they saw a compact crowd emerge on three sides, its slow footfalls raising clouds of dust. Stones flew. Each of the Franks fired his gun and killed his man, but so many more stepped in to replace the fallen that the foreigners never had a prayer. Within a few minutes, the entire caravan was in the hands of the attackers. The Nubians believed that killing a magician with one's bare hands brought on a curse, so the prisoners' death agony was more prolonged than if they could have been strangled straight off.

The king's cavalry intervened only when it was all over, taking possession of the camels and the goods the caravan was carrying and bringing them to the king. He in turn wrote that very day to the pasha. He lamented the fact that rumors of a malicious nature, no doubt spread by the Capuchins, had preceded the travelers' arrival in his country. Though he himself had treated the Franks as civilly as possible, the crowd had finally seized them. And what is a king to do, he asked humbly, when the people clamor for murder?

10

At the bifurcation of the two gulfs, a fresh breeze sprang up off the felucca's beam. The sails were raised and the craft made good speed toward the Sinai, the ocher summit of the mountain rising against the pale blue April sky. On his face and hands Jean-Baptiste had the tangy taste of the sea, and the sun dried the spray on his skin, leaving traces of salt.

Everything was coming to an end and a beginning. The three missions to Abyssinia had been stopped, and Alix was waiting for him on the shoulder of the mountain now coming into view. There were still any number of uncertainties, so that Jean-Baptiste could have gone on anxiously worrying about the moments ahead. But he did not, at bottom, expect any more big surprises. Feeling the peace that the tempestuous winds and wave-tossed waters manage at their point of contact on the mysterious surface of the sea, which so aptly represents the fate and place of man, Jean-Baptiste watched with mingled fascination and passivity, as though standing at the edge of a precipice, as the hour approached when he would finally be reunited with the woman he loved.

The Arab sailors stood barefoot around him on a deck bleached pale by sun and salt. Their long shirts flapped in the wind. They were happy to be warm, to be bringing their boat home safely. They looked at the mountain as a great and simple thing that stood over them.

Let us try to be like them, Jean-Baptiste said to himself. We must feel only what is happening and not arm our minds against happiness.

They landed at al-Tur at the beginning of the afternoon. Jean-Baptiste, dressed as an Arab, carried his European clothes in a sack. As he still had a little of the gold the duc de Chartres had given him, about ten sequins, he was able to buy a mule, equipped with a worn saddle from which tufts of gray straw poked out. With a stick in one hand to stroke the flanks of the lazy animal and a halter rope in the other to give him some control over its direction, he set off toward the interior of the peninsula.

At this point on the coast, Mount Sinai shelves to a plain from which the traveler can rise by gentle degrees toward the center of the mountain range. The desert starts immediately beyond the last gardens of the port. It is not a sand desert, where all matter seems to have disintegrated, but a landscape of bare, standing stones on a rock base. It looks like a vast expanse of monumental ruins, whose mineral incorruptibility slights every form of existence other than its own fixed and eternal one. A fine layer of white powder, carried by the swirling winds from the depths of Arabia Petraea, overlay the entire scene, giving it the aspect of a palace after the last servant has gone. Time, unable to desecrate it otherwise, had simply poured over it the fine sands of the celestial hourglass.

Jean-Baptiste rode for two hours without meeting a soul. Night would soon be coming to an end, and he tried to make his mule pick up the pace, but in vain. The poor animal had only two gaits: a full stop and a listless walk. The path now looped steeply up a large sheer face looming darkly above. By the time Jean-Baptiste reached the top, the sky had taken on an inky color, against which the black silhouettes of the rocks stood out like giants. At the juncture of the two high valleys that gouge the summit of Mount Sinai, he observed a carved rock in the midst of many unformed stones. This was the rectangular mass of the monastery's walls.

Twelve round towers broke the flat surface of the high gray walls. It looked like a qasr or desert fortress, except for the two spires of the basilica. Jean-Baptiste's mule caused him unmerciful torture—so close to the goal, it still took them more than an hour to reach the monumental gates that pierced the ramparts. The monks themselves stood guard. Two of them, built like wrestlers and wearing straight-bladed swords in the broad belts cinching their robes, stopped the traveler and carried his name in to the abbot. He was allowed to enter only after the authorizing order came back.

Inside its walls, the Monastery of Saint Catherine was in fact a town. The basilica stood at the center, but the many buildings, galleries, terraces, and chapels packed around it within the limited space of the ramparts reproduced the close jumble of walls, streets, and passages of an ordinary town in the Levant. A young monk, fair-haired as a Crusader, led Jean-Baptiste to the abbot's residence. He took Poncet's sack and advised him to leave his mule with the monks at the gate.

Saint Catherine's had been built in the sixth century by Justinian and had survived ever since because of its walls, perhaps, but also and more probably because of the protective presence of the sacred mountain, which had great moral weight with all the descendants of Moses. The Orthodox monks who lived in this sanctuary were officially under the authority of the patriarch of Jerusalem. But rather than being the instruments of a particular religion, they in fact formed an autonomous power as the guardians of a terrible and mysterious site. The fugitives given protection by the monastery were safe no matter where they came from or what crime they had committed. Some stopped there only briefly, while many others stayed on permanently, swelling the population. After a long spiritual climb, they might even hope one day to lead the community.

The atmosphere in the abbot's residence was strange and very different from what Jean-Baptiste remembered from his first visit. The monks spoke in whispers, and the odor of camphor and myrrh floated through the stone-paved hallways.

"Our abbot is very ill," the prior told Jean-Baptiste. "Three weeks ago he collapsed in the middle of a service and was carried out unconscious. He has since come to, but he has difficulty forming his words. At night he is in pain. We hear him groan and cry out sometimes. Your colleague prepared a potion that calms him and relieves his suffering, but we are still very worried."

Jean-Baptiste offered to examine the abbot. Before he did so, however, there was a question he was burning to ask.

"Tell me, where are my friends, Maître Juremi and the two ladies?"

"Don't worry," said the prior. "They arrived here two weeks ago and have been waiting for you to join them. Unfortunately, they decided yesterday to go watch the sunrise from a small chapel built by our brothers somewhat higher up the mountain. Boredom may have played a part in it, as there is not much to do here, and I regret to say that the idea was mine. At any rate they will be back here tomorrow morning."

Jean-Baptiste was momentarily disappointed but told himself he would get a good night's rest, change his clothes, and set off the next morning refreshed in body and mind to meet them.

The prior ushered him into the abbot's bedchamber, a vast room whose tall windows opened onto a balcony where laurels and fuchsias were blooming. On one wall hung a tapestry representing the Tower of Babel. The abbot had once been an architect and had lived for many years in Damascus; after the sudden death of his wife and two sons, he had left the city and wandered straight in front of him, finding the road to Mount Sinai. He had not left Saint Catherine since, becoming its superior in less than ten years. During Jean-Baptiste's first stay, he had still been wielding his compass, square, and ruler, intent on drawing up the plans for enlargements to the monastery himself. On a table in a corner were piled large rolls of paper—doubtless his still-unfinished work.

The poor man was unrecognizable—thin, haggard, his skin waxen, his mouth twisted into a grimace.

"I am glad for the chance to see you again before it is all over," he said with difficulty.

Jean-Baptiste pressed his bony hand, too moved to say anything. The old man dozed off. The doctor slipped out of the room and rejoined the prior. At most they could hope to keep the pain at bay, he told the prior, but death was inevitable.

"The most extraordinary thing," said the prior, "is that he fears neither one nor the other. It is we who are the most affected by it."

"Within two days, I would think. . . ."

The prior made the sign of the cross, brushed away his tears, and accompanied Jean-Baptiste to the apartment reserved for him.

~

At seven in the morning, walking down from the altar of repose where they had watched the sunrise, Françoise and Maître Juremi met Jean-Baptiste coming up from the monastery. They embraced him warmly and asked about his journey and arrival, but he was worried about Alix.

"She stayed behind for a bit," said Françoise. "She has wanted to be alone lately. You'll find her not far from here on the large promontory across from the chapel."

Jean-Baptiste apologized for leaving them and continued up the path. Already the day was hot, and he took off his doublet and slung it over his shoulder. The little sanctuary appeared suddenly around a bend in the trail. It was a simple stone hut roofed with irregular stone slabs. The monks had not even erected a cross on it, out of respect for the visitors of many faiths who might come to recollect themselves here. A small esplanade linked the building to a rock promontory whose vertical stone formations looked like draped figures. The ground fell away on three sides beyond it to give an unobstructed view of the sunrise. Jean-Baptiste recognized Alix in the midst of the stone forms, or rather, guessed at her presence, and she, seeing him, had a similar intuition and stood up. He ran toward her, slowed when he was ten steps away, and ended very deliberately. How she had changed! Her face, her body, and her bearing had matured, and her beauty shone all the more resplendently. She wore riding clothes, and he saw her unfettered by dresses or corsets, her hair loose. But all that is nothing, he told himself, next to her air of majesty, of insubjection. And he, whose increasingly worn image she had carried within her during his absence, now reassumed his vigorous features, his bright eyes, and the characteristic blend of strength and grace that accompanied his every gesture.

There. Every obstacle had been overcome. Nothing separated them except ten paces over pebbly ground. Their differences of birth, her father's opposition, the king's indifference, and the malice of many men no longer obstructed their path any more than the fragments of cooled lava rolling under their feet.

When they were close enough to touch, they continued to look at each other gravely. After all, the one thing they had accomplished until that point was to prepare the way for a true, an attentive, first meeting. The comedy of lowered eyes and sidelong glances was over. They were free and had first to look at each other fully, to cast modesty aside and see what they had become, now that they were more than ever themselves.

Alix lifted her hand slowly to Jean-Baptiste's lips. He kissed the ends of her fingers. They were free and no longer had to take their pleasures furtively, nor diminish them in the haste to increase their number.

The sky was full of large white clouds, cottony and serene. Jean-Baptiste dropped his doublet on a rock and embraced Alix. They were free and had no reason to hold back their passion as long as they both concurred—and it is fair to say that they did. They kissed, their mouths and caresses melting together, and there is nothing to be said about this that cannot be imagined by those who have, at least for a moment in their lives, been perfectly happy.

They stayed on the mountain all morning, walking pressed close to each other, stopping to resume the interrupted progress of their kisses. The huge blocks of basalt were stacked against each other like the leaves of a gigantic book, and different layers of the landscape were revealed by a succession of different blues, shading to violet in the farthest distance at the Red Sea. No place on earth is more tormented than the heights of Mount Sinai, which seems to emerge from the molten entrails of the earth and thrust into the turbulence of a sky veiled with rainclouds and twisted by squalls. They walked under the hot wind that made their hair fly and mingle.

"What a magical place!" said Jean-Baptiste. "Doesn't it seem as though a God might appear at any moment among the clouds?"

"And what would you do if he landed here, right in front of us?" asked Alix, laughing.

"Well, I would tell him to sit down, on this big rock, for instance, because I imagine that he is a very old man and quite tired."

"And then?" asked Alix, pushing aside a lock of hair from her lover's forehead.

"And then I would ask him to bless us. And we would talk about his life and ours."

"What if he gave you his commandments?"

"I would tell him that they have already been written into all living creatures, and that he mustn't give them to anyone in particular, at the risk of inventing priests, kings, fathers, and unhappiness."

"That would be very insolent, and he might send his lightning down on you."

"Why would he do that?" asked Jean-Baptiste gravely. "If there is a God, he loves happy men."

So passed these hours of perfect happiness, alternating between short, laughter-filled conversations and long caresses.

As they walked back down the path back to the monastery, they entered into a more detailed account of their past separation, a subject they would not exhaust for a long time. Alix was determined to reveal that she had given herself to another man, as the secret oppressed her. She said who and—briefly—why.

"Do you love him?" asked Jean-Baptiste.

"I thought only of you, and I never stopped loving you for a moment."

"Then what does it matter? I am not your master, and in a union like ours there are no conditions."

Jean-Baptiste smiled inwardly at the thought that, without having meant or wished to, he had already taken his revenge.

At the monastery, they ate lunch with Françoise and Maître Juremi. The Protestant, who was accepting his happiness in good spirits, had recovered his smile and his talkativeness. The important question was where they should go. Although protected by the Monastery of Saint Catherine, they were still in the land of the Grand Signor, where a search for them was certainly underway.

"Françoise and I are going to France," said Maître Juremi.

"France! But you are a Protestant! Have you forgotten?"

"If I forget, they'll remind me," said Maître Juremi, laughing. "Let's be serious. Which is better, to be a pariah in the Orient or in one's own country? We've reached the age where the worst thing of all is to lead a wandering life. So we'll take whatever welcome they give us."

They had made up their minds, and there was no hope of their reconsidering now. The two would stay on at the monastery for a month, to give the stir over Alix's abduction—which Monsieur de Maillet had surely announced in Cairo—a chance to subside, then they would go to Palestine and board a ship at Jôunié for Cyprus, Greece, Venice, and France.

Seeing the two of them—sturdy, calm, strengthened by their experiences, and united by a deep tenderness—it seemed that nothing was impossible to their common will.

Alix had dreamed of Abyssinia a great deal, and Jean-Baptiste spoke to her about it for hours, awakening her curiosity even more. For a short time they even made plans to go there. But it happened during their stay at the monastery that they received a letter from Murad, thanks to some sailors from al-Tur. Murad had reached Massawa and accomplished his mission there. He sent them news of Ethiopia: Emperor Iyasu had died a few months before, probably from the illness Jean-Baptiste knew him to have. His son, raised under the influence of the priests, was ill disposed toward foreigners, so much so that even Murad gave up the idea of going back to report on his mission, preferring to go instead to Aleppo or Jerusalem, where, by working as a cook, he could put to advantage his stay among the Franks in Cairo.

This news dissuaded Jean-Baptiste from attempting a journey that had been motivated at least in part by his friendship for the emperor, who would have protected them. But Jean-Baptiste, who had so ardently sought to keep foreigners from interfering with that country's affairs, could hardly be sorry now to see Abyssinia following its own historical course, in which the West and Westerners played no part.

They therefore decided to ride north, accompanying Françoise and Maître Juremi as far as Acre. From there they would follow their own inclination.

The abbot's weakness increased, and he died after a week. He was buried with fervor, and the monks elected a successor to replace him. Alix and Jean-Baptiste grew into the habit of taking long walks in the mountains, but also through the dark maze of little streets within the monastery, which they grew to know well; their favorite place, at nightfall, after the day's heat had loosed its stranglehold, was a small courtyard against the apse of the basilica. In this space, always miraculously empty, grew an unremarkable shrub that received absolutely no care. Despite this, it was the monastery's raison d'être, the sacred pivot around which the structure revolved. Though it was not the same species as the plant beside which they had first met and that Jean-Baptiste had found at al-Wah—something that disappointed them both a bit—it was, they were told, the authentic burning bush of Moses.

Epilogue

Ever since hearing of Jean-Baptiste's meeting with the Protestant bands in the hills of Provence, Maître Juremi had dreamed of nothing but joining up with them. Françoise loved him too deeply not to share his commitment to their cause. As soon as the two of them arrived in France, she used their savings to rent a small inn. Because she was Catholic, no one objected. During the day, the inn served drink to travelers, peasants, and soldiers. At night, Maître Juremi came down with the conspirators he had joined in the mountains. Less than six months later, the rebels touched off a veritable civil war in the region. An entire army, commanded by the maréchal de Villars, was needed to subdue these shirtsleeve bandits, who have come down to us in history as the "camisards." Maître Juremi, known to his fellows as Ravenel, became one of their leaders. After the rebellion was quashed, Juremi managed to flee, and Françoise in all likelihood followed him. We lose track of them at this stage, but there is some indication that they took refuge in England.

Jean-Baptiste earned enough money in Acre doctoring a few of the country's notables to move on to Syria. Alix and he rode to Palmyra, then crossed the entire desert and reached the marsh country on the Euphrates. From there they went on to Persia, where they were safe. They traveled the country as the spirit moved them and found they liked it. In Isfahan, Jean-Baptiste once again took up the practice of his art, enjoying enormous success. All the merchants, both Persian and foreign, the diplomats, the men of the people, and even the most fiery imams of that city applied to him in matters of health. He soon had enough gold to buy a large house near the Blue Mosque, where the climate was ideal for growing plants of every kind. In his medicinal garden, he naturalized the seeds he had saved in his pockets during his travels. Alix grew roses. They never wanted to leave.

When Louis XIV died, they learned after a delay of the duc d'Orléans's regency. Jean-Baptiste, of course, had almost met him when he was still the duc de Chartres. He wrote to him and the regent answered in his own hand, expressing his lively wish to receive the Poncets' visit in Paris. Jean-Baptiste conferred with Alix. In the end they decided not to leave their beloved mountains and their roses.

As to Abyssinia, after the death of du Roule, which resounded far and wide, and after the pitiful failure of the Jesuits and the expulsion of the Capuchins, it was preserved from any foreign incursion for almost a century and a half—setting aside a few rare and peaceful voyages on the part of English geographers. Only in the second half of the nineteenth century, with the completion of the Suez Canal, did colonial greed once more turn toward the Red Sea and did Abyssinia see the return of those characters Poncet had delivered it from. Perhaps because the country had preserved its original faith, its sovereignty, and its customs, it had the strength to resist them.

In the chronicles of Italian Eritrea at the beginning of the twentieth century, the name Poncet once more appears. He was an apothecary in Asmara, perhaps a descendant of one of the four children of Alix and Jean-Baptiste. There is nothing to disprove it, but nothing to confirm it either, as not much is ever known about those who are happy. They live, and their happiness takes the place of history.